Praise for Aimie K. Runyan and
Promised to the Crown

"This gripping debut brings to life the saga of three courageous women from disparate backgrounds starting over in New France. Aimie Runyan deftly guides us through the hardships and rewards of life on the early Canadian frontier. *Promised to the Crown* is an absorbing adventure with heart."

—Jennifer Laam, author of *The Secret Daughter of the Tsar*

"A captivating tale of three courageous women: Rose, Elisabeth, and Nicole, bonded by adversity, friendship, and love. In author Aimie Runyan's skillful hands, their stories are woven together as seamlessly as were their fascinating lives. *Promised to the Crown* is an unforgettable saga of strength and sisterhood, one that will stay with you long after the final page."

—Anne Girard, author of *Madame Picasso* and *Platinum Doll*

"In her original and well-written debut, *Promised to the Crown*, Aimie Runyan evokes the story of three young women who venture from France to Canada in the seventeenth century to marry and start a new life. It is a heart-wrenching and timeless tale of friendship, love, and hope that skillfully blends history and romance to educate, entertain, and inspire."

—Pam Jenoff, author of *The Last Summer at Chelsea Beach*

"An engaging, engrossing debut. Runyan's gift transports you to the distant, frozen landscape of seventeenth-century Canada, but Rose, Elisabeth, and Nicole feel as real as if they live next door. A romantic, compelling adventure."

—Greer Macallister, *USA Today* bestselling author of *The Magician's Lie*

Please turn the page for more praise for Aimie K. Runyan!

And praise for *Duty to the Crown*

"Runyan weaves a heartfelt story revealing the little-known history of the brave women who left France for the Canadian provinces to create their own destinies—for better or for worse. Their sisterhood, strengthened by formidable odds they faced, and their boldness in forging new identities in new lands, inspire this novel's fresh take in historical fiction."

—Heather Webb, author of *Rodin's Lover*

Duty to
the Crown

Books by Aimie K. Runyan

PROMISED TO THE CROWN

DUTY TO THE CROWN

Published by Kensington Publishing Corporation

DUTY TO
THE CROWN

AIMIE K. RUNYAN

KENSINGTON BOOKS
www.kensingtonbooks.com

KENSINGTON BOOKS are published by

Kensington Publishing Corp.
119 West 40th Street
New York, NY 10018

All Kensington titles, imprints, and distributed lines are available at special quantity discounts for bulk purchases for sales promotion, premiums, fund-raising, educational, or institutional use.

Special book excerpts or customized printings can also be created to fit specific needs. For details, write or phone the office of the Kensington Sales Manager: Kensington Publishing Corp., 119 West 40th Street, New York, NY 10018. Attn. Sales Department. Phone: 1-800-221-2647.

Kensington and the K logo Reg. U.S. Pat. & TM Off.

eISBN-13: 978-1-4967-0115-2
eISBN-10: 1-4967-0115-1
First Kensington Electronic Edition: November 2016

ISBN-13: 978-1-4967-0114-5
ISBN-10: 1-4967-0114-3
First Kensington Trade Paperback Printing: November 2016

10 9 8 7 6 5 4 3 2 1

Printed in the United States of America

To Katie Atkin and Maggie Trumbly,
my sisters by birth,
who taught me that loving and squabbling
are not mutually exclusive.

And to Denise Frey and Tammy Runyan,
my sisters by marriage,
who welcomed me into their family
with warmth and graciousness.

I love you all.

ACKNOWLEDGMENTS

This book would not be in your hands without the contributions of the following wonderful people:

My lovely agent, Melissa Jeglinski, who has been an amazing guide through the publishing world.

My superb editor, John Scognamiglio, and the dedicated staff of Kensington Publishing, who have worked so very hard to make this book a reality.

My brilliant sister, Maggie Trumbly, who pointed me toward some much-needed resources on the native peoples of Canada. Any mistakes are mine, but there would have been many more without her help.

The talented ladies of the BWW: Katie Moretti, Jamie Raintree, Ella Olsen, Gwen Florio, Andrea Catalano, Orly Konig-Lopez, and Theresa Alan. You're the best cheering section a scribbler like me could ask for. I love you tons.

My tribe, the Tall Poppy Writers: You embody all that is good about this crazy writing world. The same goes for Rocky Mountain Fiction Writers, the Women's Fiction Writers of America, Pikes Peak Writers, and all the other groups who give writers a place to call home. You're indispensable.

Abby Polzin, thank you for being my extra eyes. I love you, girl.

And as always, foremost and forever, to my family. The Trumbly and Runyan clans, the whole lot of you, have been so wonderfully supportive. Ciarán and Aria, you never cease to make me laugh. And Allan? You're simply the bee's knees.

Only he can understand what a farm is, what a country is, who shall have sacrificed part of himself to his farm or country, fought to save it, struggled to make it beautiful. Only then will the love of farm or country fill his heart.

—Antoine de Saint-Exupéry, *Flight to Arras*

CHAPTER 1

Manon

May 1677, Outside the Quebec Settlement

Only for her little brother would she venture onto the white man's land—especially *this* white man's land. The air had not yet lost the cruel bite of winter, and Manon longed for the warmth of her longhouse. She had several miles left to trek and medicine to brew before she could rest. Young Tawendeh was ill with fever, along with half the village. Most were not grievously ill, but it was enough for concern. She had seen fever turn from mild to lethal in an hour, so she took no risks. Her remedies were the best chance for a quick recovery, though she feared few would accept her help until they were too far gone.

The path through the forest was far more arduous than if she skirted its perimeter, but the cover of the trees protected her from view. The scent of pine danced in her nose and perfumed her skin. Manon considered it the smell of her home and her people. She cursed the feeble light of the dusk hour when the towering evergreens blocked much of the weak spring sun. When true night fell, she would be able to track her path by the stars, but only if she could see them free from the overhanging limbs. She did not fear the night or the animals that lived by moonlight. A child of the forest, she knew the most dangerous creatures lived not in trees, but in the growing town to the southeast of her village.

"What have we here?"

Manon froze at the sound of the raspy male voice.

"A bit far from home, aren't you?" he continued.

She turned, very slowly, not wanting to give the man any reason to strike. Alone in the forest, he would face no consequences if he attacked her.

"Stupid thing," he drawled. "You don't understand a word I'm saying, do you?"

"I am just passing through, monsieur," she spoke softly, but in perfect French. She did not allow the tremor in her heart to reach her voice. She would not let this dirty farmer know she feared him.

"This is my land." The man, hunched and weary from a day's labor, straightened to his full height. "You're trespassing here."

This is not your land, you foul creature. Nor any man's. Manon kept the thought to herself; it would only spark his temper.

"I mean no harm, monsieur." The courtesy tasted bitter on her tongue, but she sensed his considerable self-importance. "I am going home. This is merely the shortest route without cutting through your fields."

"I don't care for trespassers," the man insisted. "What's in your bag?"

"Nothing of interest, monsieur." Manon spoke the truth. White men had little use for plants they couldn't eat.

"Let me see in your bag, you little savage." The large man's stench nearly overpowered her as he stepped close and grabbed her wrist, snatching the deerskin pouch with his free hand. "Nothing but weeds. Are you trying to cast some kind of spell, witch?"

"No, monsieur." She fought harder to swallow back her fear. A whisper of the word *witchcraft* could see her dangling from the gallows. "I am simply gathering herbs to heal fever."

The man spat without releasing her wrist. "You were stealing those weeds off my land. I could see you hanged."

He wasn't lying. She paused for a brief moment to consider whether she could inflict enough damage on the brute of a man to enable her escape. He took a step closer.

"Don't be upset," he said, caressing her cheek with a dirty finger and moving closer still. Close enough that she could smell his rancid, whiskey-laced breath. "You're too pretty for the hangman's rope. We might be able to work something out."

Anger flashed in her eyes. This grimy man spoke as if she were the dirt beneath his feet, and he was going to force her to tell her full identity. Something she'd sworn never to do.

"I don't think so." Manon broke his grasp on her wrist and stepped backward. "This land is *not* yours. It belongs to Seigneur Lefebvre." She spat his name like a curse. The lord of these lands had once been her protector, but she hated using his name to earn her freedom all the same.

Before she could react, one of the farmer's massive hands slammed into her cheek, and stars dotted her vision.

"How dare you," Manon growled. "I know the *seigneur*. I was known as Manon Lefebvre to your people. The *seigneur* would not appreciate your behavior toward me. But please, continue, if you wish to lose every inch of your lands."

Manon saw a shimmer of fear in the farmer's eyes.

"Likely tale, you brown trollop," he said, voice wavering. "How do I know you aren't lying?"

"Madame Lefebvre's parents live less than a mile from here," Manon said. "They will vouch for me and my right to be here. I'm sure they'll welcome the intrusion over a bag of weeds that means nothing to any of you."

"You're lying," the man pressed. "Trying to trick me."

Her hunter's instincts forced her heart to slow and her breathing to steady. If he fought, she would defend herself, but killing— or even injuring—a white man would cost her life.

He had to go with her to the Deschamps' house.

"Monsieur, I speak the truth," she said, returning to a respectful tone. "The Deschamps can assure you that the *seigneur* has no objection to my presence here."

The man hesitated. Anyone might know the landholder's name, but his wife's family was not of the first circles.

"Fine, then. Lead the way, if you know it so well."

She started west, toward the cultivated fields. Her moccasins made a *slap-slap-slapping* noise on the hardened earth. She moved quickly, but not fast enough to give the farmer cause to think she would run. He trudged along a few paces behind her, breathing labored from the exertion.

Hurry up, you great moose! I need to get home.

Less than ten minutes later, Manon knocked on the door of the small but inviting farmhouse. Though visitors here were scarce, the flickering of the fire and the smell of good food radiated the kind spirit of its mistress.

An old woman answered the door. She no longer stood as straight as she once had, but moved with efficiency. No spark of recognition lit the woman's eyes as she looked with a furrowed brow at the unknown girl.

"Manon!" The cry came from behind the woman. It was the first time anyone had called her by her French name in ages, and it fell hard on her ears.

Familiar chestnut hair and soft eyes came into view. It had been five years since Manon last saw Nicole Lefebvre, the woman she once considered her mother. The years had been kind to Nicole, leaving only a few lines of experience around her eyes and a bit more fullness to her hips. Nicole dressed in fine fabrics, perfectly cut and tailored, as one would expect from a woman of status, even in her small community.

"Hello" was all she could utter as Nicole took her in her arms. She felt a few decorous tears fall from Nicole's cheek onto her own as they embraced.

"Look at how you've grown, my sweet girl! You're practically a woman," Nicole said, then seeing the red handprint on her cheek, she cradled Manon's face in her hands to inspect the injury. "What's happened to you?"

"A misunderstanding," she answered. The red print would soon be a bruise, but would fade in time. Nothing to worry over, especially with Tawendeh's condition apt to deteriorate the longer she was away. Manon did not say that the Huron people had long considered her a woman. She had learned years before that the French had the luxury of long childhoods.

"Welcome, Manon," said a commanding voice from the dining area.

Alexandre Lefebvre, her onetime foster father, entered the living area and bowed, very slightly, in her direction. Manon offered him a barely perceptible nod, like a queen acknowledging a stable-boy. The farmer shifted his weight from one foot to the other, his considerable size causing the floorboards to creak, calling attention back to himself.

"I am sorry to disturb you," Manon said, the French language still feeling odd on her tongue. "Your tenant found me gathering herbs in the forest, at the edge of your lands. I assured him that you would not object to my presence, but he preferred to hear it from you directly."

"The young lady speaks the truth, Rocher," Alexandre said to the farmer. "She is welcome anywhere on my lands and is not to be harassed, is that understood?"

"Yes, Seigneur," the man said with a bow. "Forgive the intrusion. Can't be too careful, you know." The man cast a spiteful look in Manon's direction. *Yes, because my people are the dangerous ones. You have that much to fear from a woman half your size alone in the woods?*

"Quite," Alexandre said. "You have other things to attend to, Rocher. Have a pleasant evening."

The farmer shook his head at the sight of Dame Lefebvre embracing a native girl, and bowed his way from the house.

"I'm sorry to have bothered you," Manon said, her tone still formal. "I must return home."

"Nonsense." Nicole took Manon's hand and led her to the table where the rest of the family sat. "You'll stay for supper."

"I cannot," Manon said, patting Nicole's hand. Now that Nicole was Madame Lefebvre, her hand was free of the calluses earned from a hard day's work. It pained her to refuse the hospitality of the woman who had been so kind to her, but she would not be able to sit still while Tawendeh was ill. "There is a fever in the Huron village. My brother is among the ill. It can become serious so quickly."

Nicole responded with the quizzical furrow of her brow at the mention of the word *brother*.

"Adoptive brother," Manon explained. She was an orphaned only child when she'd first met Nicole some nine years prior. Her aging grandmother had been less and less able to keep track of her young granddaughter, so Manon roamed unchecked. Her favorite thing to do was to wander into the woods and follow the brown-haired French angel who lived in the run-down cabin near the Huron village. She had never spoken to this lovely creature with her foreign clothes and creamy skin, but love-starved Manon could only imagine she was as charming and sweet as she looked. When Manon happened upon Nicole's husband, gravely injured by a Huron arrow that was meant for a stag, Manon found the angel and dragged her to the dying man. In the end, they were too late. Nicole adopted Manon and they were inseparable for the three years that followed.

"You'll be in want of supplies if the fever spreads. We'll send you with all we have." Nicole transformed at once. She was no longer just a loving mother and dutiful wife; she was a leader. The women of the house set to work gathering anything that could be of use when treating the ill: blankets, clean rags, and more food than Manon could hope to carry in four treks to the village.

Manon forced herself to keep from fidgeting as she waited for Nicole and her mother to assemble the bounty. She could be of no use, nor could she refuse the food and supplies her people needed. She stood and observed the family as they bustled about on her behalf rather than sitting down to their own supper. Nicole's parents had only spent a few weeks in Manon's company. They seemed to have a vague recollection of her and welcomed her into their home. The chatter of immaculately dressed children only served to make the small farmhouse seem all the more convivial.

"Your family has grown," Manon said, to break her awkward silence.

"Without question," Nicole said with a laugh as she folded a thick woolen blanket. She indicated a beautiful girl of eight with golden-brown curls. "You remember Hélène, of course, and Frédéric. Sabine was born shortly after you left, and Cécile and Roland arrived early last year."

Hélène was the child from Nicole's first husband, born only a few months after Manon had come into Nicole's care. She had stood by Nicole's side when the sturdy boy called Frédéric, the very image of his father with dark hair and flawless ivory skin, entered the world. He greeted Manon with wide eyes and a head cocked sideways with unspoken questions. *An imp, just like Tawendeh.* The toddling twins, blond and mischievous, were too absorbed in playing with their wooden horses on the dining room floor to notice the guest. Shy Sabine clung to her mother's skirts and looked at Manon with curiosity, weakly returning her gracious smile.

"What lovely children," Manon said in earnest. "You have been blessed."

"Amply," Alexandre agreed, taking his place at the table by his father-in-law's side as the women continued gathering. He reintroduced the Deschamps family without the slightest indication that Manon's arrival caused him displeasure. *Not that he would ever voice it.*

Nicole's parents, two younger sisters, and little brother had come to the colony nearly six years before when Manon was still a ward of the Lefebvres. Alexandre, Manon was sure, thought to please his wife by moving her family to the New World, thereby easing her homesickness and worry for their well-being. In so doing, however, he cut out Manon's place in their family and replaced it with Nicole's own sisters. Perhaps it wasn't by happenstance, either. Manon's presence with the leading woman in their small society already caused stares from the rest of the settlement. The elder Deschamps had clearly endured hard labor. Their faces showed the signs of too many days in the sun. Still, both looked plump and hardy, thanks to the bounty of their new land. They wore plainer clothes than the Lefebvres, but still fit in better in the settlement than Manon in her deerskin robes and moccasins.

Claudine Deschamps surpassed her sisters in looks, though perhaps not in grace. She was seventeen—almost exactly Manon's age, with dark brown hair and eyes that shone. Emmanuelle was almost sixteen and stouter than her sisters, but her hazel eyes that contrasted with her mahogany hair merited a second look from the young men of her acquaintance.

"You've been well, then, my dear?" Nicole asked as she placed a massive loaf of bread in a basket with a jug of soup.

"Yes." Manon paused to look at the perfectly roasted venison on the platter Madame Deschamps placed on the table, praying none could hear the rumbling of her stomach. New World foods cooked in the French tradition; foreign and familiar, all at once. "I've been trying to learn the methods my people use for treating illness. That's why I came. I was gathering herbs for a remedy for my little brother. I wouldn't have ventured so close to your lands otherwise."

"You're welcome to gather all the herbs you need here, darling," Nicole said with a glance toward her husband.

"Of course," Alexandre acknowledged, "though I would avoid Rocher. He had an unfortunate encounter with an Indian man a year or two back and is a tad leery, as you surely noticed."

"I'll bear that in mind," Manon said, keeping her less charitable thoughts to herself. Nicole flitted about the kitchen gathering more things to place in the basket. *I'll be lucky to make it home before daybreak carrying such a burden. Please do hurry.* The images of Tawendeh growing weaker and more feverish plagued her, but she would not shame herself by appearing ungrateful.

"You're sure you can't stay?" Nicole's eyes looked pleading as she scanned the room for anything else she could send along in the overflowing basket.

Claudine took a seat across the table from her brother-in-law and cleared her throat too loudly for it to be anything but a hint to her sister to sit down to the family meal. Nicole could not see that her younger sister was staring intently at the back of her head, seething impatience. Manon's view was unobstructed.

"I wish I could, truly, but I must tend to my brother and the others. And I wouldn't wish to intrude on a family meal."

"Manon, your visit is not an intrusion. Please promise you'll come see me?" Nicole took Manon's hands in hers, gripping as if to prevent her from slipping away a second time.

The thought of walking through the settlement, dressed in her deerskins, and knocking on the door of one of the finest houses in New France caused her empty stomach to churn. "I cannot promise, but our paths may cross again."

"I hope so, sweet girl." Nicole's eyes shone as she took Manon in her arms for a long embrace. Manon accepted the overladen basket that Nicole thrust at her and thanked her and Madame Deschamps extravagantly. It was enough food to feed her family for at least two weeks and one fewer worry for her as she nursed Tawendeh back to health.

Darkness had set in, though the waxing moon cast plenty of light to see Manon home. A fine carriage could not pass the rough paths to the Huron settlement; only a rugged wagon could make the journey. Nor would Manon accept the loan of a horse, so she set off toward home on foot. The faces of Nicole's abundant family flashed in her memory one by one. Nicole's darling children, proud husband, loving parents, and charming sisters. *You've filled my place admirably, Maman . . . Nicole . . . I hope, truly, that you've been happy.*

Mother Onatah looked up from her young son, who was still drenched in sweat and mumbling incoherently despite the cold cloths she applied to his forehead and face.

"No change." Manon's words were not a question.

Mother Onatah acknowledged them with a grim nod. Though the fever had yet to take a death grip on the boy, they both knew not to treat any fever with frivolity. *Yarrow tea, sooner rather than later.*

Manon added the herbs to her mortar to make a thick paste to boil into a pungent tisane. Too weak to protest, Tawendeh swallowed the potent, bitter brew and reclined back into his mother's embrace.

"What can we do now, Skenandoa?" Mother Onatah's black eyes glimmered with the unshed tears of her concern.

"We wait." The response was cruelly honest, but she would not give her adoptive mother false hope.

Mother Onatah had welcomed the frightened twelve-year-old girl as her own when Manon returned without warning from the French settlement. Onatah had stood before the council, claimed the girl as a daughter, and given her the name Skenandoa—*deer*—owing to her long limbs, graceful gait, and skittish nature. She was thus made an official member of Big Turtle clan once more, but Manon learned quickly that the Huron distrusted her French ways and her education as much as the French distrusted her brown skin and accented speech.

Still, Mother Onatah had given her a home, and it was better than no place at all. As the older woman ministered to her son,

Manon scanned the house for an occupation. The small longhouse was in disarray. Manon had been gone for hours, and Tawendeh commanded all his mother's attention. She began by organizing the pouches of dried herbs she'd strewn about that afternoon when she discovered her stores had run low. *I'll not make that mistake again. I'll gather herbs every week during the growing season for the rest of my days. My carelessness could have cost Tawendeh his life.* Chastising herself, she added more kindling to the fire and urged the flame higher in case more yarrow tea was needed.

"He's sleeping," Mother Onatah whispered to her. "You ought to do the same."

"I couldn't sleep, Mother. Not while he's so unwell."

"Then go for a walk and come back ready for rest. I'll have need of you in the morning."

"Very well." She didn't bother trying to persuade Mother Onatah to take a turn at sleeping herself. While Tawendeh was in danger, neither would sleep until her body forced her into repose.

Manon stood outside the longhouse, breathing in the midnight air—crisp, but mingled with the woodsy tang of chimney smoke. The light of the waxing moon bathed the village, preventing Heno, the chief's son, from taking her by surprise.

"There you are, my beauty," Heno said, emerging from the wood. His name meant *thunder* in their language, no doubt the Chief's attempt to inspire confidence in their allies and fear in their enemies. Thus far, the strategy had proven effective, for his son grew strong and tall—the perfect hunter-warrior.

"Good evening, my brave hunter," she said, offering the handsome young man a kiss as she took him in her arms.

"How is young Tawendeh?" he asked, pulling back slightly from the embrace and tucking a loose strand of her hair behind her ear.

"Improving," she said. "Mother Onatah ordered me to get some air while she tends him."

"I'm glad she did," he said, closing the gap between them and leaving a trail of soft kisses on her face, careful not to disturb the bruise.

"The white man?" he asked, tracing the edge of her puffy cheek with his finger.

She nodded. He growled softly in response. "How are the others?" Manon asked, resting her cheek against his broad chest to hide the injury and change the subject. She wouldn't let the stinking French farmer ruin her time with Heno.

"Fifteen more have fallen ill. No one has died yet, but a few of the elderly and one of the children look close." He spoke as though reporting back to the council about a scouting expedition or a hunt. *He has to detach himself, or else it would be too painful.*

"If only they would let me . . ." Manon began.

"I have spoken to anyone who will listen. They will come around. They'll have to." Heno ran his fingers down the thick braid of black hair that extended down past her lower back, and gripped her closer still.

I just hope they will accept my help before it's too late. There was nothing to be done, however. Any attempt to persuade them would only make them more wary.

"I need you," she breathed between kisses.

"With pleasure, my beauty." He pulled out of her embrace and led her to their favorite clearing, the place they had met for the past two years when the weather was fine. On colder nights they coupled in whatever warm corner they could find.

Though the night air bit their flesh and dew covered the grass, Heno's warm, muscled body drew her mind from the chill.

His mouth was ardent. His hands moved over her body with the confidence of an established lover. The man who taught her the art of love, despite all her misgivings in the early days. Adjusting to the ways of the Huron, where people viewed adolescent exploration as innocent and natural, took a while to accept after three years of Catholic indoctrination.

Manon lay in his arms for minutes—perhaps even hours—sated and impervious to the cold.

"I want to make a child with you," Heno said, breathing in her ear.

"Please don't start this again. I beg you. Not tonight," she said. "I can't bear to argue."

"If you have my child, Father will be forced to let us marry," Heno reasoned.

"He needn't do any such thing. And if he refuses, I'd be alone, with a child to raise." Her grip on his arm grew tighter and she had to keep herself from digging her nails into his flesh. Few raised ire in her as much as their chief.

Heno perched up on his elbows, taking her chin with his thumb and forefinger, forcing her to look into the depths of his serious black eyes. "I'd never let that happen, Skenandoa."

"You're the son of our chief. You'll do exactly as you're bid." She brushed his hand away. "You're the prince of your people, no freer to do as you please than a prince of France."

"I can't imagine the prince of a great country not being free to do precisely what he likes." Heno's jaw grew taut as it often did when she mentioned the French.

"Listen when your father speaks," she said. "His decisions have nothing to do with his happiness, but rather the welfare of his people." *And that means seeing you married to a sweet, obedient girl who cares for nothing more than the traditions of our people and securing your lineage.*

"That almost sounded like a compliment," Heno said.

"Whatever the issues I might take with your father, self-interest is not one of them," Manon said. "Though I will never care for the man who cast out his sister for taking me in."

"I wouldn't say Onatah is cast out," Heno said. "She still lives with her tribe."

"And is all but forsaken by them. Because she showed me kindness," Manon said.

Heno sighed deeply, whether frustrated by her logic or his father's irrational fear of outside influence, Manon knew not.

"I will have you for my wife, my beauty." He took her chin again, this time kissing her, claiming her mouth with his.

"Nothing would make me happier, my brave hunter," Manon said as he pulled away.

For a moment she indulged in her favorite fantasy: a life where the tribe accepted her as Heno's wife. A pillar of her community. A healer. A mother. She allowed herself to consider it only rarely; in her heart she knew it would never happen. But as she lay in Heno's arms, optimism flowed through her veins, nourishing her body like manna.

"I love you, Heno," she whispered, cupping his face and kissing his lips, savoring his taste like she would her last meal. "For now, just love me and let the future settle itself."

"Always, my beauty." He shifted to reclaim his position atop her, but Manon placed her hand on his chest. She gently pushed him to his back and straddled him, claiming her pleasure as the midnight wind stung her skin. She would have to pull away before he was satisfied and help him find his release in other ways, bathe carefully with herbs, and drink tea brewed from the papoose root as a precaution. For a few moments, however, none of that mattered. She was neither Huron nor French. She was free of everything except her love for the beautiful man beneath her.

CHAPTER 2

Claudine

May 1677

One of Alexandre's stipulations of Claudine and Emmanuelle's staying in town was that they would obey Nicole as readily as they would their own mother. Had it not been for her brother-in-law's decree, Claudine would never have agreed to wake moments after the cock's crow to take supplies to the Huron village with her two sisters and their longtime friend Gabrielle Giroux. She wanted to scoff at the idea of traipsing through the woods with blankets and food to people who had not requested and who would not welcome their interference. But she stilled her tongue. Even if it meant enduring a morning in the woods, it wasn't worth risking Nicole's—or worse, Alexandre's—ire.

"Will one of the servants be driving the carriage?" Emmanuelle asked Nicole, who had come to ensure the girls were up and preparing for the day. Emmanuelle wasn't overly fond of horses since an unfortunate accident when she first came to the colony resulted in a seriously injured leg and the loss of a much-needed horse.

"Pascal Giroux will drive us in the wagon he uses for deliveries," Nicole replied, looking over Claudine's trunk for worn clothing to add to their stockpile for the village. "It can maneuver better on the narrow roads than anything we have. He offered to drive since Gabrielle had asked to come along."

The two young Girouxes were both wards and apprentices of Elisabeth and Gilbert Beaumont, who ran the most successful bakery in the colony. Nicole and Elisabeth, along with their fellow shipmate Rose, had forged a friendship on their three-month voyage to the colony that social convention would not tarnish. An attachment between the wife of a landowner and a simple baker might have been unthinkable in France, but thankfully such lines were far less rigid in the new world.

"We'll be down for breakfast shortly." Emmanuelle smiled at Nicole, who left the room with a satisfied nod and a couple of worn chemises in hand. *Always sister's pet.*

"Why in Christendom do we have to go out all that way to haul blankets and broth to people we don't even know? Didn't we provide her with enough last night? Can't Nicole *send* someone if she thinks it's necessary to empty the house for them?" Claudine asked to no one in particular.

"Because Manon meant a great deal to Nicole, and she wants to help if she can."

Claudine rolled her eyes and bit her tongue. Emmanuelle always had a response for everything, and it was usually what Nicole and Alexandre wanted to hear. Worse, Emmanuelle offered her explanations as if she were explaining a simple sum to a befuddled child. *Maddening.*

Breakfast was a harried affair; Alexandre eating leisurely while Nicole chided the girls to eat quickly so they could get underway. There was an unspoken censure in Alexandre's eyes, but he rarely contradicted his wife. She was so often the model of propriety and restraint that he must have felt obliged to overlook her few eccentricities. In particular, her affection for the Huron girl that Claudine sensed he never fully understood.

As they left the settlement, the houses and stone buildings gave way to trees, and the wide, well-maintained roads gave way to narrow, rocky paths. Emmanuelle and Gabrielle chatted as they often did, but Nicole kept her eyes fixed to the path as though she, and not Pascal, were driving the wagon. Claudine looked at the endless evergreens and wondered why she had ever thought this would be some magical fairy kingdom where she would never be in want of diversion and handsome suitors. In her years in the settlement, she had yet to reconcile the shattered dreams of her twelve-year-old self, though she was now a young woman approaching eighteen.

Claudine, having devoured the few letters Nicole had sent home, leaped at the chance to come to the New World, where her sister had married so far above her circle. When Alexandre's agent came to offer them passage to this New France, Claudine nearly screamed at her father's hesitance to leave their barren land. It hadn't taken much persuasion in the end. The voyage provided futures for the girls and their younger brother, Georges. What was more, their elder brothers would absorb the barren land into their own farms, giving them both sizable holdings. The land could rest fallow for several years and it would bear crops again. It would still belong to a Deschamps, and that was as much as their father could have hoped for.

She'd pictured a shining metropolis and was crestfallen when she learned she'd be living on a farm much like the one where she was born. The house was infinitely better. The land was fertile. But it was still a farm, and one that seemed to be a thousand miles from anywhere interesting. The fledgling town, while nothing to the lively bustle of Rouen, was immeasurably preferable to living out on her parents' homestead. She loved her sister for taking them in and vowed she'd make a good match since she had the gift of connections to some of the best society New France had to offer. If she had any luck, she'd find a man of good sense who wanted to return to France—maybe even the excitement of Paris—and would take her away from the monotony of country life forever. Somewhere there had to be a young man with dark hair and flashing eyes who would whisk her away to a life of adventure and varied society. She clutched her wool cloak tight about her shoulders against the damp spring air. *He has to exist somewhere.*

In the meantime, Claudine lost herself in poetry. Permanently placed next to her bed was a love-worn copy of ballads by the *trouvères*—the courtly poets of medieval times—that a bookseller had given her when he realized her arresting brown eyes could actually read. It was ragged then and wouldn't have fetched more than a few *sous* from the small population interested in his wares. Claudine had read it to the point where the corners were indelibly smudged with her fingerprints. While Emmanuelle read widely, Claudine found solace in the one tome. The depictions of gallant knights and maidens took her away from the tedium of farm life and chores even after hundreds of readings.

The Huron village came into view; rows of longhouses dotted the small clearing. A few men stood at the edge of a large fire, scowling like bears awakened midwinter at the small envoy of French who had just descended upon them.

Nicole stepped down from the wagon first. Claudine waited, her breath catching in her throat, as her sister approached the men. Nicole shook visibly, but stood as proud as the Queen herself.

Please, God, don't let them be as unfriendly as they look.

Claudine had never seen such a living arrangement in her life. The building was high, even by French standards, seeming to stretch up a solid mile. There were pelts from deer, beaver, bear, and other animals covering nearly every surface of the immense building. It seemed Manon had managed to convince the council to separate the ill into a longhouse by themselves. The sick slept on beds built onto the wall like shelves—not unlike the bunks on the ship Claudine and her family had sailed on from France. The only noises in the longhouse were the chattering teeth and wheezing of the fever-riddled and the crackling of the fire under Manon's thick cauldron. Nicole stood next to Manon, who tended the bubbling mixture, while the others gathered a step behind, anxiously awaiting a command from one of them.

"You shouldn't be here." Manon barely looked away from the vapors slithering up from her pot as she stirred.

And a welcome to you, too. I guess you're too good for a wagonload of supplies and five pairs of helping hands. I won't be the one holding up the departure if Nicole bids us to leave.

"You need help, Manon," Nicole said, placing her hand on Manon's deerskin-clad back. "Please tell us how we can be useful."

"By going home. I promise." Sagging dark circles of exhaustion framed Manon's eyes.

"You heard her, Nicole. She doesn't need our help. I'm sure she's quite capable of managing things on her own." Claudine stepped forward and put her hand on Nicole's arm to lead her back to the safety of the wagon, but her sister would not move.

"Give us something to do," Nicole implored. Claudine crossed her arms over her chest and restrained a sigh. Nicole's coolness in public, her composure, was always something Claudine admired; yet in the presence of this common girl, all of that restraint was gone. Nicole was once again the awkward farm girl from Rouen.

"I need more fresh water and yarrow flowers," Manon said at length, as though speaking a dire confession.

"I'll fetch the water," Pascal said at once from the dark corner of the longhouse, where he had been lingering in silence, exiting before anyone could call him back. *He's a smart young man, probably trying to keep away from the fever. It'll be a miracle if we don't all catch our deaths.*

"What does yarrow look like?" Emmanuelle asked. Manon produced a stem with clusters of dainty white flowers like a riot of miniature daisies.

"Gather plenty of it. It's the only thing that seems to be helping."

"Let's go," Gabrielle chimed in, gesturing to the door with the basket she held firmly in her right hand. "I think I saw a patch not more than a mile from here along the road when we came in." Claudine followed Emmanuelle and Gabrielle, both of whom walked briskly to the main road that connected the Huron village to the French settlement. *Anything to be out of there and away from those people. Who knows when they'll decide they've had enough of us and choose to send us on our way by force? Or worse. I doubt her concoction even works. It'll probably do no more than give them a bitter taste in their mouths and a sour stomach.*

As Gabrielle promised, the abundant yarrow patch was a ten-minute walk from Manon's longhouse. The gentle spring rains and nurturing sun had yielded wildflower patches thicker than Claudine had ever seen.

"Let's use knives and cut the stems higher up, rather than pulling," Emmanuelle suggested.

"That will take longer and I don't want to have to come back for more." Claudine knelt and began yanking the stems from the ground, roots and all, ignoring Gabrielle's glare.

"The plants won't grow back if you aren't gentle with them," Gabrielle warned.

"I'm not wasting more time gathering weeds than I absolutely have to." Claudine gripped another yarrow stem and yanked it from the earth.

"Claudine, the Huron depend on these herbs for their medicine. Treat them carefully." Emmanuelle sounded so very much like Nicole that Claudine raised her head to see if their older sister had followed the three of them to the clearing. Claudine gritted her teeth at the rebuke. *Don't forget I'm the older sister. Learn your place.* But her censure went unvoiced. The world seemed to side with Emmanuelle and there was no winning.

"Fine. You two can sit here rolling in the weeds. I'm going back."

Claudine thought about walking back to the settlement on her own. Perhaps she could entertain Alexandre with tales of how his wife was carrying on with a pack of savages with no regard for his respectability and position, but town was miles away on a path she didn't know.

She sat down on a boulder just out of view of Emmanuelle and Gabrielle and let the tears flow down her cheeks. Nicole had told her countless times that she was supposed to be a pillar of the community and the first to volunteer her services to those in need. It was supposed to feel noble and self-sacrificing, not tiresome and aggravating. *This isn't how things were meant to be. I am going to disappoint them both and they'll send me back to the farm for the rest of my days.*

It was another quarter of an hour before Emmanuelle and Gabrielle met up with Claudine, having gathered enough of the yarrow to satisfy the demand, or so they hoped. To Claudine the overflowing basket looked like a pile of wildflowers big enough to treat several fever-ridden villages, but she didn't presume to know what went into the brewing of a tisane to cure fever.

Knowing long walks in cool weather irritated Emmanuelle's lungs and worsened her limp, Claudine took the overfilled basket and strode ahead. She was almost a hundred yards ahead of her sister and Gabrielle when the longhouse came into view. *Thank the Lord we didn't get lost. I'll learn to knit blankets for the poor after this so perhaps I might at least be able to be of service to the less fortunate from the comfort of the settee.*

In the longhouse, Manon sat beside an older woman who lay very ill with the fever. Manon held her hand and muttered words in her native tongue. The woman was petite to begin with, but the glow from sweat and the quaking of her shivering body made her look like a child. A weak child.

"I have your flowers for you," Claudine announced, trying to call Manon's attention back to her. Manon simply held up one hand to command silence. Claudine wanted to fling the weeds at Manon's head in exasperation, but stood frozen to the floor. Nicole stood a few yards away, as transfixed by the scene as Claudine was. Nicole was always the center of activity . . . always the one to organize everything . . . yet she stood immobile and useless. At seeing her sister in such a state, Claudine felt an ache in her stomach as though she were witnessing something unnatural—something wrong—like the dust flying off her father's barren field when she was a girl.

The fragile woman took a rasping breath, exhaled, and did not take another. Grim-faced, Manon closed the woman's eyes. She stood, took the basket from Claudine, and returned to her cauldron over the fire where she added new flowers to the mixture.

Emmanuelle and Gabrielle now stood next to Claudine, and their eyes followed Manon as well. Claudine summoned the nerve to look at Nicole and raise a questioning brow. Nicole looked up from the deceased woman and crossed to the waiting girls.

"That woman was Manon's adoptive mother," Nicole whispered in explanation. Claudine looked at Manon, who knelt, seemingly transfixed by the simmering cauldron. *Poor girl. No one deserves to lose a mother so young.* There were no words or gestures that Claudine could conjure up that didn't sound ridiculous, so she stood in place and waited for someone to offer up an order. It was perhaps the first time in her life she would have been glad of a useful occupation and, consequently, the first time one wasn't eagerly waiting on the tip of her mother's or sister's tongue.

After a few agonizing minutes of standing idle, a few men, mostly older, entered the longhouse. The man at the front was tall and imposing, with a face that bore more lines of experience and labor than Claudine had ever seen in her life. He was only a fraction as intimidating as the man to his right. Years younger, several inches taller, and clearly furious, he was not a man Claudine would ever dare to speak to, let alone provoke.

Claudine clutched her skirt to hide the trembling of her hands. Her breath stopped short in her chest, the lack of air causing the fire to take on an eerie halo. *We're all going to die here.*

Manon stood and approached the men, no fear discernible in her face. The oldest man spoke a few words in his language, and Manon nodded. The conversation continued a few moments longer, until a young boy, perhaps seven years old, ran to where she stood and flung his arms around Manon's waist. She spoke several words in return. Though Claudine could parse none of the words, she recognized authority and confidence when she heard it. Were it not for the crackling fear in the air, Claudine was certain she'd feel a prickling of envy at Manon's bravado.

The men exited the longhouse, the younger man lingering a few moments. He said a few words to Manon, kind ones, if Claudine interpreted correctly. She returned a terse, quiet reply and turned her back to him. The fierce-looking man's face seemed to soften for a brief moment, but almost as quickly he reclaimed his mask of hostility and followed in the footsteps of the tribe's elders.

Manon knelt before the boy, who now wept openly in her arms. Her brother, Claudine presumed. He buried his face in Manon's shoulder and sobbed for his mother. Claudine swallowed back some tears, not entirely sure why they were there. This was not her grief.

"Darling, what can we do?" Nicole said at length.

"Help me gather our things and take me into town so I can find work, please." Manon's confidence was gone, her words a mere whisper.

"Why?" Claudine blurted out.

"That man was the Chief of this clan. He has ordered me to leave. He believes the fever to be my fault."

"How positively idiotic. . . ." Claudine rolled her eyes in the direction of the door.

"Be that as it may, he is the Chief and I am no longer welcome here. I was only allowed to stay under his sister's protection as it was, and now that she is gone, I must leave."

"His own sister is dead and his first act is to banish the child she chose to raise as her own?" Nicole's jaw set, her teeth visibly clenched. This look never boded well for the person who caused it. This time, Claudine feared her sister's wrath might bring down the fury of the entire Huron Confederacy on the five of them. *Calm yourself, sister.*

"So it would seem. Would you help me?" Manon's look was at once proud and pleading. What options did she have but to ask for help? A life foraging in the woods would be no life at all.

"Manon, you needn't even ask. You will stay with us as long as you wish. We'll leave at once."

"Tawendeh must come as well. I promised Mother Onatah . . ."

"My dearest girl, I could not ask you to abandon your brother. I daresay there is always room for one more in the Lefebvre nursery."

"Thank you," Manon whispered.

"Let's be on our way," Nicole urged.

Claudine nodded, her agreement as fervent as it had ever been. She, Emmanuelle, and Gabrielle gathered up Manon's and Tawendeh's sparse belongings. In all her life, Claudine was never so thrilled to find herself in the back of a rattling wagon on a bumpy road. She hoped for Nicole's sake her brother-in-law would be as happy with the new additions to his family.

Back at the Lefebvre house, Nicole went off in the direction of Alexandre's study, Manon and Tawendeh in tow, presumably to tell the master of the house of the way the Huron chief had cast them all out and why he had two more mouths to feed. Part of Claudine would have liked to hide in the curtains to hear that conversation, but she didn't want Alexandre to know she'd had any real part in the whole debacle.

"Why don't we do another fitting on your gown?" Gabrielle suggested. Gabrielle had remarkable talent as a seamstress and had been commissioned to make Claudine's gown for her entrée into society, looming only a few weeks away. She was almost eighteen now and the hour was already late for such an affair. It was nothing so grand as a true coming-out ball, Alexandre had explained, but there would be dinner and dancing. It wasn't Paris, but it was the best she could have in their fledgling town. A good deal more than she would have had back in France, where the only future that awaited her had been starvation and poverty. It was the stuff of her nightmares.

Claudine nodded enthusiastically at Gabrielle's suggestion. After a morning trekking around in the mud and wallowing in weeds, something as civilized as a dress fitting seemed positively luxuriant. "Lunch and a good scrubbing first, though."

The staff provided the girls with a simple lunch—some ham and cheese with a loaf of the best bread from the Beaumont Bakery and some chilled cider. By the time she'd eaten her fill and washed her face and hands in a basin of heated water, Claudine felt almost herself again.

Emmanuelle curled up in a chair with her book while Gabrielle helped Claudine into the daisy-yellow silk confection she would wear for her presentation to Quebec society. It was just the color to bring out the brilliancy in her chestnut hair and the gold flecks in her brown eyes. Her eyes never wavered from the looking glass.

I doubt the girls in Paris have ball gowns any more fashionable than this. I can't wait to see their faces as I make my entrance. After the ball I won't be little Claudine Deschamps any longer. I'll be known as the protégée of the Lefebvres and the celebrated beauty of our little town.

"I'm so sorry things went the way they did with Manon," Gabrielle said, her voice muffled by the fabric as she worked her way around the skirt, making sure it lay perfectly before she tacked the hem with basting stitches. "She looked upset to be separated from her people again."

"She'll manage to get over the separation, I daresay. She'll get to live here in comfort rather than in some drafty longhouse with dirt floors. I'd think she'd be ecstatic to live in a proper house." Claudine strived to keep the exasperation from her voice. It spoiled the effect of the dress. She had to be perfect.

"There's more to life than a fine house, Claudine," Emmanuelle chastised from her seat in the corner. Gabrielle stayed focused on her hem, but Claudine could hear a small grunt of approval from the floor. "Imagine what it must be like to be cast out like that."

"To give up all your friends and most of your family? Really, Emmanuelle, do you think I cannot imagine such a thing?" Claudine broke her gaze from the mirror and looked at her younger sister. They had been young when they left France, but there were friends, aunts and uncles, not to mention their older brothers and their families whom they would likely never see again.

"We weren't exactly banished, Claudine," Emmanuelle retorted, though her eyes seemed to admit her sister wasn't in the wrong.

"We had no more choice in the matter than if we had been," Claudine reasoned. "And whatever you say, I remember how despondent Nicole was when the ungrateful little wretch left and she seems just as ungrateful now."

In truth Claudine had been puzzled at her sister's distress when Manon had left only a few weeks after the Deschamps arrived from France, and utterly perplexed as to why a young girl would leave a comfortable home to live in the woods like a squirrel.

"They were quite close," Gabrielle said, glancing upward as she sat sprawled on the floor. "Manon called her 'Maman' and Seigneur Lefebvre paid for her schooling."

"And she repaid her so nicely by running away." Claudine would not be swayed. No matter what her reasons, Manon had hurt Nicole badly by leaving and Claudine wasn't as ready as the rest to forgive her.

"I don't know the whole story," Gabrielle said, inching along the floor, rolling and pinning the hem of the delicate fabric as she spoke. "She came to live with them before I moved to town. It had something to do with the death of Madame Lefebvre's first husband." Nicole rarely mentioned Luc Jarvais, Hélène's father, who had been killed in some sort of accident. Alexandre seemed to have taken over his role as husband and father so thoroughly there was no room for Luc's memory. Such a story wasn't uncommon. New France was a harsh place to live in and there wasn't such an over-abundance of women, especially ten years before, that widows remained unmarried long.

"It seems so strange to think of Nicole married twice," Claudine said. "But all the same, taking Manon back in—with a brother besides—seems overgenerous."

"Manon was good to our sister in her time of need," Emmanuelle said, shooting her sister a severe look over the pages of her Latin text.

"Go back to your books, Emmanuelle," Claudine spat. Nothing set her on edge like her sister's piety.

"Don't be so unkind, then," Emmanuelle said. "Nicole was clearly attached to the girl. You saw how she cried that night when Manon turned up at Maman and Papa's."

Quite the homecoming, yes. Crying over a Huron girl for anyone to see? I doubt Queen Maria Theresa has ever cried in her life. As much as Claudine wanted to argue the subject, she bit her tongue. Claudine didn't trust her own temper.

"There," Gabrielle said, breaking the uneasy silence as she had enough of the hem sewn that she could continue at home. "It just wants a finished hem and time for the wrinkles to give way. You'll be lovely."

"It's beautiful, Gabrielle," Claudine pronounced. "You're truly talented."

"Thank you for trusting me with the job," Gabrielle said, gathering her notions in her sewing basket. "I confess that working with such an expensive cut of silk did wear on my nerves."

"You needn't have worried." Emmanuelle stood up and clutched her book to her chest, finally admiring Gabrielle's labors. "You sew so well, you could have your own shop in Paris."

"Yes, yes. It's lovely. Madame Lefebvre will settle the bill," Claudine said, adopting an officious tone. *You're going to be a society lady; it's time to act like it. To speak like it.*

"Of course." Gabrielle helped Claudine out of the gown and placed it carefully in her valise. "I'll hem it properly tonight and send it over with Pascal tomorrow."

Claudine nodded and Gabrielle left the room with a nod in Emmanuelle's direction.

"You shouldn't dismiss her like a servant." Emmanuelle set her book aside. Claudine could see her sister's usually placid hazel eyes bore into the back of her head from the mirror while she straightened her chemise.

"What do you mean?" Claudine asked. "How else should one speak to a dressmaker?"

"When one is a farmer's daughter?" Emmanuelle asked. "You speak to her as your equal. Gabrielle has been our friend for years. Attends classes with us. She's not a lowly chambermaid, nor are you some grand courtier."

Claudine glared at her sister as she pulled on her skirts for dinner. "I was friendly to her. I see no reason to be more than that. It's not as if I were rude. You need to learn to temper your praise a little. Learn to be aloof for once in your life."

"You *were* rude," Emmanuelle snapped. "You might be as grand as the Queen of Sheba someday, but for now you'd do well to remember that Gabrielle Giroux is every bit of the same station we are."

"Not for long," Claudine said. "Nicole welcomed us here so that we could make matches above our station. No one is taking that trouble for Gabrielle Giroux."

"As you say." Emmanuelle, already dressed for the evening meal, returned to her book, her maddening little way of saying the conversation was over. Claudine lobbed the good chemise she reserved for eveningwear at Emmanuelle's head.

"I do say." Claudine smoothed her skirt, pretending she'd not lifted a finger. "Nicole has opened up a new life for me. She'll do the same for you, too, if you'll look up from your books and let her."

"When the time comes," Emmanuelle said, tossing the garment back with less precision than her sister. "This may surprise you, but I'm no more anxious to be a farmer's wife than you. I prefer the comforts of town and varied society. I'm just not in as much of a hurry to wed."

Claudine rolled her eyes. She had never believed in the virtue of patience as Emmanuelle and Nicole seemed to.

"No one will want you if you keep poring over those books of yours. The priest himself says that reading is an unsuitable pastime for ladies." Claudine pinched her cheeks and admired the effect in the glass, desolate that Nicole forbade her to use even a hint of rouge.

"And you'd do better to pore over something other than your poetry book. Courtly knights and ladies in distress. Your husband won't know what to do the first time you sulk because he won't defend your honor in a joust."

"First of all, dear sister, I don't recall many jousting tournaments in this settlement of ours. Or anywhere of import for about the last hundred years, for that matter. Secondly, at least I know what I want." *The brave prince, gallant, strong, stoic. And wealthy, if at all possible. Preferably with a home in Paris where he will whisk me away, minutes after our wedding. That won't happen for a farmer's daughter. I must be more than a simple girl from the farm on the night of the ball, or I never will be more than that all the rest of my days.*

"I know exactly what it is you want, Claudine, but I fear he doesn't exist outside of those poems of yours."

CHAPTER 3

Gabrielle

June 1677

Gabrielle reveled in the buttery silk as it slid over her fingers, calloused by too many hours spent pulling hot trays from the oven and scrubbing bowls crusted with hardened remnants of sweet filings for Elisabeth and Gilbert Beaumont's famous pastries. She was needed below stairs to help with the supper rush at the bakery. Customers would come needing their loaves for the evening meal and Elisabeth would need her to attend to those customers, no matter how much she longed to continue her work on Claudine's gown. With a ragged sigh, she slipped a clean sheet over the precious garment, stifling the dancing golden light with the white cloth. *A shame a gown like this must be for such a proud, spiteful girl, but so long as I have the making of it, I won't complain about who's to wear it.* She tied her beige canvas apron over her tattered brown skirt and went down the stairs. That she still had work to do before surrendering the lovely dress to Claudine was no small consolation.

Pascal would be out delivering today to the customers who sent in their flour in exchange for their bread at a lesser price. It was a complicated system, but it helped them to skirt some of the regulations the Crown had set forth regarding the inventories they must keep in stock and the prices they had to set. Make no mistake, the bailiff kept close eye on the Beaumonts and a closer eye on Gabrielle herself. She was no more than eight months from her sixteenth birthday. Another edict. She would have to marry by her sixteenth birthday; else Gilbert and Elisabeth, her beloved adoptive parents, would be forced to pay a substantial fine. This would not affect the Deschamps girls. They were French-born and not bound to that decree. She, however, was a daughter of New France and did not have the luxury of time.

What pained Gabrielle more was that the edict was in her best interest. Marriage was her only chance to provide for her future. While Gilbert and Elisabeth lived, she would always have houseroom and work, but when their sons took over the business, she would have no such guarantee. Marriage would provide her with security, but suitors did not line up to court the orphaned daughter of the town drunk and his wastrel wife. Ten years ago, even five, the lack of women would have assured her a match of her choosing. But women were more plentiful now, and Gabrielle would have to overcome her family's reputation to secure a match of any kind.

Below stairs in the shop, Gilbert was removing fresh loaves from the oven while Elisabeth tidied the shop for the onslaught of customers who arrived as dependably as the sunset in the two hours before their evening meal.

The Beaumonts were a small family by town standards, with only the two boys to show for their happy union. For this reason, they were able to give Pascal and Gabrielle houseroom without difficulty. Though it was not to say the arrangement was without benefits to both sides. While the Giroux children earned experience in the bakery and had the protection and love of a family, the Beaumonts in return had two eager and willing workers. Not to mention, much-wanted children to love as their own, since it seemed an abundant family was not their destiny.

It raised suspicion with some. In a town where a new babe every year was the norm, such a small family was thought to be the result of matrimonial discord, deceit, or witchcraft. *Even though some large families haven't enough to feed their youngsters, though their fathers are cruel and shiftless, though their mothers are worn as thin as ten-year-old kid gloves—those families are admired. Lauded for their contributions to the colony.* She bit her tongue, however, when she heard the malevolent gossip, whispered loud enough the speakers could be certain she heard them. Her temper matched her flame-red hair, and to unleash it in public would do her no service. They were jealous of the Beaumonts' successful business and Elisabeth's infectious sweetness, and Gabrielle suspected more than a few wished their own unions hadn't been blessed with such fecundity.

"Sweetheart, can you call up to Pierre?" Elisabeth asked, looking up from the counter she wiped with a clean cloth. "It's time for him to come help sweep the floors."

He was not quite seven years old, but even little Pierre had his place in the running of the bakery. Only his baby brother, Fabien, sitting with a wooden toy cow in the corner of the shop, was exempt from these duties. In a few years, the babbling toddler would be expected to do his part. As with every other family in their acquaintance, when the younger brother grew of age to take over a duty, the elder was promoted to new responsibility.

Gabrielle's calls above stairs went unanswered, so she bounded back to their living area to find what detained her usually dutiful younger brother. As their home above the shop was not overly large, his absence was obvious within a few moments.

"He's not upstairs," Gabrielle announced as she descended the steps. "Is he out back?" The open space behind the shop, which housed the ovens they used in warm, dry weather, was a favorite place for Pierre to play. Gilbert emerged from the kitchens and shook his head.

"I'm sure he's gone off to the Lefebvres' to play with Frédéric," Elisabeth said. Her voice was calm, but the furrow of her brow betrayed her concern. The concern shifted to worry when Pierre had yet to return by the time Elisabeth was ready to put supper on the table. Pierre had a lot to learn about responsibility, but his punctuality at mealtimes was as dependable as snow in February.

"I can go see if he's had dinner with the Lefebvres. Go ahead and eat without me. The stew will keep well enough. I'll be back within the half hour, Pierre in tow, I'm sure."

Elisabeth nodded; Gilbert gave an unusually surly grunt. "And he'll have a tanned backside when next I see him, no mistaking that." His exterior looked gruff, but Gabrielle knew it was a pretense to hide his disquiet.

Gabrielle exited the shop and sucked the cool evening air through her teeth. The Beaumont boys did not yet understand how precious they were to their parents. Nor did they know how lucky they were to have parents who loved them so dearly. Visions of her own parents came to mind. Her father's love for the bottle and his fondness for the strap. Her mother so worn down by caring for her brood and their teetering shack that she had no strength within her to stop his whippings when they exceeded decency. *You are fortunate boys indeed. You'd do well not to frighten your poor parents into early graves.*

The Lefebvres' butler admitted Gabrielle with civility, but no ceremony. She was a friend to the family, so treated with more respect than a servant, but not of such status to merit an announcement in the drawing room where they all sat invested in their pre-dinner pursuits. Nicole and Claudine embroidering, Emmanuelle, Manon, and Alexandre entrenched in their books.

"I expect our Pierre is here, helping Frédéric give Nanny fits as usual?" Gabrielle asked after she'd greeted everyone.

"Not that I've seen," Nicole said. "But it's been at least two hours since I was in the nursery. Shall we go see?"

Gabrielle nodded and ascended the staircase in Nicole's wake. She wondered if she ought to say something to spark a conversation out of politeness, but could think of nothing that did not sound ridiculous in her head. Though Nicole Lefebvre was the picture of graciousness, Gabrielle found her stomach twist whenever she was forced to speak more than a few words in her presence.

Nicole opened the door to the nursery to find Hélène directing the twins and Sabine in a make-believe session of school. Pierre wasn't in the fray and neither, it seemed, were Frédéric or Manon's brother, Tawendeh, whom Nicole had dubbed Théodore to ease pronunciation woes in the nursery.

"Nanny LaForge, where are the boys?" Nicole demanded. "Was Pierre Beaumont here with them?"

"Yes, indeed, madame," the older woman said, standing to address her mistress. "He came about an hour ago. The boys set in that corner there hatching some devilishness, I'm sure. They said they was going to the Beaumonts and would ask your blessing before going out. I figured they were just off to pester the good Madame Beaumont for some sweets."

"They were whispering in the corner as Nanny says, Maman," Hélène interjected. "They never let me in on their fun. They say I tattle since I stopped them from leaving the frog in Claudine's bed." Hélène's large blue eyes searched her mother's face, as if to assess if she herself were in any sort of trouble.

"Do you have any idea where they may have gone?" Gabrielle took a steadying breath. There was no sense in frightening the girl. If she burst into tears, they might lose precious time they needed to search for the boys.

"Frédéric has been asking Théodore to take him to his village so he can see the longhouses. Pierre made them promise to take him with them when they decided to go. I didn't think they'd really do it, but they've been talking about it since Théodore came. Pierre wants a real Indian bow for himself."

How Théodore was able to talk such things after only a few weeks immersed in the French language, Gabrielle could not quite fathom. Apparently a trip into an actual native village and the promise of an authentic Huron bow were enough to motivate them to find a way to make themselves understood.

Gabrielle was already halfway down the stairs announcing Hélène's report of the boys' whereabouts before Nicole could finish barking orders at the nanny. *If that woman has her job in the morning, it will be an utter miracle.* Alexandre was the first to get to his feet. His older son and heir was out, darkness falling, possibly cavorting off to a village his mother and aunts had been chased out of only a few weeks before. He called out a command in the general direction of the kitchen, to which the response was the thud of boots on stone floors.

"You cannot go bursting into the village brandishing muskets and torches," said Manon, taking to her feet. She stood only a few inches shorter than Alexandre and used all of her height at that moment. Every motion she made conveyed that she needed him to listen to her.

"I can and I will," Alexandre said, ignoring Manon, continuing to organize his conquest.

"I am not doubting your ability or sincerity, monsieur. I am simply pointing out it is not the wisest course of action if you wish your son to be returned unscathed. If he has gone, they will likely send him home. If they reach the village, the worst-case scenario is that they keep Tawendeh—Théodore—and send Frédéric and Pierre back by themselves. I mean no disrespect, but I know Tawendeh is a fair hand at tracking in the woods. I don't know if your boys are as skilled as he." Manon stood, arms akimbo, defying him to question her. *How she can speak to the* seigneur *with such authority, I'll never know.*

Nicole touched her husband's arm, his entire attention shifting to her. "Darling, I think Manon may be right. She knows her people far better than we do."

"Then what do you propose we do?" Alexandre turned to his ward, his tone and expression calm. He didn't want to take her advice, but could clearly see the logic in his wife's words. He was nothing if not a rational man, and it was because of this trait that the ears of Quebec's elite bent in his direction when he spoke.

"Let me go. I may not be welcome there, but they will question my presence in fetching the boys far less than any of yours. They won't harm me out of respect for Mother Onatah's memory," Manon suggested.

"We couldn't let you go alone," Nicole insisted. "If, God forbid, one of them is hurt, you'll need help."

"I'll go with you," Gabrielle announced at once. "I won't pose any threat, either, and they've seen me there with Manon."

Manon nodded her agreement. *All the better, I was coming with you anyway.*

"I'll come along as well," Emmanuelle volunteered, placing her book on the table. "An extra pair of hands may be useful."

"You've had a sore throat, darling," Nicole said. "You shouldn't be out at night. Why don't you stay here in case they come back?"

"Your sister is right. You can coordinate efforts here and send out servants if they're found. Claudine, you will go with Gabrielle and Manon. Nicole and I, along with a few of the men, will fan out and search some of their other favorite spots nearby in case they were less foolish than we fear."

"You want me to ride along to that place just to get pitched out again? We'll be lucky not to get scalped." Claudine tossed her embroidery aside on the settee.

Manon's glare made it evident to everyone in the room that she was in danger of the very same fate right there in her sister's parlor if she continued on her current tirade.

"You're not riding anywhere," Manon declared, throwing Claudine her cloak. "We're walking."

"Of all the . . ." Claudine began.

"If we walk we won't be heard. If we're not heard, they won't be alarmed by the sound of French horses and wagons and they won't be expecting hostility. Putting them on their guard, I promise you, is the last thing we want."

"Amen to that," Gabrielle interjected. "And the sooner we go, the more light we'll have. Can we please move along?"

Armed only with an unlit lantern and a tinderbox, the girls departed into the twilight.

"When we find those boys I'm going to wring their necks," Claudine declared as they left the wide streets of town for the path that led toward the Huron village.

"Let's just hope the job hasn't been done for you," Gabrielle spat. *Your own nephew is out and alone in the woods, you cow.* Gabrielle refrained from screaming the oath at Claudine, saving her energy for whatever lay in store. Gabrielle didn't fear their fate with the natives all that much—they were just boys and accompanied by one of the tribe—but there were any manner of beasts that might decide to make a meal of them. Not to mention protective farmers too fond of shooting off their muskets before bothering to see who or what had trespassed on their land.

"I just don't see why the three of us are out here instead of some of the men."

"For once think beyond the end of your own nose." Gabrielle liked the girl, really. And she hadn't so many friends that she could afford to offend any of them, but Claudine Deschamps had a special way of dancing on her nerves. Would that Emmanuelle had been up to accompanying them that night instead of her sister.

"Don't act like I'm not worried for Frédéric and the others. I'd just prefer not to be out in the mud with dark hard on our heels." Claudine quickened her pace to bridge the gap between herself and Manon, who was several yards ahead.

"Better an inch or two of mud than two feet of snow," Manon retorted. "Now let's have some peace so we can hear if the boys are trying to call for us."

Gabrielle nodded her approval. The fewer words Claudine spoke, the better their chances she and Manon would be able to stay their temper and not shove their companion into the rushing swell of the St. Lawrence. She scanned the area for the sight of her Pierre's mop of brown curls, just as she was sure Manon looked for Théodore's jet-black hair and Claudine watched for Frédéric's dark hair and proud chin that so resembled his father's.

For the better part of a half hour, they walked along the muddy path in silence, Manon clutching the lantern at her side. The dark was looming, but not heavy enough to entice Manon to attract attention by pulling out the tinderbox and lighting the candle.

The faintest rustling from the underbrush caused Manon to start and raise her hand for Gabrielle and Claudine to remain motionless. Gabrielle was reminded greatly of one of her few hunting excursions with her brother when they spotted a deer in the midst of a meadow. As soon as she'd stepped on a twig, its ears pricked up and every sinew became taut, ready for flight. So stood Manon as her eyes scanned the surroundings for the source of the barely perceptible noise from the thicket.

"Is anyone there?" Claudine said after a few moments of heavy silence, her voice booming. *Whatever her faults, cowardice isn't one.* If Manon were annoyed with Claudine's outburst, she hid her feelings admirably. They were close enough to the settlement that whoever might be in the thicket was likely French. Manon might be their key to safe passage onto the native lands, but Claudine and Gabrielle would ensure their safety on French soil. They were from known families and meddling with any of them wouldn't be worth the consequences. Wolves, however, were not so capable of reason.

"Skenandoa!" a small voice screamed. Théodore emerged from under a pile of dried pine needles and flung his arms around his sister's waist.

The pair exchanged a few words in their native tongue, and Manon sprang into the thicket with Théodore close behind her. She dove into the pine needles and extracted Frédéric from beneath a massive pile. He was limp and looked as white as death. Théodore emerged with a branch laden with shining white berries, presenting them to his sister, his expression grave.

"Pierre?" Gabrielle croaked. Théodore pointed to a second pile of pine needles and grabbed her hand. She parted the needles as though swimming through the lake of scratchy dead flora until she felt Pierre's form beneath the mound.

Still warm. Still breathing.

His eyes fluttered and he moaned in misery, but he was very much alive. Tears of relief burned her throat, but she did not give in to them. He clearly wasn't well and she needed her wits about her for a long while yet. She lifted Pierre from the pile and placed him on the path next to Frédéric so she could examine him.

"What is wrong with them?" Claudine demanded as she knelt at Frédéric's side.

"They ate snowberries," Manon said, examining the branch Théodore had procured. "Quite a few from what Tawendeh— Théodore says."

Manon put her ear to Frédéric's chest. "His heartbeat is still strong, but we need to get them home." The boy moaned in protest, but hadn't the strength to argue in earnest.

"Are they *very* poisonous?" Gabrielle nearly choked on the words and pulled Pierre's limp form to her chest. He was everything to Elisabeth and Gilbert. He was not one of a dozen children, but the much-cherished oldest boy. Odds were good that the Beaumonts would never have another child, and Gabrielle could not imagine they would ever recover from the loss.

Manon shook her head. "You and I could eat a few and never feel any ill effects, but children don't fare as well. All the same, if they ate as much as Tawendeh says, they will be sick enough to get on with. They haven't anything like the strength to walk back to town. I'll carry Frédéric. Can you manage Pierre?" Manon asked. Gabrielle nodded, lifting the boy into her arms, not overly burdened by his slight form.

"I'll carry my own nephew," Claudine demanded, taking Frédéric into her arms from Manon's embrace.

Manon said nothing, but grabbed Théodore by the hand and led the way down the darkening path, the lantern now lit against the falling night.

"How is it our boys came to be ill and not your Théodore?" Claudine managed to grunt a few minutes into the walk.

"He stopped to ... relieve himself ... and came back to the boys feasting on a fresh crop of the berries. He tried to stop them, but they'd eaten enough to do damage already. Pierre stopped right away when Théodore told him to, but Frédéric apparently didn't believe him."

Sounds like his aunt. Gabrielle chased the uncharitable thought from her mind. Poor Frédéric was paying dearly enough for his arrogance now.

The trudge back to the Lefebvre house seemed to take hours longer than the trek into the woods, when in reality, their extra burden and the falling light only added a quarter of an hour onto the journey back into town.

Emmanuelle greeted them, her face draining when she saw the condition her nephew and Pierre were in. She barked orders to the staff with as much efficiency as either Nicole or the master himself.

Manon took charge in the nursery, freeing the boys from their soiled clothes and requesting water, rags, and other supplies from the nanny.

"They've been vomiting ... and worse ... for the better part of two hours. We must get them to take water, and soon."

Claudine did her part, making sure the staff fetched what was needed and sending orders to find the rest of the search party. Gabrielle, unsure of how to help, offered her services to Manon directly.

"Fetch me my box of herbs from my room," she said, not looking up from Frédéric's pale face. Pierre was now growing more lucid, his breathing strong. He was clearly dizzy and unwell, but he was nowhere near as ill as his friend.

Barely familiar with the layout of the upper story of the Lefebvre house, Gabrielle took it upon herself to open doors until she found the room that belonged to Manon. The austere simplicity of the nanny's quarters ... The juxtaposition of tidiness and joyful clutter in Emmanuelle and Claudine's room ... Finally, a sleeping chamber with soft pink papered walls and a massive desk of shining dark mahogany that dominated the room. A small bed was wedged against the wall to make room for the enormous wooden behemoth.

Given the quantity of books and loose papers on the desk, it had to be Manon's room. The only other family member with such a space was Alexandre, who kept a study below stairs. A scarred box sat to the side of the papers. Hazarding a guess, Gabrielle opened the lid and found numerous leather pouches bulging with pungent herbs.

Gabrielle ran back to the nursery and thrust the box into Manon's hands. Manon handled each pouch delicately until she found her prize and placed it back into Gabrielle's hands.

"It's wild bergamot. Brew it into a tincture with water. We need to settle their stomachs so they can take water and induce sweating. It will flush the poison."

With shaking hands, Gabrielle boiled water over the nursery fire, adding the dried bergamot leaves to steep in the ceramic kettle. Manon had not specified how many of the dried leaves to add, nor how long to let them steep, so she emptied a liberal amount into the strainer and let the brew steep until the water took on a yellowish-green color.

The concoction smelled strong, but Gabrielle cared not. If it restored the boys to health, it could taste as vile as death itself. Gabrielle passed off the bitter-smelling brew to Manon, who sniffed the cup and nodded approvingly. She put the cup to Frédéric's lips, and he sipped tentatively at the tincture. He used what little strength he had to wrinkle his nose at the foul liquid.

"If you keep this down and drink some water, we can sweeten the next cup with honey," Manon promised. He could only manage a few sips of the tincture before having to lie his head back down into the pillow. Gabrielle had never seen the robust boy look so weak. Mercifully, he was able to keep the bergamot from resurfacing. The unspoken fear in the room was that if they could not stem the vomiting, the boys would suffer permanent damage from dehydration.

Pierre was able to hold his head up long enough to consume half his portion of the brew, but his eyes were still glassy and his skin only a shade or two darker than the shimmering white berries that caused his illness. *You must get well, little brother. One so young as you cannot comprehend how much he is loved.*

It wasn't long before Emmanuelle ushered in Frédéric's anxious parents to the nursery, having briefed them on the events of the evening. Pierre's parents, Elisabeth and Gilbert, had gone farther to the southeast to search near Pierre's favorite stretch of riverbank, but one of the servants had been directed to find them and let them know their son had been recovered.

"Fetch the doctor here at once," Alexandre called out to the hallway.

"It's already been done," Claudine said. "He's away for the night, seeing to a patient halfway to Trois-Rivières, from what I heard. We'll have to trust Manon." Claudine's expression was grim as she admitted that Manon was their best hope for restoring their boys to health. The *seigneur* acquiesced to the truth soon enough, though the throbbing vein in his jaw looked as if the good doctor was not on the list of people he held in high esteem at the moment.

Nicole flurried about trying to find an occupation for herself while Manon and Gabrielle tended to their patients. The tisane finally consumed, and the boys resting in relative comfort, they were able to offer them sips of water at regular intervals to replenish their exhausted bodies.

With each mouthful of cool water Pierre managed to keep down, Gabrielle muttered a silent prayer of thanksgiving. When at last he was sleeping peacefully, a healthy glow resurfacing to his skin, Gabrielle finally allowed the pent-up tears to spill down her cheeks. He would be well.

She felt Manon slip her arm around her and hold her in a firm embrace for a few moments. Claudine had taken over administering water to Frédéric, who was having less success at keeping the water from coming back up.

Gabrielle was surprised to see how Claudine dealt with the boy with such tenderness. He emptied the contents of his stomach repeatedly on her favorite skirt, but she spoke not a word in remonstration.

"Is he doing any better?" The question sounded pathetic as it exited Gabrielle's weary lips.

"Slowly improving, I think," Claudine answered, her eyes never leaving Frédéric's face. "His color is a little better, and he's keeping more water down for longer. More of Manon's tincture might help."

While Manon set to brewing more, Gabrielle doused some clean cloths in cool water for Frédéric's forehead.

"Thank you," Claudine said as Manon handed her the cup. Claudine did not make eye contact with Manon, but grasped her hand in appreciation for just a moment.

"Time for bed," Nicole announced, seeing the residue of Gabrielle's tears as she entered the room. She had adopted the tone of the Dame Lefebvre, which dared not be questioned.

Emmanuelle and Nicole, joined by the recently arrived Elisabeth, relieved the girls of their duties so they could find some much-needed sleep. Elisabeth had some choice words about the doctor's absence, but thanked Manon profusely for her ministrations to the sick boys. The three weary girls stayed in Claudine's room, Manon taking Emmanuelle's vacant bed, and Gabrielle taking the spare mattress hidden under the bed for guests. With Elisabeth tending Pierre a few doors down and Gilbert notified of the situation, no one would pause to worry that she had not slept at home that night.

"I could still strangle those boys," Claudine admitted as they were settled in their beds. Gabrielle expected they were both struggling, as she was, to keep their minds from reeling. "How they could be so irresponsible I'll never understand. They ought to know better than to eat anything they aren't sure is safe. My own papa hauled us out to the woods in France to teach us which berries we could eat."

"Do you think the good *seigneur* takes the time to do those sorts of things with Frédéric?" Gabrielle found herself asking. It pained her to speak ill of a decent man who loved his children, but she could not harness her words.

"It's of no matter. I'll take the boys out myself as soon as they're well enough," Manon vowed. "Alexandre, wise as he is, doesn't strike me as much of a botanist."

Claudine laughed, her white teeth visible from across the darkened room lit by a solitary candle Manon had yet to extinguish. The idea of the proud landowner mucking about the weeds in his best boots was almost as ridiculous as the three of them dragging two sick boys from the thicket in the dark of night. It was one of those bizarre evenings where absurdity took a foothold on the day and made itself at home.

"I think you're probably right," Gabrielle agreed. "It's better we stick to our strengths anyway."

"You were good to share your expertise with us tonight, Manon," Claudine said, sincerity ringing from her voice.

"Knowledge is worth nothing if not shared," Manon reasoned.

Gabrielle said nothing, but wondered if she would ever have such a gift to share, or if she would be destined to remain forever a helping hand to those more able than she.

CHAPTER 4

Manon

June 1677

Manon had every medical text Alexandre Lefebvre owned, more numerous than she expected, piled on the massive mahogany desk Alexandre had gifted her years before when he acquired a grander showpiece for his study. She thought both desks were far more elaborate than necessary, but the gift was a testament to his admiration of her studious nature, so she accepted the offering with grace. He may not have been a demonstrative father figure, but he always seemed to take an interest in her studies, having been a scholar himself. It was at least a common chord.

She had pored over the texts so long she felt as if a hot needle were pricking the back of her eyes and the book dust, usually one of her favorite odors, burned at her nose. As the boys had recovered from their misadventures, she had resumed her research into the treatment of infectious fevers. She found nothing. No remedies that promised results better than the ones she'd used on Mother Onatah and the others. Nothing more useful than the suggestion of secluding the ill. The finest surgeons in Paris could have done no more than she did.

How could that be true?

How could the most educated men in the entire world be so

helpless against such a simple illness? That her own people, so reticent to give up their traditional ways, could fare no better against the scourge of fever did not surprise her. But the French were supposed to be better. They were supposed to be gods among men.

Some days she was still the neglected seven-year-old girl in the woods spying on the chestnut-haired angel who lived in the little cabin on the outskirts of the French town. She made up stories in her mind about what the angel's life was like. The food she ate, the friends she had, what she did to pass the time.

She never expected the angel would become her foster mother. Never dreamed that she would learn the answers to her childish queries. Nicole did not dine on fatted goose every night or drink dewdrops from lilies in the morning. She had a small circle of friends and spent her life in toil like the rest of the world. Nicole transcended from angel to woman, but it did not break Manon's heart. It was much easier to love someone on your own plane of existence.

Even so, the French were supposed to have the answers to these things.

Manon slammed the most recent medical text shut, but resisted the urge to throw it against the wall. She placed it back atop the towering stack and pinched the bridge of her nose against the thrumming rush of blood behind her eyes. She leaned back in the chair and closed her eyelids, and immediately Heno's chiseled face swirled into view as she shut out the rest of the world.

He had stood behind his father, the Chief, as he banished her from the clan. He promised to speak to his father when his anger abated. Begged her to leave Tawendeh—Théodore, damn the French anyway—with them. Despite all of his professions of love, his main concern was to keep Tawendeh, the young hunter, with the tribe. It was a trait of an excellent chieftain, but also one of a thoughtless lover.

She chased Heno from her thoughts when possible, but she could not help but occasionally seek the solace of the memory of his embrace. He had dared to love her when Mother Onatah and Tawendeh were the only people in the tribe who cared for her. Leaving Heno was almost as hard as saying good-bye to her beloved mother. The lack of finality, somehow, made it worse. Had he replaced her with a good, traditional woman who would uphold their ways and give him the brood of little hunters he longed for? In her heart, she knew the answer, but was loath to acknowledge it.

She thought of Théodore playing in the nursery two doors down and wondered, daily, if she had made the right decision in taking him from their people. His place in the tribe had never come into question. His uncle was the Chief, his cousin would become chief after him. Théodore would be Tawendeh of the Big Turtle Clan, respected and honored among his people. He enjoyed his playmates now, but how long would it last?

Frédéric was mended from their mishap with the snowberries, Pierre had barely felt the ill effects by the following day, but how soon before the innocent young boys would notice that Théodore was different? How long before those differences mattered? But her last words to Mother Onatah had been to promise she would care for Théodore until he was a man. There was no part of her that could go back on such an oath, even if she worried that she was tearing him from his heritage.

I must get out of this house, if only for a few hours; I must escape.

Just as Manon was about to escape through the front door, Nicole thrust a basket and her marketing list for the week into her hands. Their cook, Madame Yollande, was renowned in their small town, but age and rheumatism kept her from doing the marketing. Nicole usually took the task upon herself. It was a chance for her to visit with Alexandre's tenants and to mix about in town, but a charitable function at the church claimed her time that week.

In the five years since Manon had left the settlement, the town had grown like a healthy sapling. There were more buildings, robust and made from stone, much like the Lefebvre house. They were built to last the ages, against weather, fire, and other calamites. Not like the wooden longhouses that could be rebuilt in a few weeks if the need arose. There was no sense of permanence with her tribe, and perhaps it was a more natural state in which to live. People were much more like the longhouses of her people. They would come and go, be expanded or rebuilt as needed. Just as no man would live forever, neither would his home. The French so dearly loved to think their towering buildings and monuments, churches that soared to the heavens, would make them immortal.

Almost as soon as she entered the town streets she realized that her outing was ill planned. She expected that her presence in town would be met with little interest, but the settlement was still small enough that the comings and goings of one of their elite families was not something to be overlooked. A few people who recognized her from her youth stopped to greet her and enquire after the *seigneur* and Dame Lefebvre. Politeness. Small talk. One made the remark that she must be happy to be back in town and comfortably settled, to which Manon smiled and nodded as she'd seen Nicole do a million times before. *They do not know I was banished. They do not know that Onatah of the Big Turtle Clan ever existed. They simply imagine that my quarters with the Lefebvres must be more comfortable than a drafty longhouse.*

Unable to endure more conversation with the townspeople, Manon decided to finish Nicole's errands without any deviation from the required stops and return home. The cheese monger was the last of her errands and not too far from the Lefebvre house. If she were fortunate, she would be able to purchase the cheese and return home without any more than the exchange of a few words with the merchant.

A round-faced woman with thinning gray hair and a broad bosom tended the shop. The smell that emanated from the wares reminded Manon distinctly of the stink from the hunters' moccasins after they had come home from a weeklong trek in August. The shopkeeper waited on the woman in front of Manon, a tired-looking mother of four who contended with two of the youngsters tugging on her ragged skirt as she tried to conduct her business. The shopkeeper shot the weary woman the indulgent smile of one who remembered the exhausting days of child-rearing with fondness, but who was glad her brood was raised up.

The instant the young mother left the shop, the old woman's expression became as sour as the milk she curdled for cheese. She looked up and down at Manon's taut frame and fine clothes. Spite. Envy. Hatred.

"We're closing," the woman announced.

"It's only one in the afternoon," Manon countered. Shops would be open for hours yet. But Manon remembered the Beaumonts usually closed briefly for their midday meal, and the woman was perhaps overdue for food and a few moments of respite, so she clung to her civil tone. "Would you be kind enough to fill my order quickly if you're just closing for your luncheon? Madame Lefebvre sent me in her stead."

"And the King himself runs the butchery next door. Be gone with you. We're closed for the day." The woman slammed a massive round of cheese down in the case with no more trouble than if she had been laying a freshly laundered apron in a bureau drawer.

Manon cast a bitter scowl at the hateful shopkeeper. Her clothes and manner of speaking demonstrated readily enough that she spoke the truth. This woman remained obdurate out of sheer meanness of spirit.

"How wonderful your business thrives so, Madame Lagrange." Claudine's voice rang through the shop, assuming the condescending civility that her older sister adopted when speaking to those who had caused her some offense. Emmanuelle and Gabrielle stood to either side, Gabrielle losing the battle to hide a sly grin. "I know of few merchants who can boast such success. And you so new to our settlement, too. I am sure my brother-in-law will be pleased to know that one of his tenants has done so very well. I'm sure all your accounts must be paid in full, and interest paid, with such a flourishing business that allows you to close a full half day before every other merchant in town."

"Mademoiselle Deschamps, what an unexpected surprise." The old woman stammered and took a step back. Debt was the curse of the newly settled. If Alexandre pushed her to pay off the money she and her husband had borrowed to set up shop, she'd be scrubbing floors at the Lefebvre house by morning.

"It would seem so. I don't suppose you could go to the trouble of remaining open for just a few more minutes to wait on our new houseguest," Claudine purred with insincere flattery. Though Manon loathed these social games, this one time it was amusing to see them played out.

"Of course, the young lady must have misunderstood me. We won't be closing for a good while yet."

"Of course, a misunderstanding. These things do happen." Claudine offered the woman a smile that read very clearly: *Yes, these things do happen, but they had better not happen again.*

Manon relayed Nicole's order and left with her parcels nestled in her basket and a bouquet of flowery apologies from the cheese monger—all directed toward Claudine.

"Thank you," Manon said once out of earshot.

"Oh, that Madame Lagrange is the rudest old hen that ever lived. Glad to have an excuse to scare some courtesy out of her." Claudine chuckled in chorus with the other two. "Now hurry home with that basket. We were sent to find you and take you to lessons at Aunt Rose's. Nicole wanted to surprise you. Though after spending all morning with your books, I can't see why you'd care to keep on with them this afternoon."

"Rose Barré?" Manon asked. Rose had been her first teacher when she'd come with Nicole into town. She had learned French, arithmetic, catechism, embroidery, and music at Rose's side in exchange for lessons in Wendat. She was one of the few French who had showed any interest in her culture at all.

"Rose Lefebvre for years now," Emmanuelle corrected. "She was married to Alexandre's nephew Henri long before you left, wasn't she?"

Manon nodded. She preferred to remember things as they had been early on during her stay with the French. When she was a child, people overlooked her presence. As she grew into a young woman, they grew weary of her. Her lessons did not raise her in their estimation then, nor would they do so now. But like a drunkard with his ale, or a glutton before a feast, Manon was no more capable of refusing lessons than those weary souls could refuse their vices.

Rose presided over her little classroom with a smile. It was nothing like the glory days when she had a dozen Huron pupils in her charge, but Manon could see that Rose was only too delighted to have a fourth pupil in addition to the Deschamps girls and Gabrielle. Rose's four children kept her busy as well, but she confessed to the girls that relinquishing the diaper-changing duties to the nanny for a few hours each week in favor of more stimulating responsibilities did not disappoint her.

Manon sat back in her chair, the French on the page swirling like a cyclone. Poetry was nothing like the straightforward prose of the medical texts, and her brain was swimming in the metered lines. *Too many years without using the language. Too long parsing out Alexandre's books this morning.*

"Perhaps some time for embroidery," Rose suggested.

"On Thursday you should take the morning off so you can be fresh for lessons," Claudine said, throwing Manon a sidelong wink. "Too much of a good thing?"

Manon nodded and pulled out her embroidery case with the others. It wasn't her favorite task in the world, but the even stitching and forced concentration seemed like good mental exercise. Like prayer. Like meditation.

Emmanuelle and Gabrielle chatted companionably as they did their needlework, but Claudine focused intently on the pink flowers she embroidered on her soft woolen shawl. Manon favored small, well-ordered geometric patterns that resembled the beading the women of her tribe used to adorn their deerskins. She used soft pastel threads to make the effect less "foreign-looking," but it soothed her to have something familiar about her clothes and possessions.

At the end of the lesson, good-byes were exchanged, but Rose took Manon gently by the elbow as the others exited the room.

"You must pay Claudine no mind," Rose said. "She's the silliest girl in New France."

"I won't argue with you." Manon gave Rose a small smile as she packed her books.

"I'm so very glad you're back with us, my dear." Rose patted Manon's arm as she used to do after difficult lessons. "Of course, I am sad to learn the reason why. I know you're grieving terribly for your mother."

The first person to acknowledge Mother Onatah. But then again you understood the ways of my people better than anyone. And more, you know what it is to lose a mother.

"Thank you, though I am afraid you're in the minority." Manon snapped her bag shut a bit more forcefully than she intended.

"Everyone who matters is happy to see you," Rose said as she walked with Manon to the door, taking a slow pace.

"Even the great Seigneur Lefebvre?" Manon asked. "You think he's truly pleased to be housing a Huron girl? And her brother in his very nursery?"

"Has he been unkind?" Rose asked.

"He wouldn't be to my face, would he? He's a gentleman and a politician. There's no profit in being openly rude."

"True," Rose said, rolling her eyes. "He'd do well to be grateful for your presence. You might be a good influence on his hoydenish sister-in-law."

Manon, for the first time since she returned to the French, gave a genuine laugh.

"You must never repeat what I said, but you're worth a dozen flippant girls like Claudine. Though I hope deep down she's made of better stuff than she lets on."

"I sincerely hope so." Manon wrapped her arm around Rose briefly and took her time walking home in the mild sunshine.

Before retreating to the candy-pink oasis that was her bedroom, Manon made one of her frequent trips to the nursery. Tawendehnow-Théodore gleefully surrendered his Huron moniker as easily as he'd traded his buckskin breeches for woolen ones. He sat playing alongside Frédéric, Sabine, and Hélène as naturally as if they were his own siblings. Despite the linguistic challenges, the quartet made themselves understood through a secret language, sacred unto small children.

At that moment young Théodore knew not that he lived among a people who widely despised him, or would, once he was old enough to be of consequence. The Lefebvre children were unspoiled by the prejudices of their society and welcomed the raven-haired boy as an equal—much valued—playmate.

May this last for many years to come, my dear brother. And may you cherish the time. God knows you will remember the day you realize you are not a part of this world, and it will bruise your spirit if you're strong. If you're weak, it will break it.

"Soldier!" Théodore presented his sister with a wooden soldier, painstakingly carved and meticulously painted.

"Very good!" Manon kissed his cheek in praise of his improving French.

"Maman asked me to help him along." Hélène, the eldest in the nursery and uncontested chief of its residents, placed her doll lovingly in the tiny cradle and approached Manon. "I hope you don't mind."

"Not at all, my dear," Manon said, rewarding her as well with a kiss on her cherubic cheek. She was growing lither by the minute, but she still had the round face of a child. She was eight years old— just the right age to be an idol to Théodore and not too old to be disinterested in the roughhousing of children.

"I'm glad you've come back to stay with us." Hélène did not quite meet Manon's eyes.

"I'm happy to see you again, dear girl." Manon chose her words carefully. *Children's ears are too precious for the burden of untruths. They will have many adult years to hear lies and there is no sense starting them off too early on the wrong course. Though sometimes the truth hurts worse. To confess I am not happy to return would be unspeakably cruel to this lovely child who has never been anything but a loving sister to me.*

Manon recalled that day, shortly before she returned to her people, when she overheard Alexandre admit to Nicole that he did not care for Manon as a daughter, even though he welcomed Hélène without question. Manon had known that particular truth for years, but to hear it enunciated from his lips was far too much for her twelve-year-old heart to bear. That was the night that she decided to return to her people and find her place among them. It wasn't much later that she learned she had no real place with them, either.

"May I call you 'sister' again, as I used to?" Hélène's bright blue eyes looked up expectantly at Manon. She could not dash the girl's hopes as Alexandre had done to her.

"Of course you can, sweet girl. Of course."

CHAPTER 5

Claudine

June 1677

Hold your head high. Give a small, serene smile. Move as though you own the room and the adoration of everyone in it.

"You look beautiful, dear," Nicole breathed as Claudine descended the staircase. "Yellow certainly suits you." Claudine smiled at her sister, serenely, she hoped. It was her night—the night she'd been longing for—the night Nicole and Alexandre would introduce her to the small inner circles of Quebec's elite. She had to be perfect. Elegant. Refined. None of the things she was raised to be, but all the things she longed for.

Claudine had left Emmanuelle upstairs, entrenched in study; this night was the elder sister's privilege. Emmanuelle would have her chance next year. Debuts in the New World were nowhere near as formal as the grand affairs in Paris, but Nicole had made a fair attempt for Claudine's sake. Manon might be offered the same opportunity, but Claudine couldn't imagine her taking it.

"Thank you." Claudine accepted a small glass of wine from Alexandre. "Gabrielle is a treasure."

"The Giroux girl made your gown?" Alexandre asked. "Remarkable talent for one so young."

"The question, brother dear, is how do you think I look in it?" Claudine asked. "I would very much like a man's opinion."

"Like a ray of sunshine, my dear. You'd be the beauty in the greatest salons in Paris, I assure you," Alexandre said, bowing gallantly, his smile a bit exaggerated as he cast an ill-concealed wink at his wife.

"Just what a lady wants to hear," Nicole said, returning the wink and turning to her sister. "Now remember to dance with everyone who asks. Be sweet to all, regardless of your feelings. You've nothing to gain by breaking hearts—just yet."

"Spoken like a true politician," Alexandre said, a hand fluttering to his heart.

"Am I anything else?" Nicole let out a less-than-ladylike laugh. *Really, sister. People could hear you.*

"A great many things," Claudine supplied, her tone dripping in honey.

"It clearly runs in the family," Alexandre said, ushering them to their places in the foyer to receive their guests. "All the better. It will serve you well."

In the four weeks since her arrival at the Lefebvre house, Claudine imagined her entry into society with the gilded expectations of a giddy child. She anticipated dozens of handsome, young—rich—men, all vying for her favor. She had not counted on nearly an hour of curtsies, false smiles, and idle chitchat with a throng of wrinkled faces.

"The receiving line is always rather tedious, I'm afraid." Nicole patted her sister on the shoulder as they sauntered to the ballroom. Claudine massaged her cheeks discreetly as they walked. *I refuse to smile for a week after this. You can all think me surly if you want.*

"I didn't expect everyone to be so old," Claudine whispered.

Alexandre chuckled, but Nicole's eyes flashed as she rebuked her sister. "You wanted an entrée into good society. That's what we've given you. These 'old people' run the colony. You're here to entice one of their heirs, if you're lucky. Leadership is not the province of youth, sister dear."

"Now what do I do?" Claudine's whisper had an edge of panic, but her expression remained collected.

"Be your usual, charming self," Nicole said. "Alexandre and I will lead you in the right direction. And remember—don't dance with anyone more than twice. Doing so may discourage others, and it's far too early for that."

"Your sister is right." Alexandre claimed Nicole's arm, leaving Claudine a pace behind. "You don't know which families are feuding and there's no need to offend half the settlement on your first night out."

"Lovely. One dance too many and I'm a social pariah." Claudine hoped her gloves would not betray her sweating palms.

"Don't worry, dear," Nicole said. "Everyone knows it's your first ball. They'll forgive a minor blunder or two."

Claudine noticed that Alexandre did not contradict his wife, but the arch of his eyebrow clearly said *don't depend on that.*

For over an hour, Claudine mingled with Quebec's elite at her sister's elbow. She smiled for the Governor de Frontenac and his insipid mistress. She curtsied for every minor statesman in attendance, finding them all as interesting as drying paint. When, finally, the dancing began, Claudine was at no loss for partners. One by one the young men spun Claudine about the dance floor, eager to earn her attention. *Farmer's daughter indeed. I'm the sister-in-law of a leading citizen here . . . not the nobody I was and always would have been in France.*

"You'd love our estate. Beautiful view of the mountains . . . sprawling fields and evergreens as far as you can see." *What was the boy's name?* If only she had Emmanuelle's memory for such things.

"It sounds beautiful." Claudine smiled prettily for the dreary boy, but let her gaze drift about the room. Four boys in a row—all yammering endlessly about lakes and forests and mountains. Clean, solitary country living. It sounded as much fun as a hanging. She exhaled her relief as she saw Nicole hovering as the final notes of the tune sounded.

"Claudine, I wish to introduce you to our young friend, Victor St. Pierre." Nicole gestured to a young man with sandy hair and mirthful eyes. "I thought you'd enjoy a dance together."

"It would be my honor, Mademoiselle Deschamps," Victor said with a graceful bow.

Claudine accepted with a curtsy and allowed him to escort her to the center of the dance floor.

"I confess I've been waiting more than an hour for the chance to dance with you," Victor said as he expertly led Claudine about the floor. "Your brother-in-law could have sold tickets to your many admirers."

Claudine played off the compliment with a laugh, but was more than a little pleased. All evening, she could not help but notice the envious stares of the other young men as a beau walked her to the floor. But Victor, in his handsome blue *justaucorps,* was the first to merit a second glance. *The very image of my gallant prince, if a little blonder than I had pictured. It doesn't do to be too particular about these things.*

"Your sister has been extolling your many virtues to the settlement. I don't think there is a man under the age of fifty who isn't mad to meet you," he said.

"She's very kind," Claudine said in her best imitation of modesty.

"Nonsense. She speaks the unembroidered truth, I assure you." He smiled down on her as they twirled in artful circles.

"Please tell me more about yourself," she asked, deflecting his flattery. "I'd like to know more about you and your family." *For once this evening, I honestly want to know the response to that query.*

As the strains of the orchestra directed the movement of the dancers, Victor gave Claudine the usual details of his family's business and holdings. Unlike the others, he tempered his pride with good breeding, but it was clear to Claudine that his family's fortune was one of the grandest in the settlement. Better still, his father kept a house in town, despite being an active landowner like Alexandre.

"And does land management suit you?" Claudine asked.

"It's the profession of a gentleman," he said, his tone noncommittal. "Though it seems dreadfully dull here after Paris."

"Paris!" Claudine exclaimed loud enough for the couples closest to hear them. "Have you been?"

"Of course. Father sent me to the university there. It's far more established than any of the institutions here, you understand. I've not been back a full year yet. I miss it terribly."

"Naturally. I'd give anything to go to Paris," Claudine said, her enthusiasm spilling over.

"I imagine you and Paris would get along famously."

"I expect we would." *Temper your enthusiasm, you fool. Don't frighten him off.*

"Mademoiselle Deschamps, it has been my honor to dance with you tonight. I hope to repeat the pleasure in the very near future."

"Monsieur St. Pierre, you may depend upon it."

"It would be a smart match, to be sure," Alexandre said over breakfast the next morning, poring over his account books while he ate. "Well-connected family. Solid finances, from what I gather. I don't think you could do better, my dear."

"Nor do I," Claudine agreed. "He's wonderfully interesting."

"And not bad to look at," Nicole said in a wry tone. "I'm sure that doesn't hurt matters at all."

"I confess it doesn't." Claudine couldn't quite stifle her giggle.

"So you're prepared to marry a man you've only known a few hours?" Emmanuelle asked, her eyes challenging.

"I must marry. The sooner the better, really. Why wait if I've met someone so agreeable?" Claudine looked down at her breakfast plate and paid more heed to her eggs than her younger sister's chiding.

"Because marriage is for life. You cannot change husbands like you do a dress you've tired of. And I've seen you do *that* often enough," Emmanuelle said, setting her fork down forcefully.

Manon looked as if she wished to add to Emmanuelle's pronouncement, but seemed to think better of it and returned to her breakfast.

"For the love of all the saints, stop being such a pious snit, Emmanuelle," Claudine spat.

"Don't talk to your sister that way," Nicole snapped in Claudine's direction. "There is a good deal of sense in what Emmanuelle says. And you needn't rush into things. You're only just seventeen."

"Nicole, you're not my mother. Please stop acting like it." Claudine wanted to swallow the words as soon as they were out of her mouth. It was a direct violation of what she'd promised when she came to stay. Alexandre, at least, did not register offense at her remarks.

"Claudine is merely being pragmatic. If she likes the St. Pierre boy, she ought not delay and risk him finding affection elsewhere," Alexandre intervened.

"Spoken like a man of politics," Nicole said, raising her goblet of milk in his direction.

"First, foremost, and always," Alexandre said, looking weary of the female banter. "And while patience is not Claudine's chief virtue, she's right."

"Thank you, brother dear," Claudine said.

"Let's hope you don't come to regret your haste," Emmanuelle said. Claudine opened her mouth to retort, but Emmanuelle raised her hand to silence her. "I do not mean to criticize, Claudine. I just urge you caution. Take some time and get to know him. If a young man in such a territory with so few ladies can't wait a few months to court you, he isn't worth having."

"Ladies, you've put the cart a full country mile before the poor horse. No offer has been made yet. We can hope for good developments, but let's not read the banns just yet." Alexandre looked up from his account book just long enough to roll his eyes at the table at large.

"Sensible." Nicole beamed at her husband.

You really ought not be so openly affectionate, sister. Highborn ladies are cold and distant. Like the peaks of the mountain.

"Ladies, go on up and fetch your shawls and caps. We're wanted at Rose's to do some knitting for the Church."

"Oh, must we?" Claudine's tone was even more nasal than she'd intended. *So very ladylike.*

"You don't think you'll be doing your share to help the poor if you marry young Victor?" Nicole set her napkin on the table, challenging Claudine to dispute her. "I assure you the St. Pierre family doesn't take their contributions to the Church lightly. If you aren't prepared to do your part, I suggest you look elsewhere."

"Let's go, Emmanuelle." Claudine heaved a sigh and tossed her napkin on the table.

She thundered up the stairs, Manon ahead of them and Emmanuelle on her heels. As soon as the bedroom door was shut, Claudine rounded on her sister.

"Do you have to contradict me at every turn? Make them think every decision I make is foolhardy? Don't you see how lucky I am?"

"Claudine, I'm sure he's a wonderful young man, but how well can you possibly know him after the space of a dance or two?"

"I don't need to know him any better. He's young. He's handsome. He lives here in town. What more can I ask for? It's not as though we're up to our necks in such eligible suitors."

"There's at least two men for every woman here. I heard Alexandre say so less than a week ago."

"Farmers. Blacksmiths. A merchant here and there. I want more than that."

"I know you do. But there is more to happiness in marriage than a fine house in town and a smart carriage." Emmanuelle found her cap and tucked it neatly over her brown topknot.

"I'm sure there is, Emmanuelle, but you can't claim to know what it is any more than I. Heavens above, it's bad enough to be lectured by Nicole, but to be badgered by a younger sister is unendurable."

Emmanuelle crossed the room to where Claudine stood, now stooped over her trunk looking for her favorite shawl.

"I don't mean to scold. Really I don't, but I couldn't bear to see you unhappy. I just worry for you."

Claudine closed the gap between them and embraced her sister. "I know. I'm sorry to be cross with you. I just hate to have a bucket of cold water thrown over my excitement. I really think he's the one I've been waiting for."

"I hope he is. I really and truly hope he is. But slow down and share a meal or two with him before you get down on bended knee and ask him to take your hand?"

Claudine burst into a fit of giggles at the ridiculous image.

"This Victor of yours has one thing in his favor, I'll admit," Emmanuelle said, pulling away slightly and holding Claudine at arm's length.

"Don't keep me in suspense. What has he done to earn your approval to some small degree?"

"He keeps a house here in town and is likely to after he marries. I couldn't bear to be left here in town without you." Emmanuelle closed the gap again and gripped her sister in an uncharacteristically firm embrace.

"Never." Claudine gripped her sister close. "You may be bossy, and a know-it-all, and downright insufferable at times, but I love you."

"As I love you. Now grab your knitting needles and a smile. We've work to do and you can practice being a proper society lady as we toil."

"You know, little sister, I think you're more ambitious than you let on when you talk like that." Claudine laughed as she gathered her basket. *And I hope it's true, sister. For all my grand plans, I want you to share in this good fortune with me.*

CHAPTER 6

Gabrielle

July 1677

"What about the Hublot boy?" Elisabeth asked between decorous bites of crusty bread dipped in her piping-hot stew. "He always seems so friendly when he comes to the shop."

"Engaged to Lise Pierette," Gilbert answered. "Her mother was crowing about it last week. Nathanaël Lavallé?"

"A bigger prat there never was," Pascal interjected, stabbing a chunk of stewed chicken from his dinner plate.

"Surely in a colony full of men, a beautiful girl like our Gabrielle won't go begging for a husband," Elisabeth said. "Not when so many men are anxious for wives."

Anxious for wives who didn't have a drunk for a father and who have something of consequence to bring to the marriage, but I will do my duty.

"I'm not hungry," Gabrielle said, tossing her napkin on the table. *I'll apologize for my manners later.* She kissed little Fabien and Pierre on their round cheeks, but took no leave of the adults.

Gabrielle shut herself in her small room, happy in her own company, and took out the carefully cut pieces of pale pink silk for the bodice of Claudine's new evening dress. Silk required perfect stitches. One false seam and there was no guarantee that removing it wouldn't destroy the entire panel of costly fabric. It required every ounce of her attention, and for this she was grateful.

It would be a lovely gown, the soft pink offsetting Claudine's rosy complexion and brown eyes. Claudine demanded the latest in fashion, hoping to emulate the fine ladies in Paris she had never seen—and likely would never see. On the occasions Gabrielle had to sew for Emmanuelle, the younger Deschamps girl proved a far more agreeable customer. All she wanted was a serviceable garment suited for the occasion. Though Gabrielle never had the honor to sew for their elder sister, she imagined Madame Lefebvre's tastes would fit somewhere between her sisters'. Manon, on the other hand, left all of the decisions on her formal wear up to Gabrielle or Nicole, which was both thrilling and daunting.

After an hour, the bodice was basted together, and Gabrielle was pleased with the result. She removed her own bodice and replaced it gingerly with the fragile mock-up of the new one. Pink would never, ever suit Gabrielle with her fiery orange hair and freckles, but the fit was good, which meant that it would do well for Claudine. She took just a moment to embrace her vanity. She coiled her red mane on her head and admired her profile in her small mirror. She looked like a lady. The gown would cost more than Gabrielle could earn in several months, if not a year. Never would such a garment belong to her.

She exhaled and removed the bodice with care. In truth, Gabrielle didn't covet the luxurious clothes and fine things that the Deschamps girls had, or that Madame Lefebvre forced Manon to accept. Gabrielle wasn't born into a fine family, nor did she aspire to one. *But they may choose their paths, while mine was set by edict.*

The bitter thought stung like salt in a cut, so she pushed it aside. There was no use in begrudging Claudine or Emmanuelle something she had no control over. They were free by the law to marry when they chose. Whether their family was as lenient was yet to be seen. Claudine was eager enough, but Emmanuelle was more interested in her books than in the young men of the settlement. No more anxious to marry than Gabrielle herself. But when a good offer came to Emmanuelle, the Lefebvres would press her to take it. The town, in its subtle ways, would do the same.

"How thrilling for you, Mademoiselle Deschamps," they would say. *"How anxious you must be to see things settled."*

Refusal would never be mentioned as an option. The only way Emmanuelle could deny an offer of marriage or to rescind her acceptance without scorn from the community would be if there were another one made. And by a man of better standing, too. Marriage for love was mocked. Elisabeth and Gilbert were the most affectionate couple Gabrielle had ever seen, and even they did not openly display their love in the public eye. The comfort of holding hands wasn't worth the snide comments.

Gabrielle looked at her reflection in the mirror once more as she stood, clad only in her loose chemise. She unpinned her hair, letting her red curls fly down her back. *"Scrawny, freckled, red-haired, likely with a temper to match."* She heard the whispers when people thought she wasn't in earshot. *"Penniless, virtually nameless, and plain"* were the real insults they wanted to hurl, but the people in town were too kind to speak so about a girl who they had to admit was polite and inoffensive.

She had no doubt she would soon be sewing Claudine and Emmanuelle Deschamps' wedding gowns. Their weddings would be joyous events the entire town would speak of with admiration. As she looked at her own reflection, her eyes drooped; she knew her own wedding would bear no resemblance to such a lavish affair. Nor would the bride be the picture of demure beauty and sedate happiness she was supposed to be.

Though Gabrielle didn't have her foster mother's talent for pastry making, she had more aptitude for it than the men of the house. She found more pleasure in the pleats of soft linen and fine silk than in the consistency of *crème anglaise,* but did find it a good way to take her mind off other things. Elisabeth was with Nicole, sewing for the Church that afternoon, so the running of the shop was left to Gabrielle. She supplemented the dwindling stock with simple buns, savory, with a sprinkling of salt on top. It was not a day for sweet things. The hard kernels of coarse salt made a satisfying crunch between her teeth as she took a sample of her handiwork. Her sense of taste was heightened, and she knew the rich beef stew would dance on their tongues that night. She placed the warm buns on display on the shop counter, reserving some for the family, and grabbed the broom, preparing to sweep away the dirt from the morning rush before the evening rush began.

A tall man, one built for the frontier, with a scraggly beard and rough-hewn clothes, entered the shop. Gilbert and Pascal were out running bread to the outlying customers. Given the size of the man, she wished very much that one of them were home. She gripped the broom handle and forced a smile for the savage-looking man. Elisabeth's mantra echoed in her ears: *A smile will sell bread far more often than a scowl.*

"Welcome, monsieur. If there is anything you're looking for, please don't hesitate to ask." *And make no mistake: I will hit you upside the head if you look at me askance.* She took her customary place behind the counter, but kept the broom by her side.

The man wordlessly surveyed the stock.

"One of those." As he pointed to the smaller, cheap loaves, the man spoke with a voice that reminded Gabrielle of pine needles in August. Dry, brittle, scratchy. Unpleasant.

"Of course, monsieur." A false smile tugged at the corners of her mouth. It was reflexive by now.

"If it tastes of sawdust, you'll be hearing from me." The man plunked down his coins as he accepted the bread from Gabrielle.

"It won't, monsieur. I assure you." Gabrielle's customer manners melted into genuine confidence. There was nothing inferior about the Beaumonts' inventory. Gabrielle grabbed one of her salted dinner buns, still warm from the oven. It wasn't unusual for Gilbert or Elisabeth to offer new customers a small sample, so she felt certain they would not rebuke her for the gesture. "Here, try one of these before you leave, so you can pass your journey home knowing a fine supper awaits you."

The man placed his purchase on the counter and accepted Gabrielle's offering. He bit into the roll thoughtfully, like a hunter assessing the viability of a shot before loosing his arrow. Gabrielle felt the breath catch in her chest as she awaited his verdict and reminded herself to exhale.

"Not bad," he pronounced after a few moments.

"I'm very glad you approve, monsieur." The smile she offered this time was more genuine.

"If the loaf is just as good, you'll have more of my business, Mademoiselle . . ."

"Giroux. Gabrielle Giroux."

"Olivier Patenaude," the man said with a nod, grabbing his bread and exiting the shop without a backward glance.

Resuming her sweeping, Gabrielle could see him mount a massive brown beast of a horse and head west. *A homesteader for sure. He'd do better to sell his flour to Gilbert and have the bread delivered.* Gabrielle resolved to mention the service to him if he ever returned to the shop, though if he never returned, that would suit her just as well. She did smile at his pronouncement, however. She was too much a Beaumont not to take pride in her work. To hear it praised was one of the purest joys of her life.

Gabrielle went back to the kitchen and turned her attention to a small batch of wild cherry tarts for the family supper. Pascal had stopped to gather a good crop on his way home from a delivery. Elisabeth always delighted in the challenge of a new ingredient, and Pascal in procuring them for her. The fruit looked like it might be past its peak by the next day, so she decided to get the good out of it, even if it meant depriving Elisabeth of the enjoyment of concocting a new recipe.

As she mixed the water, flour, and rich butter to make the crust, she occupied her mind as she often did, with satin, muslin, brocade and damask. She imagined the cut of a perfect gown. Sometimes ornate, fit for a ball at King Louis's court. Other times the gowns were more serviceable, better suited for a stylish summer day out-of-doors by the St. Lawrence. She practiced the cuts, the stitches, the folds in her mind, since she rarely had the fabric to bring her creations to life. Claudine's ball gown provided her the rare chance to practice her craft, and it called to her. It called, but she had to ignore the allure until her duties were done.

Elisabeth encouraged her talents, but Gilbert wondered at her for choosing a path outside the shop. Gabrielle suspected he hoped she'd find a nice young man who could take Pascal's place in the delivery wagon once Pascal's duties with the Lefebvres became too great for him to continue at both. *It would be nice, dear Gilbert, but we rarely get what we want.* The pink satin called to her, but the promise of imminently arriving customers forced her to remain downstairs.

Gabrielle had the table set for supper and stew simmering over the fire when the family returned. She arranged her crisp, salted buns on a platter in the center of the table and kept the cherry tarts in reserve for dessert. So often, Elisabeth hadn't the energy to put forth much effort at dinner, so when the duty fell to Gabrielle, she tried to make more of a fuss.

"You spoil us," Gilbert said, taking his seat at the head of the table.

"What would you expect from a cook trained by me?" Elisabeth cocked her eyebrow at her husband. Even after years of marriage, Gabrielle still saw the playful smiles and knowing looks the couple exchanged. From her childhood, she hadn't realized marriage could be so friendly, appear so effortless.

"Your skills haven't gone unnoticed," Gilbert said, winking at his foster daughter as he sampled the stew.

Gabrielle stopped, spoon halfway to her mouth, and placed it back in the bowl. "What do you mean?"

"I hear you waited on a new customer?" Gilbert said. "Olivier Patenaude stopped me on my way back into town when he was on his way back to his property."

"Yes." Gabrielle nodded, smoothing her skirts with nervous hands. "He bought a small loaf. I offered him a sample as you sometimes do for new customers."

"He's not exactly a new customer," Elisabeth chimed in. "But he hasn't come around very often since he took over his homestead."

Gabrielle shook her head. Anyone who knew the Beaumonts knew their stock was impeccable. He had jibed her into giving him free food.

"I'm sorry. If I'd known, I'd never have given him anything without asking."

"No sense worrying over a small gift for a customer on the odd occasion," Gilbert said. "He told me he was pleased with you.

Thought you were tidy and a hard worker from the way you kept the broom close at hand. Said the roll you gave him was excellent as well."

Pascal, already on his third bun, nodded his agreement.

"I kept the broom handy in case I had to bash him in the head with it," Gabrielle admitted.

Gilbert's shoulders shook at his foster daughter's pronouncement and his eyes danced with mirth. "He does look the part of a wild frontiersman, but he's an honest tradesman. He asked if you had a beau."

Gabrielle felt the blood drain from her face. The man had to be fifteen years her senior if he were a day. Not to mention he looked as friendly as the bears that roamed the mountains coming out of their slumber in early spring.

"What did you say?" Gabrielle set her fork down before she dropped it on the table.

"That you were unattached and one of the nicest girls in the settlement." Gilbert's attention never wavered far from his meal, as if they were discussing the sale of a cow rather than her courtship.

"Kind of you." Gabrielle looked down at her piping hot stew, her appetite eviscerated.

"He only speaks the truth, sweetheart," Elisabeth said, patting Gabrielle's shoulder affectionately.

"He asked if he could come to dinner sometime." Gilbert spoke in between bites of stew and bread, hungry from his day's labor. Pascal and Pierre ate with no less fervor as Fabien chewed on a bun. "He wants to get to know you better."

"He'll propose within a week if the supper's as good as this one," Pascal claimed.

Gabrielle looked at her brother. He was a kind boy, but never seemed to put much stock in marriage. When people spoke of a couple being a good match, he often looked sideways. He didn't see much difference in one man or another, and didn't much see why one would suit a woman any better than another. As if one shoe would fit every foot. Gabrielle had long since given up trying to convince him that things could be otherwise. He saw Patenaude as a solution to his sister's problem and would not see the point in looking for another.

"Invite him, then," Gabrielle said, attempting to keep her tone neutral. "If you think he's a good sort of man."

"I don't know him well," Gilbert said. "But I've not heard a word spoken against him. In this settlement, if anything were amiss with his character, we'd have heard about it."

"That's true," Elisabeth said, rolling her eyes. She was the unwilling recipient of most of the town's gossip. She took pains not to relate the idle prattle; though Gabrielle suspected her foster mother's friends heard a few choice pieces from time to time, but never out of malice.

"He'll be here Thursday next," Gilbert said, taking a deep draught of cider. "So plan a good dinner, sweetheart. He'll want to sample your handiwork, I'm sure."

Gabrielle nodded and pretended to pick at her food. *So there it is. In less than a month my family will marry me off to a veritable stranger.* As soon as Gilbert had extended the invitation, the banns were as good as read. She wanted to yell. To cry. Instead, she kept a weak smile tugging at the corner of her lips and added to the idle conversation from time to time. She would no longer be a burden on the family she loved, and she had to at least pretend that the marriage was anything other than repugnant.

But she dried her eyes as she retired to her room. Now, in the waning hours of twilight, the time was hers to spend as she chose. She pulled the delicate pink silk from her basket and continued to stitch until the skirt of Claudine's ball gown swept the floor with every pleat falling artfully into place. Gabrielle set the skirt aside with a pang of loss. There would be nothing but patchwork once she married.

CHAPTER 7

Manon

August 1677

If the elegance of Paris could not be attained, supper at the Lefebvre house was served with at least as much pomp as one would find in any French country manor. Manon took the place to Nicole's right at the dining table, the place usually reserved for the eldest daughter. Hélène, the least resentful child Manon had ever met, surrendered the place at once upon her adopted sister's return. Whether Nicole prompted the deed, Manon knew not, but Hélène only had smiles to send across the table as she sat to her mother's left. Hélène was only recently allowed to dine with the adults to practice her table manners. Manon had heard that Alexandre had voiced some displeasure at allowing the practice so early, but his Parisian formalities had to be relaxed in their more rustic environs. He did admit, when Hélène was out of earshot, that the well-mannered girl was no nuisance at the table.

An adorable child who has never known suffering. None of the Huron but the smallest infants know such peace. Manon did acknowledge that the cherubic girl with golden-brown curls did have a mark of sadness on her past. The young soldier-turned-homesteader, Luc Jarvais, never knew the darling girl he fathered with his young bride out in his ramshackle cabin on the frontier. But then again, a wealthier and, from what Manon gathered, more deserving man took Luc's place before the child was a year old.

Emmanuelle and Claudine were lost in their own conversation that night, and the only addition to the family meal was Pascal Giroux, who had accompanied Alexandre to his holdings that afternoon. Manon remembered the gangly boy from five years ago, whose stomach seemed like a bottomless canyon. Manon had teased him that he must have a wolf cub living in his belly, so ravenous was his hunger. Now he sat to Alexandre's right, the place for the honored guest—a position he assumed by default of being the *only* guest in attendance. He ate more slowly now, having perhaps learned the value of chewing in the interim years. He had only grown a few inches in height, but his shoulders and arms were now those of a man and not a spindly boy.

"We need to convince the tenants on the east end of the property that they all need to diversify their crops." Pascal spoke forcefully, given that he spoke to a *seigneur*. "They'll deplete the soil far too quickly if they grow nothing but tobacco. They need to have a rotation of wheat or let the soil rest altogether."

"Have them talk to my father if they want to know how important it is to rotate crops." Nicole's tone was humorless. A few better decisions on which crops to sow from Thomas Deschamps might have meant a very different future for his daughter.

"Too right," Alexandre said, nodding to his wife as he sampled the exquisitely prepared roast quail. "And the Intendant doesn't want our tobacco crops large enough that we pose any real competition to the French holdings in the tropics. Heaven knows our tobacco isn't anything in comparison. They'd do far better with hemp or flax if they won't grow wheat. We'll have to speak with them again. I don't want to revoke their homestead, but we can't allow them to destroy good farmland. It's too hard to clear more."

Yes, trees, shrubs, native peoples . . . all difficult to clear away.

"How have your people dealt with soil quality?" Pascal asked, directing his attention to Manon. "Have you a set rotation for crops?"

"I've had little to do with the farming," Manon admitted. "But crop rotation is easy enough when you haven't the means to find or buy the seeds you like. You get what you can and hope the harvest will see you through the winter."

Pascal looked dark for a few moments. Manon remembered the condition he and his sister were in when they moved in with the Beaumonts.

"I understand the Huron tend to grow more maize than wheat," Alexandre said. "I'd be interested to see how your soil holds up comparatively."

It's not my soil. Not anymore. It never really was. "I don't think it's particularly easy on the soil, but not as bad as tobacco. But we leave fields empty frequently and move them around almost every year."

"You ought to come with the *seigneur* and me to visit with the rest of the tenants tomorrow," Pascal suggested. "You might find it interesting."

"I'm sure you and Seigneur Lefebvre will be too busy to bother with me." Manon did not make eye contact with Alexandre. She was sure that being seen by the whole settlement in a wagon with a native girl was not something he welcomed.

"You needn't be so formal, dear," Nicole said, patting Manon's hand. "You used to call him Papa."

As seldom as possible and only when you were in earshot. "Monsieur" suited both of us far better.

"Alexandre is fine if you prefer, Manon," Alexandre said, glancing toward Manon. "And you'd be welcome. If the tenants see us together it might avoid any further . . . unpleasantness like we had last spring."

Nicole beamed at the kind words her husband directed at Manon.

"As you say," Manon replied, nodding. He was providing her houseroom and education. Her brother as well. She could hardly refuse such a small request. Though she would rather do any number of things than accompany Alexandre Lefebvre as he lorded over his lands, she was not one to slight the man's generosity.

"How lovely, you both can get reacquainted with Manon. I'll make sure you have a nice little luncheon to take with you," Nicole all but purred with satisfaction. The woman did thrive on domestic harmony.

And I'm sure things were a lot more "harmonious" before I arrived.

The next morning, Manon descended the stairs to breakfast to find the table deserted except for Alexandre, who read over his account books while he sipped a very small mug of coffee and ate his toast distractedly. One of the many maids appeared silently, bearing a tray laden with more food than Manon could eat in a week, and prepared to set a place at the foot of the table.

"Mademoiselle will sit here," Alexandre said, gesturing to his right side. The maid scurried to comply with his orders and vanished without a word.

"I'm glad you agreed to come with us today," Alexandre said, placing his toast back on his plate and turning to Manon. "I was hoping to speak with you in private."

Manon looked at the massive platter before her. Pastries, sausages, eggs, rolls with an assortment of jams. The sight of so much food made her stomach roll. She took a link of sausage and a small pastry on her plate and shoved the rest away. "Is that so?" Manon asked, not looking up at his face for more than a few seconds. They'd been in the same house for months, but never alone. Mostly because Manon spent as much time in her room as she could without offending Nicole.

"Yes. You know your leaving wounded Nicole." Alexandre shut the account book, his expression the one he used when dealing with particularly challenging tenants or when negotiating for something of grave importance. "She was disconsolate for weeks."

"She seems to have recovered," Manon said, eating as quickly as decorum would allow.

"Yes, but I can't allow her to be wounded again. She is my wife and it is my first duty to ensure that I spare her from pain whenever I can."

"Admirable," Manon said, her words as flat as the table where they sat.

"You're rather a heartless thing, aren't you?" Alexandre said, his voice dripping with a mixture of sarcasm and incredulity. "The woman cared for you for years and one day you decided to pick up and leave with little more than a 'fare thee well.' Is that any way to repay her?"

"Yes," Manon said, raising her head so her black eyes could sear into his gray ones. "Considering the hateful stares she pretended to ignore every time we were in public, every veiled insult she deflected on my behalf. Yes, I thought leaving was a great kindness. When I was a small girl, it didn't seem to matter as much. Perhaps because I was just a child, people could forgive her indulgence toward me. As I grew, and especially after you married her, people were less forgiving."

"She didn't care about all that," Alexandre said, his tone softening slightly.

"No, but you did," Manon countered.

To this Alexandre had no reply.

Alexandre set his mug of coffee, more expensive than his finest cognac, down on the table with precision. "Let us come to a right understanding, shall we? If you leave her and leave this house again as you did before, I won't allow you back. Do I make myself perfectly plain?"

"As always, monsieur. I never intended to hurt her. I missed her bitterly. I only left because I wanted her to be happy. I wouldn't be here if it weren't for Tawendeh—Théodore, if you must. If I can't find work among the French and my own people are ready to see me cast out as an evil spirit, I haven't many choices, do I? If it were me alone, I'd do my best to live off the land, but I won't see him suffer."

"You deserve better than a life foraging out in the woods as well," Alexandre said. "You're a capable young woman. You'll stay here, and your brother, too. But once you leave this house, you will stay gone. I won't have you break her heart again."

"Understood. I hope to find another situation so my brother and I needn't trespass on your hospitality for too long," Manon said, regaining her civility.

"Let's have none of that. Nicole wants you to feel as one of the family, after all. If you leave, let it be for a good marriage so she has the pleasure of seeing you well settled. It would be a far better repayment for her kindness than skulking away." Alexandre took on his officious tone. *It's business to the French, after all. Any true affection in marriage is just a nice, if unnecessary, windfall that precious few experience.*

Manon welcomed the silence from Alexandre and Pascal as they drove along the dusty path to the Lefebvre estate. The largest holding, by a wide margin, was tended by Nicole's father, Thomas Deschamps. Every inch of the land was tended with the utmost efficiency and modern methods, thanks to Alexandre and Pascal's guidance. Thomas followed his son-in-law's directives like gospel, and it worked to good result. The other farmers were less convinced by Alexandre's suggestions. Manon supposed they saw his soft hands and shining leather boots and assumed he wouldn't know which end of a hoe to use to till the soil. They wouldn't be entirely wrong, but as she saw the Deschamps farm with its thriving fields of wheat, barley, oats, and peas, Manon admitted his notions must have merit.

When they arrived at the eastern border of the Lefebvre homestead, Alexandre gave order for Manon and Pascal to stay with the horses. The other tenants had been happy to see the *seigneur*'s young companions, but he warned it might not be the case here. The Giles were good people, but the patriarch, Hubert, would feel intimidated if Pascal and Alexandre both presented their suggestions. Manon's presence would only confuse him. Pascal offered Manon a hand down from the wagon so they could stretch their legs and enjoy the summer sun while Alexandre spoke to his tenants about his tobacco fields that had continued to grow more and more feeble for the past three years.

"The old man needs to listen," Pascal said. "Two years. Let half the land rest fallow and grow wheat on the other half one year and then swap the next. It would liven the soil up for another ten years."

"I thought you hated farming," Manon said, remembering the diatribes of his youth. "I thought you'd be in commerce with the Beaumonts for the rest of your days."

"Time softens harsh memories, I suppose," Pascal said. "Though I confess there were too many hungry nights to forget completely. It must be in my blood. Seigneur Lefebvre and I fell into a conversation about his estate two years back, and I've been training with him on the running of the place ever since."

"And you enjoy playing landlord?" Manon asked, looking out over the expansive fields that butted up against the forest of her youth.

"I do," Pascal admitted. "If I can help ensure the farms are well run, it means fewer people go hungry. I can't think of a better trade than that. Since Alexandre's nephew Henri was granted an estate of his own, Seigneur Lefebvre needed a hand, and I'm grateful for the chance."

Manon nodded. Starving Frenchmen made for poor neighbors to the Huron.

"The *seigneur* tells me you've taken up where you left off—nose in the Latin and Greek and all that?"

"Yes," Manon said. "And other things. Medicine, history . . . and domestic skills when I can't escape them."

"I never understood how you could read that stuff," Pascal said with a playful nudge to her arm. "Though I can sit down with a book more easily than before."

"There may be hope for you yet, then." Manon smiled at the tall young man with his dark hair and serious eyes. "You certainly put enough effort into resisting your lessons. I'm amazed Monsieur Beaumont had the patience to teach you."

"He may not look it, but he's as stubborn as a worn-out donkey when he wants to be. It's a good trait in a father."

Manon gave a full-throated laugh. "I imagine it must be." Her mind flitted back to Heno, Manon tucked in his arms, her face pressed against his muscled chest and her fingers in his flowing jet-black hair. He'd begged her for a child, but would he have had the patience to teach their son the skills he would need in life? The image of the brave hunter and the forbearing father seemed too sharp a juxtaposition for her to reconcile.

"I do have a bone to pick with you, you know," Pascal said after a while as they looked out from atop a hill at the St. Lawrence rushing several miles away.

Manon sighed and did her best to look meek. "What have I done now?"

"You never told me good-bye, all those years ago. I had to hear from Gilbert that you'd left." His jovial tone was gone. He didn't look to her, but out across the valley he'd come to love.

"I had no idea you'd notice that I was gone." Manon looked up at him, trying to read his expression. "We played, we chatted, we were friendly. But you had dozens of other children to play with."

"I promise you, I noticed."

Manon blinked with understanding. She had broken his sixteen-year-old heart when she was little more than a girl. Far too young to understand feelings deeper than friendship. *I knew leaving had been the right choice, and now I've been given more proof. I'd have caused his ostracism from the settlement for sure.* Now that Pascal was a man of twenty-one, he had a better understanding of the repercussions of a life with a native woman. She hoped he would let his good sense guide him away from her.

And her mind traveled once again back to the hunter she'd left behind. She was no suitable wife for an honest Frenchman. Even a sweet-natured man like Pascal could not look past her years with Heno. Though her adopted culture told her she ought to be ashamed of her midnight embraces, she could not bear to think of them with embarrassment. Especially now that the memory of those nights was one of the few comforts she carried with her from her time with the Huron.

It seemed indecent to think of the looming winter on one of the most gloriously sun-kissed days in August, but Manon had to admit that Nicole's plan made sense. Certain crops were beginning to come in, and everyone was beginning to preserve their winter rations. They set to salting meats, preserving vegetables in brine and fruits in sugar, putting hardy crops in the coldest areas of their root cellars, and making sure they had flour and grain to last the season. It seemed like most farms ended the harvest with a surplus of one crop or another, so Nicole had it in mind to create a store of the extra food for the Ursulines to keep on hand for the families that would inevitably fall on hard times that winter. If the more prosperous farms gave a few jars of brined vegetables or a few sacks of flour, or a spare blanket or worn pair of trousers, they would have a formidable supply to help the struggling farms survive.

Manon remembered more than a few weeks in her village when

rations grew sparse in the winter, even with the support of everyone in the tribe. She imagined that many isolated homesteaders would struggle terribly in the long white months that would be upon them. She volunteered to help Nicole gather the stock, knowing she would sleep better in her warm bed that winter for her efforts. Claudine, Emmanuelle, and Gabrielle pitched in their support as well. Manon sensed Gabrielle's kindness stemmed from having known her share of lean winters, and Claudine's from her eagerness to appear industrious and benevolent to the St. Pierre family. Emmanuelle, however, was always happy to help where she was needed.

Gabrielle, having learned how to drive a wagon at her brother's side, would take Manon and Claudine to some of the nearer homesteads to the west to ask for donations. Emmanuelle, Nicole, Rose, and Elisabeth all focused their efforts in town and to the east.

"It's a shame all charitable works can't involve a wagon ride out into the country on a lovely summer day," Claudine mused.

"Then we'd all be philanthropists," Manon agreed. "We'll have to remember today when we're sitting in the parlor knitting our endless blankets for the unfortunate this winter."

"Too true," Gabrielle said. "The Mercier farm is just ahead. She's a kind woman and will be sure to have something in her pantry to spare."

"From her figure, she's not known a hard winter, either," Claudine said with a derisive snort.

"It might be best if you refrain from such talk when we get there." Manon rolled her eyes as she gazed off toward the inviting farmhouse. Claudine's tongue would earn them no great support from the homesteaders they canvassed if she would not keep it in check.

Manon walked aside Gabrielle, who, knowing the woman best, took the initiative to knock on the door.

The woman was every bit as stout as Claudine had led them to believe, and her mouth was quick to smile at the sight of the girls, proving Gabrielle's assessment of her character to be true as well.

"The Sisters are seeking donations for the Indian children, then?" Madame Mercier's brow furrowed at Gabrielle's explanation of the winter stockpile scheme. She looked at Manon's French clothes contrasted by her thick, black braids, clearly not sure what to make of her.

"It's possible the Sisters would help any of the families in the area that came to them for help, but our thoughts were really of those on the outlying homesteads and those newly settled who will have difficulties this winter."

The woman nodded, but did not appear convinced of the tale. She sent them on their way with a half dozen jars of preserved fruits and vegetables from her larder and a small sack of flour.

"Well, if every stop is this successful we'll have something to show for our day, aside from the benefits of fresh air and sunshine," Claudine said, satisfied.

Manon agreed, and did not voice her annoyance at the woman's assumption that Manon's involvement meant the rations would be distributed to the Huron and other neighboring tribes. *We fare the winter far better than your people do, because we do not scatter like seeds in the wind. This whole exercise of Nicole's would be unnecessary if you lived as a tribe, but you do not look beyond your own families and closest companions.*

They visited eight more homesteads before they began to circle back to town. The families all had far more to spare than the single men. The wagon didn't sag under the weight of their donations, but every last potato and frayed jacket would be helpful.

"Let's make a last stop at the Faillon place," Claudine suggested. "We have a bit of room left and he's always one to leave his *sou* in the collection plate."

Gabrielle nodded her assent and guided the horse down the path that led to the well-ordered farmhouse.

A spindly man of forty years came from the fields around the east side of the house, having seen the wagon approaching. This time, Claudine announced their business, her smile perfectly posed to charm the weary farmer. Manon appraised his work-worn face and decided she would do best to stand behind Claudine and Gabrielle, rather than at their side.

"I ain't got food to spare for them that can't help themselves," he replied with a growl.

"We're so sorry we interrupted you while you were in the fields, monsieur. We know your farm is one of the best tended in all the colony and you must work yourself like a plow horse to keep it so," Claudine purred. "We just know that the winter can be such a treacherous season, even for the hardest-working among us. Crops fail; kitchens burn, taking a winter's worth of food with it—any number of things can happen. We just want to have a modest supply on hand for families who find themselves in distress."

"More like, those Sisters of yours in that convent want a big, fat larder to bribe those Indians into converting." Faillon looked directly at Manon. "Don't let them fool you. They don't care for us once we've pledged our souls. They're just looking for new recruits, you mark my words."

Claudine thanked the man with such frost encrusting each syllable that it sent a frigid breeze to quell the August heat.

Back in town, Pascal waited at the door of the Ursulines' storeroom to help unload the bounty. The room was already lined with abundant donations. Their addition to the stock would hardly be noticed.

Nicole looked over the various foodstuffs and goods Manon and the others had been able to amass. She furrowed her brow for a moment and gave the order to Pascal to unload them according to the system she had devised.

"You visited all the farms I suggested?" Nicole asked Manon with a weary eye cast at Claudine.

"And two others besides," Manon said, acquitting Claudine of the unspoken accusation of convincing the others to shirk their duties.

"Well, we all know that some farms do better than others. And who's to say what their situations are." Nicole smiled and patted Manon's shoulder before returning to the storeroom.

Manon felt the muscles in her neck and jaw tighten, and she forced herself to breathe deeply so they would not clench any further. If she did not, she would be down for hours with another one of her headaches. *The farmers donated less because of me, I'm sure of it.*

She wanted to go into the storeroom and join Claudine, who teased Gabrielle companionably about her upcoming nuptials to Olivier Patenaude as she sorted through and organized the donated clothes. Manon saw the invitation in Pascal's eyes to come and help sort the various foods. She had thought a little too often of his confession two weeks prior, and knew she was not indifferent to his kind eyes and easy smile. She wondered what it would be like to take his hand, ever so briefly, knowing full well the simple gesture would likely set into motion a course of events that would see her as his bride before the following spring.

The face of the surly farmer, the shrewish shopkeeper, and all the sidelong glances from the rest of the townsfolk convinced her that such an act would doom him to a life of obscurity. He could achieve so much more than that, with Alexandre's guidance. He could, in time, become a *seigneur* himself, and she could see the glint of pride in his eyes when he spoke of their improvements to the land. Not only did he deserve to climb in social prominence, his efforts made the lives of Alexandre's tenant farmers infinitely better.

If he yoked himself to her, she would be denying him his chance, as well as depriving the tenants of a skilled and compassionate manager. Worse, as her husband, the dubious gazes in town she endured would be cast onto him as well. Doors would close in his face, just as they had for Mother Onatah. Even occasionally for Nicole, though marrying Alexandre had opened them wide once more. She could not bear to see him shunned. Her own happiness seemed a reasonable price to spare him from the ostracism that he had no idea he would face.

CHAPTER 8

Claudine

August 1677

Less than three hours from schoolroom to ballroom, not bad. Claudine followed Nicole and Alexandre into the St. Pierre ballroom. The unexceptional sextet played to welcome the guests; their notes soared to the lofty ceiling as Claudine surveyed the room that sparkled with the glint of candlelight against crystal and jewels. As had become her custom, she scanned the room to see if any of the young women outshone her. She smiled in satisfaction, seeing none.

Claudine spotted Victor across the room, chatting with one of the governor's deputies and a throng of old women. *Poor boy, what dreary company, but you'll find an excuse to break away soon enough.*

Claudine's reverie was shattered when Nicole grabbed her at the elbow and dragged her before a man deep in conversation with Alexandre. He was a man of middling height, nondescript brown hair, and no particular charm. He had rather a round face to match his stout form. Were his eyes not surrounded by a few lines of experience, they might have been described as mirthful. It was the only aspect of his appearance that Claudine thought merited any notice.

Another stolid, respectable old man.

"Seigneur Laurent Robichaux, I'd like to present my sister, Claudine Deschamps," Nicole said as the men broke their discussion.

"How very kind of you." Robichaux bowed slightly to her. "Such lovely young ladies are so rare in the settlement, it's a real pleasure to make the acquaintance of one."

Oh, deliver me from this boor. Do these old men study from the same stale book of flattery?

"Very nice to meet you, *seigneur*." Claudine curtsied low. She only just kept from gritting her teeth. *Why must everyone outrank me?*

"Would you do me the honor of a dance, mademoiselle?" Robichaux asked, extending an arm.

Sure of yourself, aren't you? Claudine knew of no polite means to refuse him, so she accepted his escort to the dance floor.

The dance was prim and gave the couples ample time for conversation, much to Claudine's dismay. Endless prattle about tenants, crops, and livestock. Not a syllable about people or society or anything that mattered. Victor shot her a roguish smile as he danced with a gray-haired woman. Claudine answered Robichaux's questions with all the grace expected of a Lefebvre, though the charm she aimed in his direction was as false as some of the glass jewels the lesser women wore.

Victor intervened as the next dance started, much to Claudine's relief. The next number was more exuberant than the last, so Seigneur Robichaux looked none too disappointed to relinquish Claudine into the arms of a more skillful partner.

"Darling girl, how funny to see you wasted in the arms of that old man," Victor whispered with a low chuckle.

" 'Funny' was the last word I would have used," Claudine said, suppressing a giggle.

"You are such a lovely creature," Victor breathed. "Every time we're together I long to be alone with you."

Claudine's eyes widened at his familiarity. She knew she ought to be shocked at his suggestive undertones, but the warmth of his words spread to her very core. It was a flame she could not quench.

"Come with me," Victor whispered. "There's a room where we can go. . . ."

He's going to ask. It will all be settled. I will be his wife.

Victor whispered instructions and left the room first, Claudine following a few minutes later so they wouldn't be seen leaving the room together. In the dark of the side corridor, he offered his arm and led her to a small but lavishly appointed bedroom. His mouth was upon hers and his hands roved over her breasts. He expertly loosened her stays and exposed her bare skin to his.

"Let me . . ." he asked.

He's going to ask Alexandre tonight. He wouldn't ask me to do this if he weren't. What's the harm? I'll simply insist on a short engagement. He continued to kiss her hungrily, invading her mouth with his tongue. These were not the sweet, lingering kisses he stole in shadowed hallways, and she found she missed them. His hands were rough with her tender flesh, pinching and probing in places she'd never dared to touch herself.

"Slowly," she urged in a whisper, hoping he could temper his eagerness. She moved her hands to caress his buttocks over the smooth silk of his breeches, her touch featherlight, demonstrating how she wanted him to love her.

"Shh," he said, pulling her hands away and loosening his breeches, entering her with one swift movement. She began to cry out at the rush of pain, but he covered her mouth with his hand as he gyrated above her, grunting. *Won't you look at me? Whisper sweet things to me, my darling?*

She'd pictured this moment more times than she could ever admit to her confessor, but she did not expect the discomfort. She had dreamed of his soft hands bringing her pleasure with gentle caresses, but he only took what he wanted.

He's young. He's impatient.

She said this to herself, and the words were true, but they gave her no comfort. No matter how she justified his behavior, she could not ignore the lack of warmth in his touch.

Almost as soon as he'd begun, he gave a final thrust and climbed off her at once.

"Hurry," he said, fastening his breeches and straightening his hair as he steadied his breath. "They'll notice we've gone."

Claudine succeeded only marginally at keeping her tears in check. *Perhaps it was just the excitement of the moment? Nerves?*

Victor left without a thought to helping her dress or restoring her to a presentable state. The truth twisted in her gut like the rusty blade of a hunter's dagger: No part of this had been about her, not a solitary second. Victor had claimed his prize and had not spared her another thought. But men of his class, Alexandre had often explained, were not like the farm boys she was used to. He would have to be taught to consider of her needs when they were married.

She straightened her skirts and smoothed her hair in the mirror to little avail. There was nothing to do about her stays without the help of a lady's maid. *What in God's name am I going to do? Go out into the hall half dressed? Why would he leave me like this?*

She peeked into the hall, praying to see a maid who could be bribed into silence, but instead saw Nicole and Alexandre scanning the hall. She'd been missed. *Why couldn't Nicole be alone?* She swore under her breath and called to her sister in a loud whisper.

"What's happened to you?" Nicole said. Alexandre took one look at his sister-in-law and his expression darkened instantly. Nicole placed her hand on his arm and he stepped back out into the hall. "Did someone hurt you?"

"No, not exactly," Claudine said. *I know he didn't mean to.*

Nicole said nothing, but rearranged Claudine's dress and fixed her stays. She did what she could with her hair without the benefit of a brush or pins.

Back in the hall, Alexandre greeted them with arms crossed over his chest and his teeth clenched so tightly the vein along his jaw protruded. There was no question that he knew what had happened and no doubt in Claudine's mind that he would make her pay for her transgression.

"I don't know what you're playing at, young lady—" Alexandre hissed.

"Please, it won't matter," Claudine said, her expression panicked. "He's going to ask you tonight. He wouldn't . . . wouldn't have otherwise . . ."

Alexandre's expression was no less murderous, but a call for attention from the ballroom interrupted what was certainly destined to be a scathing lecture. They returned to the room, Alexandre leading Claudine by the arm instead of his wife. *Shortening the leash already.*

Aubin St. Pierre, Victor's father, stood near the orchestra, the room's attention fixated in his direction. "My dear friends. We thank you so much for joining us this evening. We do hope you're enjoying yourselves. To that end, we wish to impart some glad tidings to bolster your enjoyment further. We are pleased to announce that our eldest son and heir, Victor, is engaged to Mademoiselle Nadine DuLaurier, daughter of Seigneur Antoine DuLaurier. Please join us in wishing the young couple well."

Victor approached his father, arm in arm with a fair-haired girl with a narrow, weasel-ish face and an opulent gown, who smiled with the happiness of a well-matched bride.

Claudine looked at her sister and brother-in-law in horror.

She was ruined.

"What in God's name were you thinking?" Alexandre barked an hour later in the privacy of the Lefebvre parlor.

"I thought he was going to ask you," Claudine said, staring at her hands, unable to speak above a whisper. "Truly I did."

"He never gave you any understanding? No false promises?" Nicole asked, sitting ramrod straight in her chair—the face of the *seigneur*'s wife in place. Claudine knew the look. She was looking to minimize damage.

"No," Claudine admitted. "But I heard the rumors in town. I didn't think he would . . . well, I didn't think he would take liberties if he wasn't going to ask."

"How very naïve," Alexandre said.

"I feel responsible," Nicole said. "We heard Victor's mother discussing the announcement. We came looking for you to take you home to spare you the public embarrassment. If only we'd come a bit sooner."

"It's not your fault," Alexandre scolded his wife, taking a deep swig of his fine brandy that he usually reserved for happy occasions. *There are always exceptions, I suppose.* "She ought to have behaved herself until she was certain things were settled, whatever she thought he was going to do."

"Alexandre, don't you think you're being a bit hard?" Nicole's cup contained only cider, and it seemed to give her no more comfort. "After all, he led her on."

"Unfair as it may sound, her virtue is the only one that matters,"

Alexandre said, then turned the full force of his glare to Claudine. "You're going to go back to your parents and hope for two things: First, that no one saw what happened, not so much as an eavesdropping housemaid. Second, that St. Pierre hasn't saddled you with a child."

Claudine's heart fell to the pit of her stomach. *A child.* She had never entertained the possibility. Stuck in the wilderness on her parents' farm with a squalling baby to care for. Her parents' heartbroken expressions every time they saw their disgraced daughter.

"Please, not the farm," Claudine said.

"There's no other choice," Alexandre said. "If there is a child, I can't have people knowing I housed you. I can't risk the scandal."

"Alexandre, isn't that—" Nicole began.

"What? Too harsh?" Alexandre slammed his glass down on the table with a *clank*. "No. I don't think it is. She came with the understanding that we would give her houseroom here if, and only if, she behaved. Sending her back to her loving parents to avoid tainting the whole family doesn't seem harsh at all."

"But won't her leaving cause talk anyway?" Nicole asked. *Well played, sister, you do know his weaknesses, don't you?*

"Everything causes talk," Alexandre said. "If there isn't a child, nor any malicious gossip, we'll bring her back in a few months' time for a visit to dispel any rumors. We'll invent an excuse—some malady best cured by fresh air—headaches or the like. People will believe it if they choose to."

"Well, you've thought of everything, haven't you?" Claudine said, regaining her composure. "May I leave in the morning, or will you have one of the manservants steal me away to the farm under the cover of night?"

"Don't be silly," Nicole said. "Of course you may wait until morning."

"I wasn't sure your husband wanted me sullying your house another night," Claudine said.

"Don't be hateful," Alexandre said. "St. Pierre acted unpardonably, I'll admit."

"How gracious of you to say so, *seigneur*," Claudine said, curtsying with an affected flourish. "I promise not to trespass on your hospitality a moment longer than necessary."

Claudine spun on the ball of her foot and climbed the stairs to her room. Thankfully her entry didn't disturb Emmanuelle, who stayed fast asleep. She indulged in the weakness of tears, wishing that her sister's presence didn't impede her from giving in completely to her grief.

"Perhaps Alexandre will allow you back—after," Emmanuelle said the next morning as she helped Claudine arrange her plainest clothes in the trunk. She was too delicate to speak the rest of the sentence: *after you're sure you're not with child.* Manon sat next to Emmanuelle and held her hand. The youngest Deschamps girls had never been separated from each other before, and Claudine expected Manon knew something of what they were going through.

Claudine raised her hand to silence Emmanuelle on the subject. She didn't want to hear the words spoken, as if it might make them true.

"I won't set foot in this house again," Claudine said. "I see Alexandre Lefebvre for who he is now, and I want nothing to do with him. I'm just sorry Nicole will never be free of him."

"He's a good and generous man, Claudine," Emmanuelle said.

"Until you make a single false step," Claudine said. "As soon as you risk staining the Lefebvre name with the bright red ink of scandal, then his generosity is nowhere to be found."

"Claudine—" Manon interjected, wrapping her arm around Emmanuelle.

"Don't, please, Manon." Claudine stepped away and crossed her arms over her chest. Pity was unendurable. "Step off your pedestal for one moment, Emmy. I'm ruined. I was a fool and I don't blame Alexandre—or Nicole—for my folly. I *do* blame him for not lifting a finger to help right things. To come to my defense or my aid. It's not as though I acted alone. But while Victor is free to live the life he wants, I'll be cast out from good society. Possibly forever."

"I'll miss you," Emmanuelle said at length.

"And I you," Claudine said. "We may have driven each other mad, but you've been my friend when there was none other to be had."

"I could come home with you," Emmanuelle offered.

"No," Claudine said without pause. Not long ago she would have begged her sister not to leave her alone on the farm, but now she could not deprive Emmanuelle of the benefit of Alexandre's assistance in society. *At least one of us can make a life.*

A knock at the door startled the trio. Rose entered the room, bearing a stack of books for Emmanuelle and Manon.

"Your brother-in-law informs me that you're returning to your parents for some rest," Rose said, looking to Claudine as she passed the books to Emmanuelle. "I was surprised to hear it."

Claudine emitted an unladylike snort. "Rest indeed."

"That's what I thought, which is why I insisted on bringing the books up to your sisters myself." Claudine arched her brow at the plural but said nothing. Rose took a seat in the plush green chair nearest the window. She was ready for a long tale. Claudine sat on her bed and indulged her with one, relaying more detail than she had in her brief confession to Emmanuelle and Manon. All sat stunned as Claudine recounted the sorry tale.

"The vile little slug," Rose said in an uncharacteristically acid tone. "Taking advantage of a girl moments before announcing his engagement to another."

"Yes, but Alexandre places the blame squarely on my shoulders." Claudine sorted through her wardrobe, selecting only the items she'd brought with her. "I know I was in the wrong as well, but at least I wasn't being deliberately false like Victor. But apparently that counts for nothing."

Rose took a place next to Claudine on the bed and wrapped her arm around her. The gesture startled Claudine at first, Rose not having been openly affectionate with her in the past. After a brief hesitation, Claudine returned the embrace, if awkwardly.

"It counts for more than you think," Rose said, releasing her. "Come with me."

The pair found Alexandre in his library, deep in contemplation over his record books.

"Ah, how nice that Claudine was able to say good-bye before her retreat to the country," Alexandre said. "Are you packed?" *"Don't dawdle about it,"* you'd say aloud if it weren't for Nicole.

"It's not much of a task," Claudine said, keeping her tone in check. "I'll have no use for evening gowns. I've left most everything for Emmanuelle."

"Sensible," Alexandre said with a nod.

"I'm afraid you'll have to reclaim your wardrobe from Emmanuelle," said Rose. "You'll have need of your finer things if you're to stay with Henri and me."

"Rose, I'm afraid you don't understand the circumstances—" Alexandre began.

"I understand them perfectly well," Rose said. "While Claudine did act irresponsibly, the young man in question was malicious and cruel, which is far worse. I won't see Claudine deprived of her education because of his misdeeds."

"Do you really think Henri would appreciate you inviting scandal into his house?" Alexandre asked. "What if the worst happens?"

"We'll know soon enough," Rose said. "And we'll make arrangements if we must. In the meantime, I would rather answer to my maker and my conscience for scandal than heartlessness."

"Very well, if I cannot persuade you, I won't waste my breath," Alexandre said, crossing his arms over his chest. "Though I'm curious as to why you champion her cause so vehemently. She's not been a prize pupil, of your own account, and you've not been the best of friends."

"Perhaps not, but Claudine is bright and has potential," Rose said. "What's more, I had three years of my life wasted in a stinking death trap when my own family cast me out. If I can spare Claudine any part of that heartache, I will." Rose had only mentioned her years stuck in the bowels of the Salpêtrière charity hospital a handful of times. Each time, she grew pale and withdrawn. Such horrors, Claudine didn't care to imagine.

"As you wish," Alexandre said.

"Run along and pack the rest of your things, dear," Rose said, her tone significantly softer.

Claudine nodded, still wide-eyed in shock at the kindness extended to her. It wouldn't be quite as gracious a life as she had with Nicole, but it was infinitely better than no life at all. *But what if the worst happens? If there's a baby I can better conceal it if I stay in the country. And there's Emmanuelle to think of. I won't have her tarnished by my stupidity.*

"Thank you, Rose." Claudine embraced her teacher again and kissed her cheek. "But I'm afraid I ought to go back to the country for at least a time. If . . . things . . . change, might I take you up on your offer in a few months?"

"Of course, darling. But you know you mustn't hide if you don't wish to." Rose wiped an errant tear that Claudine didn't know she'd shed.

"I know, but the rest may be good for me." Claudine took Rose's hand and gave it a reassuring squeeze.

"Those may be the first words of sense I've ever heard you speak, Claudine," Alexandre scoffed from behind his desk.

"Don't be fooled, *seigneur*. My decision has positively nothing to do with making things less awkward in your social circles."

They have far more to do with me avoiding the sight of Victor St. Pierre. And you.

CHAPTER 9

Gabrielle

Early October 1677

The date had been pushed as far back as possible. Any later in the year and the weather could turn in a moment and make travel to the homestead a monstrous chore. Not to mention Advent would be hard upon its heels, making a wedding impossible. And, of course, her sixteenth birthday was only a week away. Despite assurances that the Beaumonts would be happy to pay the fine if she remained unmarried until the spring, Gabrielle remained adamant that they should not pay a single *sou* on her behalf.

Gabrielle walked down the aisle in a plain but new dress. No satin and silk for a farmer's wife, but she made it herself, taking more care than she usually did with her own garments. She may not be the blushing princess bride bringing pride to her kingdom by way of a match well made, but it was her wedding day, and it deserved some small attention. The Beaumonts and her brother were in the first pew, an assortment of Lefebvres and Deschamps behind them. The groom's side of the aisle was empty save a gruff-looking old man named Jacques Verger who called himself Olivier's friend. He dressed in ragged hides and more dirt than a wild bear. She struggled to keep her nose from wrinkling against the stench of unwashed flesh as she walked past him.

These will be my friends and companions now. Men who look as savage as the land they steward. Gabrielle banished the uncharitable thought from her mind and spoke her vows with a smile that at least went skin-deep, if no further. She felt nothing as Olivier placed a decorous kiss on her cheek as the priest pronounced them husband and wife. As they turned to make their way down the aisle to the front of the church, she saw bailiff Duval duck out of the last pew. He wanted to witness the marriage for himself to ensure he could not find any way to further harass the Beaumonts.

Scum. At least they're free from you. On my account, at least. Go bother someone else, preferably one who is actually doing wrong, for once in your miserable life. She tried to push the man from her thoughts to allow some form of bridal felicity to enter them, but Duval's mere presence had the ability to fill her spirit with rancor.

The small assembly walked back to the Beaumont home and enjoyed a simple stew accompanied by Gilbert's good bread and Elisabeth's best pastries. Nicole and Emmanuelle chatted merrily, and Manon was deep in discussion with Pascal over various livestock practices. Gabrielle smiled and made small talk whenever someone engaged her, but found herself observing her nearest friends and her new husband. While Pascal and her friends visited companionably, Olivier sat in stubborn silence, seemingly uncomfortable with the number of people in the room.

Make allowances, Gabrielle. He lives alone. This may be daunting for a man so used to his solitude. You can bring him around. Make something of him.

Gabrielle studied the man, who was tall and proud with a thick black beard and dark eyes. He'd washed for the wedding and wore what appeared to be a new suit of clothes for the occasion. He cut a handsome figure, she realized, and his sturdy frame had been chiseled from hard labor. He would be a good provider to their family. She hoped he would be. In truth, she'd seen him three times since the marriage had been decided upon. Each occasion was at the Beaumont dinner table and in the presence of her adoptive family. They had exchanged a few dozen words at each meal, but no more. She had not seen his home or his land. She was entering blind into the marriage and battled her nerves at each moment.

Gilbert and Pascal had contrived a reason to visit the Patenaude homestead, however, and assured Gabrielle that the house, while not luxurious, was sound and the land was cleared. Everything a girl was taught to ask for was seen to. *Heaven knows the likes of me isn't entitled to ask for more.*

As soon as his plate was cleared, Patenaude stood, indicating his desire to leave without bothering with ceremony or civility.

"We've just finished eating. I think the Beaumonts . . ."

The look on Olivier's face silenced Gabrielle at once.

"It's fine, sweetheart," Elisabeth said. "It's a long drive for the horses, we know, and not an enjoyable one after dark. We've thrown together a few gifts for you. The men can see them loaded in a trice."

Olivier nodded curtly to Elisabeth and followed Gilbert and Pascal down the stairs. The rest of the assembly took turns embracing Gabrielle and giving her their best wishes. Elisabeth hung back for last.

"My sweet girl, how I will miss you." Elisabeth folded Gabrielle in her arms, gripping tight, fortifying them both for the imminent separation. "You must send letters into town as often as you can, my dear, and come in with Olivier whenever he makes the trip."

Gabrielle nodded and kissed Elisabeth's damp cheeks. She doubted the trips would be frequent, but she didn't add to Elisabeth's suffering by pointing that out. She looked around the small house, taking in all the familiar sights one last time as a resident. The cozy kitchen, the tiny parlor that Elisabeth bemoaned as the only fault in the house, the small bedroom that was her own corner of the world. None of it was hers any longer. It never really was, but the Beaumonts never made her feel it. For Elisabeth's sake Gabrielle kept her tears at bay, but she longed to run to her soft mattress and indulge in them one last time.

Pascal and Gilbert had been truthful when they said Olivier's home was sound. They also didn't exaggerate when they said it wasn't the Palace of the Louvre, either. Olivier made quite the show of putting his aging stallion, Xavier, away in his barn stall. Olivier gave a derisive grunt when Gabrielle offered her help with the tack and hay, so she went to inspect the house. The walls were solid, and it would keep out the chill of winter. It was a simple, wooden one-room affair with a big stone fireplace and rough-hewn furniture that looked as if Olivier had fashioned it himself. There was a large table for eating and cooking, a pair of straight-backed chairs, and a bed in the corner. The sight of the latter caused Gabrielle's stomach to rise to her throat. She'd tried to avoid thinking of that aspect of her marital duties, but the moment when she would have to submit was soon at hand.

"I believe I shall be comfortable enough here," Gabrielle said to break the silence as Patenaude returned from the barn, removing his new coat and placing it gingerly in the trunk at the end of his bed.

"It won't be the posh city life you're used to, no mistaking that," Olivier said, hefting her trunk to the end of the bed. "And I won't abide any sniveling about it, either."

"Of course not," Gabrielle said. *I'm not exactly prone to sniveling, and I could tell on our first meeting you weren't one to tolerate it.*

"So long's we understand that." Olivier opened her trunk and rifled about her clothes.

"Is there anything you're looking for?" Gabrielle was puzzled as to what might interest him among her chemises.

"Whatever I see fit, girl." Olivier did not look up from her trunk as he tossed her garments around.

"If you tell me what you're looking for, I can help you," Gabrielle said, picking her clothes off the filthy floor. "And please be careful with my things."

Olivier stood to his full, considerable height and took his hand down across her face. She'd had worse from her father—certainly it was nothing compared to the last beating she'd received at his hand—but Olivier's slap was enough to make her stumble backward.

"Don't you ever give me an order, girl. Is that clear?"

"Y-yes," she said, looking up, bewildered by the man she'd married only three hours before.

"While we're on the subject, let me set down a few rules. They'll be no backtalk from you. I won't have it. Better yet, you'd be smart to keep your lip shut unless you're spoken to. I expect my supper on the table at dusk, else you'll get another taste of what you just had. Anything I ask you to do, you do without question, and you'll hand over every last *sou* that crosses your palm. Is that clear?"

"Yes." Gabrielle took a step back and looked him up and down. He stood as tall as he could, clearly trying to intimidate her as her father had done so many times. Her sharp tongue had earned her a number of beatings, and now she was destined for more of the same.

"Now, seeing as how you roped me into a marriage, it's high time I took what's owed to me. Take off that dress before I take it off you."

It was clear from his face that he meant his words. If she didn't comply he'd rip it from her and there would clearly be no replacing it. She complied quickly, but covered her nakedness with an arm across her breasts and her hand shielding her sex. *Do what you must, but do it quickly, bastard.*

"Don't cover up. I want to see what I've bought." Olivier grabbed her wrists so he could see her form—all of it. His eyes looked her over, just like a farmer inspecting a dairy cow or a brood mare. She felt just as much dignity as the beasts, for in that moment she knew she had even less value to the man who examined her.

"Scrawny and redheaded. A mass of freckles to boot, but I guess a man can't be too particular when there's so few women about. Besides, you redheaded ones are all alike. Sluts, the lot of you. Just mind you keep yourself to my bed and no other, clear?"

Gabrielle's green eyes flashed with indignation at his implication, but she spoke not a word.

"Don't look at me so defiant-like." He brought his hand down on her cheek, causing her to fall back on the bed. Before she could get to her feet, he was atop her, breeches down, claiming his due as her husband. *Just be done with it. Have pity on me and be done.*

She stared up at the ceiling, waiting for his grunting to desist. She refused to let her tears come to the surface no matter how her cheek ached or how roughly he'd claimed her maidenhood. She would not give him the satisfaction of seeing her cowed by him.

God in heaven, I escaped my father's house only to find myself in a deeper circle of hell. I don't know what I've done to offend, but I think it's You who must make amends now.

The following morning, Gabrielle escaped from the sweaty confines of Patenaude's bed to prepare the morning meal. Stale bread.

Some salted meat. A few questionable vegetables. Little else. The worst bachelor's larder she'd ever seen. Thankfully, Elisabeth had sent her with a hamper of groceries so she was able to make a proper breakfast. She prepared the meal in silence and set it on the table, but did not dare to eat her portion or rouse her husband from his slumber. Remembering her father's temper, she knew either action would be certain to raise his ire. Thankfully, he stirred not long after she set the meal out, so it wasn't cold. That wouldn't earn her credit with him, either.

He grunted at the sight of the meal, which Gabrielle took to be a sign of his appreciation. *You're not an eloquent one, are you? Not that I mind. I'm not sure you allow me to mind anything at all.* The couple ate in silence, the porridge and toast with jam tasting as appealing as ash on her tongue. Patenaude ate ravenously, which she guessed meant he enjoyed his meal. Though the Beaumonts weren't particularly highborn, they took table manners as the first mark of civility. Had Olivier Patenaude made such a display at their supper table, they never would have allowed yesterday's wedding.

"Where did the food come from?" Patenaude asked once the meal was concluded.

"The hamper that Elisabeth sent for us," Gabrielle said, clearing the plate from in front of him.

"The food we can keep; the rest of the gifts that can fetch a price are to be sold."

"But, surely—" Gabrielle began. There was a nice length of wool from Nicole she'd planned to make a winter jacket from, good linens, and other gifts that had been chosen for her with care.

"Are you questioning me, girl?" Olivier's eyes flashed in Gabrielle's direction and she was glad not to be within striking range.

"No, I only meant to point out that some of the guests might be offended. . . ." *Some of the embroidery took weeks. And they're tokens of love from* my *friends. Not yours.*

"Do you think they'll travel all the way out here to see you?" Olivier looked at Gabrielle, the disdain dripping from his voice like poison. "And if they did, do you think they'd look to see what sheets you have on your bed?"

"I do think the Beaumonts will come from time to time. Surely Pascal will." She took care not to sound patronizing or insolent, but in that moment she prayed any one of them would come through the door to prove him wrong.

"Oh, the Beaumonts may come 'round once or twice, but you're not their kin. They'll forget about you soon enough. That brother of yours is thick with that high and mighty Lefebvre. No mistaking that; he'll have no time for his little slut of a sister for too much longer. He's got big ideas, and don't forget it."

"I know he has," Gabrielle agreed. It was a source of pride for her that her brother, despite his upbringing, aspired to do something with his life. To improve the lives of others. To be a credit to the colony.

At the same time, she looked at herself and saw that, for all her hopes and hard work, she'd landed in a worse predicament than her own misguided mother.

Patenaude stood and grabbed his hide rucksack, a filthy affair covered in bits of fur and traces of animal blood, from a dusty corner of the room.

"What are you doing today? I thought it might be time to harvest?"

"Harvest what, you dolt? I ain't got time to waste farming this frozen soil. If we were down south, maybe. Not here. I just keep the land clear to shut up the deputy. Fall's trapping season. Only reason I married you was that they wouldn't let me hunt and trap if I didn't get married."

"Oh." Gabrielle registered his words. She was just a hunting license to him. In all fairness, to her he was only a means of sparing the Beaumonts from difficulty. Perhaps on that score, they were even. "Will you be gone long?"

"Don't ask questions. I'll be gone as long as it takes. Maybe a few days. Maybe weeks. Sometimes as long as a month. Depends on the snow and the hunting. Make sure to care for Xavier while I'm out. Hay and water every day and walk him about the fields to keep him limber, but you're not to ride him. I don't want you out gallivanting in town for people to chat about." *You care more for the damned horse than your own wife.*

Gabrielle bit back her rebuke. "Won't you have need of him?"

"Not as far as we're going. He'd be all but useless in the woods. Canoes. Snowshoes if the weather turns. Faster and more reliable.

No feed to carry neither since there won't be much in the way of grass soon."

"Of course," Gabrielle said, looking down at her hands, trying to conceal her smile. *Go, and go far. If there's any mercy, there'll be a late start to winter, and just enough creatures to keep you hunting, but not enough to satisfy your greed.*

Patenaude threw the rest of his gear in the reeking bag, along with a huge portion of the food from Elisabeth's hamper that would keep on the hunt, and hoisted the pack onto his back. He nodded in Gabrielle's general direction and left the cabin without a word.

May your trap snare the real beast.

CHAPTER 10

Claudine

October 1677

Claudine threw her most personal possessions, few that they were, into her little satchel, emptying of any signs of life the small bedroom she had shared with Emmanuelle at their parents' house. Claudine was returning to the Lefebvre house for Emmanuelle's wedding. With any luck she'd be invited back to stay with her sister or Rose, though she didn't expect it.

For almost three months she fed the horses, scrubbed floors, and minded Georges without complaint. She plodded along in her Latin grammar in the evenings when her mother had the energy to polish up her rusty skills. Nicole and Emmanuelle, sympathetic to their sister's banishment, sent letters with the news from town, but Claudine burned them after she scanned their contents for any real news. The prattle of all the social events was just a cruel reminder of all she missed. There was no mention of Victor's wedding. At least they had the good sense to give that wound time to scab over.

Bernadette entered the small bedroom, knocking softly, but not waiting to enter.

"All packed, my darling?" Bernadette asked.

"Not much to gather up, Maman, but yes. I'm ready when Papa

is." Claudine smoothed the last wrinkle out of her freshly made bed. Claudine stood a full head taller than her petite mother, but they might have been twins, but for the age difference. The same even features and mahogany hair. If nothing else, her months back on the farm without Emmanuelle had given her the chance to know her mother better.

"I've never seen a girl so altered as you since the spring." Bernadette took her daughter's hand and violated one of her strictest rules—sitting on a tidy bed more than five minutes before someone was to crawl into it. "I'm not complaining about your hard work, but I do wish you'd talk to me about why you came back."

"It doesn't matter, Maman. Let's just say that Alexandre and I quarreled."

"I'm sure he will forgive you, dearest. He may be stern, but he's a kind man." Bernadette patted Claudine's hand. *Not just a little spat, Maman. You can think he'll forgive me if it comforts you, but I know better. I crossed over his imaginary line of conduct and he'll never find it within himself to look past the transgression. And I'm not sure I can forgive him.*

"Is Papa nearly ready?"

"I imagine so. We'll miss you while you're gone, dear."

"You'll be there on Tuesday for the wedding, Maman. I expect I'll be coming back with you."

"Don't be so downtrodden, darling. Whatever happens, you'll make the best of it." Bernadette embraced her daughter and escorted her to the front room, where Thomas waited. "Of all your talents, it's the most valuable."

Claudine returned the embrace with a weary smile. As usual, her mother was right, but it didn't necessarily mean that her talent didn't come without a healthy dose of sacrifice.

When Papa's wagon pulled up in front of the Lefebvre house, Emmanuelle, for once in her life, ignored the rules of decorum by racing into Claudine's arms before she had the chance to cross the threshold. Usually the doting daughter, Emmanuelle only offered her father a hasty kiss by way of greeting before dragging Claudine up the stairs to the room they had shared, which they would share again only for a few more nights before Emmanuelle's wedding.

"I missed you so much, Didine!" Claudine fought for breath as her sister's arms cinched like a blacksmith's vice around her rib cage. "It's been so strange here without you."

Claudine smiled at the nickname, shelved for years, but hoped it would not find its way back into daily use.

"I've missed you, too. At least you had Manon for company." Claudine wiped the warm tears off her sister's cheeks. "Not to mention Nicole and the others."

"Manon is lovely," Emmanuelle agreed. "But she's not you. Why didn't you write more often?"

"Do you really want to hear about which cow was stubborn at milking time and how the wheat crops are faring?" Claudine held her sister close as the chortle escaped from deep within.

"Yes. And about Maman and Papa . . . and Georges and you. You promised you would write." Emmanuelle's words sounded more pleading than angry.

"I'm sorry, Emmy. I really am. I just couldn't bear to write the truth. 'Today I scrubbed Maman's best pot and made pork stew for supper. I burned the bread again.' Those tasks are endurable once, and only just, but not worth the reliving of them."

"I just want to hear about *you*, Claudine. I feel like I've been missing my right arm these past few months. I hope you weren't too desolate out on the farm."

"I've felt just the same about you, Emmy. Let's not waste time worrying about my solitary mornings with Marguerite the stubborn milk cow. Since you're to be married in three days, this all ought to be about *you*."

Emmanuelle tilted her head back, and her laughter tinkled like tiny bells. "It seems ridiculous to think of me married. And before you, it just seems utterly impossible."

"But you are happy, aren't you, Emmanuelle?" Claudine finally escaped from her sister's embrace long enough to remove her cap and cloak, which she hadn't had time to discard at the entry. "That's what matters."

"Laurent is wonderful, Claudine. The kindest man I've ever known. Truly."

"Then I am happy for you both." Claudine took Emmanuelle in

her arms again and smoothed her hair. "For you are the sweetest girl who ever drew breath. If he is as kind as you say he is, then you will be the most blissful couple in the settlement."

"You must promise to stay in town, Claudine. I hated being apart." Emmanuelle kissed Claudine's cheek. "Promise me."

"I wish I could promise, Emmy . . . but you know the decision isn't mine. Besides, you'll be a busy married woman and won't have time for your old spinster sister anymore."

"A spinster at eighteen. I think you make our settlement out to be harsher than it is." Emmanuelle laughed and began to unpack Claudine's case.

"I've learned to think it harsh so that I can be pleasantly surprised when it is not," Claudine said.

"You've grown wise in your months of exile, Didine." Emmanuelle placed Claudine's treasured volume of courtly poetry at the bedside table where she had always kept it.

"I hope so, Emmy. I hope the time was well spent. Now let's go down to our biscuits and cider so Nicole can gush about the wedding plans, shall we?" Claudine took Emmanuelle's hand in hers and led her out the bedroom door.

Claudine doubled back briefly, took the worn tome from her bedside table, and placed it up on the top shelf of her armoire before following her sister down the stairs. *There is a library of books in this house. It's time I tried out another.*

Emmanuelle stood before the glass, a vision in pale pink silk. While Claudine was usually open with her criticism, she never told Emmanuelle what she—and most public opinion—held to be true. Emmanuelle was the least of the Deschamps girls in age and looks. Nicole had a warm expression and soft eyes that endeared people. Claudine's shining mane of mahogany hair attracted second looks all by itself. Paired with her mischievous smile and flashing brown eyes, she was regarded as a blooming beauty. Emmanuelle, for all her kindness and intelligence, had narrow-set eyes, a stout figure, and a long nose that caused her to fade in the presence of her sisters. Today, however, as she smiled for the mirror as she planned to smile for her groom, any fault of nature was varnished over by the radiance of a joyful bride.

"Laurent Robichaux will be the proudest man in the settlement tomorrow," Nicole proclaimed as she adjusted the skirt to lie perfectly against the three petticoats that gave her a bell-like silhouette. Claudine, Manon, and Nicole were there to make sure the ensemble was perfect and the bride properly swooned over. To have Gabrielle absent from the fitting seemed unnatural, but no one marred the day by mentioning it.

"And if he's not, he's a fool." Claudine kept the venom from her tongue, but not all of her vehemence. The night she'd learned her sister's betrothed was none other than the stodgy man she'd danced with at the disastrous St. Pierre ball, she'd wept bitterly into her pillow. How could such a dullard be a companion for her bright, sweet sister? The thought of Emmanuelle's best years wasted on him sickened Claudine, but she voiced none of it. As reprehensible as she found the marriage, she would never aspire to make such a match herself. Not now. The nightmare played over in her head. She would find a boy from the right family and the right situation. He would court her and propose to her. The wedding would be as grand as any in the highest Parisian circles. Then he would take her to his chamber that night. He would discover she had been unchaste.

And he would fling her to the wolves.

Of course, none of that was certain. He might take pity on her. Certainly, most boys didn't go to the marriage state unsullied—more here than in France, perhaps, owing to the scarcity of women—and they couldn't sow their oats alone. Many young men were sensible enough to know this and didn't necessarily expect a virgin bride. But a boy like Victor St. Pierre clearly had drawn a divide between the women for marrying and the women for bedding. Most of his kind would. No, she had to find a nice farm boy. One who didn't care overmuch for the rules and regulations of society as long as he got three good meals a day and a soft, warm body beside him in bed.

It wasn't the life she'd hoped for, but it was the best she could expect.

Claudine affixed her smile and pretended the blessed event was the happiest thing she'd ever experienced. If anyone thought she was insincere, they'd just ignore it as the sort of affectionate envy the older sister feels when the younger marries first.

"Not a pleat out of place," Nicole said, hands on her hips, surveying the gown with satisfaction.

"You're brilliant, as always, sister," Claudine said, squeezing Nicole's shoulder. The tender gesture caused a few raised eyebrows in the room, but Claudine paid them no mind. *Let them think I'm being sentimental on the occasion of my sister's wedding. By all means.*

"Dear, why don't you help me with the linens downstairs. Manon can see Emmanuelle out of her dress." Nicole put a gentle hand on the crook of Claudine's arm with a gentle tug toward the door.

Claudine knew full well Nicole would have seen to it a week prior that ample linens were laundered, pressed, and ready for the festivities tomorrow, but she obliged her sister without question. Nicole led her sister to the green-and-pink oasis of her sitting room rather than the stuffy storerooms below stairs.

"How have you been managing at the farm?" Nicole gestured to a plush chair and took the one opposite. "With all the excitement, I've hardly had time to draw breath, let alone see to you."

"I'm perfectly well. Why would I be otherwise?" Claudine tried, not all that successfully, to keep her tone flighty. Insincerity didn't come as easily as it once did. She amended, "I'm as well as you might expect."

"I've worried for you. Maman wrote just two weeks ago to say she'd barely recognized the girl we sent back to her. I'm glad you used the time to be helpful to her." Nicole patted her sister's hand, but fire blazed back from Claudine's eyes.

"What use am I now, other than washing, cooking, and tending other people's children?" The resignation in her own voice startled Claudine.

"Claudine, this isn't court, you know. You do have options." Nicole sat back in her chair, looking rather more pensive than usual.

"Not like I did," Claudine said, looking at the grain on the wood floors rather than up at her sister.

"No," Nicole agreed. "Some things cannot be undone, but lucky for you the gossip has been minimal. St. Pierre has been married and there is no child. There's no reason you can't have a life."

Claudine cursed the tears that stung in the corners of her eyes.

"What is it, my dear?" Nicole leaned forward and brushed a lock of hair from her sister's forehead. "You know you can tell me."

"I—I thought he loved me," Claudine stammered between tears.

Nicole stood and knelt by her sister's chair and took the girl in her arms.

"I know, dear, I know."

"Why would he do such a thing to me?" Claudine fought to keep the pain from her voice. "Why would he mislead me? I never would have . . ."

"You answered your own question, love," Nicole said. "He wanted your virtue and was willing to shame you to get it. I'm glad you're rid of him."

"Too late though," Claudine said, wiping the salty brine from her cheeks.

"Never, my dear." Nicole cupped Claudine's face in her hands. "I've lived through a broken heart myself. The best revenge is to build a life better than the one you might have had."

"Your husband who died?" Claudine arched a brow at her sister's mention of revenge in connection with little Hélène's father.

"Him too," Nicole said, nodding, her eyes misting over with memory for just a moment. "But you don't remember my beau back in France, do you?"

"Jean something-or-other?" Claudine supplied. "I never knew what happened."

"Jean Galet. Papa and Maman wouldn't have talked of it, not in front of you. When Papa's farm started to fail, he had to use my dowry to save it. Jean married another girl just three weeks after he was supposed to marry me."

"How awful!" Claudine said, looking into her sister's brown eyes, understanding where a few lines around them originated. "So soon!"

"I know. In my heart of hearts I knew his affection for me didn't run as deep as mine did for him. I was so embarrassed. So ashamed. When the recruiters came offering ladies places on a crossing to New

France, I begged Papa to let me go. I just wanted to escape it all. I was weak. I see that now, but I wouldn't change things now."

"I know that feeling. All too well," Claudine confessed. "It's why I haven't raised a fuss about coming back to town."

"It's too bad you can't go back to France. Paris would be ideal for a girl with your wit and spark, from what Rose and Alexandre tell me."

"I used to long for Paris. Not anymore," Claudine said, looking out the window onto the settlement town.

"What is it you do want, my dear?"

"My pride back," Claudine said. "Or at least most of it anyway."

"That will come. In time. But thankfully you had more than enough to start with."

For the first time in many weeks, Claudine wallowed in the delight of a girlish giggle and the warmth of her sister's embrace.

The next afternoon, Claudine watched as Emmanuelle became Dame Laurent Robichaux. As witness, Claudine wore a duly inferior dress and what she hoped was a sincere smile. From her heart, she wished her younger sister all the joy in the world, but the doubt that sweet Emmanuelle could find it with the bland man crept through her veins.

Robichaux's round face beamed at Emmanuelle when the priest declared them man and wife, and sealed the union with a demure kiss. *I hope you know what you're doing, sister. A comfortable house and position aren't the only solaces life can offer.* Claudine kept a placid smile plastered to her face as she exited the church behind the bride and groom and the Lefebvres. With a sigh she conceded that she was in no place to judge her sister's choices. Emmanuelle's life was shaping up far better than her own.

The reception Nicole and Alexandre hosted was among the grandest affairs the renowned Dame Lefebvre had ever thrown together. The eldest of the Deschamps girls was the most skilled at keeping a neutral expression, but Claudine saw the glimmer of pride in Nicole's eyes at the success of the evening. Claudine watched as Emmanuelle danced primly in the governor's arms. An honor conferred only on a bride of status. It was everything Claudine had longed for. *Once upon a time, perhaps. But the gallant prince of mine is long gone.*

Not far from her, Victor St. Pierre danced with his young bride as well, though he rarely looked at her face. Alexandre had warned her that St. Pierre would be on the guest list. To slight him would only give credence to any rumors. She averted her eyes before he could see her looking at him and moved in Nicole's direction to seek out some office that surely needed someone's attention.

"I was hoping I might have a dance with my new sister-in-law." A hand lightly touched Claudine's shoulder, causing her to start.

Behind her, Robichaux stood expectantly. Claudine eyed Emmanuelle off with one of the governor's deputies, so she had no excuse to refuse the groom his dance. Claudine nodded her assent and allowed him to escort her to the dance floor.

"Who would have dreamed the last time we were dancing that our next would be as brother and sister?" Laurent asked. "Life can bring such unexpected changes, can't it?"

"Monsieur, you speak the unadorned truth," Claudine agreed. *Such a boor for my sweet sister. How will she endure it?*

"I confess, I'd hoped to see you after that ball." Laurent's voice was just above a whisper. "I saw the look on your face when young St. Pierre announced his engagement. I can only guess what happened, and I wanted to tell you how sorry I am the knave toyed with your affections. I surmised that's why you went back to be with your parents." *Thank God you didn't guess the whole truth.*

Claudine exhaled with relief. *Plausible, to be sure. Hopefully everyone else believes the same.* "Exactly, monsieur. I was foolish and let myself believe his affections were greater than they were. Going back home allowed me to see things more clearly."

"Very wise, my dear sister-in-law. Many in town have said you were a flighty thing, but I think those tongues wag out of sheer jealousy."

They do, do they? Claudine could not help but shoot Laurent a wry look as they danced.

"My apologies; that sounded uncharitable. I meant to pay you a compliment."

"I'm sure you did, monsieur," Claudine said. "And I will take it as one."

"I'm glad. I do hope you'll come back to town now. Emmanuelle will be so happy to have you near. She talks of little else, you know. You and her studies."

To know that even in her disgrace, Emmanuelle had pined for her sister caused Claudine's heart to ache. She looked over at her younger sister, who smiled politely and exchanged pleasantries. Emmanuelle's studies were at an end now, if not her education. Rose would miss her probing questions and keen intellect. If Claudine came back and resumed her studies, she would be a poor replacement for her sister.

"I cannot say, monsieur," Claudine said. "The decision lies in the hands of others. I cannot risk being an imposition." *And I'm not sure I have it in me to prevail upon Rose's offer. I must retain something of my dignity.*

"Nonsense, I'm sure," Laurent scoffed. He motioned to Alexandre, who was between bouts of conversation. The sextet's tune came to its end, so Claudine found herself at the edge of the dance floor once more.

"I was just speaking with my dear sister-in-law," Laurent said to Alexandre. "Emmanuelle—and I—would love to see more of our Mademoiselle Deschamps here in town. You were meaning to have her back now that Emmanuelle will be out of your nest, surely?"

I did not put him up to asking you! She hoped her eyes screamed the thought to Alexandre. *I wouldn't stoop to begging my way back into town.*

"Of course. I don't think her elder sister would permit otherwise. She's going to miss Emmanuelle painfully." Alexandre wore the playful face of a long-suffering husband who secretly adored his wife. In some ways, Claudine felt his social façade was more truthful than his cold demeanor in private.

"Wonderful news, Lefebvre. And tell your delightful Madame Lefebvre that I won't keep our Emmanuelle a prisoner. She'll be free to keep her sisters company as often as she likes." Laurent glanced Emmanuelle-ward. He clearly cherished her, which showed that he had good sense in women at least.

"How very accommodating of you, monsieur," Claudine said, masking her husky voice with a polite cough. "I'll ask you to excuse me for a little while. I'm in want of a drink."

The gentlemen nodded her away and she grabbed a glass of the champagne that Alexandre and the fashionable set in Paris were becoming so fond of, and escaped into the vacant hallway.

"There you are . . . I had hoped the wedding would bring you back in from the woods." Victor's voice slithered across the marble tile to her unwilling ears.

"And I'd rather hoped to avoid you." Claudine forced herself to turn and look him in the eye.

"Oh come now, we had a bit of fun, didn't we?" He approached her with a swagger and brushed her cheek with the back of his finger.

Claudine met the gesture with a smart slap across his face.

"Fun, you call it?" Claudine felt her throat constrict but fought to remain mistress of herself. "Leaving me in disarray to be discovered by anyone?"

"I suppose that was a bit careless, wasn't it?" He had the good graces to blush into his champagne flute as he took a decorous sip.

"More than careless. It's a wonder I wasn't cast out forever. As it is, my family will never forgive me." Claudine spoke in a hiss, careful not to be heard.

"Don't be so melodramatic, Claudine. Family always forgives these little missteps. What else is family for?"

"You forget I am not a man, Victor. These sorts of things aren't so easily forgiven in a woman. But let me make myself rightly understood—I will never forgive you. Either leave me in peace or your horse-faced wife will know every detail of how you acted. I've nothing left to lose."

Victor stared at Claudine for a moment. He hadn't expected the attentive, sweet girl from a few months ago to become the wrathful shrew who stood before him. *And the shrew of your making, you heartless ass.*

Without further conversation, he nodded and escaped back into the ballroom. She smiled at the sight of her handprint, still red on his cheek. *Explain that to your wife, cad.*

Alone with the echoes in the corridor, she took a minute sip of the curious fizzy wine and allowed it to slowly trickle down her throat, savoring each sip of the chilling sweet-tart liquid as tears flowed down her cheeks. *My sisters are beloved wives. Nicole is a doting mother. Emmanuelle won't be far behind. And I, for all my scheming and dreams, am left with nothing.*

CHAPTER 11

Manon

April 1678

The Robichaux parlor, while charming in its simple elegance, did not aspire to the same grandeur as the Lefebvre sitting room. It was for this reason that Manon preferred when Emmanuelle hosted them for refreshments and handiwork. It was to everyone's advantage when fully considered, for Manon and Claudine had far more time for social calls than Emmanuelle, who now had a husband and the running of a house to attend to. Manon imagined Claudine was happy to have a few hours out of the Lefebvre house. While it was clear Claudine was happy to be settled back in town, the peace between Alexandre and her was still a fragile one.

"How are lessons at Rose's?" Emmanuelle asked, leaning forward in her seat.

"Rose pines for you," Manon answered. "It's not the same with just the two of us to teach."

"No, it's not," Claudine agreed. "I think it's a shame you've had to quit."

"It wouldn't be seemly for a married woman to continue her schooling," Emmanuelle said, though she hid the longing in her face poorly. "And at least Laurent has a good library. I haven't had to take up Nicole on the use of theirs yet."

"That *is* a compliment to Laurent's collection," Manon said. Books were not plentiful in the colony, but those who could read had at least a few volumes. Alexandre's library had to be one of the largest in the colony outside of the seminaries and convents.

"I've thought of bringing up the idea that she invite some more girls to tutor. Manon and I will have to move on eventually, as you and Gabrielle have." Claudine's knitting needles clicked furiously as a blanket unfurled at a steady pace.

"An excellent thought," Manon said. She was no more eager to give up her studies than Emmanuelle had been, but the time was coming, and soon. Not only for her own good, but Rose's as well. If the Church or any other authorities got it in mind that Rose's lessons were enticing women away from marriages, they would put an end to her little school. There would always be "visits" where they might discuss topics of greater interest than the price of flour at the market, but it wouldn't be lessons as they had in the past.

"Are you still waist-deep in all of Alexandre's medical texts?" Emmanuelle asked. The quaver in her voice caused Manon to look up from her hemming. "I've been meaning to ask you for some time now."

"On occasion," Manon said, placing her work in her lap. No one really asked about her interest in the tomes out of more than idle curiosity or vague amusement that she'd taken a fancy to medicine. "I've read most of what Alexandre has in the way of medical texts already. I've not been able to learn any more about the spread of disease than I didn't know or hadn't supposed to be true already."

"Have you considered studying something other than poxes and such?" Emmanuelle took a long breath and set aside her work, which appeared to have been neglected the entire visit.

"Emmy, what's wrong?" Claudine demanded. "If something's the matter, send for Guérin."

"Nothing's wrong, Didine. It's just ... the midwives I've met here don't strike me as kind women. I thought Manon might be better suited for the work."

Claudine shrieked and crossed the room to plant a kiss on her sister's cheek as soon as she'd registered the significance behind the statement.

"When do you expect the little one?" Claudine asked.

"I really have no idea," Emmanuelle said, laughing quietly. "It's not as though Rose ever covered the topic in our lessons. I'm no longer sick in the mornings and have a bit more energy back."

"Why have you said nothing?" Claudine asked, clearly exasperated.

"I wanted to be sure," Emmanuelle said. "It's so terrible when mothers announce their news only to have their hopes dashed."

"Have you spoken with the doctor?" Manon asked. Birth was the province of midwives, but it wasn't unusual to have a doctor oversee the pregnancies of ladies of standing like Emmanuelle.

"Oh, old Guérin has no interest in seeing women safely delivered of their babies. He says he'll intervene if there is a problem, but he says more often than not there's nothing to be done. If a birth goes badly, it's just God's will and we're not to question His why. Or so the doctor says."

"What a pompous..." Claudine muttered, saying the oath under her breath, so as not to disrespect her sister's home.

"That's not entirely true," Manon said. "I confess I didn't read all the information on childbirth in the volumes I read, as it wasn't the information I was after, but there are things midwives and doctors can do to help a mother or baby in distress."

Emmanuelle stood and sat beside Manon on the settee. "I knew you'd have answers. You're always so clever, Manon. And calm. The way you nursed Frédéric back to health after he ate those cursed berries, you were like an anchor to us all. Please say you'll help me when my time comes?"

"I can certainly study and learn what I can," Manon said. "I've only seen birth twice, when Mother Onatah was asked to help. I am no trained midwife."

"You have three times the brains of anyone in this settlement," Claudine said, patting Manon's knee with vigor. "You'll read enough to be a trained surgeon in Paris before her time comes, I'm sure."

"I'll do it," Manon agreed. She had few dealings with the town midwives, but they did seem a surly lot.

"I think you could be wonderful at it," Emmanuelle said. "I'm sure half the women in town will seek you out."

Manon shook her head. "No they won't, Emmanuelle. The

Church will never give me a proper license and not everyone is as kind-spirited as you are. But I expect I can be of use to a few. Women like Gabrielle who are so far afield must go wanting for help when the time comes."

"True," Claudine agreed. "She may be in need of your services before much longer."

"Oh, I wish she were closer. I would love for our children to be friends," Emmanuelle said, sighing. Emmanuelle looked visibly relieved to have enlisted her friend's help, and Manon now wondered how she had missed the obvious radiance of an expectant mother. Emmanuelle's abdomen would begin to swell noticeably with child very soon. She had less time to study than she would have hoped, but at least she had some texts at her disposal that would be of use.

The trio parted ways not long after, with Manon promising to spend her hours studying that week and to return in a few days to assess when the baby might arrive and to start giving her an idea of what to expect when her time came. Emmanuelle was born on a farm, so she understood the rudimentary principles behind birth, but she had been quite young when Georges was born, and not allowed to be of use to her mother.

"Thank you," Claudine said as they reached the top of the Lefebvre house and were just about to part ways to change for supper. "Emmanuelle is such a gentle soul, she can't have some vicious old crone to help her along."

"I'm happy to do it," Manon said. "I hope I can help her through the ordeal with as little worry as possible."

"If anyone can do it, you can," Claudine said, her voice confident. "She'll be lucky to have you."

Manon spoke no thanks, but gave Claudine a brief embrace and retreated to her room. She longed to dive into the medical texts, but dinner would not wait. She had never envisioned making a life for herself as a midwife, and she was certain she would never get the blessing from the Church to serve as one in any real capacity, but the trust that Emmanuelle—and Claudine—conveyed in her ability was humbling.

Once dressed for the evening meal, Manon caressed the spine of her favorite medical text with her index finger lovingly, with a promise she would return by candlelight to learn its secrets.

CHAPTER 12

July 1678

In the hour after supper, Claudine and Manon watched as Frédéric and Théodore played companionably with the youngest Lefebvre children as Hélène directed the scene. They waged a dramatic war between the girls' cloth dolls and the boys' toy soldiers. The dolls fared better than one might expect against a well-trained military regiment, wooden or otherwise. Claudine had to battle valiantly to keep her smile in check, lest the children believe she didn't take arbitrating the skirmish seriously. Were that the case, Nicole or even Alexandre might have to be summoned to take her place, and while these wars were terribly important to the smallest members of the Lefebvre house, they were less compelling to the older residents who had other, though far less dire, matters to attend to.

Just as the wooden soldiers were preparing to unleash a brilliant counterattack on the dolls' fort, a soft knock at the door was immediately followed by Nicole's entry into the nursery.

"Dear, the Robichauxes' man has just come for the both of you. It sounds like Emmanuelle will be wanting you soon."

Claudine kissed her nieces and nephews, Manon kissed Théodore's cheek, and they left the flurry of questions about Auntie Emmanuelle directed to Nicole. Manon's case, fully stocked with supplies, was long-since packed in preparation for the day. Emmanuelle would soon bring the Robichaux heir or beloved daughter into the world. As promised, Manon had spent the last four months studying the best information on midwifery that Alexandre could procure from France. Claudine promised to go for support of both mother and midwife. While she wasn't the scholar Manon was, she studied sections from the books that Manon had indicated were the most useful. She was both excited to be of use in the delivery and terrified of it in equal measure.

Claudine fought to steady her breathing as she settled into the Lefebvre carriage. Manon sat, seeming placid and calm as ever, but Claudine saw how her hands clutched the handles of her case. She was ready to pounce out the door the minute the horses' hooves slowed. Claudine offered Manon her hand and gave a gentle squeeze as she interlaced their fingers.

"We've got to calm down. I know I won't be any use to her if I don't." Claudine took a deep breath and focused on the rhythm of the horses' hooves as they sped along.

"Quite right. Just focus on her and what she needs. She'll be grateful you're there." Manon's lips turned upward slightly.

"I hope you're right. Please be sure to tell me if you need anything when—when the time comes. I want to help."

"Depend on it. Things happen quickly at the end and I'll need an extra pair of hands." Manon offered Claudine a smile and was pleased to feel the slowing of the carriage as the Robichaux house came into view.

As Claudine expected, Laurent paced the floor in the Robichaux foyer, looking as lost as an abandoned child. *Poor man, the world has taught you that you must have the answer to every question and the solution to every problem, but you find yourself for the first time in the dominion of women and can do nothing. Like all fathers, though, you'll come through the birth unscathed. Perhaps a little more humble?*

A maid saw the young ladies to the birthing room, where Emmanuelle lay panting through the pain. She managed a weak smile for her sister and friend, clearly relieved to have more support than one worried-looking servant.

Claudine held her sister's hand and talked her through the surges that already grew in frequency and intensity as Manon emptied her medical supplies from her case onto the top of the bureau and organized the room. The labor escalated faster than the books had said they should anticipate for a first child, but Manon did not seem overly concerned. Claudine only hoped she wasn't concealing any fears for Emmanuelle's sake.

Less than a half hour after their arrival, Emmanuelle writhed on the bed and shouted for relief when she could draw enough breath to speak.

"It's time to push, Emmanuelle," Manon said. "Don't pull any faces, just take a deep breath and focus all your energy on pushing."

Emmanuelle nodded, unable to speak, and within twenty minutes, the Robichaux heir took his first breath in Manon's arms. He was a fat young lad with a mop of black curls to match his father's. Claudine took the little one in her arms and cleaned and dressed him so he could be presented to his mother and father properly. She kept the baby in Emmanuelle's line of sight as she worked so that mother could see the baby as Manon attended her. As Claudine swaddled the plump boy in the pristine linens, she felt a warmth rise in her bosom as she looked into his dark blue eyes.

So love at first sight is real, little man. You may not be my prince charming, but trust that I will dote on you as much as your parents will allow.

She placed a kiss on the baby's soft forehead and went to place him in his mother's arms, but as she turned to her sister, she saw that Emmanuelle's color was far too pale. She placed the baby in his bassinet and rushed to Emmanuelle's side.

"I can't stop the bleeding. Nothing is working." Manon did not look up, her hands working furiously to stop the flow of blood.

"Fetch the doctor! Now!" Claudine yelled out into the hallway where a throng of servants awaited orders.

"I'm so sorry, Claudine. It's too late."

The baby began to cry in his bassinet, his wails punctuated by Laurent's anguished shout from the hallway, as Manon imparted the news. Claudine clutched the baby close to her breast and made no attempt to stifle the tears that flowed. She took the baby over to his mother and laid him on her chest. She took her sister's hand and placed it on his back so he would feel secure in his mother's embrace. She kissed her sister's forehead and brushed the hair, damp with the sweat of her labors, from her brow. *I know you longed to hold him, sister. I won't let that be taken from you.*

"What . . . ?" was all Laurent could stammer as he entered the room.

"She always . . . I just thought he should know what his mother's arms felt like. . . ." Claudine explained. *He'll think I'm daft.*

Laurent nodded in understanding, or at least in acceptance. Claudine took the babe from Emmanuelle's arms and handed him to his father.

"You have a healthy, beautiful son, my dear brother," Claudine rasped.

"But at what cost?" Laurent did not look down at the boy in his arms, but rather at the lifeless form of his wife on the bed.

"It was one she was willing to pay to give you a child. Repay that sacrifice and love him for the both of you." Claudine stroked the baby's cheek as he settled back to sleep in his father's arms.

"I'm not sure I have it in me, Claudine. I'm not sure I can."

"Then I can help you love him, brother. For Emmanuelle's sake. For his, too." Claudine took the baby from her brother, seeing the wet nurse had arrived and was waiting for her charge along with the nanny who would oversee his care. She handed him to the young woman, who looked appropriately mournful.

"Take good care of this boy," Claudine ordered. The nurse nodded and departed for the quarters designated for her and the child. *He is more precious than you could ever realize.*

Laurent stood at Emmanuelle's side, his face pale and beyond emotion. Still trying to wrap his mind around his loss. He would sit with her for hours, until they took her body from the house, Claudine imagined.

"Brother, I know this is cruel to ask, but I would very much like just a few moments with my sister before I leave you with her." She cringed at her own words, knowing it was the last request he wanted to grant in that moment, but it would be her only chance to be alone with her sister.

"Of course," he whispered, his voice soft as gravel. He exited the room, and from the sound of scurrying feet in the hallway, Claudine knew he had commanded the remaining servants to await their orders elsewhere until he could return to his wife.

Claudine pulled a chair over to the side of the bed where Emmanuelle lay, so peaceful and calm. She looked precisely as she did on the rare occasion that Claudine woke first and had to rouse Emmanuelle in the next bed over. The days of lazy Saturday mornings had passed already. She had already mourned for their girlhood late-night chats as they braided each other's hair and ruminated about the wonders in their future. Now she mourned for Emmanuelle as a woman, a person she'd just been getting to know. She mourned for a life that wouldn't be lived.

She took Emmanuelle's hand in hers and kissed the cool skin of her knuckles.

"I will miss you so much, Emmy. I know your Laurent is about ready to pull me from the room by my hair, but I promise I will take care of your boy. I'll see to it he has every happiness I can give him. And I'll try to do more. To be better. To be like you. I love you."

She took a few moments to commit to her memory the exact shade of her maple-brown locks, the curve of her long lashes, the angle of her proud nose contrasted with the swell of her soft cheeks. That she would never see a smile on her lips or laughter in her eyes burned a fire in her gut she was sure would never be quenched.

She could have stayed for hours, but Laurent had to be given his rightful place. She dried her tears on her apron, knowing he didn't need to shoulder more grief than his own, bent down and kissed her sister's forehead for the last time, and went to Laurent's side.

"I will never be able to thank you enough for letting me have those few minutes, my dear brother. Go to her now." Laurent clasped her bicep briefly, a sign of appreciation, and walked past her into the room that held the worst of his nightmares come to pass.

There must be something that needs attending to. Claudine hurried down the stairs in search of an occupation; Nicole nearly collided into her as she raced up to Emmanuelle. Any trace of composure was gone. Her face was lined with tears, her hair askew.

"A maid came. . . . It can't be true, Didine." Nicole's voice warbled as she fought to speak intelligibly.

Claudine shook her head and took Nicole in her arms.

No, it can't be . . . but it is.

CHAPTER 13

Manon

July 1677

Doctor Guérin had the decency to come examine Emmanuelle's body. After only a few moments with her, he announced that she had simply bled to death.

"I've seen it happen more than a few times," Guérin told Laurent. "Once, it was a countess in the finest hospital in Paris surrounded by the best doctors and surgeons in the country. There was nothing to be done then, and I doubt I, or anyone, could have helped this time. Based on what I've seen here and how the child was taken care of, the Huron girl was an exemplary midwife to Madame Robichaux."

Claudine wrapped her arm around Manon, and Laurent offered what appeared to be an appreciative nod in her direction. *You don't blame me. I wish I could say the same.*

"You need some rest." Nicole's voice was raspy, in brief reprieve between bouts of tears. "Why don't you have a lie-down in one of the guest rooms? It may be some time before we go home. If you're hungry, one of the maids will find you something."

Manon nodded, but did not follow the corridor down to the guest quarters, nor could she abide the thought of food. She detoured a few doors down to the family rooms to the new nursery that Emmanuelle had planned out herself. The nanny, Madame Simon, paced with the new baby in her arms, her eyes slightly red though she'd only met Emmanuelle a few times. She looked up as Manon entered the room, her expression softening at the sight of her. *It might be easier if you all blamed me. It would be easier to bear if I didn't feel I was alone in casting the blame at myself.*

"Might I hold him for a few moments, Nanny Simon?" Manon asked. "I won't leave the room."

"Of course, Mademoiselle Lefebvre. I confess I wouldn't mind a brief escape to the kitchen and the privy while the nurse is napping." She passed the sleeping boy over into Manon's arms with expert grace. "I won't be more than a quarter of an hour, if you don't mind staying that long with the wee man."

"Take your time. It's been a long night for all of us." Manon took a seat in the plush chair covered in soft green velvet and looked down at the sleeping babe. His full round cheeks and strong chin were replicas of his father's while his beautifully chiseled nose was identical to his mother's. His eyes, when they were open, were a lovely gray-blue, but it would be months before they decided between his father's handsome brown or his mother's hazel-green or some shade in between. His black curls framed his forehead, making him look as angelic as the drawings of cherubs she'd seen in some of Alexandre's books.

"Sweet baby. I'm so sorry your mother won't be here to comfort you. She longed to hold you. I hope you will be just like her. I would gladly trade my life to bring her back, but since I can't, I'll tell you every chance I get how wonderful she was. How much she loved you even before you were here with us."

With this, Manon placed the sleeping babe in his cradle and rocked him with the edge of her boot. She watched as the minuscule chest rose and fell with steady breaths. She admired his perfect fingers and impossibly long eyelashes. Manon recalled the fuzzy images she had of her own parents. Her mother's flowing jet-black hair and her father's broad chest, which was always warm against her soft five-year-old cheek. The dear boy would not even have those faded memories of the woman who gave her life to give him his.

Nanny Simon returned as promptly as promised, looking far more comfortable than before. The good-natured old woman patted Manon's shoulder with an encouraging smile, and bone-weary, Manon stumbled back to the guest rooms. She found the room that looked the smallest and easiest to restore to cleanliness. She removed her boots, jacket, and skirt and climbed in between the cool sheets, clad in her loose chemise.

Manon focused on relaxing every muscle from the tips of her toes up to her legs, her abdomen, her chest, her arms, her neck, and her face. Willing sleep to claim her. Praying that she might have a brief respite from the pain and guilt—and the kindly stares that implied she needn't feel either.

They held the funeral mass and internment on a hot July day whose cheerful weather seemed to mock the sobriety of the mourners. Robichaux bore his anguish with dignity befitting the most battle-tested Huron hunter. Nicole and Madame Deschamps had less success in restraining their pain. Alexandre propped his arm around his wife, while Monsieur Deschamps and Claudine did the same for Emmanuelle's mother. The rest of the mourners, some close friends, others simply paying respects to the wife of a well-liked citizen, all wore the expression of those who saw the injustice of a healthy young woman taken too soon. Emmanuelle was only one woman in the long history of women who sacrificed their lives to bring their babies into the world, but that did not comfort a community who lost one of its kindest members.

The injustice was highlighted by the presence of the child, christened Zacharie for his father's father. There had been a brief row when Madame Deschamps suggested that little Zacharie might stay home with Nanny Simon during the funeral. Robichaux, normally very respectful of his mother-in-law, had snapped at her, saying it was the child's last chance to be with his mother, whether he knew it or not, and that he would at least be able to tell the boy he'd been there to see his mother laid to rest. No one dared propose an argument to counter his wishes.

At the burial, Manon stood toward the back of the congregation, not wanting to impose herself on the Lefebvres, Deschamps, and Robichauxes in their moment of grief. Elisabeth Beaumont wordlessly placed an arm around Manon's waist and led her to where Pascal and Gilbert stood, Gabrielle having sent her condolences with a neighbor. The priest droned on, his voice spiritless as he eulogized Emmanuelle, but Manon tried to absorb his words.

"Do not mourn for the dearly beloved Madame Robichaux. A woman of kindness, duty, and honor has surely found her place in heaven. . . ."

You may feel we should not mourn for our Emmanuelle, who has gone on to the heaven you Catholics have created for yourselves, but do not begrudge your flock the sadness they feel at the separation from one so much beloved.

Manon remembered the kind girl who never mocked her accented French or less than impressive stitches. She was always happy to discuss the plays and poetry that Rose shared with them without judging Manon for her point of view that was influenced by a culture so foreign to the French girl. She showed kindness not only to her, but to all who crossed her path, whether the kindness was returned or not. Manon could no longer restrain the tears, allowing them to drip off her cheeks and chin down onto the crisp linen of her bodice. Manon felt a hand claim her own, and she accepted the affectionate gesture, not bothering to look down to see who had offered it.

It was not long, owing to the heat of the morning, before the priest dismissed the congregation. Even he, who had buried so many of his followers, seemed affected by the loss of the sweet girl. Those who didn't know could still see that she had endeavored to fulfill her duty to King, Church, and her fellow man. *She did all you asked of her, but it could not save her in the end.*

"Let's go for a ride. You need to be away from all this." Manon looked up to see Pascal's tall frame standing over hers. His fingers were the ones entwined in hers. Manon knew the propriety of the French dictated that she should refuse to go anywhere unaccompanied with Pascal or any other young man, but the weight on her heart kept her from refusing the chance to escape her guilt and grief for a few hours.

"I-I should let Nicole know where I'm going. . . ." Manon mumbled.

"I'll take care of it," he said. He succeeded in catching Alexandre's attention and gestured from Manon to the wagon with his left hand. The right still clasped her own. Alexandre raised an eyebrow, almost imperceptibly, but nodded his assent.

Pascal released Manon's hand to guide the horses on the way out of the city, but sat as close to her as he could comfortably do with the reins in his large hands. Less than an hour later, they were on a large clearing, not far from the Deschamps farm. They perched on the back of the wagon and looked out over the valley from under the shade of a massive evergreen.

"When was the last time you ate?" His words sounded like a gentle rebuke. From the way her dress hung, it must have been obvious to anyone she'd lost weight.

Manon shrugged, unable to remember the last time she'd sat down to a proper meal. The Lefebvre cook had not prepared a hot meal since Emmanuelle's passing the week before, but threw together small morsels when they were called for. Only the children took their regular meals. Manon realized she hadn't called upon Madame Yollande's services as often as she should have done.

"Eat this." It was a firm request, but not a command. He offered her a large slab of cheese and fresh bread, baked no more than an hour or two before with the good hard crust and decadent soft interior that Manon had pined for in her absence from the French. He pulled out a second portion for himself and they ate in silence. It was no chance encounter; he'd planned her escape from town before the funeral. She fought against the lump in her throat at the idea he'd been able to anticipate her need. When she was finished, she brushed the crumbs from her skirt and leaned her head against his muscled shoulder. He smelled like a man should—sweet pine entwined with the tang of honest sweat.

"Thank you," she said at last.

"I knew you'd need to be away from everything for a while. It's not your fault, you know."

"I should have been able to do something to save her. To save Mother Onatah. To save all of them."

"You can't take the responsibility for the world on your shoulders, Manon. That's not fair to you or anyone, even God. You have to leave some work for Him to do, after all." Manon's reply was a dry laugh, but the first she'd had in days.

"It's right to be sad, you know. She was taken from us far too young, but there was nothing we could have done. She wouldn't blame you, and you shouldn't disrespect her memory by contradicting her."

"You know me too well." She found herself edging closer to him. He welcomed the gesture by wrapping his arm across her shoulders.

"Of course I do. I love you."

Manon lifted her head and looked into his earnest brown eyes. "I know you do." She pressed her lips to his, ever so gently. He responded with inexperienced enthusiasm blended with tenderness and genuine affection. He hadn't perfected his art on a string of willing young companions as Heno had done.

She wrapped her arms around him and let her own enthusiasm bloom like a reluctant flower in the chill of early spring. After minutes, perhaps even hours in his embrace, she allowed him to lay her down on the bed of the wagon and take her away from the pain, if only for an afternoon.

Wordlessly she guided him in lovemaking the way Heno had taught her. She slowed his kisses so that they quickened her heartbeat with their sweetness. She showed him how to handle her breasts, caressing them delicately but firmly. He didn't break her silence, but awaited her instruction with such earnest devotion that Manon felt her heart, and her resolve, melt away.

If you allow this, he will beg you to marry him.

She willed herself to stop his wandering fingers, but her body would not respond.

You will cost him every opportunity to make a real life for himself. To build something more than Pascal's father could have ever done for his children.

He cradled her neck in the crook of his arm, kissing her deeply, then gently biting her bottom lip with a low growl. She felt her hands loosening his trousers and grasping his length, causing him to gasp with pleasure. There was no denying him now, or denying herself. She tried her best to hide the warm tears that spilled onto her cheeks. She wanted this as much as she'd wanted anything in her life, reveled in the feeling that she was wanted and loved by someone as kindhearted as Pascal.

But soon enough, when the town shuns him for loving me, that desire in his eyes will turn to resentment, and my heart will never mend.

CHAPTER 14

Claudine

September 1678

Claudine paced the nursery floor, baby Zacharie in her arms, giving Nanny Simon her much-needed hour of respite in the afternoon. The sweet old handmaiden had been offered an assistant on numerous occasions in the three months since the baby's birth, especially since the wet nurse wouldn't be with them for much longer, but she refused to hand the child over to anyone except a family member. Mercifully, the child was growing well and sleeping for longer stretches, which gave her more rest. Knowing Nanny Simon's reluctance to leave the child except with the nearest of kin, Claudine visited every afternoon she could be spared. She felt it was the least she could do for Emmanuelle's baby. Many times she felt it was far less than Emmanuelle would have done had the situation been reversed, but she dedicated herself to the classroom and served as Nicole's assistant in all things. Every charity event Nicole worked for, every company meal she planned, every accounting of the books Nicole made with Alexandre was done with Claudine at her elbow.

A knock sounded at the door, Laurent emerging without invitation shortly after. Claudine let out a short squeak at the sight of her brother-in-law. These past months they had seen each other only a handful of times and exchanged only the bare minimum of words to maintain civility.

"I'm so sorry to disturb you, sister dear. I just thought I'd take the time to see how you both are getting on."

"Fine, thank you," Claudine said, looking down at the boy's curious eyes, which had settled to a greenish-hazel, just the shade of his mother's. "He's such a sweet boy."

"That he is. And you do well with him, so Nanny Simon says. And her praise is not given freely." Laurent crossed the room to the green plush chair that Nanny Simon favored and motioned for Claudine to take the spare.

Claudine smiled. "No, I don't believe it is." Nanny Simon had taken to Claudine after Emmanuelle's death and she enjoyed the older woman's company far more than she had expected to.

For a moment, Claudine considered placing her nephew back in his crib, but knew he would resist sleep with all the power his healthy lungs could muster. He stared too eagerly at his aunt, enjoying her attentions. Claudine herself wasn't ready to put him back, whether he was ready or not.

"I must say, when we first met, I didn't think you'd be the maternal type. I pictured you with a troupe of nurses, nannies, and governesses when your time came."

Claudine looked away, the color rising in her cheeks. *You thought of me as a mother? How generous of you. I never really did before, and certainly don't now.*

"I'm sorry. I've made you uncomfortable." Laurent looked down, seemingly at a blemish on the toe of his impeccable boots.

"No, not really. Things have just changed, that's all." Claudine placed a soft kiss on Zacharie's forehead and was promptly rewarded with joyous coos punctuated with bubbles of spittle.

"That they have. I pictured my entrée to fatherhood very differently, I must say."

"I imagine you did. No one excepted . . ."

"No . . . we didn't." Laurent leaned over and stroked the black curls on his son's forehead. "Poor chap. He'll never know how wonderful his *maman* was."

"I tell him every day. It's not the same, but it's the best I can think to do for him. For her. Though Emmanuelle was the most selfless creature there ever was, she wouldn't want to be forgotten."

Laurent looked toward the window for a few long moments and cleared his throat. "No. No, she wouldn't. I'm grateful to you."

"Please don't mention it." Claudine did not speak to offer a modest platitude, but rather to implore he drop the subject.

"I mean it truly, my dear. You knew her better than anyone. You'll be able to help him know. . . ." A single tear escaped down Laurent's cheek. He wiped it away once he realized his lapse from manliness, but looked as if the effort to restrain the rest of them cost him dearly.

"I'll do what I can for him, I promise you that. For Emmanuelle's sake and yours."

"Thank you. He'll at least know something like a mother's love in his early days. Nanny Simon is incomparable, but she's not family."

"No, sweet woman though she is," Claudine agreed.

"It seems impertinent to ask for anything else since you do so much already, but I was hoping I might ask you to stay to dinner from time to time. This place does get lonely after a while."

Claudine stifled a giggle at the thought of feeling alone in a house full of staff, but of course a man of his status couldn't converse with a maid or a cook as he could with his sister-in-law. A wave of remorse washed over Claudine.

"We've all been so worried about seeing to the baby, no one has thought to see to you."

"Oh, speak nothing of that. To be honest, I'm only now feeling equal to any sort of company." Laurent's tone was low.

You wouldn't tell us even if you needed us. "I can well understand that. Of course I can come to dinner as often as you like."

"I don't wish to impose upon your time. Perhaps Thursdays would be convenient? You mustn't feel obligated."

You may well be the only person in Christendom who feels Emmanuelle's loss as keenly as I do. You might not be a dashing conversationalist, but I can brave a few lackluster dinners.

"You can depend upon me, brother. It would make Emmanuelle happy for me to keep you company in these hard times."

"It will be the highlight of my weeks. Now if you'll excuse me, I have a few things to see to before evening. I will see you for supper tomorrow."

Claudine nodded, offering a weak smile for her brother-in-law. *I would not wish your pain on anyone, dear man.*

"Let's turn our attention to embroidery for a while, shall we?" Claudine recognized Rose's signal that conversation, rather than academics, was called for and opened up her embroidery basket. She was finishing a large tablecloth that Emmanuelle had started. She planned to pass it along to Laurent's housekeeper so it could grace the table for which it was intended. The last few weeks, there had been a great deal more sewing and quiet chatter than literature and arithmetic.

"Lovely work, dear," Rose said, peering over her pupil's shoulder. "Your stitches are growing so small and even. My favorite governess said it was the sign of patience and maturity when a woman's embroidery becomes so fine." *Almost as fine as Emmanuelle's, but I'm not sure I'll ever have her gift of patience.*

Claudine tried to keep her laugh from sounding too derisive. "Patience is our lot in life, is it not? It's not a question of having it, but learning to embrace it."

"Therein lies the maturity," Rose countered.

"I suppose you're right," Claudine admitted. "Have you heard anything from the Beaumonts about Gabrielle, Manon? Nicole said you were visiting yesterday."

Claudine thought she might have seen the color rise in Manon's cheek, but she dismissed it. "Elisabeth hasn't heard anything in close to a month. I do think Pascal's close to going out to visit the homestead, with or without an invitation."

"I expect she's very busy keeping house," Rose said, pulling out her own mending. "She hasn't the benefit of any help."

"That's what I tried to tell Pascal, but he insists she'd find the time to write unless there were something amiss. These pillowcases will be for her as I'm sure she hasn't the time to do them herself."

"A lovely gesture, my dear," Rose said, smiling at Manon.

"Yes, you must see to it that Pascal asks her if she is in want of anything. I'm sure we can provide her with anything she'll need before winter." Claudine, almost as familiar with Nicole's store cupboards as the mistress of the house and the housekeeper alike, knew that there were plenty of linens that would be put to better use in Gabrielle's little cabin.

"I'll do that," Manon said, nodding, in line with Claudine's thoughts. "Surely Nicole won't mind."

"I wish Sister Mathilde were alive to see you both," Rose said, exhaling deeply and setting her mending down. Claudine had a few vague memories of the barbed-tongued but good-natured woman of the Church from her early years in the settlement. Life on her parents' homestead kept her removed from the social circles in town, but she knew her sister and her companions had grieved bitterly when winter claimed their mentor and guide in the New World. "This was exactly the New France she had envisioned. 'While the men are out to carve a living for themselves, the women must band together to weave a life.' She would be so proud of you."

"It's just a pair of pillowcases, Rose," Manon said. This time there was no mistaking the color rising in her cheeks.

"It's more than that, Manon. You're single women living in comfort. You could be doing anything with your spare time that you choose, but you're spending your time improving the lot of others."

Claudine looked down at the tablecloth, knowing that Laurent Robichaux or baby Zacharie would never notice or care about the tablecloth she stitched. They had a dozen others, and heaven knew that a man would hardly pay attention to the table at which he ate so long as the food was savory and plentiful. But it wasn't for them that she finished it. It was to make sure that, in some small way, Emmanuelle's work on earth wasn't left undone. There was so much of her life left unlived that Claudine couldn't bear to see her sister's little projects remain incomplete. Though it was silly, perhaps even wicked, to think it, Claudine imagined Emmanuelle's spirit restless in heaven for all the work she didn't finish.

Claudine's mind wandered to the sweet black-haired baby, presumably taking his afternoon nap under the watchful eyes of his devoted nanny. Some projects Emmanuelle left were bigger than others.

"I wish I could do more," Claudine said.

"You're doing more than you ever did before," Manon chimed in. "Everyone has taken notice."

"That's precisely what I don't want. People must think I'm just doing things to get attention." Claudine removed a wayward stitch made in anger, pleased she didn't damage the cloth noticeably.

"I don't mean to sound harsh, dear, but I'm sure there are some who do," Rose said, looking at Claudine with a somber expression. "You spent years portraying yourself as a girl who never made a gesture for her fellow man that was not in her own interest first. Your youth and vivacious nature helped many to overlook your flaws, but I'm sure some did not. But the people who love you know your motives and that's all that truly matters."

Claudine looked down at the yellow, green, and pink stitches on the stark white fabric, willing the tears to stay where they belonged.

"It's all right, my dear. You *should* feel proud."

Claudine nodded, not wanting to contradict the woman she had grown to respect so much. *I don't feel one ounce of pride. If I had come to realize how poor my behavior was and corrected it on my own, I might. It took my ruin and my sister's death to bring it about, however, so I can't see much cause for pride in it. Only shame. Embarrassment. Humiliation. All I had to do was look at either of my sisters for a model of good behavior, but I continued on my broken path, stubborn as a damned mule.*

"I think Pascal *is* worried for his sister. More than he lets on," Manon said as they walked back to the Lefebvre house. "It's not like her to be so silent."

"I confess I wasn't the friend to Gabrielle I should have been, and don't know her as well as you, but that does seem out of character for her. She's always seemed very devoted to her brother."

"Very much so. And he to her. I'm certain he plans to check on her tomorrow. He has some deliveries to make near enough to their homestead to justify an uninvited visit." Manon's eyes glanced to the northeast in the direction of the Beaumonts' shop. Claudine wondered why Manon had spent so much more of her time of late at their shop, but held the question back. Perhaps Manon had spent more time there in the past than she realized, but Claudine had never paid attention.

"Do you think we ought to go with him? Gabrielle might appreciate the company." Claudine knew that Gabrielle would sooner expect the Pope himself to show up at her doorstep, but she hoped that her past behavior wouldn't make her unwelcome. "We can raid Nicole's larder for all sorts of good things to help set them up for winter."

"A sound idea. As highly as I think of Pascal, we might have better luck discerning if anything is wrong."

"I think you might be right," Claudine agreed. "We'll send over a message to Pascal, but I can't imagine he'd object to our company."

Manon nodded her agreement and opened the door to the Lefebvre house for Claudine. They cast off their cloaks and disposed of their books before descending upon the kitchen. Claudine fetched one of the largest marketing baskets and placed it on Madame Yollande's expansive worktable. The two peered into the pantry with an assessing eye.

"Certainly the jams would do," Manon said. "The salted beef and pork?"

"Nothing better," Claudine agreed.

"And what are you two doing?" Nicole's voice sounded behind them.

"Putting together a hamper for Gabrielle. We were sure you wouldn't mind," Claudine said, turning her head back to the pantry shelves.

"Of course I wouldn't," Nicole said, looking over the jars they'd placed on the table. "I know Gabrielle is partial to the gooseberry jam. Be sure to take all but the largest jar. I'm glad you girls have decided to go. Elisabeth has been wanting to for weeks, but you can understand how hard it is to get away from the shop and the little ones."

Claudine gripped her sister's shoulder. Their own *maman* didn't make the trip into town as often as Nicole would like. Their mother wasn't fond of cities, even one as rudimentary as Quebec, and it took a good deal of convincing to get her to agree to the trip into town. Nicole's duties made frequent trips to the farm impossible, so though they were half a world closer than they once had been, they were still very much separated.

"Why don't you come with us?" Claudine offered. "It would be good for you to get away."

"Kind of you to include me, darling, but you two go visit with your friend and repay me for depleting my stores with all of her news. Does that sound like a fair exchange?"

Claudine embraced her sister, not worrying about crumpling Nicole's lovely evening dress. "More than fair. Especially if you have any of that soft yarn you used for Zacharie's blankets. She may be in need of it soon."

"Oh, I think I can dig up a few skeins for her, but you're a worse cheat than any British tradesman I've ever encountered," Nicole said, placing a kiss on Claudine's temple.

"So long as we don't encounter any of those on the road tomorrow, I'll be happy," Manon interjected.

"Amen," Claudine said with a scoff. "Let's go upstairs, Manon. We can go through our things to see if we have anything that might be of use to Gabrielle."

"Wonderful idea," Manon agreed, following Claudine up the stairs. The sweep of Manon's wardrobe didn't take long. Most of her things were new and she hadn't been with the Lefebvres long enough to build up an extensive wardrobe. She removed from the corner of her armoire a pair of sturdy leather shoes that looked like a cross between boots and bedroom slippers and blew off the layer of dust.

"Moccasins," Manon explained. "Heaven knows I can't be seen in them here, but they'll be serviceable for Gabrielle."

"Sweet of you to give up such a remembrance of your people," Claudine said, adding them to the basket.

"I've given up so much, what's a pair of shoes?" Manon followed Claudine into her room, sat on Emmanuelle's long-vacant bed, and issued her opinion on Claudine's pieces. A few of her everyday dresses had grown a bit worn for city wear, but with Gabrielle's skill with a needle she'd be able to make them better than usable for country life.

"I don't suppose you'd agree to sleep in here, would you?" Claudine aimed her words into her armoire. *Don't be such a coward. All she can say is no.*

"Pardon?" Manon looked up from one of Claudine's poetry books she'd left on the bedside table.

"It's just . . . it's so quiet in here. I'm not used to being alone."

Claudine folded a gray wool dress neatly and placed it atop the others in the basket.

"I don't see why not," Manon said, her eyes wide.

"Thank you," Claudine said, her voice barely above a whisper. "You could keep your old room as a little study. A room to yourself, just like Alexandre has."

"As grand as the *seigneur* himself," Manon said with a chuckle.

"I'm glad. I've not always been the kindest person to you. I suppose I was jealous." Claudine stared at the wooden floor and the tips of her boots with great interest rather than look at Manon directly.

"Jealous of me? Why on earth would that be?" The disbelief in Manon's words echoed against the stone walls.

"Aside from the fact that you're one of the smartest people in all of New France? When we arrived here, my sister loved you so much; I thought you'd taken my place. More than her sister, you were her daughter. I worshipped Nicole when I was little. Worshipped the memory of her when she left France. So when I showed up ready to be her cherished little sister again, and saw you by her side, beautiful and dressed in finer clothes than I had ever owned, I hated you. I thought she'd never look at me again. I'm ashamed of it now, but it's how I felt."

She felt Manon's arms slip around her, and Claudine nearly jerked away when Manon's warm tears spilled against her own cheek.

"I left because you had come to claim that place back in her heart," Manon said simply.

"She never got over you leaving, you know." Claudine clung to Manon a few more moments before taking a step back and taking her hands. "And I was foolish to treat you as I did. Please forgive me?"

"Friends," Manon agreed.

"What I need is a sister," Claudine said, squeezing Manon's hands.

"I always wanted one," Manon said, her tears spilling over once more.

"Look at the pair of us," Claudine said, laughing as she dried her cheeks. "Acting so foolish."

"It's been a hard few months. I think we're entitled to a little sentiment."

Claudine nodded, steadying her breath. "I hope Gabrielle will be happy to see us." Claudine fumbled to change the subject.

"Well, with a hamper like this, I can't imagine she wouldn't be." Manon turned back to the task at hand, arranging a few of Claudine's cast-off chemises more carefully.

"I think she'd be happy to see us both, with or without the hamper, but I'm sure she'll be all the more pleased for it."

Chapter 15

Gabrielle

September 1678

The following morning, Gabrielle stood to see the sounds of Pascal's horse and wagon, laden with Claudine, Manon, and their hamper, traversing the ill-kept path to the cabin. *Oh, why couldn't you have waited three weeks? He'd have been gone by then.* She peered down into her washbasin filled with murky water. She didn't see any visible bruises or scrapes on her face, but she wasn't surprised. Patenaude was careful to avoid hitting her face, claiming he couldn't abide ugly women and didn't want to risk breaking teeth or ruining the shape of her nose. It was the closest he'd come to paying her a compliment in the span of their married life. A good meal was met with what might be construed as an appreciative grunt. A clean home was merely expected. Well-mended clothes were ignored and the new shirt she made for him was scorned as frivolous.

"My brother and friends are coming; you might want to get dressed." Gabrielle spoke just above a whisper. He preferred women who spoke softly if they had to break their silence at all.

"You invited them here, you little slut. I told you I'd take the strap to you if you pulled such a trick. How did you get a letter out?"

"I did no such thing. They're likely here *because* I didn't write and haven't written for weeks. If you'd allowed it, I could have assured them I'm well."

"Likely story, liar. Your brother, let alone the *seigneur's* sister-in-law and heathen whore he took in wouldn't be bothered to check on the likes of you if you hadn't written to complain."

So you say, bastard, but they stand not ten paces from your door. "You can believe what you like. I know nothing I say will sway your opinion in my favor. However, if you don't want our company to see your lazy arse without breeches, I suggest you get out of bed and dress." The sass would cost her later, but it was well worth it to release a small morsel of her temper.

Patenaude did not speak, but the anger that flashed from his muddy brown eyes needed no voice to be heard. He pulled on his filthy buckskin breeches and tucked in his shirt. *The Olivier Patenaude approach to making himself presentable for company. Charming.*

The knock sounded at the door and Gabrielle shook her head. *I'd rather be dead than have you see me in this miserable place.*

Gabrielle took in a breath and opened the door to the ramshackle cabin for her guests.

"What a lovely surprise," Gabrielle said, embracing her brother and the girls. She was surprised that Claudine greeted her so warmly, but did not question it. *Kind people who love me. I thought you were a race gone from this world.*

"You had us worried sick," Pascal said. "Not a word in over two months? What were you playing at, girl?"

Gabrielle longed to leer a "told you so" toward Olivier, but it was not worth the subsequent rage. Enough trouble awaited her as soon as the guests departed.

"I'm so sorry," Gabrielle said. "It's been so hard to find a moment."

"Of course it has," Claudine said, taking the liberty of emptying the contents of the basket in the cupboard Gabrielle used as a pantry. "But we're pleased to see you're well."

"And surprised to see you here, Patenaude. We figured you'd be in the fields this late into harvest season." Pascal's tone was even, but Gabrielle recognized a challenge in her brother's voice when she heard one. *Tread lightly, brother. You have no idea what I will pay for this.*

"I'm spending my time hunting, if it's all the same to you. Fur season starts soon and I'll be off trapping." Patenaude stood to his full height, a show meant to intimidate the younger man. Though Patenaude was a broad, tall man, he stood an inch or so shorter than Pascal, which Gabrielle was sure irked her husband greatly. He could not stand to be second in anything, and nature had not graced him with all that many advantages. *Life must be a disappointing venture, you slow-witted beast.*

"And what of my sister? Are you just going to leave her alone out here when winter sets in?" Pascal's anger raged in his brown eyes as Gabrielle had only seen him direct toward one other man—their father.

"She fared fine last winter," Patenaude countered. *Indeed I did. It was the most peace I had all year. Please God that you're gone three months this time instead of three weeks.*

"I've been tending to the fields, Pascal," Gabrielle supplied. *Though it was hardly worth the trouble. Only a bushel of potatoes and a pound or two of wheat as reward for hour upon hours frying in the sun like fatty bacon on a hot griddle.*

"You mean to say you—" Pascal moved so close to Patenaude their noses nearly touched.

"It's fine, Pascal. Leave him be. Please." Gabrielle shoved her arm in between the two men. She couldn't bear to see Pascal hurt and she didn't want the bother of nursing Patenaude's wounds.

"Listen to your sister. She's speaking sense for once. I'm going out for the day. Have supper ready by dusk, woman." Patenaude left the cabin without a backward glance at his wife and without acknowledging Claudine's or Manon's presence.

"You'll have to forgive him. He's not used to company." Gabrielle turned to look at her newly stocked cupboard. Enough food to last for weeks. She gave a dry, barking cough into her hand to chase the emotion from her voice. She'd barely made it through the previous winter from the contents of her wedding hamper. In preparation for the next, she'd gathered berries and made an attempt to farm on her own, but her little crops would only last a month at most.

"Not *fit* for company, more like," Pascal said. "Pack your things. I won't leave you here with him."

"And do what, Pascal? Wait for him to come back to town and drag me back by the hair? I'm his wife now. I have no choice."

"Are you unhappy?" Manon asked. "Truly, if you are, there must be something that can be done."

Perhaps your people don't see marriage as the life sentence that mine do. I'm French. It means I'm stuck until I die or he does. "Forgive me, but I don't see the relevance of the question. I'm married. I'm doing the best for my husband that I can."

"But is he doing the same for you, Gabrielle?" Claudine looked at Gabrielle, her expression one of genuine concern. "You know that Alexandre is a powerful man. He can help."

"I seem to remember the priest saying something about 'what therefore God hath joined together, let not man put asunder' or something along those lines. The last I checked, Alexandre Lefebvre is not God, so I don't see what he can do."

"We don't mean to meddle," Manon said. "We just care about you."

Gabrielle could not find the strength to hold back her tears and let them flow freely. Most barely traced her cheeks before they dotted the front of her grimy dress. "Of course you do. I'm sorry."

Gabrielle felt herself swept into Claudine's arms. Her friend stroked her red hair like she might for a disconsolate child.

"I'm going to talk to Patenaude. And hope to God I can keep my temper." Pascal was halfway to the door before Gabrielle raised her head and wiped her face.

"Don't, Pascal. It will just make things worse. It's just the way he is. He's gruff to outsiders. I can make things better. We'll figure things out."

Even as the lies came from her mouth, she imagined her mother saying the same things to her loved ones in her early-married days and her stomach turned. There was nothing she could do to make Olivier Patenaude happy, but she had to cling to hope if she was going to endure this marriage.

* * *

October set in, and Patenaude grabbed his tattered rucksack and tracks, making his way out into the depths of the forest to liberate creatures from their hides. *For a man who treasures animal hides so much, he hasn't much respect for mine.* The bruises on her legs and thighs were still violently purple; those on her arms and abdomen were finally fading to a yellow that reminded her of pus. She languished in bed as long as she liked these days. Patenaude was not there to demand his breakfast or that she lie still while he grunted over her. The cabin was barely worth tending, nor were her clothes worth mending.

I could just end it all now. The slash of the sharp kitchen knife across her wrists appealed too much for comfort some days. She knew what fate the Church said would befall her if she humored these dark thoughts. She thought of Patenaude's face if he came home to the sight of a bloodstained mattress and a dead wife. She saw shock, then a roll of the eyes. Annoyance that he had to go into the backfield and take the time to dig a hole for her corpse. He wouldn't call a priest. He wouldn't bother to tell her family unless they came to demand her whereabouts. She'd rot in the ground she hated without a word said over her body. *I will not give him the satisfaction of doing that to me.*

Gabrielle swung her feet over the edge of the bed. She was loath to leave the warmth and relative comfort the lumpy mass of goose feathers offered, but she forced herself up to make some breakfast. She'd thrown together a few small loaves with the generous sack of flour Manon and Claudine had brought, and sliced a portion to eat with her gooseberry jam and milk. The bread was tough, nearing the end of its lifespan, but the jam usually softened and sweetened it into a more than palatable breakfast. That morning, her stomach rolled and she found herself emptying its contents into her waste bucket.

Maybe God is listening to my prayers today, sending an illness to take me away, but he could have found a less painful method. Gabrielle crawled back into the bed and stared at the pattern in the rough logs that comprised the wall of her home. She studied the pattern, trying to make sense of the randomness, but could not and began to wish she'd thought to rinse her mouth with cool water before retreating back to the bed. Now, only the apocalypse itself would raise her from beneath her covers.

She knew not how long she lay there, willing her stomach to cease its churning and cramping. She focused on taking deep breaths for a while, but then let her mind wander. After a time it wandered to the basket of clean rags she kept for her monthly courses. She realized she hadn't touched them in close to three months.

Gabrielle sat upright and calculated. She removed all her clothes for the first time in months and felt her abdomen. Though she rarely took the chance to look over her bruised and scraped flesh, she could see and feel that the shape was beginning to change, just slightly. She'd worried about this once before, but it was last spring when the lack of food had caused her body to skip its courses. The summer had been a time of relative plenty, and the hamper from her friends replaced the absent harvest and more. Her body was healthy enough to conceive and nourish a growing child.

When Olivier beat her for her "transgressions" after Pascal and the girls left, the baby was too small to be impacted, or else his blows never hit her womb. She forced herself to look down at her blackened skin, to take inventory of every scratch the man had inflicted upon her. She had stayed because she thought she had no choice. Now she knew she had to find another. *I spent a childhood at the mercy of a cruel father and I will not see this baby subjected to more of the same.*

Gabrielle found her large case that Gilbert had given her on the occasion of her marriage and loaded it with every jar of preserves, every scrap of salted meat, every stitch of clothing she owned. She would not leave one thing of value behind for Patenaude. She left behind the bare store cupboard, made the bed with the threadbare quilt so filthy that Gabrielle was certain it was stitched together by dirt, and hauled the spare traps and musket to the wagon. She hitched the loaded cart to old Xavier, who grunted and fussed as if Patenaude had left him instructions to continue making her feel unwanted. The horse eyed her with suspicion as she climbed onto the driver's perch, and refused to move when she prodded him forward.

"Get me to town, you broken-down pile of bones, and I *might* consider sparing you from the butcher." She took the crop and slapped him—hard—across his rump. Xavier, surprised by the ferocity of his usually gentle mistress, moved forward. Not with the speed Gabrielle might have liked, but she had to make allowances for his advanced age. She exhaled with relief as they approached the bend in the road. She did not look back at Patenaude's dank cabin and vowed she would never enter it again.

"I'm going to kill him." Pascal punched the wall for emphasis, but ended up shaking his hand in pain at his own folly. Elisabeth, Gilbert, and their adopted Giroux children sat at the dinner table, mulling over Gabrielle's fate, each with a glass of expensive cider in hand. The Beaumonts usually saved their cider for Sunday dinners or company, but Elisabeth, now standing at her worktable, often said that bad situations could often be chased off by good food and drink. It wasn't the case that night, but Gabrielle admitted that the fear, the anger, and the loathing she felt for Patenaude were all better endured with a full stomach and good drink than without.

"Sit back down and don't say anything of the sort like that ever again. Or even think it. If something *should* happen to that louse and you've been shooting off your mouth like that, you'll be the first one they go to." Gilbert's pragmatism was likely the only thing keeping him from a fit of rage to equal Pascal's.

"I don't care what happens to him, but I won't see you hurt, Pascal." Gabrielle's voice was stronger than she'd dared to speak in over a year. "He's not worth it."

Elisabeth placed a plate of Gabrielle's favorite apple pastries on the table and embraced her from behind before taking the adjacent seat. "I just don't know why you decided to stay as long as you did." It wasn't an accusation. Elisabeth took Gabrielle's hand, very much looking as though she wished to know what had compelled her beloved daughter to submit to Patenaude's brutish treatment.

"You sit in church every Sunday. You hear what the priests say. Until death, I am bound to Patenaude. It doesn't matter if he was cruel to me. I was to bear it. If he sold everything I had that was worth anything, it was his right as my lord and master. But when I realized . . . when I realized there is going to be a baby . . . I couldn't risk starving. I couldn't risk him treating the child the same way Father treated us. If it were just me . . ."

"You should have come back the moment the beast laid a hand on you," Gilbert said, the grinding of his teeth audible from across the table.

"Gilbert, enough." Gabrielle was surprised to see a flash of temper in Elisabeth's eyes. "Do you think he would have let her come back? Do you think she could have reasoned with him? Be sensible."

"You're probably right." Gilbert looked into the depths of his mug and seemed to find no answers there.

"All of this comes to nothing." Pascal banged his fist down on the table like a weary judge calling for order. "The past is the past and we have to figure out how to move forward."

"Amen," Elisabeth said. "You'll stay here, of course."

"And you can resume your duties in the bakery until you don't feel well enough," Gilbert added. "The community will think better of your situation if you're actively working and making a contribution to our family and the town."

"And Patenaude may likely stay away. If he was truly only interested in marrying you to reinstate his hunting and trapping rights, he may just as soon prefer you stay in the settlement." Pascal sat back in his chair, that moment looking very much like Alexandre Lefebvre, as though thinking three moves ahead in a game of chess.

"I appreciate this very much. And I don't see any choice but to stay here for a while. But when the baby comes—" Gabrielle began.

"We'll make room," Gilbert said. He placed his mug smartly on the table to punctuate his words. The thing was done in his mind, Gabrielle could see it.

"I don't *want* you to have room made for me. For us." Gabrielle absentmindedly touched her slightly distended belly. She'd not yet adjusted to the knowledge that a tiny life grew inside her. All she knew was that more than her own future was at risk if she did not plan the next steps of her life meticulously. "I want a life of my own. A home of my own. And I'm no great baker, either. Nothing compared to any of you. You're gifted at your trade, and I at mine. I'd rather make a living as a seamstress."

Gilbert, Elisabeth, and Pascal sat silent for several moments.

Never before had Gabrielle laid so much before them. She'd always been the first to go along with the plans proposed by the others. She'd always tried to follow the rules. Always tried to be kind, to be gentle, and to think of others before herself. *And a great deal of good it did me, too. But now I must think of my child. And what's best for me is likely best for her . . . or him.*

"And how is it you plan to go about all this?" Pascal's question was the one Gabrielle dreaded.

"I have some of Olivier's things. I was going to sell them before he could prove they were missing. It's not wrong. He's sold most everything you ever gave me. It may not be much, but I thought it might be enough to find me a little place of my own. And I can sew to make my way. Most of the women here don't need ball gowns, to be sure, but most of the ladies in town don't want to do all their own sewing, either."

"True enough," Elisabeth agreed. "But when Patenaude comes back into town and clears out your coffers? Then what? The deputies wouldn't stop him even if they wanted to. He's entitled to anything of yours he wants."

"I thought about that, too. What if I were to petition for a separation of person and property?"

Gabrielle's words silenced the room once more.

Few women dared to do it. Fewer still were successful at it. Those who were found themselves on the outskirts of society, never welcomed by the finest members of the elite, and barely acknowledged by the rest. *I'll be alone anyway, but I might as well have the security of knowing that what's mine truly is mine.*

"Such a thing won't be easy." Gilbert's expression betrayed that he knew his words were needless before he spoke them. "And I wouldn't sell all his belongings. Not yet. The judge won't look at that as the act of a dutiful wife, no matter what he's done with your things."

"Of course it won't, but if I stay married to him, my life will never be my own. It's my only chance to provide a real life for my baby." Gabrielle almost smiled at the trace of confidence in her voice.

"I'm just ashamed I ever let you get into this mess at all," Gilbert said, sitting back in his chair. "If I could go back and slap myself for walking you down that aisle, I would."

"Don't blame yourself. I agreed to the marriage out of fear. I'm leaving it for the same reason, but I'll never allow it to rule me like that ever again."

As Gabrielle spoke the words, she hoped with all the goodness inside her that they were true.

CHAPTER 16

Manon

October 1678

Tuesday afternoons, Manon abandoned her studies to retreat with Pascal to the Lefebvre fields. Sometimes Pascal made deliveries for the Beaumonts or called on a tenant for Alexandre, but most often they escaped to be alone. After the noon meal, Manon began to feel a sensation of anticipation tinged with guilt. She loved being away from the activity of the Lefebvre house for a few hours. She enjoyed Pascal's company. She'd tutored him in the art of lovemaking and his fumbling was not so inexpert as it had been a few months prior. But she did not love him as deeply as he wanted. She wouldn't allow herself to. She knew she risked breaking his heart. She'd tried to let him go, but she'd left so many people behind that his affection filled a void she hadn't known was there.

Were he from her clan, she could enjoy his intimacy without any pretense that they must agree to spend the rest of their natural lives together. *You French tend to take things to extremes. Marriage until death. Monarchies that stay in families for centuries. Change is not evil if you learn how to embrace it.* Manon knew that in this settlement, where tradition ruled as absolute as the Church and its monarch, her ideas were an anathema—even blasphemy—so she kept her mouth closed.

That particular afternoon, Pascal had no task but to devote his time to Manon, which suited her mood well that day. He'd held her hand the entire drive once they left the settlement, trusting the dutiful horse not to take advantage of a slack rein. He pulled the wagon to their favorite clearing, a secluded spot by the edge of the woods that allowed for spectacular views of the mountains and a dazzling array of wildflowers in the spring. In October, the crimson, orange, and gold leaves painted the hills against the backdrop of the stately evergreens.

"Manon, I wanted to—" Pascal began. She silenced his words with a long kiss. He tried to pull away for a moment, but then melted into her caresses.

"My sweet . . ." He breathed in between her kisses as she took some air.

"Let's talk later, please," Manon begged, her fingers busy unbuttoning his shirt.

"As my lady commands," Pascal said, nimbly unfastening her dress.

He met each kiss, each caress with fervor until he could wait no longer. He loved her slowly, deftly, as she had taught him. Slower, deeper movements caused delayed and heightened pleasure until her sighs let him know he could release his seed on her abdomen, a safe distance from her sex, as she'd commanded Heno to do as well.

He cleaned her skin gently with the soft cloth he'd brought for that purpose, and then reclaimed his position at her side, cradling her in his arms. The cool October air nipped at her skin, but Manon was too busy breathing in Pascal's honest scent to bother with trivial things like physical comfort.

"You make me so happy," he whispered into her jet-black hair while caressing the soft skin between her shoulder blades. He kissed her again, this time without the urgency of his need to rush him.

"I love you." He pressed his lips to her forehead, then to each of her eyelids, as delicate as a butterfly landing on a budding leaf.

She gripped him tighter, kissing the scruffy hollow of his neck where his beard was beginning to fill in. She longed to repeat the words he'd uttered a dozen times before. The words he meant more and more with each moment they shared, but she would not lie to this man whom she respected to the core of her being.

"You make me very happy, too, Pascal." It was as close as she dared come to making the declaration herself. And it was the truth. Aside from Tawendeh, no one else in the settlement lifted her spirits like Pascal could. *I did not think to miss my people as I do. I was never welcomed—not really—but in truth I was more a part of my tribe than I will ever be a part of the French society. Nicole can put me in satins and silks and lace, but she cannot whitewash my brown skin.*

"Then marry me, my love." Pascal's words floated soft on the brisk October wind, so faint Manon almost imagined she'd heard them. She'd dreaded this moment, but knew they had been approaching it for weeks. Months. He was a man of honor, and would only be comfortable with a dalliance for so long.

Sit up right now. Put your clothes back on and tell him, as kindly as you can, that this all must stop before both your hearts are broken. Before a mistake happens and you are with child. Before you ruin him and he ruins you. Manon tried to listen to the sensible if cold-hearted words from her conscience, but the idea of removing herself from Pascal's embrace caused her chest to tighten and her stomach to constrict.

"Can't everything just stay as it is?" Manon asked the question to no one in particular.

"No." Pascal's voice rang with a man's confidence. "Of all the promises a man can make to a woman, that's one I could never make, because it's the first I'd be forced to break."

"Lovemaking has made you philosophical." Manon chuckled as she conceded the point, but not her grip around his muscled torso.

"And you are a philosopher always. It's why we'd make a good match."

"You aren't wrong. But I'm not the right girl for you." Manon buried her face against his chest.

"I think I'd rather be the judge of that than this mysterious 'they' you think might disapprove. Frenchmen have been marrying native girls here for over half a century. What choice is there when there are so few Frenchwomen to be had?"

"If by marriage, you mean Frenchmen have taken native mistresses . . ."

"That's not what I meant. You know there are legal marriages, too."

"A handful."

"So let us be one of the few. It might be unusual, but it won't be scandalous."

"Pascal, you're under the wing of Alexandre Lefebvre. You stand to run one of the largest estates in New France as his agent. You could have your choice of a dozen French girls. He could import one for you for all I know. And it would be far better for your social standing to make a smart alliance with a Frenchwoman than with me."

"You speak of importing a woman like he might import a length of silk from the Orient. That sounds awfully coldhearted for you. And I don't care a fig for 'smart alliances' as you call them."

"I'm thinking about your future, Pascal, even if it sounds coldhearted to you. You may not care about alliances and making a good match now, but the time may come when you wish you had cared a good deal more. What if your involvement with Lefebvre puts you in line for an estate of your own? Do you think the governor will give holdings to a man who has married a native woman?"

To this, Pascal had no reply.

"Don't you see? I won't stand in the way of you making a grand future for yourself. Of all the people in the settlement, there's none who deserves an estate and a name more than you. It won't happen if I'm your wife."

"You're the ward of Alexandre Lefebvre and his wife. You've been convent-educated. Do you honestly think any of the Frenchwomen in the colony can boast much more, if we must look at things this way?"

"Possibly not," Manon admitted. "But be sensible. No one in town outside of our families will see beyond my brown skin. They don't care if I read Latin and Greek or with whom I've lived. They'll only see an Indian girl. And if anything, my education will make them more dubious."

"If you think that being Lefebvre's ward won't have influence on the governor's opinion, you're mad."

"It's not worth the risk," Manon said, finally listening to her inner voice and searching for her chemise. "I won't gamble with your future, and neither should you."

Pascal had asked Manon to coax his sister out of the house, and she felt she couldn't fail him in such a simple request. Gabrielle had expressed that she didn't feel it was appropriate for a married woman expecting a baby to continue with her lessons, but Manon and Claudine arrived at the Beaumont house prepared to pull Gabrielle to Rose's classroom by force if she wouldn't submit to an afternoon out. Gabrielle, mercifully, didn't put up much protest and accompanied her classmates to the home of the younger Lefebvres.

If Rose were surprised to see Gabrielle return to the classroom, she said nothing and masked her astonishment with the expert skill that took years on the stage—or as a parent—to master.

"Why don't we just work on our sewing and have some spruce beer today. You've been working hard lately." Manon nodded in agreement with Rose's impromptu curriculum change. Manon and Claudine *had* in fact been working very hard over the past weeks, Claudine's dedication a shock to all who knew her, and there would be no way for Gabrielle to keep up after her prolonged absence.

Both Gabrielle and Claudine produced small garments in need of finishing ruffles and lace. Claudine's was destined for her small nephew and Gabrielle's for her unborn child. Manon, having no such enticing project, pulled out one of her own skirts that was in need of a new hem, having rent the last one while out riding with Pascal some weeks back. She thought of the babies from her imagination, black-haired and tanned in the past, but now fairer and tawny-haired like Pascal, and could not repress her pang of envy. Little Tawendeh grew to be little Théodore more and more each day. He grew to be a Lefebvre, and not a child of the Big Turtle clan. He grew further away from his sister as well.

"How are you feeling these days?" Claudine asked. "Emmanuelle said the first months were simply exhausting."

"She wasn't wrong," Gabrielle said. "I hardly can get through the day without falling asleep on my feet. I tumble into bed at night as if I'd been plowing the fields all day."

"And so you have been, more or less," Rose said, smiling. "Making babies is hard work."

"Amen," Gabrielle agreed. "And I am so sorry about Emmanuelle, Claudine. I wish I could have been here for you. And to pay my respects."

"You had your own burdens to bear," Claudine said, her voice dropping as it tended to do when she spoke of her sister.

"Speaking of which, I heard that the elder Seigneur Lefebvre was going over to counsel you on . . . your legal matters." Manon hesitated to mention the separation aloud. "Did you make progress?"

"As much as you might expect. We'll have to present to the judge. We'll have to show proof of cruelty. It won't be easy."

"But you'll have our support," Claudine vowed. "We'll not see you sent back to that monster."

"Thank you." Gabrielle wiped her eyes on a scrap of cloth and giggled into it. "I've never been one to blubber, but these tears are always at the surface anymore. It's so ridiculous."

Rose returned the giggles as she handed Gabrielle a spare handkerchief. "Oh, I remember those days. It's maddening to feel as if you don't have a grasp on your own feelings."

Gabrielle smiled and nodded in agreement. "Let's change the subject, shall we?"

"Do let's. It seems as though my brother-in-law is very pleased with your brother Pascal's work. I'm hoping he'll name him as his agent." Claudine barely looked up from her stitches, so focused she'd become on her task.

"That would be a wonderful chance for him," Gabrielle said, the clang of pride unmistakable in her voice. "It seems like he's born for management. You've been a good deal of help to him, Manon. I'm grateful to you."

"Not at all," Manon said. "I've just helped him learn the various types of native plants and a few of the better techniques my people have used on their farms. We know the land, but you French are the real farmers."

"All the same, I appreciate it. To see him make his way in the world gives me pleasure when I didn't think I could feel it again."

"I'm happy to help," Manon said, going back to her hem. *And*

*for your sake as well as his and my own, I will not allow him to pay
me court anymore.*

"He did seem out of sorts on Tuesday, however," Gabrielle continued. "I suppose there was some unpleasantness with a tenant?"

"You might say that," Manon answered. "But these things always figure themselves out. It just takes time."

Gabrielle returned to the Beaumonts' on her own, and Thursday afternoons saw Claudine nestled in with her nephew, so Manon took the opportunity to run errands for Nicole. While Manon had no particular love of marketing, she was happy for a diversion that day. Being among people would keep her from dwelling overlong on her thoughts. Over the last two days, she'd come close to running to the Beaumonts' home, seeking out Pascal and begging him to renew his offer.

She knew he would.

She still knew it was wrong.

She let the daily details of marketing for meat and cheese claim her mind since her more academic pursuits could not keep her distracted. The Lagranges' cheese shop was impeccable, and the family who ran it one of the most respected in town, but Manon had no great desire to visit since her encounter with the patroness when she first returned to live with Nicole.

Two people waited in line before Manon, so she admired the attractive display and well-ordered shop. When the other customers trundled off with their odiferous goods, Manon approached the counter and offered Madame Lagrange a shallow smile that did not reach her eyes. Her efforts were rewarded with a scowl.

"Madame Lefebvre would like a wheel of the country cheese and a crock of the cream cheese, please."

"Madame Lefebvre has put you to work, then? Can't say as I blame her. Damn kind of her to take you and that brother of yours in at all. I'd have you scrubbing the floors, make no mistake of it."

"Have you any other suggestions for me to relay to Madame Lefebvre?" Manon's voice seeped ice like a stream in early spring.

"None of your sass, girl. I won't take guff from the likes of you."

"Then give me her order and I'll be on my way."

With a spiteful look, the wiry woman thrust the cheese into Manon's hands and stalked off to her back storeroom.

Shriveled old witch. If there were another cheese monger in town, rest assured I'd make sure the seigneur *sent his custom elsewhere.*

Manon shoved the cheese in her basket, not bothering to inspect her purchases. No one would dare sell inferior goods to the *seigneur* or his household, no matter who did the shopping.

The butcher was more convivial as he filled the order, but Manon's ruffled demeanor did not inspire friendly chatter. Rather than retreat to the solace of her bedroom to pore over her books as she normally did, she passed her marketing basket off to the cook, Madame Yollande, and retreated back out into the October air, which grew crisper as the light grew feeble.

Manon pulled her cloak tight around her shoulders and walked aimlessly for nearly an hour until she found herself at the edge of the river. Not wanting to spoil the fine woolen cloak Nicole had commissioned from Gabrielle on the occasion of her return, Manon sought the cleanest, driest patch of grass she could find and watched the coursing water.

"Something bothers you, my dear pupil?" Rose's soft voice caused Manon to start, almost painfully.

"And now heart troubles to make matters worse," Manon said, rubbing her chest dramatically. "You're stealthier than the Huron's best hunters."

"Well, it's good to know I have employment opportunities if my teaching career fails me." Rose winked as she pulled her skirts to the side and claimed the spot next to Manon.

"What brings you here?" Manon asked, not unkindly, though not particularly happy with the interruption to her solitude.

"You're not the only one who enjoys mulling over her thoughts by the river." The faraway expression on Rose's face told Manon that she must be recollecting her previous visits. What her sweet-natured teacher had to ruminate over in years past, Manon knew not. Any other day, the question might fascinate her. "Truth be told, I've never seen you more distracted in class. I was picking up a few things in town when I saw you leave the Lefebvre house and thought you might need company."

"You could have let me know you were following me rather than scaring me half to death." Manon plucked a blade of grass and twirled it between her thumb and forefinger, watching the swirl of green against the rushing river.

"I didn't mean to startle you, but I did think you needed to be alone with your thoughts for a while." Rose tucked her legs beneath her in an attempt to find a ladylike posture.

I still do, if you don't mind. "You're not wrong."

"So what have you told Pascal?" Rose didn't make eye contact with Manon and kept her tone from sounding too prodding.

Manon sat up and looked over at her teacher. "Did he tell you?" Manon's eyes were wide at the idea he'd spoken of his proposal to anyone, let alone someone so far removed from his usual circles.

"No. I have eyes. I have ears. I see you two driving off together every Tuesday. I can see as plain as the nose on his face that Pascal is in love with you. I'm shocked it's taken him so long to propose, to be honest. All it took was a glimpse of your face to tell me that he had. And I'd wager he didn't get the answer he wanted, either."

You needn't be so perceptive. It's rather ingratiating. "I couldn't chain him to a native girl. Not when he has such good prospects. If he were a simple farmer, perhaps. I won't see him robbed of an estate for my sake." Manon hugged her knees to her chest and looked out at the coursing water.

"I wouldn't sever ties with someone I cared about because of something that may or may not come to pass in many years to come. Henri had to wait years for the governor to notice him."

"And when the governor finally noticed him, he saw a man with a gracious upbringing who was married to a woman suited to his station. If the governor looks to Pascal and sees a man married to a native girl, he will look elsewhere as fast as his eyes can travel."

"What does Pascal have to say?"

"He says he doesn't care. He's being foolish." Manon found a flat rock in the grass with her right hand and threw it out into the rushing water.

"Most men in love are." Rose patted her hand, but Manon withdrew it just as quickly.

"I care about him too much to break his heart."

"My dear, I think you're well beyond that point. Why don't you take a chance? Lord knows I did and I'm much happier for it."

"I don't love him the way he needs me to, Rose. He needs a woman who will love him with the innocence of a girl. I can't do that."

"I think you give him far too little credit for knowing his own heart, but I won't press the matter further, darling. But remember, our time on this earth is fleeting and those who are able to sow some small seed of happiness while they are here are lucky beyond measure. Don't throw it away unless you're sure."

CHAPTER 17

Claudine

October 1678

Though Laurent Robichaux was the most gracious of hosts, there was nothing that could make Claudine feel at ease while sitting in her sister's place to Laurent's right side at the supper table. While only the two of them dined, the cook prepared the finest dishes— good cuts of pork or beef in well-seasoned sauces, vegetables braised to perfection, good crusty bread, succulent pastries, and fine wine. Just when Claudine thought the meal would surely be coming to its close, another course was served, another glass poured.

"Zacharie is getting so big," Claudine said to break the silence. Zacharie was their default subject of conversation, and while Claudine adored her nephew, there was only so much to discuss about a child whose development had reached as far as grasping a rattle and smiling.

"Indeed he is," Laurent agreed, his face darkening. "I confess that it had been a few days since my last visit to the nursery. When I saw the two of you together today I could hardly believe the changes."

"I'm sure your business keeps you occupied," Claudine said, sipping at the rather remarkable red wine the servant poured. She was certain it was the same quality of vintage that Alexandre reserved only for the most important guests.

"It does, but that's not what keeps me from the nursery. He reminds me so much of her."

Claudine noticed that he had hardly touched this course, and the previous hadn't been more than picked at, either. The wine bottle had emptied considerably, however, and not much due to Claudine's efforts.

"I know. There is so much of her in his countenance. But it's all the more reason to lavish your affections on him. She would want it that way." She placed her left hand on his right, to which he placed his free hand atop hers and caressed it gently.

"Thank you. It doesn't make the pain less, but it's good to know that someone understands what I'm going through. Someone who loved her so dearly."

Claudine didn't bother to fight the tears that welled up in her eyes. It had been a week or more since her last good cry over Emmanuelle, and she was due for another.

"She was lucky to have a husband who cherished her so," Claudine said, thinking of Gabrielle's drawn face and barely concealed bruises. "You were good to her, and that thought should give you comfort."

"I wish it did, but nothing does." His hands still grasped hers, though she could remove it if she chose. She wanted to, but hated to hurt the feelings of a man so clearly in pain. "Your visits are the only solace I have."

"Then you may depend upon them, dear brother. But you needn't empty the pantry for my sake."

Laurent barked a dry laugh. "The cook thought I was mad. I didn't know what you might like, so I told her to prepare the best of everything. I want you to enjoy your visits here."

"I do," Claudine said. "But you mustn't go to any fuss on my account. I'm family, not company."

"Thank you, my dear. I can't tell you how much your kindness means to me."

"Think nothing of it. If there is anything else I can do for you, you must ask."

Laurent's probing brown eyes searched hers. Before she could react, he placed his hand around her wrist and pulled her to his lap. He lowered his wine-perfumed lips down to hers and drank from them as though she were an oasis and he a man who had been wandering the desert for a month. She wanted to protest, but she could not bring herself to voice it. She let him kiss her for some minutes, but did not return his ardor.

At once, Claudine found herself standing on her feet, Laurent bracing himself with a hand on each of her arms, catching his breath and cursing softly.

"My God, I'm so sorry. Please forgive me."

Claudine nodded, her eyes wide, her brain unable to process fully what had just taken place. "I-I should . . ." was all she could stammer. She turned to the doorway and grabbed her cloak from the hall, drying her tears on her sleeve, praying her lips didn't look too swollen from Laurent's kissing. The last thing she needed was more gossip about her virtue as she left the house of a single man.

Claudine forced herself to make pleasantries when she entered the house. She longed for the solitude of her bedroom, where only the memory of Emmanuelle would bother her. *How I long to speak with you, dear sister. I've quite the matter to discuss with you about your husband.*

Instead, she remained in the parlor with Nicole, Manon, and Alexandre, claiming a book from her brother-in-law's library to occupy her thoughts. Mending and embroidery gave her mind too much liberty to run into dangerous territory that night.

"Monsieur Robichaux is here to see you, *seigneur*," the butler, Paul, announced at the parlor door.

"Show him to my study," Alexandre said. "Here to talk about the border tenants again, to be sure. I may be awhile."

Claudine was vaguely aware of a Lefebvre tenant and a Robichaux tenant on neighboring farms who disputed a boundary line, but she'd paid the matter little mind. *And I'll wager my best dress he's here to speak of nothing like border disputes.*

Claudine made a weak excuse and took her book upstairs to read at the feeble light of her oil lamp. Rather than resume the text on modern French livestock practices, she tossed it on her bedside table, wondering what had possessed her to choose such a dry tome. She removed her boots and threw herself, fully clothed, on the bed.

He's going to tell them I'm a wanton whore who seduced him. He's going to ensure that I face the full shame I barely eluded with Victor. She imagined herself returned to her parents' homestead and eventually marrying a plodding farmer. Living for her visits to town thrice a year. Miserable.

She was grateful the bookish Manon was holed up in her study, rather than reading in Emmanuelle's old chair as she sometimes did. Curled up on her bed, Claudine lay still and allowed her tears to flow freely down her cheeks as she let herself wallow in her self-pity. With no Emmanuelle to comfort her, it was the next best balm for her aching soul. *Don't let him exaggerate the truth at least. It was a kiss. Nothing more. I didn't mean to entice him.*

Perhaps a half hour later, a soft knock sounded at the door and Nicole entered without invitation.

"Alexandre wishes to speak with you, darling." Nicole's expression was not lined with anger or frustration. *Let's just get this over with. I'd have done better to pack my things rather than sulk.*

Alexandre sat behind his desk, a cognac in his hand, his eyes wandering his bookshelf, looking as though he marauded about the jungle of his thoughts. He snapped back to attention when he noticed Claudine and Nicole enter the room. He indicated to the empty chairs in front of his desk. Claudine's was still warm from Robichaux's backside, the thought of which made her stomach both sink and twist into knots.

"Laurent Robichaux came to apologize for his unseemly behavior tonight. He didn't think you'd listen to him directly, so he conveyed his regrets to your sister and myself in the hopes we would relay them to you." Alexandre sipped his cognac as he leaned back in his chair, as informal as he might be with his nephew or other close male friend. Claudine exhaled audibly, relieved at her brother-in-law's pronouncement. Robichaux's half-consumed cognac still sat before Claudine's seat. She took the glass and sipped its contents thoughtfully, painfully aware that his lips had been on the same glass only minutes before.

"He's grieving. He's not himself." Since he didn't cast her off as a whore, she could afford to be generous.

"Kind of you to say," Nicole said. "But he had no right to force his attentions on you if they weren't wanted."

"I was too shocked to protest," Claudine admitted. *But would I have done so if I hadn't been so shocked?* The question had plagued her for the past two hours. She could have cast him down for his actions. Should have done, probably. But, even with the events of her past considered, she could not find it within herself to deny him the few moments of escape from his grief.

"I can imagine not," Alexandre said. "He's greatly embarrassed by the whole thing. He hopes you'll find it in your heart to forgive him and continue to visit the child, even if you won't join him for supper."

"Of course," Claudine said. "I won't abandon Zacharie over a lapse of a man grieving for his wife. I'll write him a letter to soothe his feelings."

"Sweet of you, darling," Nicole said. "I'm sure that will reassure him greatly."

"I think it best you suspend your suppers for a while, though," Alexandre advised.

"I've no objection," Claudine said, rising from her chair. "A meal grand enough for Queen Maria Theresa herself is no treat when paired with awkward conversation. I'll write the letter before bed." Claudine rose, considerably lighter, perfectly happy to write her brother-in-law a very cordial letter of forgiveness.

"That's not all," Alexandre said. Claudine arched her brow and sat back in the plush blue chair.

"Claudine, Seigneur Robichaux has asked permission to pay you court after Advent." Nicole took her sister's hand. "He thinks it the honorable course of action given the events of this evening. He also thinks it would be best for Zacharie to have you as his mother since our Emmanuelle is no longer with us. I cannot fault his logic there. Such a dutiful aunt has never been seen."

"It's what I thought Emmanuelle would want" was all Claudine could stammer. She took Robichaux's cognac glass and downed the rest of the sweet amber-brown nectar in one swallow.

"Were you my daughter, the matter would be settled already," Alexandre interjected. Nicole met this statement with a hard squint in her husband's direction. "He's one of the most respected men in New France. He has both fortune and position enough to please most any noble family in France, let alone here. You could not do better, especially considering past events."

"Which you will never let me forget," Claudine said.

"There's no need to browbeat upon it, Alexandre," Nicole said, taking an unusually harsh tone with her husband. "No harm came from it."

"Because luck smiled on her," Alexandre said. "Claudine, the fact remains that you have the chance to make the match you aspired to for years. I can't imagine such an offer will ever be repeated. If you wish to make anything significant of your future, I urge you to accept him."

"And you, Nicole? What do you think?" Claudine turned to look at her sister, whose face was lined with concern for her younger sister.

"I think Laurent Robichaux, despite his lapse in judgment tonight, is a very good man. He was more than kind to Emmanuelle and will be the same to you."

"Don't you think it odd that he wants to marry his late wife's sister?" Claudine asked to no one in particular.

"Not in the least. In many respects you're the logical choice. You've already proven yourself as a compassionate mother to the child. No one has more of a vested interest in his future than you, aside from Robichaux himself. I've seen it happen numerous times in the best families in France." The prudence of the alliance only now made itself apparent to Claudine, but it was undeniable.

Zacharie. The thought of any other woman caring for him as a mother, or worse, ignoring him in favor of her own children with Robichaux, caused a cold sweat to form on Claudine's brow. A man like Robichaux would not remain single. Men in his station rarely did. If Claudine did not accept him, the day would come when another woman would take over care for her dear nephew, and she would not be likely to welcome her involvement.

"You don't have to make a decision tonight," Nicole said, squeezing her sister's hand.

"But you must make one. And soon." Alexandre's words left no doubt that he believed there was only one right answer to the question put before her.

It was her afternoon to visit Zacharie at last, and both anxiety and dread churned in her core as she walked to the Robichaux house for the first time since Laurent had approached Alexandre. Would she see Robichaux? Would he *want* to see her? *Do* I *want to see* him? She couldn't answer the question with any real satisfaction.

She handed her cloak to the butler and summoned enough courage to add, "Please tell Seigneur Robichaux I've come to see the baby. He needn't feel obligated to come visit, but he may wish to."

"Very well, mademoiselle."

Zacharie greeted her with his usual smiles and coos, and Nanny Simon looked almost as pleased to see her as the gurgling infant. Claudine could not help but smile at the lovely woman and empathize with her joy at a few hours of liberty.

Less than a quarter of an hour eclipsed before Laurent's tall frame emerged at the nursery doorway.

"I was afraid you wouldn't come," he said by way of greeting.

"I wouldn't abandon Zacharie. Not even for a worse offense than . . . your little misstep. I could never forgive myself." Claudine motioned to the empty chair next to her own, to show he was welcome.

"You're a good woman," he said, claiming the seat and caressing the back of his son's head. *Not "girl."* She offered a small smile at the sign of respect, combing her brain to think if anyone had ever used the term in reference to her before.

"I'm learning to be. I have a far better idea of what that means than I used to. At least I hope I do."

"Indeed you do. You're becoming every bit the good woman your elder sister is and your younger sister certainly was becoming."

"Thank you for that," Claudine said.

"Please tell me you forgive me. I couldn't live with myself—"

"Laurent, there's nothing to forgive." Claudine knew that using the first name of a *seigneur* was bold, but formalities seemed awkward, given the intimacy of their last encounter. "You're grieving and lonely. Let's put it behind us."

"Thank you," he said. "I don't want things to be unpleasant with us."

"Nor do I."

Despite the words, an uncomfortable silence settled over them for several minutes.

"Did your brother-in-law and sister mention what I asked them to?"

"About you courting me come January? Yes." She looked down at the sleeping babe in her arms. *Should I accept him? For your sake?*

"I hope it wasn't too presumptuous. I felt it the honorable—not to mention practical—course of action."

"And you won't mind taking Emmanuelle's sister as your second choice?" *Taking second to Emmanuelle is something I've never done in my life. Can I do it now? When it really matters?*

"My darling Claudine, I wanted to pay you court from the first moment we danced together. Please don't misunderstand; I loved your sister as much as any man could do, especially given the short duration of our marriage. But I've never been able to forget you. Not entirely."

Claudine felt the tears spill over and angled so they would not waken the sweet baby who was still asleep in her arms. She rose and, gently as she could, placed him back in the safety of his crib.

"I'm ashamed to make such a revelation to you. You must think I was a rake to marry your sister when I still felt this way for you. But I knew you'd never say yes to me. You needed someone younger. More exciting. But I hope that since things have changed . . . you might at least consider."

Laurent remained seated, but his eyes never wavered from Claudine. They seemed to implore her for an answer. Since her arrival in New France, she dreamed of a handsome young man of good standing to raise her fortunes. This man wasn't particularly young. He wasn't overly blessed with good looks. But he was, she had to admit, one of the best men she'd ever known. For all of his dark good looks, Claudine would not exchange Laurent's affections for Alexandre's. Gabrielle's husband was good-looking in his rustic way, and he was no prize for a husband. Laurent would never be cruel.

"Laurent, I don't want you to pay me court in January." With her words, his face fell. "I'd prefer to call it a done thing and be married in the New Year."

Laurent's eyes welled up, and he made no move to manfully hide his emotions. "May I please kiss you?"

Claudine smiled at the modest question he would have done better to ask a week prior and nodded her approval. This time the kiss was slow, chaste, but no less charged with his repressed desire for her.

I'll do the best I can for them, Emmanuelle. For both of them. I hope this is what you would have wanted.

CHAPTER 18

Gabrielle

November 1678

Gabrielle sat in her old bedroom, bundled up against the coldest afternoon they'd seen in the budding winter, hemming one of the skirts that Laurent Robichaux had commissioned for Claudine. A year ago, she'd spend the entire time sewing with a dose of spite, begrudging the smug girl her happiness. Now she was able to sew with a heart grateful for her friend's upcoming nuptials. No one outside of the Lefebvre and Beaumont families knew of the engagement, and the new wardrobe was to be kept in Gabrielle's closets until the vows were spoken. *I do not envy you your fine clothes or your kind husband-to-be, dear friend. You deserve a second chance at happiness. As do most of us.*

The soft yellow linen was a joy to touch, let alone craft into a flowing skirt for everyday occasions for the smart young matron. It made for more amusement than baking for Elisabeth or doing her own sewing, which now consisted of letting out the waists of her own skirts to make way for her swelling abdomen. The even stitches kept her mind from wandering to the upcoming hearing. She would be forced to see Patenaude for the first time and she would have to stand before a judge and beg for her freedom. Both of the *seigneurs* from the Lefebvre family would testify for her.

Gilbert, too, though the word of a baker, even a successful and well-liked one, would count for far less.

Patenaude's bearded face and foul breath crept into her mind. She recalled an evening when he grabbed her by the hair and threw her against the hearth, causing a deep gash by her right temple. The scar still gleamed pinkish-white. *You've marked me, Patenaude. You've bruised me from head to foot, but you've yet to leave a mark on my heart. It will remain unblemished so I can give it to my child in the perfect condition every baby deserves from her mother.*

She cursed as she realized she'd rumpled the fabric, her hands tensing at the vision of Patenaude's hulking form towering over her. She poked her finger with the needle in her anger, and tossed the fabric to the safety of her clean bed so it would escape soil. She found an old rag and wrapped her bleeding finger until the flow of red subsided.

Do not let him upset you. He's not here. He cannot hurt you. He is not worth ruining one of your old aprons, let alone a length of new linen.

She felt the prick of tears at the corners of her eyes and kicked her bedroom wall. *Leave me be, you damned brute. Can't you even leave my mind in peace?*

The bleeding stopped; she limped back to her bed and placed Claudine's dress in her basket, to be revisited another hour. She lay down on her bed and forced her breath to slow until she could no longer feel the pulsing in her face or the racing of her heart against her rib cage. *The baby needs you to be calm. The baby needs you to be healthy.*

She looked down at her little bulge and patted the growing mound. She'd not felt a proper kick yet, but got the occasional sensation of movement. Elisabeth dismissed it as her stomach churning, but Gabrielle was certain her child was moving within her. *My darling baby. I will keep you safe, as my mother was unable to do. You will never know pain or suffering. You will grow to a fine woman and I will see you happy. Rose can be your auntie and will help you in society. I'll make and mend every stitch of clothes she wears for the rest of her days without charging her a* sou *in exchange for lessons.*

Her heart lightened as she imagined the life her daughter would have with the help of her friends. Privilege, rank, respect. All the things Gabrielle witnessed but never had for herself. Because she had married, people did not look down on Gabrielle. They knew she worked hard and was no burden on the town. They gave her credit for no more than that. She was what a woman ought to be and no more. Once word circulated that she petitioned for a separation from Patenaude, the measure of respectability she had would be lost. They would see a willful woman and a fatherless child.

Better to be the scorn of the town than to risk her at his hands. He cannot be allowed near her. I will not go back to him.

She had escaped Patenaude's grasp once, and she would not see herself thrown back into his clutches. She had a child to protect. Her own health to protect in order to care for the child. No longer would she allow a man to raise a hand to her. She would place her trust in the good judge and in her friends. They would see her and the baby protected.

Claudine and Manon helped Gabrielle dress for the hearing. They put together an ensemble of their own clothes in better repair than anything she owned, but they made sure they were plain. They could not have the judge thinking she'd squandered Patenaude's money on frivolous new clothes, but she couldn't appear unkempt, either.

"It's going to be fine," Claudine said, smoothing Gabrielle's unruly hair into a tidy knot and covering it with a fresh white *coiffe,* as all dutiful married women wore.

"You're in the right," Manon said. "We can hope the judge will recognize this and do his duty." Manon shot Claudine a warning look that Gabrielle interpreted with too much ease. *Do not raise her spirits with false hopes.*

"Don't be cross with Claudine. Whatever the judge decides, I have to try," Gabrielle said. "I have to protect my child from Patenaude. If I don't make the effort, I'll never forgive myself."

"Too right," Claudine said. "Have you decided to tell the judge you're expecting, then?"

"No," Gabrielle said. "Alexandre seemed to think it would work against me. The courts would assume I would have to rely on charity to raise the child without a father. I'm better off pretending I don't know about the impending arrival just yet."

"Wise," Manon agreed. "But you'll earn no affection from the judge if you're late."

The hearing had created enough gossip in town that quite a crowd had gathered in the little courthouse. The judge had the right to decide if the hearing would be public or private, but chose to admit as many people as the room would hold, seemingly uninterested in keeping the private affair from becoming a public spectacle.

"It's just as well," Alexandre said. "It's better the gossips hear the news firsthand. The more witnesses we have, the less opportunity they have to embroider the tale."

Gabrielle nodded, but wasn't convinced. These were not the details of his personal life being brought out before the town. He could afford to be objective.

Patenaude took the stand, cleaner and more respectable-looking than he had appeared on their wedding day. He was the very image of the hard-working homesteader as he stood before the judge, though he'd never sown as much as a single seed in his life. Even his scruffy friend Jacques Verger appeared to have taken a bath, though despite a good washing, he hadn't been able to scrub the sour expression from his face. Gabrielle forgot the old man and fixed her eyes forward as the judge questioned her husband.

"*Monsieur le Président,* I haven't the slightest inkling as to why my wife is seeking to break up our home. I've done what I can for her. I work from sunup to sundown every day but the Sabbath, and many's the time I've come home with no proper supper to eat, nor any kind attentions from her, if you understand my meaning."

Shiftless lout, you helped yourself to my "kind attentions" whether I was willing or not.

"Madame Patenaude claims you've hit her to the point where she blacked out. Is that true?"

"Never once, *Monsieur le Président.* If she fainted, it was because she took to the drink when I wasn't looking. I know her father was powerful fond of it, and I fear she's gone the same way. It's the devil's nectar, and a damned shame if you ask me. Begging your pardon, monsieur. Wish I could have kept a closer eye on her, but a man has to earn his way."

"You liar!" Gabrielle stood from the hard wooden bench across the courtroom and pointed her finger at her husband. "That man fills your ear with lies, *Monsieur le Président*. I've never drunk to excess in my life. Even if I had the taste for it as he claims, I never had so much as *sou* for bread, let alone drink."

"Quiet, madame. We will question you in due course." Judge Arnaud grimaced as he shifted in his seat and glared at Gabrielle for her outburst. Claudine took her hand in solidarity, both shaking in anger at the judge's censure.

"You see what she's like, monsieur. There ain't no pleasing a woman like that."

The judge said nothing, but his expression looked sympathetic. Gabrielle guessed Madame Arnaud was not the dutiful wife the judge yearned for. She listened to the rest of the judge's questions with only vague interest. Patenaude had won the sympathy of the courts and she could say nothing to change his mind. *He is going to punish me to make an example. I'm absolutely finished.* Still, she stood dutifully when called by the judge. She would not admit defeat while she had a small chance at freedom.

"Madame Patenaude, with what implements did your husband hit you?" The judge's dark eyes bored into her, looking as though he were furious with her about her imposition on his time. Her palms slickened with sweat and the taste of metal coated her mouth.

"His hands, mostly. His belt on occasion."

"I see. And were these lashings, as your husband says, as a result from you neglecting your domestic duties?"

"*Monsieur le Président,* if ever my husband was denied his supper, it's because there was none to prepare. More than once I went without so that he might eat."

"Because she's a poor manager, that's what." Patenaude stood up from the bench. The judge made no move to silence him. "I always gave my wife the means to keep a proper home. I don't know what she did with the money, monsieur. I can only suspect." He made a motion as though he were taking an imaginary cup to his lips.

"*Monsieur le Président,* I never misspent a *sou* of my husband's money because I was never given one to spend. He would bring home the odd kill when he couldn't sell it. A sack of flour or vegetables on occasion. Otherwise we lived on the hampers from the Beaumonts and my own poor attempts at farming. I confess, monsieur, I am not much at cultivating the land, but I had no help from my husband on that score."

"That will be all, madame."

Alexandre, Gilbert, and Henri all came to Gabrielle's defense. They spoke of the lack of provisions, the abuse. The judge spent the entire hearing with pursed lips, clearly unimpressed with the tales of her plight.

He took no time to deliberate.

"I have heard no proof of wrongdoing on Monsieur Patenaude's side. He is free to discipline his wife in the manner he sees fit. So long as he does not beat her with a switch thicker than his wrist, it is not for this court to tell any man how to run his house." Gabrielle looked over at her husband's hands and arms. A few blows with a switch that large would have killed her. *So kind that such stringent laws are in place to protect women from the cruelty of men.* "Madame Patenaude will return to her home with her lord and master, and I suggest that she use the voyage to contemplate how she can better fulfill her duties as a wife, rather than troubling the courts with her complaints."

You're sending me back to my death, you heartless monster.

While Gilbert looked as though he would gladly throttle the judge in front of the entire courtroom, the rest of the men circled Gabrielle, shielding her from Patenaude. Claudine and Manon stood beside her, as though ready to defend her against him right on the very courtroom floor.

"Just let me go," Gabrielle said. "My life apparently is of no consequence to this court, so I might as well go and spend what I have left of it in misery."

She made no respectful exit of the court, but spat in the direction of the judge, not caring what any of those assembled thought of her crass behavior.

Outside the courthouse, Pascal and the other men gave Gabrielle the wide berth she'd asked for, but blocked Patenaude from his cart.

"You will never lift a hand to my sister again, you piece of gutter sludge, or I will bury an ax in your skull. I swear it." Pascal stood only a few inches from Patenaude's face, this time with a public audience to witness his display.

"You can try, you scrawny girl," Patenaude said, shoving Pascal out of the way. He turned and grabbed Gabrielle by the arm. "Get in the wagon, you tiresome slut. I've had more than enough trouble from you."

At this, Gilbert's fist, made strong from years hauling sacks of flour, connected with the sickening crack of bone. Blood poured from Patenaude's nose and he doubled over on the street.

"Let me repeat what my son said. If you lay a hand on my daughter again, it will be the last act of your life. Do you understand me, you despicable son of a bitch?"

Patenaude stood up, nose still cupped in his hands, but a vicious look in his eyes still plain to see. Any normal man would understand that Gilbert was perfectly serious in his threats, but Gabrielle knew *she* would be the one to pay the price for Gilbert's aggression.

The entire ride home through the snow and biting wind, Gabrielle refused to look at her husband, keeping her eyes on the decrepit horse or on the scenery that grew more and more savage as they left the town. Patenaude made no attempt at conversation and she was grateful for that small mercy. *I'm sure you'll have plenty to say soon enough.*

Her instincts proved correct. As soon as they were indoors and the hamper of food Elisabeth had thrust at her placed on the dining table, he crossed the room and slapped her hard.

"You stupid bitch. How dare you make a fool of me like that?"

"Why on God's green earth did you challenge it? You could stay here on your own and hunt all you damned well pleased. You'd have what you wanted and you'd be rid of me."

"Because people would think I let you get the better of me. The only women who leave their husbands are sluts, and I won't let you free to whore about."

"I'm not a slut, you babbling fool. I just want to go more than a day without you or anyone knocking me about."

"Today ain't that day." Patenaude struck her across the cheek so hard she fell to the floor. Then he went to work with his boots. Kicking everywhere but her face. She covered her abdomen, but his boot found its mark more often than not.

When he grew tired of beating her, he threw her on the bed and forced himself atop her. She gripped her eyes shut and tried not to cry out when his rough treatment upset her fresh injuries. *You will not have the satisfaction of hearing me call out, you worthless shit. You will not.*

The following morning, Patenaude arose with the sun and helped himself to the bulk of the contents of Elisabeth's hamper. He ate a generous breakfast from it and put the rest in his knapsack.

"That damned hearing of yours cost me almost a week on the caribou hunt. I'll be back in the New Year. Be here when I get back or you'll be sorrier than you are now."

He shut the door and left into the cold and snow. Gabrielle sat up and made to stand from the bed, hoping to salvage something like a breakfast from the remains of the hamper. As soon as she stood, she doubled over. A pain, like a hot knife buried in her midsection, sliced through her and she collapsed on the cold floor. She felt the warm blood gush from her sex and knew that Patenaude had exacted the worst possible revenge upon her.

I am so sorry I couldn't keep you safe, little one. He can't hurt you anymore though, my darling. No one can.

For a long while, she lay on the floor, unable to summon the strength or the will to move. She let the sadness have her and reveled in it. Her sweet baby, who Patenaude never knew existed, deserved a mother's grief.

She wasn't sure how long it was before she stood and made some attempt to gather herself. The pain in her abdomen was still sharp, and her joints stiff from too long lying out on the floor. She bathed herself as well as she could and tore her chemise to strips. There would be no salvaging it, and it would serve her better as rags to stem the flow of blood from her broken body.

Where do I go now? She could not petition the court again. The judge would send her right back, angrier than before with her for disrupting the natural order of her marriage. He would expect that Patenaude would have punished her. Would dismiss the loss of her child as an act of God—or worse—the result of her own stubborn and unfeminine temperament. No one would show her clemency from her own marriage.

Were she to return to Elisabeth and Gilbert, the town would find out and alert the judge. It might allow her a week or two of sanctuary, but no more.

By nightfall she was dressed, clean, and able to control her grief with some small success. She still ached with every movement, so she sat in one of the stiff kitchen chairs and surveyed the room. The gleam of the muzzle of the musket she returned with all of Patenaude's belongings caught the sun and commanded her eye from across the room. Beckoning. *Thank God Gilbert kept me from selling it.*

Patenaude had claimed this one had misfired one too many times, and spent money they did not have to spend to replace it.

It looks in good enough repair to me. Good enough for one last shot.

CHAPTER 19

Manon

December 1678

Say what I might about the French, their Christmas is a marvelous way to muddle through the middle of winter. Manon helped Nicole festoon the parlor with fragrant boughs of fresh evergreens accented with squat cream-colored candles that would give off a warm glow to ward off the chill of the December evening. The smell of molasses and cooking spices wafted in from the kitchen, and Manon felt more relaxed than she had in weeks. In the years she spent with the Huron, Christmastide was the only time she really yearned for the French.

The Lefebvres had cultivated a custom of hosting an intimate gathering for their friends and family two days before the church services would keep them occupied. The feast was the most magnificent of the year, and the company far more enjoyable. No governors, deputies, judges, intendants, or other royal envoys. The younger Lefebvres, the Beaumonts, Claudine, Laurent Robichaux, and a handful of other friends welcomed in the splendor they would otherwise reserve for the likes of King Louis himself.

"Perfect," Nicole declared once the last of the boughs were placed. "We'll have Nanette light the candles at the last moment so we don't risk fire. It will be lovely."

"As usual," Manon agreed. "The smell. It's a shame we can't contrive a reason to keep boughs indoors all year long."

"Then we'd soon grow immune to the scent, and that would be a real tragedy," Nicole said with a smile. Nicole wrapped her arm around Manon and kissed her temple lightly. "Now go get dressed. We'll have company before you know it."

In her room a gown of velvet, the color of her beloved evergreens, waited for her. Gabrielle was not in town to fashion it, so another, far less capable seamstress had taken the task. Though the services of a lady's maid were available at her request, she and Claudine preferred to help each other dress and style each other's hair. Manon examined the tall woman with rich brown skin and almond eyes, who looked in contrast with the rich fabrics and European fashion. *You can't exactly go down in deerskin. Just smile and make the best of it.*

Rose and Henri had already arrived when she descended the stairs, and they stood in the parlor with glasses of fine port. Manon soon found a glass in her own hand and sipped at the rich wine, glad for its restorative warmth and pungent sweetness as it trickled down the back of her throat. Pascal entered with the Beaumonts a quarter of an hour late. *I'm not sure I've had enough port for this, but I'm not going to make a fool of myself.*

She buried herself in conversation with Rose, but it only provided a diversion for so long. Pascal loomed about the edges of the room looking ready to pounce on Manon at the first sign of a break in the conversation. Mercifully, the butler announced dinner before he had his chance, and for the next two and a half hours they were treated to six courses of the richest, most elegantly prepared food in New France. Duck, fish, chicken, beef, cranberries, squash, and other dishes too numerous to remember laden down the table and were all paired with wines carefully selected by the *seigneur* himself. Manon only sampled a spoonful from each dish, but still found herself straining at her corset stays by the end of the meal.

You serve enough food to fifteen people in one meal to feed my clan for a week. Despite the excess, Manon could not find it within herself to scorn her adoptive family that night. Their celebrations might be more elaborate than those of her people, but they were entitled to their happiness. *If only you would extend the generosity beyond your inner circles.*

As the meal dissipated, the men assembled in Alexandre's study to sample some cognac while the ladies congregated in the parlor. *If I sit on the settee to gossip, I'll never stand again.* Manon made a signal to Nicole and escaped to find her cloak and boots in the hallway. There was only a thin layer of snow that night, so a quick turn in the evening air didn't seem like such an unpleasant affair.

"Couldn't abide the chatter?" Pascal said, catching up with her a few houses down. "I couldn't either, truth be told."

"You ought to be making up to Alexandre Lefebvre like a good prospective agent would," Manon chided, keeping her eyes forward and not slowing her pace.

"It's no night for business, is it?" Pascal asked. "Christmastide and all."

"I suppose you're right." Manon pulled her cloak tight, having misgauged the coolness of the night air.

"I'm glad to have caught you alone." Pascal's voice dropped considerably.

"Please don't, Pascal. I meant what I said."

"I know you did. I know you still do. But I wanted to apologize. I've badgered you, trying to convince you to do something you don't want to do. No matter how much I want you to be my wife, how much I want to build a future with you, it means nothing if you don't want it too. Haranguing you about it was unkind."

"Thank you," Manon said. "I'm glad you see it that way."

"I didn't say I agree with you. Far from it. But if all I can have is your friendship, I'll take it and be grateful."

"Friends," Manon said, extending her hand.

He took it in his own, large hand, shaking it warmly and holding it just a moment longer than was decorous. "Will you accept a small gift for the season?"

"If you insist, though I have nothing to offer you." The double meaning of her words caused her to draw in her breath. She had no wish to be cruel.

"Never mind that. Please take this and open it later." He handed her a very small parcel. "Not until after the party, please. Speaking of which, I'm going to retreat back to the bakery for some sleep. It will be an early morning at the ovens."

"Good night, Pascal."

Without preamble, he placed a soft kiss on her cheek and turned in the direction of the shop.

Manon returned to the party before anyone else missed her and did her best to be charming for another two hours. The whole time the small parcel in her cloak pocket in the hall beckoned her. When finally convention allowed her to retire, she fetched the package and retreated to the privacy of her bedroom while Claudine was still occupied helping Nicole entertain the remaining guests.

Instead of tearing into the package, she decided to savor it. She placed the parcel aside and unburdened herself of her heavy gown and restrictive stays. She loosened her hair and reveled for a few moments in the comfort of her loose chemise before sitting at her dressing table with Pascal's gift. Inside the package was a small wooden box, no doubt one that Pascal had carved himself. She spent several minutes looking over the extraordinary detail and estimated that it must have taken each spare moment he had for the last three months to complete it. Inside was a single pearl attached as a pendant to a thin gold chain. It was in the shape of a perfect teardrop and its luster could match the finest specimens in Nicole's treasury. It must have cost him a king's ransom. She clasped it on and admired the contrast of the warm ivory pearl against her tanned skin.

Pearls are tears, and this one is yours, Pascal. Let this be a sign that you have finished weeping for me, my darling man. I wish I could be what you need. Wish I could let myself love you as you deserve, but you're much better off without me.

Manon frequently felt restless in early January. The cold had kept her indoors too long and she felt drawn to the woods and the hills as songbirds were to the trees in spring. Manon bundled up against the chill and strapped on the snowshoes Alexandre had given her as his token of the season.

She walked north, ignoring the stinging in her lungs from the cold air. The exertion caused her muscles to scream where they once would have rejoiced, but she trudged on until she left the settlement behind and found herself in the thickest part of the woods. The air was cleaner, the animals active, the trees stretched to the heavens, unaware of their worth as building material and fuel.

"You've come back to us, Skenandoa." A deep baritone voice sounded to her right.

Heno.

"I had no idea I'd ventured so far," Manon confessed, the Wendat feeling foreign on her tongue.

"It's easy to wander when you follow your heart," Heno said.

"The warrior has become the poet. You're a good way from the village. What brings you this far south in winter?"

"Nothing could take me from my people but you, my beauty."
Your beauty? Am I still?

"What do you mean, Heno?"

"Father has died. I came to bring you back. And Tawendeh."

"What was your plan? To knock on the door of every Frenchman until you found me?"

"If I had to."

"Chances are you wouldn't have knocked on many doors before someone closed it with a musket. You're lucky I found you." Manon shivered at the thought of the welcome he would have had at the hands of the French. "I am very sorry about your father, Heno."

"He died well. On a hunt. Not from the white man's fever or in his bed like an old woman."

Thinking of Mother Onatah, she stifled a hiss. "I'm pleased for him. He deserved a good death after living a good life."

"That's very gracious of you to say. I know you weren't particularly fond of him."

"No, but I respected him. He was a selfless leader, though I thought he was a misguided one at times."

"I hope I will follow in his footsteps. At least in that regard." Manon's eyes widened at the realization. Heno had been elected the chief of their people. He had been groomed for the task his entire life. His father's life's ambition had been realized.

"As do I, Heno," Manon said. "Our people need a strong leader and I hope they will find it in you."

"You don't belong with those people, my beauty. Come home and be my wife. Stand by me and help me lead our people."

Manon looked at Heno, the picture of the Huron ideal. *You're strong. Confident. An upholder of traditions. Is that who I am?*

She found herself walking to the village, three paces behind Heno on the narrow path. *Why am I doing this? What do I hope to accomplish?*

As she entered the village, Heno took her hand and called the clan together. All of them openly stared at her French clothes and well-crafted snowshoes. *They won't know who I am in these ridiculous weeds.* Her people stood before her all dressed in the same shade of deerskin that made her Bordeaux-colored dress look garish.

"My people, Skenandoa has returned to us." Heno spoke with a voice loud and true. The voice of a leader.

"Your father banished her." One of the old men pushed his way to the front of the assembly. "You should not treat his memory so lightly, young hunter."

"I am the elected chief of this people, old man, and I won't have you speak against my wishes." Heno took one step in the direction of the withered man's frail frame and he relented immediately. *That works, for now. But for how long, Heno? You cannot bully your people into submission. They get enough from the French. The British. Any white face that covets their lands.*

"Where is Tawendeh?" a woman demanded. "Where is Onatah's boy?"

"In the French town," Manon said, her Wendat halting after months of disuse.

"She will go to fetch him at first light. Once we've spoken our vows." *He's serious. He means to marry me.* Two or three young women in the crowd frowned deeply. One looked openly hostile as she glanced in Manon's direction. *So true you've been to me, my hunter, though it's not as though I've been faithful to you.* The ice congealed in her stomach as she thought of Pascal. Sweet Pascal who did not order her about. Who did not command her before a throng of people.

"Heno, perhaps it's best we wait. The clan might be happier if they get to know me again," Manon whispered. She could not be seen questioning him in front of his people.

"Their happiness does not matter. You will be my wife and they will accept you as such."

And I will be your undoing. Because of me, they will question your judgment. Question your loyalty to the clan.

She was an outsider, more now than she had been as Onatah's daughter. If she married Heno, the people would have to be kind to her. They would never really welcome her as the wife of their leader. His positions would be challenged just because it was she who defended them. She pulled Heno away from the throng of her clansmen, far out of earshot.

"Heno, your father was right. You need a traditional woman to make a proper wife to a chief. That can never be me." Manon was surprised not to feel the pang of regret return to the pit of her stomach.

"But I want you." Heno moved forward and placed his hands on the sides of her arms. "My beauty, you cannot refuse me now that we are free to do as we choose."

"My hunter—Heno—" she said, hastily dropping her former endearment. "Take a lesson from your father's example. In your heart do you think I am the best wife you could choose for the sake of our clan?"

"That doesn't matter, Skenandoa." Heno's grip tightened.

"It's *all* that matters. All that *should* matter to you, Heno."

"If that is your choice, then so be it." Heno's hands dropped to his side. "Do you think a Frenchman will offer what I do? Love? A place of honor? Respect?"

Manon's eyes narrowed at the last word. Few Frenchmen cared for the wits their wives possessed, it was true, but Heno was an exception among their people as well.

"Heno, I cannot."

"You'll end up a Frenchman's whore, then," Heno spat. Manon thought of Pascal. Heno had no idea that she had already cast aside the love of another good man for much the same reason. Her hand rose to the pearl at her throat and she thought of the contrast in their reactions to her refusals. She thought of the lazy summer afternoons in the back of a wagon with Pascal and compared it to her nighttime trysts with Heno. *Which man would put my needs above his own? I don't think there is much question.*

"You don't understand them, Heno. And I will not waste my breath trying to convince you. You will just have to trust that I am doing what is best for you, for me, and for our people."

"So be it," Heno said. "But you should send young Tawendeh back to us. His place is here."

At that very moment, Tawendeh—Théodore—was likely playing with the Lefebvre children in the warm glow of the nursery fireplace. He was cared for and loved. He was learning his way in the world, even if it was not the way of the hunter.

"He will stay with me. It was our mother's wish that I would care for him, and that is precisely what I will do."

"You have turned your back on your people, Skenandoa—or should I say Manon? Father *was* right. You're no Huron."

"No. I might have been once, but I am not anymore."

Manon returned to the Lefebvre house only moments before dinner was set to appear at the table. She discarded her cloak at the stand in the hall and took a few moments to warm her hands before the fire. *The next time you go wandering in winter, be smart enough to return early enough to change into a dry dress before dinner.*

After the numerous feasts in honor of the Christmas season and New Year, the fare in early January was plainer, much to Manon's relief. A simple stew with a portion of good bread was a welcome change after the endless courses of fine cuisine. Manon felt the muscles in her shoulders relax as the warm medley of beef, potato, onions, and carrots slid down her throat and restored her after a day in the cold.

She rarely added overmuch to the dinner conversation, but tonight she reveled in silence. She watched as Alexandre, Claudine, and Nicole chatted companionably about a visit from the governor. She watched as Hélène practiced her table manners, studying her mother and Claudine with an attentive eye.

I have judged this family too harshly. Nicole has taken me in—twice—without any thought for the effect it might have for her among her people. It's not her fault that the rest of the town won't ac-

cept me. But I can accept Nicole and her kindness. Alexandre's be-grudging affection, too.

Though Pascal crept into her thoughts, and his image proved as stubborn as the man himself, refusing to leave, Manon stayed below, conversing in the parlor for a solid hour after dinner. It had been her custom to retreat to her little study with a book or to the nursery to visit with Théodore. Tonight she spent time with her family, making the effort, for once, to be part of them.

When she finally retreated to the solitude of her bedroom, she looked at her reflection. She admired the creamy pearl at the base of her throat and thought of the young man who had so thought-fully bestowed the gift on her. He was a hardworking man. He cared for her. Not her looks. Not her position, or lack of one. He truly cared for her.

She went to her desk in the next room over, pulled a piece of parchment from the massive wooden desk, and dipped her quill in the black mire of her inkpot.

> *Dearest Pascal,*
> *You say that you have loved me since I was a mere child. I was far too young to understand what romantic love was. I was a girl only aware that I had no place in the world. I was so heartbroken by the rejection I felt, I was unable to see the gifts I had in my possession. I am ashamed to admit my heart had not grown any wiser in the years since. Until now. I am sorry for the pain I have caused you, and I will try never to hurt you again. Our relationship will continue on in the manner of your choosing. If you cannot forgive me for the events of recent weeks, I will hope to—in time—regain your friendship. If you can forgive my foolishness, I will accept your previous offer with open arms and an open heart.*
> *Whatever you decide, please know that my love will always be with you.*
> *Your Manon*

With the note, she included a small golden brooch Nicole had given her for a birthday in years past before her return to the

Huron, which she cared for greatly. It had a clever little compartment where she had kept pine needles to remind her of the scent of home. She emptied the dried needles into her chamber pot and removed the scissors from her desk. Carefully she snipped a lock of jet-black hair from the back of her head and twisted it into a coil until it was small enough to fit in the brooch. She sealed the note and trinket into a small pouch and descended the stairs, where she spotted one of the footmen.

"Place this in Pascal Giroux's hands and none other," Manon commanded. The footman looked at her in surprise. So often Manon went out of her way to avoid soliciting the help of the servants, even when they offered it to her readily. To see her give commands with such confidence would have startled any of the household within earshot.

The next step is up to you, Pascal. Please choose wisely, my love.

Manon went back to her room and removed all the trappings of the French culture until she wore nothing but her chemise and Pascal's pearl. *There is a woman somewhere between Manon Lefebvre and Skenandoa of the Big Turtle clan. I must discover her. Invent her if I must. The people of this settlement may not accept me, but they will. Manon Giroux will have a place in this land. And our children as well. I will not fail them. I will not fail myself again.*

CHAPTER 20

Claudine

January 1679

I hope this makes you happy, darling baby sister. Claudine stared out the window and clutched her bouquet of evergreens and holly. *If you disapprove, now is the moment to send down the lightning bolt to strike me down.*

"What are you doing, darling?" Nicole asked, fluttering about and straightening every fold and bit of lace on her sister's gown.

"Just checking the weather. It's of no matter. Are we ready for church?"

"It won't be long. Alexandre will signal when it's time to go. I'll leave you alone for a few moments to collect your thoughts, darling." Claudine nodded her appreciation to her sister as she exited the room with Manon. These were the last moments the room would be her own, and she wanted to savor them.

Claudine looked critically at the reflection in the mirror. She wore a fine gown of rich blue velvet with a cream underdress. The lace trim matched the cream, highlighting the blue against Claudine's creamy skin. Gabrielle had nearly finished the gown before she was hauled back into the wild. Nicole herself had finished the last of the detailed sewing. She didn't have Gabrielle's skill, but her stitches were even and true.

The dress was modest, despite the luxuriant fabric, and would serve well for many an event that called for elegant but not extravagant dress. This was not the elaborate gala the Lefebvres had thrown for Emmanuelle, nor anything like the grandiose social event that Claudine envisioned only a year or two before. Claudine insisted on a simpler affair out of respect for Emmanuelle and out of deference for the fact that this was Laurent's second marriage. It was just grand enough to befit the Robichaux and Lefebvre family standings, but no more.

Alexandre knocked at the door, and Claudine descended the stairs.

"You look so gorgeous, my baby girl." Bernadette cupped her daughter's face in her hands and placed a featherlight kiss on each cheek. *I'm not really your baby girl, Maman. I'd trade my life to bring her back to you.*

"To church, everyone," Alexandre announced, opening the door to the wintery morning for his family. "The groom and the good Father await us."

The snow required the wagons and carriages to be stored until spring, making sleighs and sleds the main mode of transportation. Despite Claudine's pleas to keep the event as simple as decorum would allow, Alexandre had out his finest sleigh, polished to the luster of shimmering crystal, and four magnificent horses to pull it through the center of town. It was just before midday on a Tuesday, and more than a few people exited their homes and businesses to see the glinting equipage passing by.

Claudine stood at the door to the nave, Thomas Deschamps at her right side. The church was festooned with evergreen boughs and red winterberries, the only flora readily available. Though it didn't have the delicate grace of spring flowers or summer blooms, nor the dramatic punch of color of autumn leaves, the scent of pine and the pop of the red berries against the green backdrop were inviting enough to make Claudine forgo any regret about not marrying in the warmer months as so many others chose to do.

Laurent stood at the altar, tall and confident. He wore an expression that reflected the solemnity of the occasion, but still radiated happiness. *Because I said yes. Because I am here.* The reality of the depth of his affection both flattered and frightened her.

"You're so beautiful, my angel," he whispered as Thomas Deschamps placed his daughter's hands in Laurent's.

"And you as well." Claudine smiled up at Laurent, speaking with sincerity. His blue velvet *justaucorps* matched her gown and masked the slight sag in his midsection rather well. She clasped his hand as a sign of solidarity and turned to face the priest.

Within moments they were man and wife. Claudine accepted Laurent's chaste kiss and let him lead her back down the aisle.

Well-wishers filled every corner of the church. The Robichaux and Lefebvre names commanded too much respect for the settlement to ignore a wedding that tied the houses—even if it was for a second union. Despite this, Alexandre agreed only to invite their closest friends and a few of the most important dignitaries in town. Most understood the reasons behind the modest nature of the celebration, but Claudine was certain that some would feel slighted.

It doesn't feel right to dance, to laugh, to celebrate, so soon after Emmanuelle's passing. Less than a year. No one seems to think anything of Laurent taking her sister as a wife. It's as though she never existed for you.

The more rational part of Claudine realized they had known Emmanuelle but for a few months as a part of their social circle. She had been a quiet woman, a sweet-natured woman, but never one who called much attention to herself. All they knew was that a good excuse for a joyous social gathering was being passed over, and there were not so many occasions that the loss wasn't felt. The less understanding part of Claudine's nature spited those who had not instantly recognized Emmanuelle's kindness, grace, and largeness of spirit.

Claudine had left all the details of the nuptial luncheon in Nicole's capable hands. Claudine didn't care to be bothered with the particulars of the menu and the guest list when there was such an accomplished hostess at her disposal. When Claudine took her place at the table between her new husband and her sister, she realized that she'd done well to entrust the meal to her sister. Four courses—and all her favorite things. Rich onion soup, roasted goose with apples, the best bread from the Beaumont Bakery, a wonderful light cider procured by Alexandre for the occasion, and Elisabeth's incomparable *millefeuille* pastries for the capstone. Had the dinner been a family-only affair, she would not have been able to resist licking the pastry crumbs from the back of her gilded fork.

"You've got a gift," Claudine said to her sister in a moment of quiet as the meal had faded and the party spread to the parlor.

"Nothing too good for my sweet sister," Nicole said, kissing Claudine's cheek.

"Thank you, Nicole. You've been better to me than I deserve."

"Not a bit. I think your husband is anxious to get home, though." Laurent was in conversation with Alexandre, but never appeared more distracted in all his life.

"I think you may be right."

"Just remember, dear. Let him lead. These things will all work out."

Claudine hugged her sister and hoped that Nicole's optimism would spread to her own heart.

Claudine surveyed the rooms that would serve as her personal bedchamber and sitting room at the Robichaux house—her house— for the rest of her marriage. The room that had been Emmanuelle's. Laurent had bid the servants to remove Emmanuelle's personal effects, but her presence was still there. The furniture was a deep mahogany that contrasted with the powdery, pale blue papered walls without being too harsh or discordant. It was nothing like the pinks and yellows with light oaks and pines that Emmanuelle would have chosen for herself; but still, she lingered. Whether it was her scent, her spirit, her sweetness that remained behind, Claudine knew not, but she was convinced she shouldn't find the room a peaceful place for all its comforts.

She sat at the dressing table, her sable hair brushed into a sheen. She wore a chemise of the softest muslin, gifted to her by Nicole. She was a vision of bridal beauty, as her duty sounded at the door. She opened the door to Laurent already *en déshabillé,* forgoing his *justaucorps* and breeches for a dressing gown.

"Do you like your rooms?" His voice wavered just slightly as he spoke.

"Very much. They're very beautiful." The second sentence, at the least, wasn't a lie. One would have to be blind not to appreciate the well-crafted furnishings and soft linens.

"I'm very glad," Laurent said. He stepped closer, shutting the gap between them. He wrapped his right arm around her waist, pulling her close. Slowly he craned his neck down and placed a kiss on her lips. This time he needn't ask. She was his to claim as he liked.

She closed her eyes and waited for him to finish. When he pulled back, he surveyed her face with a curious expression. He cupped her breasts with his hands and rubbed her nipples with his thumbs, causing her breath to catch uncomfortably in her throat.

"You're so beautiful, my angel." The same words he whispered at the altar. He kissed her again, his lips hungrily seeking her own this time. She willed her breathing to slow, but her nerves prevented her from relaxing her muscles.

"To bed?" His expression was hopeful, nervous, almost fearful as a boy's moments before his first tumble with a girl in a hay pile in the barn. Claudine nodded.

He did his best to keep his heavy frame from pressing her uncomfortably into the mattress. But he wasn't entirely successful. She raised her chemise dutifully and allowed his fingers to explore the depths of her sex, made damp by his caressing of her tender breasts.

"May I?" His question was loaded with all the expectation she could imagine. She wanted to spread her legs and let him claim her as his wife. *It's your duty to him, to the colony, to the Church, and your king. Your duty to yourself.* But as she breathed in the sweetly perfumed air of her new bedroom, laced with dried rose petals, she could not let Emmanuelle's husband have her.

"Just hold me, Laurent. For tonight, just hold me."

He looked pained as he rolled off his young bride, but did not utter a word of complaint. He rolled her to her side pulled her to his chest, his arms tucked protectively around her, his stiff manhood pressing into her buttocks until it finally grew flaccid. For long minutes—perhaps hours—she listened to his breathing as he drifted off into sleep.

I had no business taking my sister's husband as my own. I will look after Zacharie at least and finish the job my sister started, even if I can't be a proper companion to her husband.

His arm grew heavy on her torso, but she dared not move. She willed sleep to take her away for a few hours, but it eluded her like the answer to a riddle she ought to have been able to solve. When the dawn light crept through her window, she thanked the stars that she would soon be free to stretch and move, despite her lack of rest. It would be a very long day, but no longer than the night of purgatory she'd just spent.

Zacharie filled her days with endless gurgles and gassy smiles. He was a darling baby, but she did not know how Nanny Simon had managed to spend so many hours alone in his presence without going stark raving mad for want of conversation. She was free to spend her time as she chose, but she felt compelled to spend as many hours mothering the sweet boy as she could bear. It was what Emmanuelle would have done. It was the least she could do for Laurent. Four times he had come to her room, and each occasion found her with some sort of an excuse not to give herself to him. The time would come when he would either force the issue or ease his frustrations elsewhere. Neither thought gave her any comfort.

In a moment of desperation, Claudine wrote to Nicole in hopes she would be able to visit and relieve her from the doldrums for a short while. The missive was returned with an apology, that an essential dinner demanded her attention, but as the note was returned with Manon, who brought along her sewing basket, the blow was of short duration.

Settled in her parlor, the maid sent off in search of refreshment, Claudine pulled out her own embroidery and set to work with Manon, who continued her progress on a large quilt made from lovely scraps she had cut into squares and triangles, which she pieced together into an intricate geometric pattern resembling a compass rose. It was large enough for a married couple's bed rather than a single woman's but Manon didn't volunteer the recipient of the quilt and Claudine wasn't in such spirits as to try to pry it out of her.

"So Rose is left with just one pupil," Claudine commented, to make conversation. She still had time for her studies, but people would look askance at a married woman continuing her schooling. If nothing else, Claudine endeavored to make no more disturbances in her social circles than she already had. "That must be lonesome for her. For both of you."

"She's pining for you all," Manon admitted, smoothing her completed square on her lap to inspect her stitches. "She told me as much. Without her students she has little to do outside of her domestic duties. I think it grows tiresome for her. And I'm afraid I won't be able to offer my distraction, little as it is, for much longer."

"What aren't you telling me?" Claudine's playful nudge entered her voice for the first time since Emmanuelle had died. "You know a secret is worth gold in this place."

"All the more reason to cling to it," Manon retorted with a laugh. "No, to be honest, I just think it's time I focus on life outside the classroom. I'm eighteen years old, after all. Nothing more interesting than that."

Claudine nodded her understanding. She tried to enjoy her lessons as her sister had done, but she could never conjure up the same enthusiasm, even once she'd recognized their utility.

"I feel bad for her," Claudine said, thinking of the sleeping boy upstairs. "It can be wearisome to stay at home all day with nothing all that interesting to do."

"Especially for a woman like Rose," Manon agreed. "She's too well educated to take idleness in stride."

"I expect she'll become more active in her church activities. They need someone like her to organize the charity work." The *R* on her monogrammed handkerchief was not to Claudine's liking, so she started it over again.

"Anything to give her some diversion would be welcome, I'm sure." The pieces of Manon's third square hadn't quite taken shape, but Claudine studied her method as she went along. *Something else you excel at. I shouldn't be surprised. But sewing, charity work, children . . . what else is there for us?*

"Has Pascal heard from Gabrielle?" Claudine asked. She thought with guilt about how rarely her friend's fate crossed her mind. Between her marriage and caring for the baby, the world outside her front door now seemed like an abstract problem for others to handle.

"I haven't heard anything from Pascal in several days," Manon said, her eyes never deviating from the scraps of yellow and blue fabric in her hands. "But I'm confident that he would have called on the Lefebvres or sent a note if he had word from her. They know we worry as they do."

"Is everything all right?" Claudine asked, setting her embroidery down.

"Oh, fine," Manon said, still not looking up. "He's just extremely busy, you know."

"Of course," Claudine said. *And you've quarreled, but I won't pester you.* "I do worry for Gabrielle. I hope Patenaude learned his lesson from the hearing."

Manon shook her head. "If anything, it probably made things worse for her. He's not the kind to ignore such public shaming."

"If indeed it was a shaming for him. It seemed like the judge placed all the blame on her shoulders, though he was the one who did the beating." The handkerchief was now wrinkled from her angry grip and would have to be pressed before she could continue embroidering.

"I won't disabuse the judge for deciding within the confines of the law, but it was cruel to send her back for more abuse." Manon's expression was as solemn as Claudine had ever seen. The effort to restrain her venom against the French laws was clearly not easily borne. "And it was silly she was forced to marry at all."

"I suppose they need more children to help hold the colony safe from the British. It does seem unfair that she was forced to a different standard than I was just because of where we were born." Claudine sat back in her chair, feeling tremendously grateful. *I might be a terrible wife to Laurent, but at least the choice was my own.* "I'd suggest we venture back out to the homestead, but I don't think the roadways out there are in any condition for it."

"I'm afraid you're right," Manon agreed, looking out the parlor window. There was a thick blanket of snow that coated the buildings, making them appear as though encased in clouds. "And I don't think we'd be welcome any more than we were the first time."

Claudine nodded her agreement, smoothing the rumpled handkerchief with her sweaty hand. The crackle from the fireplace and the warm cider chased the chill of winter from the Robichaux house, but she doubted Gabrielle was as fortunate.

Chapter 21

Gabrielle

January 1679

For weeks she planned out the task in her mind and dreaded killing herself in the process. She barely knew how to fire a musket, but she had to repair Patenaude's discarded weapon well enough to function properly. She took the rusted old musket to her kitchen table and looked it over. Patenaude didn't care for the fussy trigger and claimed that it tended to lock up when he was loading it. That's how he justified spending their last few *sous* to replace it, but Gabrielle hadn't questioned him. She didn't dare speak unless he asked her a direct question. *It makes for a much nicer environment. Almost as nice as when he's gone. Almost.*

Carefully she scrubbed away at the rust and let the amber flakes fall onto the scarred tabletop. She took a light coating of grease made from rancid butter to free up the trigger as it bound up when she squeezed. She was certain it wasn't good for the gun, but it only had to work once.

After an hour of her inexpert tinkering, she took the gun out into the snow-covered pastures that lay fallow with no plans for a crop the next season. She loaded the gun as she had seen Patenaude and her own father do countless times.

This is lunacy. You're going to get yourself killed. Or worse, maimed. He'll know exactly what you did and you'll be all the less able to defend yourself with a missing hand or foot. Stop being a damned fool.

But Gabrielle did not heed her inner voice. She took the loaded musket and aimed it at a knot that sat heart-level on a tree about thirty feet away. With her first shot, she made her mark, blasting away bits of bark from the tree. She would only make the one practice shot. She couldn't risk the gun breaking beyond repair or the neighbors becoming suspicious of the musket fire. She only had the chance to make one shot. She had to make it count.

She returned to the house and sought out Patenaude's oldest patched woolen breeches, which would never cease to smell of alcohol. She cinched them with a leather strap, but still they hung ridiculously off her slender frame, like brown skin off a sickly leper. It was necessary though, as they were easier for moving about in the snow than her tattered skirts. She strapped on Patenaude's old snowshoes, slung the musket over her shoulder, and went back out into the biting cold January afternoon.

She trudged along the trail that Patenaude favored, hoping he wasn't days out. He ought to be on his way home by now—the last snowstorm would have driven the animals into shelter and the trapping wouldn't be worth his time. An hour from the cabin, she found the tree she'd been looking for. It would shelter her from view, but allowed for a clear shot onto the path that Patenaude always took on his way home. She climbed the tree, perched on a solid branch, and lay in wait. Her prey had to be along soon.

It was less than an hour before she heard the crunch of footsteps on virgin snow. She raised the musket and closed her left eye. She took a deep breath and exhaled to steady her hands. The sound of male voices wafted as far as her tree despite the dampening of the sounds in the snow. They were too far away to see clearly, but there were at least three men. *Damn it to hell and back. He isn't alone.*

Gabrielle hadn't counted on that possibility and cursed herself for her folly. He'd brought home his hunting companions before, charming men such as they were. She'd imagined the perfect scenario in her head and didn't allow for any deviations from her plan. *Dolt! They're less than an hour from home and here you stand in*

these wretched pants with a loaded, perfectly functional musket.
Women have been hanged for less.

With a colorful oath, Gabrielle descended the tree and tossed
the musket into the brambles. She could fetch it later if it was
missed. She'd think of an excuse for its absence later. She cut
through neighboring pastures to reach the farm before Patenaude
and his companions, trudging as fast as the snowshoes allowed. She
hoped her head start, light load, and cross-country path would give
her a few minutes' advantage over the men.

Seeing no trace of Patenaude when the cabin came into view,
she flung open the creaky door and threw herself through the doorway. Her lungs were screaming from the exertion, but she did not
dare pause. She tore off Patenaude's cast-off clothing, placed them
in his trunk, and donned her ragged skirts and patched woolen
jacket, the chief virtue of which was that they had been lying by the
warm hearth. She stoked up the fire, adding two logs and standing
as close as she dared to chase away the frost from her fingertips and
toes. She scanned the room—nothing seemed out of place that anyone would notice. There were tracks from the snowshoes, but there
were any number of explanations as to why she would have ventured out on them in the past three days since the last snowfall. *Act*
normally and be a model hostess. Maybe he won't beat you when
they've left if you treat them kindly.

She had to trust that she looked as normal as possible, and settled into her chair with some mending. She forced her breathing to
slow and her hands to steady with reasonable success. Not five
minutes later, a knock sounded at the door. The sound of two, perhaps three, male voices wafted in through the door. *Why did I leave*
the musket behind? It may not have been him on the road at all. God
knows who's at the door. Patenaude wouldn't have knocked.

In the space of a moment, visions of her dead body splayed, her
crimson blood befouling the sparkling white snow, danced in her
mind. *I will not have survived Patenaude only to meet my end at the*
hands of a few haggard bandits. She scanned the room for a weapon
but only saw a convenient stick of firewood that might serve well to
bash one of them in the head. The other two would disarm her before she could inflict more damage, but she would at least do her
level best to defend herself.

"Who are you and what do you want?" Gabrielle summoned her voice from the depths of her chest, trying to make herself sound forceful.

"Jacques Verger," one of the voices answered. *The smelly man from our wedding.* Gabrielle rolled her eyes and cast the firewood aside. He might have been crude—he might have had an aversion to soap that Gabrielle couldn't understand—but he was not dangerous. She opened the door and allowed Verger and his companions in.

The other man with him was just as gruff-looking, and just as foul-smelling. He had to be Verger's grown son she'd heard of but never met. Between them, Patenaude was draped with an arm over each shoulder, his head drooped. *Drunk again, the swine.*

"Oh dear. Bring him in and lay him on the bed, please." Gabrielle shook her head at the sight of her unconscious husband. He'd awake with a monstrous headache and a mood to match. The men didn't look her in the eye, nor did they follow her instructions, leaving Patenaude's limp form just inside the door. *Kind men, to be sure, but if they tell Patenaude you were rude, you'll pay.*

"Thank you, gentlemen. Is there any refreshment I can offer you? I might have a little spruce beer left if you like. Lugging him about must have been thirsty work."

Jacques and the boy who must have been his son exchanged a glance.

"You needn't feel awkward. I'm sure my husband would want me to be hospitable even if he's not at his best." Gabrielle mentally scanned the meager contents of her cupboard. Little to serve that wouldn't embarrass her.

"Not at his best?" Jacques gave her a questioning look.

"Too much drink on the hunt again, I assume," Gabrielle said, rolling her eyes in the direction of her husband passed out on the floor.

"You might say that," Verger said, his expression humorless. "And while he was neck-deep in his flask, he ended up shooting a rock and getting himself a chest full of rock and musket ball."

Gabrielle walked over to Patenaude's form and pulled back his coat. There was so much blood she couldn't begin to determine how badly he was hurt. She'd been so consumed with appearing normal when the men arrived, she didn't notice the mud and blood on her husband's clothes.

"Will he be all right?" she asked. The thought of weeks—months—as his nursemaid sent her heart thudding against her rib cage. He would be horrific.

"That all depends on how you look at it, ma'am. Ain't nothing going to bother him ever again, so I'd guess you could say he's all right as a man can be."

"You mean he's—"

"Dead, ma'am. I'm sorry to bear the news, but there it is." Verger's expression, to his credit, did show a trace of compassion. "We'll leave you to see to things. I'm sure you'll want to let the folks in town know so he can have a proper funeral and all."

Funerals cost money I don't have. Gabrielle kept herself from speaking the thought aloud, and managed to indicate they should move him to the corner of the house farthest from the fire. It would keep the stink from spreading sooner than it had to.

"Would you be so kind as to help me take him into town in the morning? I'm sure we can manage with the wagon and Olivier's horse." Her husband's Christian name felt foreign on her tongue, but she would not win favors by appearing to be anything less than dutiful.

"We've delivered him to you and you'll have to take care of this on your own," Verger said. He offered her a curt nod of the head, gave his son a smart rap on his chest with the back of his hand, and they backed out the door.

Gabrielle ran her fingers through her hair, exhaling. She crossed the room over to her husband's broken body and delivered a swift kick to his ribs that resulted in a satisfying *crack* of bone that, for once, was not her own.

The sun hung low in the sky. It was easily a two-hour walk into town without the cover of snow and it would be dark long before she was able to make her way there.

I will not spend another night here. Not with his rotting corpse. I will be free of him tonight.

Once again, she donned her snowshoes and bundled up in her thickest cloak and Patenaude's as well. He wouldn't be needing it. She thought longingly of the woolen breeches—or a cleaner facsimile thereof. It would make the trek into town far easier than carrying her skirt and petticoat up above her ankles as she walked as deftly as she could across the packed snow. She could not be seen in the settlement in men's clothes, however, so her skirts she would wear no matter how cumbersome they were.

She was not a mile into her journey when she realized her claim about taking the body into town by horse and wagon was completely unfounded. The road would only be passable by sled and nimble horses. She'd have killed old Xavier in the attempt, not that the loss would be all that great. Were it not for the snowshoes, the trip would have been impossible for her as well.

Trudge on, she told herself as she shivered in the dying light of the day. *Trudge on.*

And so she did until she reached the door of the Beaumonts, promptly fainting in Pascal's arms at the most welcome sight of the only man who had always loved her.

Elisabeth kept Gabrielle in bed as she had done in the weeks after her father had beaten her, left her for dead, and ran off into the Canadian wild for the last time. Gabrielle was lucky to have escaped any frostbite or permanent injury, but she was weak and frail. She was certain Elisabeth imagined the least ailment carrying her off, and Gabrielle hadn't the energy to contradict her. Gilbert enlisted Alexandre's equipage and manservants to fetch the body. Pascal arranged for a simple service that only the four eldest members of the Beaumont household bothered to attend.

"You're a brave woman," the priest declared after the blessings were spoken for the departed. She had not shed a tear for the cruel man. "But time will heal your wounds, my daughter. You will find another lord and master as worthy as your first. You must pray for it, and I will do the same."

I'm afraid my prayers will not resemble yours, Father. I will pray for a life of solitude and deliverance from cruelty rather than submit to another marriage. You cannot force me to live through that hell again.

Gabrielle only nodded and accepted the condolences of the priest, who thought he was comforting a woman bereaved instead of a woman freed from the shackles of a hate-filled marriage. For the rest of her days she would be forced to ignore Olivier Pate-naude's shortcomings and speak of his memory with deference. It was a cruel joke to offer such a man this level of consideration, but she had the chance to live as a respectable widow. She had to take it.

She only spent an hour out of bed for the service, and found herself ushered back to the comfort of her bedroom by Elisabeth. There were days in the confines of the cabin she thought she would never feel truly warm again, but the quilts and well-tended fires at the Beaumonts' home soon thawed her body. The ice in the pit of her stomach took longer to melt. It was only when Elisabeth gave up her protest and allowed Gabrielle a length of fabric so she had an occupation that she began to feel more like herself. It was just some plain brown wool she could fashion into a serviceable skirt, but it was the first new garment she'd had since before her wedding and would be the only one in good repair.

Though Elisabeth meant well, and wanted to see the girl she loved as a daughter returned to health, the long hours in bed only gave her time to feel every sore muscle, every bruise, every scrape from the falls onto the rough wooden floor. It gave her mind every chance to replay every scene of Patenaude's cruelty over and over again. Worse, she was able to recall each moment of the days where she lay in bed, bleeding and cramping, as her child slipped away from her.

I'm so sorry I failed you, baby. I can't say I dreamed of you. I can't say I wanted you to have the father you did. But I was honor-bound to protect you, and I wasn't able to. I am so sorry.

Sleep only relieved her for a few hours at a stretch. It left her more irritable than if she hadn't slept at all. She felt trapped in the four stone walls, and often imagined them turning damp and grow-ing with moss. The imagined smell of mold and decay overpowered her. She had the sense of foreboding that they would soon close in upon her, the muck crushing her, enveloping her. Ultimately eras-ing her very existence.

Of course the room was bright, warm, cheerful . . . and plentiful, appetizing food arrived along with Elisabeth, Gilbert, and Pascal's lively company frequently. She doubted whether King Louis and Queen Maria Theresa's babies and all the other royal bastards re-ceived such care from their nurses, maids, and valets. Certainly those ministrations were not given with the same love as Gabrielle felt flooded upon her.

All the same, her womb felt hollow and her heart encased in ice for the life she'd been unable to protect. For the months of suffering. For the cruelty of the men—first her father, then her husband—who had failed *her*.

All she had now were a few yards of brown wool and some thread to keep her mind from the pain. She made sure each stitch was tiny and even—painstakingly so. She made no haste, and was none too hesitant to remove a stitch and start anew. The wool would give long before her stitches, and this gave her pleasure to create something durable. But at last the hour came when she could no longer work on perfecting the seams, else the fabric would fray irreparably.

I will ask Elisabeth for all the mending, despite her protests, too. And all the Lefebvres and the Robichauxes. I must have an occupation or I will go mad.

She smoothed the wool over her like a blanket. It was warm. It was clean and new. It may not have been a thing of beauty, but it was a thing created of her own hands, and she felt pride in her accomplishment.

"Thank you!" Gabrielle said, smiling to the point of discomfort at the sight of Elisabeth ushering in Claudine and Manon. Gilbert and Pascal entered behind them, both carrying in heaping baskets of mending. Alexandre's breeches, Zacharie's nightgowns, their own chemises. Tattered hems, worn cuffs, holes in need of patching. A treasure trove of activity to keep her company. She sat up straight in her bed and ran her hand over the textures of linen and wool and muslin in the nearest basket. *I will make them whole again.*

"It's not every day you're greeted with a smile when you bring someone a pile of work." Claudine chuckled as she placed her basket of mending within reach of Gabrielle's bed.

Elisabeth shook her head in disapproval. "You need to be resting. Not working."

"I promise, I will rest better with something to do," Gabrielle said, looking up at her foster mother, hoping she conveyed all the sincerity she felt. "A little exertion will help me sleep."

"She's not wrong, Elisabeth," Gilbert said, a gentle scold in his voice. "Let her have something to do."

"I think we can trust our Gabrielle to mend while she's mending," Manon said with warmth. Pascal set his basket down wordlessly and headed back out with a brief nod to his sister.

"Heaven knows I don't mind passing on the chore," Claudine confessed. "Of all the domestic duties I've inherited, mending will be the last to endear itself to me."

"I've no great talent for it myself," Manon agreed. "And Rose has sent over a few things as well. She's not been feeling her best. Nothing serious from what I understand, just the unborn babe making his presence known, but she's grateful for the help."

Gabrielle smiled wider than she had in over a year. She could breathe new life into the clothes and make them not only wearable, but also beautiful again.

"Sit, please," Gabrielle said, gesturing to the empty chairs that Elisabeth, Pascal, and Gilbert occupied of an evening.

"I'll get you all something to nibble at while you chat," Elisabeth said with a dubious glance at all the clothes that now dominated the small bedchamber.

"Thank you," Gabrielle said, watching the sweet-natured woman exit the room with a martyred sigh. *I know you're trying to protect me, but the real threat was buried three days ago, sweet lady. I promise you I will be well.*

"I'm so grateful you all came to visit me," Gabrielle said. "And you've given me a gift."

"I can understand the agony of being idle," Manon said. "Hopefully you'll get some hours of occupation out of the mending, if not amusement."

"I'm sure I will," Gabrielle said.

"I'm just happy you're back with us," Claudine said, sipping from one of the glasses of cider Elisabeth placed on the small bedside table as they spoke. There was also a plate of the good cream puffs Gabrielle had longed for in her absence. In the past they had seemed too cloyingly sweet, but now they sated her hunger as nothing else would. Elisabeth kissed Gabrielle on the forehead and left the girls to their discussion. Gabrielle supposed it took a good deal of effort not to tack on an admonition that she ought to rest.

"As am I," Gabrielle said earnestly. "If only that damned judge had listened, the baby might . . ."

Claudine crossed over to the bed in a flash and cradled Gabrielle in her arms. "I'm so sorry" was all she was able to mutter. It was all Gabrielle needed to hear. No platitudes about another child. A kinder husband. A better future. She let the tears fall, knowing that she was in company who would not expect her to conceal her grief.

"He ought to have listened," Manon said. "And he'll be made to understand his folly. I'll see to it that Alexandre writes a letter to the Intendant and the governor, since anything I write wouldn't be read by anyone who matters."

"And Laurent, too," Claudine said, still holding her friend. "It may not help your baby, but it may save someone else."

Gabrielle, unable to speak, nodded her appreciation as she dried her tears on the sleeve of her chemise.

"I'll take it," Gabrielle said, reaching for the basket heaping with four large loaves of bread along with an assortment of rolls and sweet pastries. The Sisters did their own baking most of the time, but commissioned Elisabeth to furnish finer breads and baked goods when they were expecting company of particular importance. Gabrielle knew not who the Sisters were entertaining, but she was ready to escape the confines of the bakery for an hour or two.

"Are you sure—" Elisabeth began, moving the basket out of her reach.

"Yes, she's sure," Gilbert interrupted, taking the basket from his wife and handing it to Gabrielle. "It's been three weeks since she left this house and a short walk will do her a world of good."

"Very well." Elisabeth sighed, returning to the mound of dough before her. "But be home before dark, please." Elisabeth hadn't made such an admonition since Gabrielle's earliest days at the bakery.

"Of course." Gabrielle grabbed the basket and her cloak.

Her muscles screamed at the exertion, but she fought through the discomfort. The convent was only a quarter of an hour away on foot, and while she was thrilled for the escape, she was equally glad she hadn't farther to travel.

Sister Marie-Jeanne, a young nun with a round, kindly face, opened the door and accepted the basket with a smile. "Bless you, my dear. Sister Catherine will settle the account."

"Naturally," Gabrielle said with a dismissive nod. Even if the Sisters forgot to settle the account for months, there wasn't a soul in the Beaumont Bakery who would ask for the money. Elisabeth remembered her months living at the convent before she married Gilbert with too much fondness to let accounts trouble her.

"Is that Mademoiselle Giroux come to visit?" Sister Anne, now the most senior of the order below the Mother Superior, walked into the entryway. Gabrielle remembered her from her first days in the settlement after the Beaumonts had taken her on. She'd been portly and spry, if not young. Now she was stooped, and her face lined with the burden of leading the daily running of the Ursulines.

"Madame Patenaude for quite some time, Sister, but it is me."

"You'll come and have a cup of coffee with an old woman, won't you?" Sister Anne turned to allow Gabrielle entrance to the common room.

"I've not had it before, but I'd be happy to join you, Sister." Gabrielle removed her cloak and placed it in the waiting hands of another one of the younger nuns. The King hadn't sent young ladies as brides for the settlers in more than five years, and there was something of an air of loneliness left behind.

"Come sit by the fire, my dear." Sister Anne had rearranged the room somewhat since her last visit. She had appointed her favorite chair along with a sturdy little table next to the fire. A graceless earthenware kettle and two cups filled every inch of the table. "Try this, my dear. I confess it's one of the little luxuries I miss most from France. The good Seigneur Lefebvre sent me a tin when the last ship came in from the mother country."

"Kind of him. I remember Madame Beaumont saying he was as giddy as a schoolboy when it arrived. He ordered a massive platter of pastries to go along with it. He'll be desolate when his supply runs out."

"I'll be none too pleased myself, but it will give me enjoyment to share a cup with you and hear all your news."

Gabrielle sniffed at the dark brew as decorously as she could before sipping. *Lord, it's bitter. How could anyone enjoy this?* But she could not refuse the Sister's hospitality and would have to leave an empty cup behind her.

"I am so sorry to hear about your husband, my dear." Sister Anne looked into the crackling blaze thoughtfully.

"Thank you, Sister." Gabrielle shifted in her seat. *I'm not sorry. Not one bit, but I can't tell you that.*

"Have you made any plans?"

"Nothing definite, Sister. But I've some ideas." To cover the taste of the thick, bitter liquid, Gabrielle nibbled at one of the buttery biscuits Elisabeth had sent with her.

"Very good, very good. No need to rush into things. Especially while you're in mourning."

Gabrielle fought not to snicker in her coffee mug. *I mourn for him like I'd mourn for the loss of a gaping wound. Indeed, that's what I feel like I'm healing from. The gaping wound he left on my body and on my heart.*

But then the image of her baby's face popped into her mind. She was in mourning, just not as the Sister understood her to be.

"What are the Sisters doing?" Gabrielle asked, looking for a means to change the subject. Four of the Sisters sat at the long table nearest the window, bent over statues and an odd sort of paper that caught the light and caused it to dance off the convent walls. *Far too jolly for such a reverent place.*

"Gilding the statues for the Church. That is, covering them with gold leaf. The bishop is coming to look at their handiwork this evening. They've more than a little skill, my fellow Sisters."

The nearest Sister labored over a statue, the subject of which Gabrielle did not recognize, but the face was one of sorrow and suffering. As the nun applied the gold coating, the expression became softened—almost blank.

"So it would seem. You'll pardon me, but the statues seem lovely enough without the extra adornment." Gabrielle took another sip of the coffee, the flavor growing less acrid as it cooled.

"I don't disagree with you, my dear. I much prefer to see the statues painted true to life. But alas, the decision is not mine. The good bishop wants his cathedral to be as grand as Notre Dame de Paris, and my opinion matters not."

"It's so frequent that we must hold our tongues. Hide from the truth. It's a shame." Gabrielle started as a log snapped in the fire. She set down her mug, glad she hadn't upset the contents all over herself.

"How true, my dear." Sister Anne looked at her, apprising. "We must gild the truth, make it more pleasing to the eye—or ear, if you prefer. I suppose it's the price of living in society."

"I suppose it must be. Perhaps it's why I've never been very good at being a part of it."

"My dear girl, you'll find your place here again. I'm sure of it. You're a good woman. A good worker. People will see your value."

"As you say, Sister." A child raised by Elisabeth Beaumont would never contradict an Ursuline, even if she said the sky were green and the ocean a vibrant red. *I don't know if you speak of wishes or truths, but I fear at best it's a truth as gilded as your lifeless statues.*

CHAPTER 22

Manon

February 1679

While Manon missed Claudine's companionable chatter before bed, and even her grousing at the early morning sun, the solitude of having the room to herself before facing the day was a blessing at times. She took the note she'd sent to Pascal, the one in which she'd confessed the depths of her feelings and asked for his forgiveness, from the little box on her night stand. He had opened it, presumably read its contents, and wrote a missive on the back:

> *You must think little of my dignity if you think me capable of accepting a vow of fidelity from a woman I saw in the arms of another man only hours before she sent this letter. Good-bye, Manon, and farewell.*

The servant Manon had sent with the note and brooch returned, both in hand, within the half hour. It wasn't long in such a settlement before Manon learned that Pascal had gone off after her when he'd seen her walking toward the woods on her snowshoes. He managed to follow her as stealthily as one of her own Huron hunters. Whether to ensure she didn't come to harm or to renew his pledge of affection, Manon could not know. He had seen her walking off to the Huron village with Heno and spent an agonizing afternoon wondering if she would ever return.

She tried to put herself in his position. To imagine what it would have been like for her to see Pascal in the arms of another woman. She recalled the nights when the thought of Heno replacing her with a dutiful Huron girl had kept her abed for hours. She could imagine Pascal's pain and was sorry she had been the cause of it. For all of this, she hoped that she would have listened to Pascal or to Heno had the situation been reversed. To know if she had misinterpreted their actions as Pascal had done.

There was no unpleasant scene, no raised voices or teary oaths from either side. The note was the extent of his rebuke.

She had tried on occasion to get him to acknowledge her. To explain the scene he witnessed. He would not return anything more than a simple nod. There was no anger in his eyes, only resignation. Heno would have raged like an angry sea and then begged her forgiveness. It was somehow easier for Manon to palate Heno's volatile moods than Pascal's placid acceptance. Worse, his stubborn refusal to hear her reasons for her brief departure.

For weeks she'd borne her shame quietly and cried in private over her heartbreak. She could not bear to have Nicole console her or have Claudine revile him for his pigheadedness. She could not burden Gabrielle, the girl who would have been her sister, with more sorrow than she already bore.

She dried her eyes and stowed the note. It was one thing to indulge her sorrow for a few solitary moments before greeting the world in earnest, but it was quite another to bask in it like summer sunshine. Gabrielle's pain was far more acute than her own, and Manon would heal. Gabrielle would bear her grief for the rest of her days.

Since Gabrielle's return, Elisabeth still kept her nestled in the safety of the Beaumont home, and in the comfort of her bed for as many hours as Gabrielle would allow. Gabrielle insisted she was well enough to be of use in the shop, but aside from the occasional pass with the broom or minding of an oven, the Beaumonts coddled her like a lamed child. Manon knew the bakers acted from a kindness that ran deeper into their souls than most people could comprehend, but it did not keep Gabrielle from the brink of madness. She and Claudine visited, bringing some sort of occupation, every afternoon they could be spared.

Manon and Claudine had respected Gabrielle's need for silence regarding Patenaude's untimely demise, despite their longing to know the truth. That afternoon, however, Gabrielle confessed the hell she had endured since the trial.

"If he hadn't died in the accident, I was going to do it myself." Gabrielle's hands shook as she spoke.

"I'm sure you were tempted to stop things. He was a monster of the worst kind." Manon handed Gabrielle the spool of thread so she could continue mending the rent in Nicole's chemise, but Manon herself could not pay heed to the embroidery she'd brought with her.

"You don't understand my meaning," Gabrielle explained. "I repaired his old musket. I was going to wait on the trail and kill him on his way home. If he hadn't gotten too deep in a bottle and done the job for me, I would be a murderess."

"There's no way anyone could find out what you . . . were planning. . . ." Claudine whispered, also failing to make progress on her embroidered nightdress for Zacharie. The Beaumont parlor was quiet, but no one could be certain his or her conversation couldn't be heard in the shop below.

"I don't see how. I left the musket out in the brambles, but I'm not sure anyone could tell it had been mine." Gabrielle spoke softly as well, but there was an edge of anger to her voice that Manon didn't recall hearing before Gabrielle's unfortunate marriage.

"The important thing is to act as if nothing other than a tragic accident has occurred," Manon said, hands busy with some of Gabrielle's mending. "Because, in truth, that's all that *has* happened." Her mind wandered some years in the past when she'd come upon the bleeding body of Nicole's first husband, Luc Jarvais, when she was a young girl. She had been afraid to approach him, in case he tried to shoot her out of fear. She'd run off to the chestnut-haired angel from the French settlement and dragged her to him instead.

Gabrielle's plans were deliberate, but Manon could not fault her for them. Olivier Patenaude had deserved his fate, and a good deal worse. She had lived among the Huron, who treated all living things as sacred. She now lived among the French, who considered the taking of a human life to be one of the gravest of sins. For all this, Manon could not condemn Gabrielle as the rest of her people surely would if they learned the truth.

"Manon is right," Claudine agreed. "Appearances are everything, as my brother-in-law is wont to say. You are the widow of a good man and faithful subject to the King. You mourn for your loss each day and regret all the strife the two of you had in your past."

Manon nodded. As much as it made her ill to think that Gabrielle should take any amount of the blame for Patenaude's actions, it was what the authorities wanted to see. The penitent widow.

"Devote yourself to your mending business. It shows you're industrious and don't want to be a burden on anyone," Manon said.

"Nor do I," Gabrielle said, her eyes looking up from the frayed chemise she repaired. "I hope to set up my own shop and home soon enough. I can't bear to impose on Elisabeth and Gilbert anymore. They've done enough for me as it is. It's too much to ask them to look after me now that I'm of age."

Manon held her tongue, for she knew Gabrielle meant no offense. Manon was more than two years her senior and still living in the care of a family that was not her own. *Perhaps it was time you thought of forging out on your own and starting a life for yourself as Gabrielle is doing.* Manon remembered Alexandre's lecture and knew that the next time she moved out of the Lefebvre house she would not be welcome back in it. She would need something more solid than a drive for greater independence before she left.

"For now, stay here," Manon encouraged. "Showing yourself as a dutiful daughter will cast you in a good light. Not to mention, it will be safer for you here than in your own home."

"Perhaps for now," Gabrielle said, her hands shaking as she tried to stitch. "I've become accustomed to my solitude though. Sitting through dinner with a tableful of people seems almost chaotic. I used to love a bustling family dinner."

"It will take you some time, but you'll adjust." Manon surveyed the patch on the knee of the trousers she mended, pleased with the result. "After quiet meals with Mother Onatah and Théodore, I thought the Lefebvre house was pandemonium itself. It took weeks to enjoy my food." *Not to mention the rich sauces and unending courses that tore at my stomach. How I longed for plainer fare.*

"But what... what if someone... somehow finds out...?" Gabrielle asked.

"No matter what your intentions," Claudine said, "no one here would suspect you."

"What we need is someone to stand up for you," Manon said. "Your family is one of the most respected in the town and it's time they acted on your behalf."

Manon said her farewell to Gabrielle and went out behind the Beaumonts' shop, where Pascal hid from Manon while loading flour into the storeroom. Steam rose off his warm skin. She could see his body, made strong by honest work, and she felt a tug of desire—and something more. He was a good man and she was fortunate to know him. Even now.

"I come in peace," Manon said, when he looked up and scowled in her direction.

"I don't want to talk," Pascal said, throwing a fifty-pound bag of flour onto the pile with the others as if it weighed no more than a feather.

"I don't need to talk about us," Manon said. "Not now. I'm worried about Gabrielle."

"As are we all. It's not your concern. We'll take care of her." Gilbert flung another sack of flour from the cart with a *swish* as it flew through the air and a dull *thud* as it came down.

"It *is* my concern. She's my friend. One of the only ones I have, it seems. And she doesn't need to be swaddled and taken care of. She needs your support in town so she can rebuild her life."

Pascal looked up briefly, his brown eyes flashing at her. She could see him bite his tongue against the scathing response he wanted to hurl at her. *Go ahead and speak plainly to me for once. Stop being so damned French!*

"What would you have me do?" Pascal said, hands on his hips. "As much as I wish I could influence the people in this place to think differently about certain things—certain people—I'm not all-powerful."

"You've got more influence than you give yourself credit for," Manon said, keeping her voice even, though she yearned to scream at him. "Just mention your sister's mending business. If you know of someone who needs a new suit of clothes or a dress, suggest her. Find ways to mention her industriousness, her goodness, as often as you can. Encourage Elisabeth and Gilbert to do the same."

"Elisabeth doesn't want to see Gabrielle working so much just yet." Pascal wiped the sweat that pooled on his brow with the back of his hand.

"Elisabeth needs to trust Gabrielle to know what she's capable of. You all do. If she doesn't have something to do she'll run mad. She doesn't need to be making ball gowns yet, I'll agree. But patching trousers and hemming skirts keeps her hands busy and her mind from venturing into the shadows. Certainly you see that. She's been through hell and she needs the chance to come back to the real world."

Pascal nodded. "That much I won't argue with. I'll talk to Gilbert and Elisabeth."

"Thank you," Manon said. "I know you don't want to talk to me—even to see me—but I can't bear to see Gabrielle hurting if there is anything, however small, that can be done to help."

"That's good of you," Pascal said. He looked at Manon square in the face and exhaled deeply.

"What aren't you saying, Pascal?" *Do not beg. You're not going to stoop to that.*

"You're a good friend to my sister, but you've shown me a good deal less consideration." Pascal's gaze now did not waver. She knew it cost him dearly to say these things aloud. In many ways he wasn't unlike the Huron hunters of her youth.

"Pascal, I've tried to apologize. Tried to explain. I offered you my heart and you hadn't a word to say to me. I don't know what else to do or say. I'm so tired of the silence. Of feeling guilty. Of feeling angry. Just so tired. Bone-weary."

"Why did you go back?" Pascal asked. "Why did you leave me again? You didn't even tell me you were going. I went looking for you at the Lefebvres and no one knew where you were. Then I saw you walking back with . . . him. Who's to say you won't go again?"

"I was gone for a few hours. I had to be sure, Pascal. I had to pay respects to my Chief and see if there was a place for me with my people. You belong here, Pascal. There's no question of it. You live with the people you were born into. No one has ever questioned your place. Since I was eight years old, people have looked at me like an outsider. Something unknown. Dangerous. Even as a child . . . and then when I went back all those years ago? No one except Mother Onatah would speak to me. Acting as though I were tainted. You can't know what that's like, Pascal."

"It doesn't make it hurt less when you leave," Pascal said.

"I know it doesn't, Pascal. But I had to know. There is no place for me among my people anymore. I knew within the hour of my arrival at the village I would be an outsider there for the rest of my life. There isn't much of a place for me with the French, either . . . but I have to try to carve one out for myself. By and large, I think it's better for Théodore, if not both of us. I tried to explain that to you, but you didn't care to listen."

"I couldn't bear to hear it," Pascal said. "All I could feel was the pain when you left. I thought I'd never see you again and you didn't have the decency to say good-bye."

"I didn't know I'd be leaving. I didn't plan any of it. I had to see for myself. I was gone the length of an afternoon, but my place isn't there. It's here."

"I know . . . I can see that now. I couldn't then. I was just too angry. I couldn't be your second choice."

"And you had a right to be angry, Pascal." Manon took a tentative step toward him. "I didn't mean to hurt you, but I know I did. Do you think now you might start to forgive me? We could at least be friends again? I've missed you." The truth in her words stole Manon's breath like an unexpected punch to her gut.

"No, Manon," Pascal said. "I can't be friends with you."

An unwelcome, unexpected tear stung at the corner of Manon's eye and rolled down her cheek. *Be strong. Do not show your pain to him.*

"Manon, you and I could never be friends. You're too much more than that to me. Either you'll be my wife or we'll be nothing at all." He stood, shoulders broad, waiting for her words like he would brace for the kick of a mule.

"Wh-what?" was all Manon could stammer.

Pascal took two long strides and closed the gap between them. He took her hand in his and knelt down on one knee.

"Manon Lefebvre, will you please be my wife?" The words were spoken so quietly she might have mistaken them if he weren't on bended knee.

This was her last chance. If she didn't take Pascal now, he would never repeat the offer again. Their friendship would be forever severed and he would never speak to her more than the exchange of pleasantries between two distant acquaintances. He would be lost to her. The pain at that thought was so great she had to breathe through it to be able to clear her mind.

"Yes, I will," Manon agreed. A warmth flooded her as Pascal scooped her up in his arms and covered her mouth with his as he stroked the length of her black tresses that hung loose past the middle of her back. *My future is tied to yours, Pascal, and I know I shall be happy. I only hope you will be able to say the same.*

CHAPTER 23

Claudine

February 1679

I dreamed of my gallant prince. A fine palace. A dozen beautiful children. A life filled with excitement. I don't dream anymore. Alone in her room, Claudine brushed out her long mahogany mane into smooth, rippling waves that flowed down to her lower back. She massaged the crick in her neck and looked at her reflection in the vanity mirror. She recognized the reflection of the girl who dreamed of her coming-out ball and dreamed of a dashing prince to take her away from the monotony of daily life. She recognized her, but that girl had died months ago, buried with Emmanuelle. There was more understanding in her deep brown eyes, a furrow of concern in her brow, and something she refused to acknowledge as the start of fine lines of experience forming in the corners of her mouth.

She wore a nightdress of soft white muslin that did little to keep out the February chill, but it was not her thin gown that caused her to shiver that night. The fresh memory of Gabrielle, barely able to leave her bed, bereft of her child, enshrouded in grief and guilt . . . all at the hands of a cruel and callous husband. Her eyes flitted to the door and thought of Laurent across the hall in the master suite. Never a cross word. Never had he voiced a single complaint about her lack of affection. A more attentive father had never been seen.

And yet, you do not love him. You're a dolt. A fool to treat a good man with such coldness.

A tear rolled down her cheek as she thought of Gabrielle alone in that cabin all those months. Worse, the weeks when Patenaude graced her with his presence. The darling boy in the nursery might not be Claudine's own, but he was close enough to it that she could at least imagine the flavor of Gabrielle's anguish, though she'd not tasted it herself.

So many hours Claudine spent in the nursery kissing toes and playing mindless games with more and more patience. She never thought she'd grow so fond of tending to a child, but he'd charmed her with his big eyes and black curls. When she held him in her arms, a hollowness ached in her core. She longed to give Zacharie little brothers and sisters. She longed to give Laurent the tribe he wanted. That he deserved.

But that would mean telling Laurent the truth.

The time will come, sooner or later. You ought to make it the time of your choosing. Better to come forward and soothe his feelings. Perhaps he won't cast you to the wolves if you're honest with him.

Claudine placed the silver-plated hairbrush back on the vanity with a shaking hand. *You must go to him and do it now.*

She gave her reflection a stern look and rose to cross her bedroom. Few women would be so bold as to knock upon her husband's bedroom door and ask for his favor, but she knew he was past asking. Too many excuses and rejections.

She padded across the hallway and rapped decidedly but softly at the door. *Please, God, let him be kind.*

"Is everything all right, Claudine?" Laurent asked, his eyebrows lifted at the sight of his wife at the bedroom door. *Not "my dear," "sweetheart," "darling" . . . just Claudine.*

"Yes." *Though perhaps not for long.* "Might I come in?"

Laurent stepped aside and made way for her to enter the room.

Claudine paused for a moment to take in the candlelit room. The furnishings were dark, sturdy, and masculine, much like Laurent himself. The bedding and tapestries favored threads in deep reds and gold hues that made the room seem warm despite the chill.

"Please, sit down," Laurent said, gesturing to a plush chair by the fireplace, formal as though he were welcoming a maiden aunt into the parlor.

"I hope you don't mind me barging in like this." Claudine became acutely aware of how sheer her nightdress was as she sat before him. He kept his eyes respectfully on her face, but she could sense they wanted to explore the rest of her.

He's your husband. He can look all he likes. And if you didn't want him to, you should have worn your dressing gown.

"Claudine, you're my wife and this is your home. You're welcome in any room in this house whenever you like." Laurent pulled a second chair close to hers and patted her hand affectionately. The first gesture he'd dared show in weeks.

"Laurent, I know I haven't—that we have yet to—" Crimson crept up from her navel to the tip of her scalp in the matter of a moment.

"Consummate our marriage?"

"Precisely." She rubbed the velvet of the chair with her pinky, unable to look into his face, but grateful he'd voiced the issue when she could not. "I wanted to tell you there's good reason."

Laurent scooted closer to the edge of his seat but refrained from offering any verbal encouragement to continue.

"You know that I had been terribly keen on Victor St. Pierre. What I hadn't told you is that I let him . . . that is . . . we . . ."

Speak, you fool! He deserves the truth. Not your stammering.

"On the night of his ball, not an hour before he announced his engagement to another woman, he persuaded me to let him . . . have me." Now that the truth was spoken, never to be unheard, she let out a jagged breath she didn't know she'd been holding.

"I see" was Laurent's only reply.

"It only happened the one time. I was foolish enough to think it was *me* he was planning to propose to. I never would have otherwise. But I knew that once we . . . once I let you . . . you would know the truth. And then you'd hate me. I couldn't bear it."

"Claudine, of all the things I am capable of, I don't think hating you could ever be one of them."

"I want to be a good wife, Laurent. A proper wife to you. If you wish to set me aside it's your right. I should have told you before."

Try though she might, the lump rose in her throat as she thought about what that future would hold for her. She would spend the rest of her days on a remote homestead, no chance of a family. Cut off from Zacharie forever. Not seeing Laurent, the loss of which stung more than she realized it would. Enduring his condescending gaze if they ever crossed paths. Seeing him married to another woman. She hadn't expected the twinge of jealousy in the maelstrom of emotions that besieged her.

"Yes, you should have." Laurent sat back in his chair, his brow creased as he looked down at his interwoven fingers.

"It was dishonest." The truth spilled from Claudine's lips and she could no longer dam it up. "I hope you will come to forgive me, in time." Claudine leaned forward to smooth a wayward lock of his dark tresses. She lowered her hand slowly to caress his check, but he stilled her hand with his own.

"There is nothing to forgive," Laurent said, standing. With three strides he was back at the bedroom door holding it open for her. "Thank you for telling me the truth."

It was a dismissal.

Claudine did not look at his face as she left the room and kept her countenance until she shut the door to her own bedroom behind her. The moment the door clicked shut she slumped against it, slowly sliding to the floor, and let the tears come forth in a torrent. She bunched up the hem of the nightdress and bit against her howling sobs. She would not let him hear. She would not give the staff the satisfaction of knowing she was an unfit mistress to the house of Robichaux.

She would play the part until Laurent decided to end the charade.

The following morning at breakfast, Claudine took her place at the table, waiting for Laurent to scream at her. To drag her by the hair and fling her into the street. Instead, he chatted with her companionably as he had done every morning since they married. *This is worse. If he raged at me, at least I'd know he cared. Hatred might be painful, but his indifference is insufferable.*

"And what have you planned for today, my dear?" Laurent

asked. *Oh please, anything but idle chatter! Call me a whore and cast me out, but don't make small talk.*

"I had thought to pay a visit to Rose." Claudine invented plans out of thin air. While visiting Rose had been on her list of things to see to, it had in no way been a fixed plan before now. She had to find some occupation to take her from under his nose.

"How thoughtful of you. I've heard she's not been in the best of health or spirits with this child. Your visit will cheer her up."

"I hope so." *I'd like to bring some joy to someone today.* "I'll take her some of Elisabeth's almond tarts. I know they're her favorite."

"Excellent notion," he said, pushing his chair back and rising from the table. "Have a lovely visit. Don't hurry back."

No, don't hurry back. Stay away and keep your sullied self out of my home. Claudine shook her head at her ungenerous thoughts. There was no sense in putting the hateful words in his mouth before he took the opportunity to say them himself.

Less than an hour later, Claudine knocked at Rose's door, basket laden with pastries and needlework, armed for a solid day away from the Robichaux house. The manservant escorted her to the parlor, where both the lady of the house and her husband found some repose.

Rose, plump with child, lay with her feet propped up on a decadent-looking settee opposite the fire, a small gown coming to fruition in her hands. Henri sat in an armchair trying, and evidently failing, to concentrate on a novel. He looked very little like his uncle Alexandre. His hair was a much paler shade of brown than his uncle's, his skin swarthier, too. While the elder Lefebvre was tall and lean, Henri was shorter and more muscular. In truth, Claudine always thought he looked like he was built to work a farm, not manage one.

"Perhaps I'll leave you ladies to your conversation?" Henri suggested, setting the book on the small table by his seat with an air of relief. "I believe I can trust our young Madame Robichaux to keep my wife from overexerting herself?"

"Of course," Claudine said with a smile, hiding a wince at his use of her title. "I'll keep her happy and entertained for as long as you need."

Henri offered her a smile and bounded out of the room before anyone contrived a reason to call him back.

"Poor Henri. He feels as though he has to entertain me at every moment, else I won't take the bother to rest. He's been so sweet about it, but it drives him mad."

"He's the sort who can't bear to be idle," Claudine agreed. "It's not a bad quality in a man."

"Not at all," Rose agreed. "But he's hardly restful company if he can't sit still for more than a few minutes at a time."

"True. But soon you'll have another delicious baby and his worry will be over." Claudine busied herself setting a pastry in front of Rose on her table and pouring some spruce beer the maid had brought for them.

"Elisabeth is a miracle worker," Rose declared with her first bite into the flavorful tart. "From simple ingredients like flour, water, and yeast she makes heaven on earth."

"I'm glad your appetite will allow you to eat," Claudine said. "Emmanuelle was sick for so long when she was expecting Zacharie." With a tug at her heart, she realized it had been weeks, maybe as much as a month or two since she'd spoken her sister's name aloud.

"Thankfully, that hasn't been a problem this time," Rose said, sampling one of the buttery confections. "You're a dear to come visit me. Though I sense your visit isn't completely altruistic."

"You're too perceptive for my taste, always have been," Claudine said, clucking her tongue.

"Then get on with it. I'm languishing for want of news." Rose sat up a little straighter on her settee, folding her hands on her lap in anticipation.

"Laurent and I . . ." Claudine felt the sting of tears and battled through them as she recounted it all—her inability to do her wifely duties and how she had confessed to Laurent the entirety of her dealings with Victor at the St. Pierre ball—all of it in one tidal wave of confession.

By the time she was finished, Claudine was seated on the floor by Rose's settee, doubled over with her head on her knees. Rose gently stroked her hair, making motherly, encouraging sounds, but never interrupting Claudine's litany.

"He pretended as if I'd said nothing this morning," Claudine repeated, leaning her head against the edge of the settee, trying to keep the churning bile in place. "He dismissed me from his bedroom. He must despise me."

"My dear, Laurent Robichaux, of all people in Christendom, is probably the least capable of despising anyone. You're simply imagining how you yourself might react, rather than truly paying attention to his words and actions. I'll say this, while I'm glad you've dulled that razor-sharp tongue of yours a bit, your backbone is good for him to see."

"So you don't think he hates me, but that he's a fool not to?" The tears cool on her hot cheeks, Claudine looked up at her beloved teacher.

"That's not what I said," Rose said, visibly stifling a chortle. "You must learn to listen, my dear. I think Laurent may indeed be hurt by the truth. He may just need some time to adjust his thoughts on the matter. I'm sure he appreciates that you've finally owned the truth."

"A bit late," Claudine said, wiping the brine from her face. "The information would have done him more good before we were married."

"Perhaps, but it's a done thing now." Rose leaned back to her original position, looking weary from sitting up overlong. "He's a good man, Claudine. He will learn to look past it all, I'm sure."

"How can you be convinced?" Claudine asked. "He could cast me out this moment with the clothes on my back and nothing more and no one would think ill of him once he divulged the truth. What's to say he won't be pleased to be rid of me?"

"Darling—"

"Good men have cast out wives before. You can't deny it." Claudine buried her face in the plush settee cushion next to where Rose sat. *Good settee, be a dear and swallow me whole. It will spare me the pain of returning home only to be turned out by my husband.*

"No, no, I can't," Rose admitted. "But you must not act like a woman defeated. You have spoken your piece, apologized, and now you must wait. Wait, and hope that he will forgive your folly."

"I hate waiting, I hate that he holds my fate in his hands. It's so incredibly unfair."

"It is, my darling girl. But so is the fate of being born a woman. We are placed on a higher pedestal than man. We have further to fall when we stumble."

"It's unfair," Claudine repeated.

"Many would disagree with you, sweet girl," Rose said, reprising her caress of Claudine's wavy brown locks. "But I am not among them."

A few hours later, Claudine left a rapidly fatiguing Rose in Henri's care. She tried to contrive an errand to keep her from home, but with an insincere curse of her efficient staff, she could think of none. Furthermore, the brisk February air and blanket of snow dispelled any desire she had to delay her return when she began the trek, and she was happy to find the warmth of her foyer a quarter of an hour later.

In the nursery, Nanny Simon diverted little Zacharie with small wooden animals that Claudine's father had sent for the boy. Each of the Deschamps children had their little menagerie, and it seemed his grandchildren wouldn't be deprived of the tradition. Claudine took a spot near the fire and warmed her hands so she wouldn't shock the baby with her cold skin, but he was crawling up in her lap before the job was done. Despite the cold hands that enveloped him, he rewarded her with a lopsided grin punctuated with bubbles of spittle in the corners of his bow-shaped mouth.

"Sweet, darling boy," Claudine cooed, burying her face in the soft skin of his neck. *Please, God, don't take him from me.* "Nanny Simon, please go enjoy some rest. I'm sure you're in need."

"With pleasure, Madame Robichaux." Nanny gripped the side of her solid chair to lift herself off the floor after a bit of struggle and grunting. "You seem a bit out of sorts, if I may say so, madame. Is there anything I might help with?"

"No, my dear lady. Not a thing." *Just care for my boy if his father sends me away. Not that I need ask it of you.* "Enjoy your afternoon. I plan on being here for quite some time. I'll call for you when you're needed."

"Very good, madame." The kindly woman did not look convinced at her mistress's assurances, but did as she was bid.

For a long while, she sat and held the sweet child in her arms, drinking in his scent and memorizing the exact pattern of his riot of black curls. He was able to sit on his own and crawl with some success, but he was still content to let his aunt cradle him for as long as she desired. These days were numbered, and Claudine knew to cherish them.

"My own sweet boy. I love you. . . ." She rocked back and forth watching his eyes grow heavy with the swaying motion. "I don't know how many days we have left together . . . nor if I'll ever be able to cradle any little brothers or sisters for you . . . but thank you for letting your auntie hold you for now, my love."

"May I intrude?" Laurent asked from the doorway, waiting for Claudine's acknowledgment, as was his custom. Claudine looked up from Zacharie's face and wiped away the tears she hadn't known were there.

"Of course. It's your home." *And only you know how much longer it will be mine.* Her arms wrapped tightly around her nephew as though Laurent might grab him from her embrace at any moment.

"Please don't take him from me, Laurent. I beg you."

Laurent dragged the spare chair next to Claudine's and wrapped his arms around her and the child. "My angel . . . I would not dream of separating our family." Emotion caught in his throat and he buried his face in her hair. Claudine adjusted the baby so that her body more easily melded to Laurent's. She'd never noticed how he smelled of fresh leather and heady spices.

He's not sending me away. I can stay. She placed a kiss, ever so gently, on the soft skin of his neck. *I will repay your generosity. Your kindness.*

"I'm so sorry, Laurent. I should have told you sooner," she whispered sometime later.

"Indeed you should have, but perhaps you were wise," Laurent said, gripping her tighter. "If I had known how St. Pierre used you, I can't promise my temper would have held. But knowing that you're mine helps me to keep things in perspective."

"I didn't want to hurt you. I hope you know that."

"I confess, these weeks I had no idea what was going on in that head of yours. I can only imagine how uncomfortable you must have been. Here in our own home. The thought of you in distress hurts me deeply. I know I haven't helped matters today, but I just needed some time to consider the matter." *Just as Rose said.*

"I can well understand you needing some time. It was no small confession." Claudine felt she could afford to be sympathetic now that she knew she wasn't going to face the world alone.

"We need never speak of it again," Laurent said, sitting up and kissing her temple and twirling one of his son's curls with his thumb and forefinger. "He ought to call you 'Maman.' I don't wish to erase Emmanuelle from his life, and I want him to know about her . . . but it doesn't seem right for a child to grow up without someone to call his *maman.*"

"Many do," Claudine said, her voice hollow, kissing Zacharie's smooth brow and placing him in his crib.

"Not in this house." Laurent stood from his chair and held out a hand for Claudine. Little Zacharie's eyes were shut fast in sleep and did not stir as she pulled the soft woolen blanket up to his chest. Claudine asked the maid who was sweeping nearby to listen for any fussing from the nursery while she worked so Nanny Simon could still enjoy another hour to herself. Laurent took Claudine's hand and led her down the corridor in the direction of the master bedrooms.

"It's only midafternoon," Claudine said as they stood outside Laurent's bedroom door.

"Yes, my angel, but I think we're far overdue for our wedding night, don't you think?" Laurent opened the door to his cozy bedroom, the fire already blazing several hours before it normally would have been lit. The bedcovers were turned down, inviting them to spend the afternoon wrapped up in their warmth.

Laurent kissed her neck as he freed her from her clothes. With shaking hands, she helped Laurent from his, waiting for him to take what he wanted.

The image of her tall, dashing prince vanished as Laurent placed her gently on the bed and began to caress her. She drank in his clean scent and rubbed her fingers on the soft skin of his back that had never been tanned from a hard day of labor or sport in the sun. *He is not young and dashing . . . but he is good. He is kind. He is mine. . . .*

Claudine let him claim her as his wife. There was no pain or discomfort this time. Nor any pangs of regret or remorse. *There is no great crash of lightning when I look into his eyes, but perhaps the love in storybooks is better left to the page.*

CHAPTER 24

Gabrielle

March 1679

Gabrielle surveyed the small room that was slowly transforming from a bland, disused space in a rickety building into her workshop. The one she'd dreamed of since she learned how to hem her first skirt. There was not a useless piece of bric-a-brac in her possession, but the essential nature of every object in place gave the otherwise unremarkable room a conviviality. It breathed function and utility. Efficiency. *It may be small and drafty, but it's mine. Or at least as much mine as most shop holders can claim.*

"I insist you take the chair," Elisabeth said, as Gilbert brought the solid piece of furniture into the shop from the wagon. "You need a comfortable place to sit while you work."

"It's one of your best pieces of furniture. It's too dear." Gabrielle stood behind the shop counter putting her sewing notions in order.

"We can buy another easier than you can. It's none too dear for you." Elisabeth shot Gilbert a look that conveyed an order he dared not countermand. The chair was placed in the corner by the window where she could sew by the natural light and there, Gabrielle realized, it would remain. It was beginning to look like a proper shop after three days of cleaning and another two moving all of Gabrielle's supplies and personal possessions to the shop and the small apartment above stairs. The soft blue silk for the skirt of Manon's wedding gown fell into soft, gentle folds from the makeshift mannequin she used for marking and hemming skirts. She'd never seen a proper dressmaker's shop in Paris, but she couldn't imagine they had fabric much finer than the silk Alexandre Lefebvre had secured for his ward. Both Manon and Claudine had spent hours scouring the floors and helping Gabrielle make the space her own. Gabrielle wished they could be there at that moment to help defray some of Elisabeth's flutterings.

The proceeds of the sale of Patenaude's homestead and most of his worldly possessions enabled the endeavor. Though the cabin was nothing to speak of, the land was good, and partially clear. It would save the next habitant a few weeks of backbreaking labor to have a few acres cleared for planting in the coming weeks. *If there is one mercy in this untamed land of ours, it's that my husband's goods came to me and no other. The women in New France are treated far better than our sisters in the old country on that score.*

She wasn't left a wealthy woman, but even Gilbert and Elisabeth acknowledged she now had the hopes of being self-supporting. She would never earn an enormous sum making clothing. Too many of the settlers had to make their own clothes from cloth they spun themselves. Few in the settlement had expansive wardrobes, but there was at least a small population who could afford to send their mending to her. A few could afford the occasional dress, but those would be rare and enjoyable exceptions to mending frayed trouser legs and patching holes. But if nothing else, it was a living. It was a life.

There was still work to be done, but her vision for the shop was becoming a reality. The Beaumonts had shown her how to keep a meticulous shop. Pascal taught her his methods for tracking his flour deliveries in a ledger, which she could apply to her mending jobs. Rose's tutelage in arithmetic and keeping household accounts would be invaluable. For all of Elisabeth's disquiet, there were few shopkeepers in the settlement as well trained as Gabrielle.

"I think Gabrielle can take care of things from here," Gilbert said, seeing that Gabrielle was reaching the stage in her preparations where outside help would only be a hindrance. "Let's leave her be to get organized in peace."

"But—" Elisabeth looked about the room, her eyes clearly hunting for a chore that required her personal attention. She found none and heaved a sigh.

Gabrielle crossed the room and gave Elisabeth a reassuring hug. "I'll be fine. I promise. I'm not more than five hundred feet from your front door." *I won't abandon you. I know how much this hurts you. Things will be better—not just for me—than they have been since before I married. I am sure of it.*

"You'll join us for Sunday supper every week, yes? And any other night you wish to." Elisabeth stood almost half a foot taller than Gabrielle and rested her chin atop her head.

"It's a bargain," Gabrielle said. "You're the best cook in the settlement; you won't need to work all that hard to convince me."

Elisabeth managed to laugh through the few tears that spilled down her cheeks. "Sweet girl."

"And you'll have what you need from the bakery whenever you like," Gilbert said, ruffling her red curls as if she were a child of six. "Consider it back payment for years of loyal service."

"Thank you." Gabrielle gave Gilbert a tight hug and gripped his bicep for a moment as he pulled away. "If nothing else, I may come by to use your ovens when they are free. It will save me the trouble of lighting the one here."

Gilbert nodded his approval. The bread oven included in the use of the rented building was a small affair and had not been particularly well tended. Her little fireplace would do well for her humble soup, but the time she saved using the always-running Beaumont ovens could be spent sewing. What's more, she could take her basket with her and mend while her bread baked, and have a good visit.

Gabrielle felt the air catch in her chest as the two people who had been better to her than her own parents walked away from her shop, but only a small part of her longed to rush after them and return to her old girlhood bedroom. *They're leaving me in better condition to provide for myself alone than they did when they left me with a husband. I'll manage fine on my own. Better than manage. I will thrive.*

* * *

The supper Gabrielle prepared for herself was nothing of note, but far better than the meals she'd pieced together from odd bits of whatever she could scrounge when she was living on the homestead. Her soup, thick with salted pork and chunks of fleshy potato, was restorative against the spring chill. With the addition of the hearty bread Elisabeth had stocked in the kitchen, she was amply fed and reasonably warm, given the shoddy construction of the floor. The draft crept in on occasion, chilling her ankles despite her long skirts and petticoats. *It's no secret why the rent comes so cheaply.*

The light was too feeble for more mending, and her eyes too sore for the strain in any case. She wandered about the house for half an hour, dusting, tidying, and rearranging, but with Elisabeth and Gilbert's help that morning, there was little left to be done. No book would hold her interest, nor had she any other leisure activities she could indulge in. These had been the hours she devoted to her sewing, but now her pastime was her profession and she could not afford to grow weary of her work. It was her first night in the home that was hers alone. Few women in the settlement would have that experience. Her friends moved from their fathers' homes to their husbands', never to know the feeling of true solitude. Gabrielle had spent weeks on her own when she was married to Patenaude, but his presence was always there.

Gabrielle had craved a space of her own. She loved the Beaumonts so dearly, but she was a woman now and was loath to be dependent on them or anyone. Now she questioned the wisdom of seeking out her independence. Perhaps women didn't live alone for good reason. A scratching of a tree branch against the side of the house sent a shiver through her marrow. *I'm a bloody coward and a fool.*

Though she knew it had to be a solid hour before she usually retired, she changed into her chemise and sought out the solace of slumber. Her bed was the same she'd had for the duration of her stay at the Beaumonts, so as familiar as her own two hands, but felt foreign now that it was ensconced in her little room, barely larger than a broom closet. The glint of the moonlight bounced to the wall from her hand mirror, which rested on her tiny vanity table.

The pattern it reflected on the walls was menacing, a gnarled hand reaching out for her in the night.

Anyone could break in at any moment. The doors are not strong. The bolts far from impenetrable. Any number of people know I am alone.

She pulled her patchwork quilt tight under her chin, closing her eyes against the errant moonlight and willing sleep to come. *Calm down, you simpleton. No need for your heart to be racing. God knows you've faced enough real danger in your life. You don't need to go inventing more.*

Each time she closed her eyes she saw Patenaude. Smelled his putrid breath. Felt him looming over her when he was drunk and lustful. Remembered the sting of his hand coming down against her cheek. Still felt the ache of where his massive fists connected with her ribs. The blow of his boot against her abdomen.

And the pain, the agony that she thought—she prayed—would claim her as the baby lost his battle for life. She still offered up prayers that her hope of carrying a healthy child was not forever lost.

I'm not sure whom I have offended, or how I have offended. If only God would show me what I have done to merit the treatment I endured at Patenaude's hands, I would make amends. Somehow. Though I am not sure what sin merits such cruelty. And surely, if nothing else, I deserve a good night's sleep.

Over and over, she would dip into sleep . . . only to wake doused in sweat and choking back her bile until she was forced to heave into her chamber pot. Shaking, she wiped the corners of her mouth on the cloth she used for cleaning her face in the morning. She descended the stairs to her kitchen to find water to clear the acid taste from her mouth.

She sat at her kitchen table, head in hands, fighting to slow her breath, which heaved from her uncontrollably. Muscle by muscle, sinew by sinew, she made herself relax until she felt like the mistress of her own body once more.

Leave me in peace. Leave me in peace. Leave me in peace.

She breathed in time with the words, making order from chaos. Gabrielle didn't know if an hour or three elapsed as she sat at the kitchen table, battling with the horror of her memories.

* * *

It's perfect. Her head cleared from her lack of sleep, and she surveyed the shop with satisfaction. Every spool of thread, every needle, every scrap of cloth she used for patching had a place. A real Parisian tailor couldn't find fault with her systems and organization. Though she longed to attend to Manon's wedding gown, Rose and Henri had sent over a large basket of mending that took precedence, so she settled herself in the comfortable chair by the window and set to work on the hem of one of Rose's frayed skirts.

She was deep in concentration when the shop door opened unexpectedly.

"Heavens above, you frightened me!"

"Have I?" A man of middling height with blond hair and blue eyes looked as though he wanted to laugh at her shock. "You clearly are new to running a business."

"I've tended the Beaumont Bakery since I was twelve years old. Worked there since I was nine. I would hardly say that's the case." *Keep the fire from your voice, git. He might be a client.*

"I apologize, that's not what I meant. Those accustomed to tailoring become accustomed to interruption." The man gave a sincere-looking bow of apology.

"Indeed. Baking is different work. It doesn't require the same concentration."

"I should imagine not. And now that I've made myself look like an inconsiderate fool, let me introduce myself. I'm René Savard, deputy to His Excellency, the governor. He has commissioned me with greeting—and encouraging—all of those who open an enterprise within the settlement."

"Gabrielle Patenaude." She curtsied deeply, honoring the distinction in rank. "How very kind of the Governor de Frontenac. I hadn't thought my little shop worth his notice."

"His Excellency cares a great deal about commerce. And he has a great attention to detail." He surveyed the shop, and Gabrielle could see him mentally cataloguing the contents for his report to the governor.

"May I offer you some refreshment?" Gabrielle was now exceedingly glad for the heaping hamper of baked goods from Elisabeth and the bottles of young cider from Gilbert. The cider was over-tart for Gabrielle's liking, but it was at least something more suitable to offer her company than water or milk.

"I shouldn't waste your time, Madame Patenaude, but I confess I had to leave early this morning and have barely had a moment's peace since." Gabrielle motioned for the deputy to sit in the spare, far less inviting chair while she fetched her bounty from her small kitchen.

"Compliments of the Beaumont Bakery." Gabrielle placed the tray with pastry and cider on her worktable in front of the deputy and distributed a plate and glass to each. She'd thought to save her pastry as a dessert after her evening meal, but she could not resist when the deputy's visit called for hospitality.

"Your former master and mistress are unequalled in their craft," René pronounced as he lifted a forkful of pastry filled with cherries and almonds to his lips. Gabrielle shuddered at the terms *master* and *mistress*. Never had they treated her as a mere apprentice.

"Indeed they are," Gabrielle said, acknowledging the compliment.

"And an asset to the community. As I'm sure your business will prove to be as well." The deputy leaned forward as he spoke. *A man who cares deeply about a thriving economy in our little town. What a refreshing change in a politician.*

"That's my fervent hope, monsieur." Gabrielle looked into her cider cup hoping it contained something interesting for her to say to the deputy. Sadly, it contained only the beverage she'd poured.

"I understand you were living on a homestead until very recently. I am very sorry to hear of the loss of your husband."

Gabrielle nodded soberly. *You may be the only one.* "Very kind of you, monsieur. Though it seems you have all the advantage here. I know nothing of you. A rarity in our small settlement, to be sure."

"A very simple explanation, madame. My wife and I made the crossing just last year at the governor's request. We've been in the settlement only eight months."

Gabrielle's heart made an uncomfortable thud against her rib cage at the word *wife,* but she ignored it.

"Ah," Gabrielle said. "It was fortunate your wife was willing to make the journey. Few women are."

"You speak the truth. We were married shortly before our departure. I knew it would be far easier to bring a wife along than to find a suitable bride here."

You speak of your wife as you might bring along a case of your favorite wine with your trunks.

Gabrielle cast the spiteful thought from her mind; he was right. Marriageable women for a man in his station were scarce.

"And how does settlement life suit you?"

"I'm dreadfully fond of it. The people here are better than you'll find anywhere."

"It can be a lonely life," Gabrielle said, her fork tracing the edge of her uneaten pastry.

"Yes, I confess Madame Savard agrees with you. She was raised among the first circles, you see. She doesn't find many peers here. Nor much in the way of diversion."

Foolish to bring a lily into the ice and snow. "I can imagine it might be hard for her. Of course the ladies of the Alexandre and Henri Lefebvre families would make fine acquaintances for her."

"Madame Savard hasn't the easiest time making friends. But still, I hope she'll continue to adjust."

"We haven't much choice, do we? We must adapt or perish, as is the way of all life, is it not?"

"A very astute observation. One wouldn't expect a seamstress to be so insightful."

"One oughtn't underestimate seamstresses, monsieur. We must maintain an eye for detail."

"Quite so," René said with a chuckle. "I hope our paths will cross again. I assure you the Savard house will be sending you some business. My wife is none too fond of mending."

"I would be grateful, monsieur." Gabrielle gave a slight curtsy as she opened the shop door for him. "Business often begets more business."

Gabrielle watched the deputy ... perhaps for a bit longer than propriety would have allowed. She noticed his clothes for the first time. Well tailored, well cut, impeccably clean, but made of sturdy, serviceable fabric. Taste and practicality. She contrasted Alexandre Lefebvre's fine clothes and Gilbert's sturdy work breeches and plain shirts. The deputy had found a pleasing middle ground. *A harmonious match we don't see often enough. It's a pity, really.*

She forced herself back into her seat and returned to Rose's skirt hem, covering the worn edge with a new ruffle. She made sure each stitch was small and even, as though they would be inspected at length. As soon as it was complete, she saw to patching a chemise and two pairs of breeches. She cursed the fading light that forced her to abandon her toils, knowing full well the deputy's face would linger in her dreams.

CHAPTER 25

Manon

March 1679

Manon took in her reflection in the long mirror in Nicole's private sitting room and was unconvinced by her adoptive mother's flattery. The blue silk complemented the rich hue of her skin. The folds of the gown Gabrielle sewed so expertly gave her the illusion of hips and a bust. Pascal's pearl shimmered perfectly at the hollow of her neck. It was the *fontange* hairstyle, with its pile of ebony curls, which seemed to take on the form of a frightened crow showing off its plumage, that gave her pause.

"Are you sure my hair isn't . . ."

"It's perfect, darling." Nicole patted Manon's shoulder affectionately.

"The maid did a lovely job," Claudine agreed, with a note of hesitance. "But you don't look like our Manon."

Manon looked in the mirror at Claudine's reflection, eyes widened momentarily at the endearment. "I don't feel like her, either."

"Is it the dress?" Gabrielle said. "There isn't much time, but I might be able to fix it somehow."

"No, the dress is . . . well, nothing short of remarkable." Manon never offered false praise, nor did she adopt the bad habit on the occasion of her wedding. The lovely length of blue silk was not only well sewn, but the beading and embroidery that covered the majority of the fabric, and the modest cut of the neck somehow called to mind the patterns her own people used in their clothing and textiles. Manon knew Gabrielle's thoughtfulness; this wasn't a happy accident.

"It *is* your hair," Claudine said. "It's simply too much. It might work for us, but on Manon it's simply gilding the lily. Especially with all the embroidery on the gown. Hand me the brush, please, Nicole."

"But—" Nicole protested, as Claudine picked up the silver-plated brush with its stiff bristles.

"It will be *fine,*" Claudine said, loosing the curls so they flowed down Manon's back.

Manon closed her eyes as Claudine worked on her mass of hair, forcing herself to drink in the air of the perfumed salon and exhale it deeply. Her heart sill raced; she hoped the powders and rouge wouldn't slop down her face with all the sweat.

Pascal would be waiting at the church by now. *Would that we were merely alone in your wagon out in the countryside. Yet to church I must go . . . you would never abide another broken promise. Nor should you.*

"There," Claudine said less than ten minutes later. "If you hate it we can call the maid back in and see what can be done."

Manon opened her eyes to see the massive tower of hair reduced to a fraction of its original height. The rest of her hair was now swept up with a few hairpins, but was mostly left in loose curls that Claudine swept gracefully over Manon's right shoulder. *I don't exactly look like me, but a damn sight closer.*

"You were right," Nicole admitted, gracious enough to leave any trace of rancor out of her voice. "But we're also late. We must get to the church before they bar the doors on us."

"It's her own wedding and you're a Lefebvre. She could keep them waiting three quarters of an hour and no one would dare complain." Claudine winked at Manon conspiratorially.

"Best not to press our luck," Gabrielle interjected, picking up the short train of Manon's skirt from the floor so she might walk with ease down the stairs.

Below stairs, Alexandre awaited, arm outstretched to escort Manon. The grim-faced butler wrapped a fine fur cloak at her shoulders and opened the door out onto the square. Manon blinked when she saw more than a few of their neighbors standing in their doorways, waving at her as she entered the gleaming sleigh with matched horses, as though she were a princess bride from one of the fairy stories Nicole read the children. She offered them a timid wave, and to her surprise, many returned the gesture with a smile.

"It's rare they get to see such a display of beauty," Alexandre said, as if to justify the attention.

Théodore sat to Nicole's left, Alexandre to her right, Nicole, Claudine, and Gabrielle on the bench opposite, as the sleigh glided over the late-winter snow.

"You look scared," Théodore said. "Don't you want to marry Pascal?"

Alexandre laughed at the innocent question, for once unreserved; throwing his head back to the white flash of teeth brightened the dark interior of the carriage. "I think all brides are a bit nervous on their wedding days, young man."

"Not as nervous as the grooms, my dear," Nicole chided with a wink.

Please, enough with the banter. I know you mean well, but it does nothing to ease my stomach.

Manon listened to the cadence of the hoofbeats as they crunched down on the snow and ice. She let the steady *slosh, slosh, slosh* of the hooves over the melting snow transport her away from the here and now . . . let the sound ease the knots from her neck and shoulders so that she might face her husband with her back straight.

The doors to the church opened. Théodore escorted Nicole to her seat and claimed the seat to her left, leaving a space to her right for Alexandre. Gabrielle and Claudine followed and would stand to Manon's left as her pillars of support.

I would never have imagined that you two would be the ones by my side, but I am pleased you're there all the same.

On Alexandre's arm, Manon took her first steps from the bright noon sunlight into the dark church, lit only by low candles. The dust and incense bit at her nose, but the soft glow from the votive candles was warm and somehow inviting.

Manon saw Pascal, haloed by the dim light, through the sea of people who had come to see the spectacle of a Lefebvre wedding. He struggled to keep the proper visage of the solemn groom that all expected, but he could not help but smile through the mist of incense at his approaching bride.

She took the decorously slow march down the aisle and listened to the words of the priest, responding in perfect Latin when prompted. *My studies prove useful again. Perhaps for the last time?*

Within a quarter of an hour they were married and Pascal claimed his bride with a chaste kiss on the lips.

Manon. Manon Lefebvre. Manon Giroux. Skenandoa is no longer.

"Madame Giroux, out of bed with you!" Pascal flung open the bedroom windows, letting the brisk morning curl around her sleep-warmed flesh.

"You cruel, evil man!" Manon said, sitting up, pulling the covers over her bare breasts. "A good husband would let his wife sleep after her wedding night."

"It's nearly noon," Pascal said, arms akimbo. "And it's not like I slept any more than you did."

"I should think not!" Manon said. "Else I think we were doing things horribly wrong. Come back to bed and let's make sure." She held out her hand, inviting him back to the large, plush bed that dominated the finest guest quarters in the Lefebvre house. Nicole had insisted the couple spend the first days of their married life in the best comfort she could provide, and so the room would serve as their honeymoon cottage until they found a place to settle. It was far finer than Pascal was used to, and by the tense way he moved, Manon guessed he worried about breaking or spoiling anything he touched.

Rather than submit to Manon's gentle tugging, Pascal pulled Manon from the covers, exposing her flesh to the cold air.

"You're too beautiful to be real," Pascal breathed, before covering her mouth with his and sliding his hands down the soft skin of her back and cupping her buttocks.

"But not so beautiful that you won't come back to bed? And *men* like to tease *women* for being contrary?" Manon let out a soft chuckle against the soft skin of his neck and nipped playfully.

"I'm too excited to spend the day in bed, my sweet. I've something to show you." She felt herself lifted in the air and swung around like one of Hélène's dolls during one of the "great cyclones" the boys reenacted. "Get dressed, as much as it pains me to ask it."

"So this is the married life you waxed on about it?" Manon scoffed as she pulled her chemise over her head. "Lying in bed and making love all day. Mooning over each other as long as our bodies can stand to remain ensconced in our covers . . . it didn't last long."

"Quit your grousing, woman, and get moving." Pascal strode over to the armoire, found a sturdy woolen skirt and jacket, and thrust them at Manon, his every muscle dancing with the impatience of a small child.

She longed to tease him further, but as they'd been married less than a full day she decided to bite her contentious tongue and don the clothes he'd tossed in her direction. She shook her head at the mismatched ensemble and, from the armoire, selected the jacket that was meant to accompany the skirt while Pascal paced.

Manon descended the stairs on Pascal's arm, surprised when he curbed her attempt to enter the dining room.

"Am I not allowed to a simple breakfast before you drag me from the house? I had no idea you were such a heartless brute." Manon winced at her own words, thinking of the hell Gabrielle had endured at the hands of a true monster. "I *am* hungry," she added, her tone soft.

"First of all, Madame Giroux, it's time for luncheon, not breakfast. Secondly, we will eat our feast in the great out-of-doors. It's waiting in the sleigh for us. The more you stall, the longer you must wait." Pascal pulled her from the house where waited one of Alexandre's small sleighs hitched to the fine chestnut horse Gilbert had gifted him on the occasion of their wedding. He wasn't a large beast, but strong and a willing worker—necessary for a beast of burden to be worth his feed. Manon patted his neck affectionately before taking Pascal's proffered hand and assuming her place by his side in one of Alexandre's smaller sleds.

"Now will you tell me where we're going in a foot of snow?" Manon asked.

"Patience, Wife." His tone was chiding, but his expression couldn't hide the joy he felt in using the term lawfully.

The familiar roads let them to their favorite clearing, where they had spent many clandestine afternoons wrapped in each other on the wagon bed.

"For pity's sake, we could have stayed at home in a warm bed if you wanted . . . that." Manon slid down from her seat and stretched her legs, looking out over the rolling hills that would soon come to life with the bloom of spring.

"That's not why I brought you here, my sweet." Pascal approached her behind, his fingers tracing the curve of her waist and trailing down to her hips.

"You're not very convincing. . . ."

"Darling wife . . . this is ours. All ours. Alexandre has gifted it to us. The rest will pass to young Frédéric in time, but he's given us fifty acres for our own to cultivate and pass on to our children. It's ours."

Manon looked out over the fertile land and felt her stomach lurch. *Because a man gave us a paper. . . . Now it belongs to us? How does it belong to anyone?* Manon wanted to scoff, but she knew the gesture was too generous to rebuke.

"I didn't think you ever wanted to farm?" Manon tucked her head against the hollow beneath his collarbone. "Would you be happy here?"

"Fifty acres is no great enterprise. I'm here mostly to set an example to the tenants and to oversee things on site as it were, as his nephew Henri used to do before he got his own lands. We'll take over their old home once it's been repaired a bit. I'll be in his employ and we won't be solely at the mercy of the land. That's what I've always loathed, though now that I'm older I see it was largely my father's laziness, rather than bad harvests, that caused us to starve. That will never happen to us."

"No, it won't." *Whatever the future holds in store, I've no worry that Pascal and I will be able to care for our family. He's stubborn, and I am cunning when I need to be. We're the kind that survives.*

"I thought you might be happier here than in town. Some distance might be good for you?" Manon relaxed into the brawn of his arms and breathed in the scent of soap and pine.

"You're probably right." It would be hard not to feel welcome here. It could be their haven. A legacy for their children.

It was a place to call home.

"You must see it makes more sense to keep him here." Nicole set her fork next to her dinner plate with a metallic *clack* against the polished mahogany.

"Tawendeh stays with me." Manon dropped the French moniker, her hands clasped until her knuckles shone white in the candlelight.

"It's too much for you to put a home together and look after a child. Be reasonable, dear. He's happy here with the other children to play with. Think of the education we can provide for him." Nicole sat tall in her seat at the foot of the table, prepared for battle like a seasoned general.

And think of the education you cannot *provide for him. He would never know anything of his people.*

"I promised that I would care for him and keep him with me. I cannot fail on that promise." Manon spoke each word as if the edges were sharp enough to cut her tongue if she didn't pronounce them with precision.

"He'll be taken care of beautifully. What difference does it make if he's here or with you?" Nicole wasn't completely successful in keeping her serene façade.

What does it matter to you? *You know we can provide for him.*

"Dearest, I'm sure Manon is aware of her capabilities. Younger women than she mother children without trouble, and she's sensible enough to ask for help if the need arises." Alexandre gave his wife a pointed look from the opposite end of the long table and took a long draught of wine from his goblet.

"Alexandre, I don't think she understands how much work it will be to set up a home." Nicole placed her napkin at the side of her place, food clearly no longer a priority.

"We won't have a home anywhere as grand as this. We intend to live simply." Manon lowered her voice, but did not avert her gaze. It would do no good to appear confrontational.

"And she won't be alone. I'll be there to help her." Pascal rarely interjected in the mealtime conversations at the Lefebvre house unless the discussion centered on farming, but his voice rang true as he voiced his support for his wife.

"I don't see what the fuss is about. The cabin won't be ready for another month or two at best. The tenants who lived there last acted like they lived in a run-down tavern rather than a home, so let's not borrow trouble before it knocks on our door, shall we?" Alexandre clearly was reaching his limit of patience with the conversation, and Manon agreed with him.

"That seems wise to me," Pascal agreed, his expression lined with gratitude for Alexandre and his peacekeeping.

"And it's not as though the boy couldn't stay two or three weeks longer while they get settled, in any case." Alexandre returned his wife's mutinous glare with a wry one of his own. *Sometimes it's like living with two moody bulls. Their personalities can be too big for one bull pen . . . or house.*

"That seems reasonable." Pascal's brown eyes shot purposefully and Manon gleaned their meaning in an instant. *Don't be stubborn. It's a good compromise.*

"Of course." Manon took a few bites of the stew before her in a pretense of politeness. *It is reasonable to leave him here for a few weeks as we set up housekeeping. I know Nicole will argue when the time comes to take him with us, but he is my brother.*

Alexandre shifted the conversation as deftly as he could, but Manon could see the longing in Nicole's eyes. She wanted to keep the argument alive. She didn't want to lose a single chick from her nest. She would have gladly kept Manon and Pascal in the guest room for the rest of their days if they'd been willing. *Let it be, please, Nicole. You can't control everything.*

That night, Pascal removed his wife's dress with the reverence of a priest unwrapping a precious relic of the church as he prepared to worship.

"My raven-haired beauty is upset." He twirled a wayward strand of her ebony hair around his finger for a moment, then traced the edge of her jaw with his calloused fingertips. "Please be happy, my dearest one."

"I am." Manon turned to face the mirror and pulled his arms around her waist, rubbing the soft skin of her buttocks against him as she drew him close. "When you and I are alone, the world is a place of calm and peace."

"Don't fret so." He cupped her right breast with his hand and nipped at her earlobe. "You know she only wishes to help. She wants to make sure young Théodore has the same advantages as every child under this roof. Considerable ones."

"You think I should leave him here, don't you?" Manon turned back to face him so she could read his expression.

"No, I don't. If for no other reason, it would make you unhappy to do so." Pascal drew her back in his arms and brushed a stray lock of hair from her face.

"I promised I would take care of him. I promised he would know where he came from. If he stayed here he would be French. He would lose all that he was."

"And in turn, so would you." He kissed her temples with feather-soft brushes of his lips. "I would not have that. I love who you are and would not change you. He is your link to your people."

"Pascal . . . Sometimes I think I'm all alone in the world and then you say things like that." She did not attempt to check the tear that rolled down her cheek.

"I know you, my sweet. You forget. There hasn't been a day since I met you that you haven't been in my thoughts. Not a time that you've been in my presence that your actions haven't been the most significant doings in the room for me."

"I love you, Pascal." She breathed the words into his bare chest and closed her eyes as she let her damp cheek absorb his warmth.

"I love you, too, Skenandoa. Manon. Madame Giroux. I will help you build a life with me. We will find our place."

Manon thought of the familiar meadows and hills that would soon be their home. The little stone house that would welcome them as man and wife. The little black-haired boy asleep in the nursery who would grow to a man there under her care. Away from the prying eyes of town, it seemed no better place could be their nest.

Though the doubt lingered in the pit of her stomach, she relaxed into Pascal's arms and trusted that he would endeavor to keep his promise, though she knew the world worked against him.

CHAPTER 26

Gabrielle

May 1679

"Monsieur Savard, what a pleasant surprise," Gabrielle said, looking up from the tattered chemise she mended and offering the governor's deputy a smile. She wiped the sweat from her palms onto her apron as discreetly as she could manage. He'd visited the shop a handful of times in the past months, bringing a torn waistcoat or a chemise in want of a new hem. Madame Savard never sent commissions. From the rumors about town, Annette Savard would sooner discard a garment than take the trouble to mend it.

"I've a pair of breeches that have become frayed and thought I'd ask you to take a look at them."

"With pleasure," Gabrielle said, extending her hand for the garment, which he produced from his satchel. There was the slightest hint of some loose silken threads at the cuff that hit just below his knee. The deputy dressed impeccably, especially by settlement standards, but this attention to the state of his clothes seemed excessive.

"I can trim the threads and rebind the cuff for you in a trice, monsieur." It was a pity she couldn't take longer at the task or contrive a reason to have him return, but it violated her sense of industry to take longer at a task than she had to—or to keep a customer waiting more than necessary.

"Would you mind if I wait then?" Gabrielle thought she saw a spark of hope in Monsieur Savard's eyes, but convinced herself it was of her own invention.

"Of course you may." Gabrielle gestured to the seat next to the one she preferred and selected the closest matching thread for the breeches from her stores.

They sat in silence as she repaired the cuff, Gabrielle trying not to be unnerved as he watched her stitch. A half dozen times she tried to start up a conversation, but stopped the words before they plunged off her tongue. *He's educated, well traveled, refined. Nothing I have to say would interest him.*

His throat cleared and she looked up from the brown silk. *Say something, please.* She met his eyes for a few moments, but he didn't open up the gates of conversation.

"Does this meet with your approval, monsieur?" The cuff was repaired and there was no sense in dragging out the uncomfortable silence any longer.

"It's sturdier than when I bought it, madame. You're as skilled a seamstress as ever I've seen." His fingers traced the minuscule stitches against the fine fabric, eyeing them with genuine appreciation.

"Thank you, monsieur. It's always a little thrill to work on good fabrics." *And he couldn't care less about what fabrics you enjoy sewing on, you fool.*

"I can imagine. Like a carpenter who comes across a stock of fine mahogany when he must so often craft his goods from soft pine." The deputy placed his carefully folded breeches back in his satchel but made no move to leave the shop.

"Well said, monsieur. For a man born to your sphere, you seem to understand the heart of the craftsman."

"I do try to. As the governor's interests in commerce are keen, it's my duty to understand it as best I can." *Business, Gabrielle. It's not about you.*

"Of course." Gabrielle stood, replaced her thread in its case, and took back up the chemise she'd put aside.

"I must confess, Madame Patenaude, the mending wasn't the chief reason for my visit this afternoon."

Gabrielle could feel the blood rushing in her ears. *What could he possibly want? A new suit? Perhaps he wants to surprise his wife with a gown. . . . It must be something of that nature.*

"Seigneur Robichaux is having a small party at his home in a few days. The governor is the guest of honor and so I'll be in attendance. I was hoping you might have been invited as well."

"I'm sorry, Monsieur Savard, but while I'm friendly with Madame Robichaux, I'm not exactly part of the same social circle." She looked down briefly at her plain dress and smudged apron. *Me? Dine with the governor? Perhaps he's a bit addled by the aroma of the spring wildflowers in the air.*

"You must think our settlement grand indeed if you think there is more than one social circle." Claudine's voice tinkled with laughter from the entrance of the shop.

"I didn't hear you enter, Claudine—Madame Robichaux," Gabrielle said, correcting herself for the deputy's benefit.

"Claudine as always," Claudine responded, scoffing at the formality as she set her basket of mending on Gabrielle's workbench. "And of course you should come. It was thoughtless of me not to include you."

"Very well." Gabrielle drew in her breath and forced herself not to scold Claudine in front of the deputy.

"Wonderful. Madame Savard is in Trois-Rivières visiting friends and I was worried I might feel out of place, so to speak." Savard looked anxiously at the door and his usually confident demeanor seemed ruffled. *Claudine's presence, perhaps? But he is used to socializing with people of her rank.*

"I'll be sure to seat our Madame Patenaude next to you at dinner, monsieur." Claudine smiled graciously. "We want you to have a pleasant evening, naturally."

"How terribly kind of you. I'll be looking forward to it." He bowed slightly with a harried "*Mesdames*" as he left the shop.

"Madame Robichaux? Really, Gabrielle? When have you ever referred to me as *madame?*" Claudine set to work unfolding her mending.

"You've only been married a few months; I haven't much had the chance to use the title. I supposed you'd prefer it when we were in the company of the deputy." Gabrielle looked over Claudine's shoulder to inspect the job in store for her. A couple of torn hems and some missing buttons. Quick work.

"Nonsense. Perhaps in the presence of the governor himself at a formal function, just as I would call you Madame Patenaude."

"Lord, how I loathe being called that. If only I could take back Giroux. At least my brother brings happy associations with the name if my father didn't."

Claudine rubbed Gabrielle's arm, her eyes wide with sympathy. "With any luck, you'll cast off the name Patenaude when you find someone new. Someone worthy."

"I'm not sure I want to marry again." Gabrielle busied her hands with a bodice whose boning needed to be re-cased. She couldn't bear to see the judgment on Claudine's face.

"I can imagine you wouldn't." Claudine tucked some coins into the tin where Gabrielle kept her payments. Claudine always over-paid and would never allow her to return the overage. Gabrielle had stopped trying to persuade Claudine to pay what she charged everyone else. The truth was that she couldn't afford to refuse her generosity.

"You—you needn't have invited me. If it was just to please the deputy, I can come up with an excuse if you like."

"Nonsense. I'm only ashamed at myself for not having thought to invite you." Claudine gathered up her basket and checked her reflection fleetingly in Gabrielle's small mirror. "We'd love to have you."

"I'm the widow of a poor fur trapper. I have no business at a dinner with the governor," Gabrielle said. "I wouldn't want to embarrass you."

"I'm the daughter of a farmer whose land was depleted and only has a roof over his head because my brother-in-law was good enough to save us all from starving." Claudine placed both her hands on Gabrielle's shoulders, forcing her away from tidying the already-immaculate workbench. "I'm no grander than you, no matter whom I married or what idiocy I said in the past."

After Claudine took her leave, Gabrielle sat down with the

frayed bodice in hand and resumed her work. She wanted to believe Claudine's pronouncement, but couldn't bring herself to own it. Claudine was a lady now with fine things, a solid stone house, a staff, and a doting husband. She'd announce her pregnancy any day and the town would celebrate for them. No one, save the Beaumonts and their inner circle, would have noticed if Gabrielle had died alongside her husband.

By the time Claudine had her stuffed into a corset, dressed, powdered, and fitted with shoes that pinched her feet, Gabrielle was ready to crawl into the warmth of her bed and hide from the world for a week.

"I look ridiculous." Gabrielle studied her reflection and sighed. *I don't know who that woman is or if I want anything to do with her.* The ivory gown she had borrowed from Claudine was so delicate, the golden embroidery so fine, Gabrielle was certain she would spoil the dress simply by breathing.

"You speak nonsense. You look beautiful." Manon kissed her cheek and patted Gabrielle's tamed curls.

"Indeed. It's quite bad taste to look better than the hostess, you know, but I suppose I can ignore it this once. We old matrons can't hope to compete with the lovely unmarried ladies like yourself." Claudine pinched Gabrielle's arm playfully. "Madame Savard will have to be careful or the deputy will be swept away by your charms."

Gabrielle felt herself choke as if a breath had caught sideways in her throat, though the flippant remark was made with the obvious twinkle of mirth in Claudine's brown eyes. *It was a harmless jest, but it wouldn't be harmless if it fell on the wrong ears.*

"Don't say such things." Gabrielle swallowed, forcing the air back into her lungs.

"She's right, Claudine, she's nervous enough as it is. Don't tease." Manon, beautifully dressed and hair styled in an elaborate knot, looked at herself in the mirror and sighed at the reflection. "I can't say I love these dinners any more than you do, but with Pascal's position, I can't very well refuse."

"I expect not," Gabrielle mumbled, turning away from the mirror. "Are you sure people won't think me ridiculous? I'm a seam-stress. I have no reason to be here."

"Yes, you do. I invited you. Now enough balking and let's go downstairs before Laurent sees us all flogged for leaving him alone in company. There's nothing he hates more."

Chuckling at the preposterous notion that the kindly Seigneur Robichaux would ever threaten violence, the three women were able to descend with ready smiles for the assembly. The guests had congregated downstairs, sipping champagne. From the landing, their chatter might sound like the shrill chirping of birds as their words bounced off the hardwood of the floors and walls. The candle-light cast a welcoming glow over the foyer that prevented even Gabrielle from feeling completely ill at ease.

"Deputy Savard, we knew you were counting on our enchanting Madame Patenaude to keep you company this evening as your lovely bride is out of town. You'll promise to take good care of her for me tonight, won't you?" Claudine all but purred like a well-fed barn cat as she passed Gabrielle over to the deputy.

" 'Enchanting' is the precise word I would use, Madame Ro-bichaux. I shall, to the best of my ability."

As she was the sister of the best hostess in all of New France, Clau-dine's efforts could be no less than exemplary. Platters with delicately prepared pigeon haloed by sprigs of dried herbs...mounds of golden rice...an array of vegetables such as Gabrielle had never seen. Deputy Savard kept up a flow of charming conversation as course after course was presented in a perfectly choreographed dance by an impeccably trained wait staff. Servants from the Ro-bichaux and Lefebvre households worked along with a few more engaged especially for the evening. The temporary staff hoped to gain notice of the families and to land a regular place in one of their households. It was steady, well-paid work. More dependable in-come than farming. Gabrielle could see the appeal, and couldn't help but notice the barely concealed nerves of a few. Their families had likely instilled in them the importance of the opportunity be-fore them, and they were desperate to impress.

"Ah, your friend has paid a king's ransom for this meal's capstone," Deputy Savard proclaimed as the waiters sashayed about with the silver trays laden with delicate glass goblets filled with what appeared to be a pudding or sweet cream of sorts. His eyes sparkled in anticipation, but Gabrielle looked askance at the foamy concoction placed before her.

"I've never seen a brown pudding before," Gabrielle confessed, eyeing the dessert with distrust, waiting for the others to sample the dish before she did.

"You wouldn't have, as you were born here," the deputy explained. "I expect the governor gave this supply of chocolate to the Robichauxes himself. It's worth more than its weight in gold, especially overseas."

"So *this* is chocolate. Elisabeth has described it so many times; I thought I would recognize it. She never described the color. . . . I expected it to shimmer. When she spoke of the taste I always imagined pink silk."

"You've the heart of a seamstress, despite your training as a baker. But ignore its drab color and appreciate the taste, my dear Madame Patenaude. You won't be disappointed."

Not wanting to affront the deputy or her hostess, Gabrielle dipped her small spoon into the sugary brown foam, took a minuscule dollop on the end of it, and placed it to her lips. Bitter yet sweet, the texture was somehow creamy, yet lighter than air, having been whipped into a frothy cloud by an expert chef. She took pains to remember every detail of the confection; Elisabeth would want a full account of it.

"Your thoughts, madame? You look like a woman falling in love."

Gabrielle felt the heat rise to her cheeks. *The mousse, you fool.*

"I-It's remarkable, monsieur. Truly," Gabrielle stammered.

The deputy seemed to recognize her momentary misinterpretation, the color in his face rising to match her own. "You will make a young man very happy one day, as I am sure Monsieur Patenaude was."

Gabrielle forced the sip of sweet wine to descend her throat without sputtering. It had been weeks since she'd given her late husband a lucid thought outside of her nightmares. *Does that make me a bad person? A bad wife, surely, not to mourn for a husband, no*

*matter how cruel. I would much rather spend my time thinking about
your blond curls and blue eyes, but of course that would be wicked.*

"I cannot speak for the dead, Deputy Savard, but I genuinely
hope I gave him happiness in the short time we were married."
Gabrielle did not look the deputy in the face, but took another
spoonful of the decadent mousse. *It's too dear to waste, and I may
never have the chance to sample it again.*

"How thoughtless of me. I am sure the mention of your late
husband is still very painful. Forgive my lapse in tact, please."

"There's nothing to forgive, *monsieur le député*. You find me in
a pensive mood this evening." Gabrielle looked at him and gave
him a smile that went only as deep as her lips.

"Then I am remiss in my duty to you as a companion this
evening. On a night such as this, one's thoughts should be of naught
but the fine food, the pleasant company, and of course the dancing."

Dancing. The strains of the music wafted into the dining room
like the enticing aroma of the roasted chickens coming from the
kitchen. The blood drained completely from Gabrielle's face and
she looked for Claudine or Manon to help her make an exit.

The deputy stood and, offering Gabrielle his hand, said,
"Come, let us dance away those sobering thoughts of yours."

Gabrielle accepted his hand, but took a step back once she found
her feet. "I'm terribly sorry, Monsieur Savard, but I don't dance."

"Nonsense, there's nothing to it. Just follow my lead and listen
to the music." He smiled broadly, his eyes danced. She could not
refuse him.

She nodded her assent and he led her to the dance floor, where
they joined seven or eight other couples who had already begun
twirling in time with the music.

"Just breathe and look into my eyes. Don't worry about your
feet." He took her in his arms expertly and she found immediately
that he was right. All that mattered was his arms and the music. All
else had vanished.

"You truly *are* enchanting, Madame Patenaude." Savard murmured his words a little too close to her ear to be completely decorous. She thought for a moment she'd felt his soft lips brush against
her skin, but dismissed it as her imagination. A married man would
not be so bold. Not in public.

"As are you, I'm afraid," Gabrielle whispered at a slightly greater distance.

"Afraid? Do I frighten you, madame?" There was a twinkle of mischief in Savard's eye that made Gabrielle's heart stir. She'd never seen the slightest glimmer of mirth in Patenaude.

"More than I should let on, monsieur," Gabrielle said, her green eyes wide with sincerity.

CHAPTER 27

Claudine

July 1679

"The green suits you beautifully, but I'm not sure if the reddish-pink isn't better with your skin." Gabrielle held the fabric up to Claudine's face, alternating between the two shades of precious silk that Laurent had procured. She'd been given first choice of the lot, but the rest would be sold to the other ladies of standing in the settlement. She wouldn't need more than one fine gown that year and the other women would never speak to her if she monopolized such a fine shipment. Claudine had come to admit that she preferred her woolen jackets and sturdy skirts to the frills of evening wear most days. Still, it was always a joy to know she had a few delicate pieces when the need arose.

And it's not like the wool I wear is the coarse homespun I wore as a child, either. A little money can procure much softer stuff. She looked over at the lovely length of navy blue wool that Laurent had secured for her jacket and skirt for cold weather. Though the July sun warmed her now, there was comfort to know that she'd have new, warm clothes for winter.

"The pink," Claudine agreed. "If the green were darker, I wouldn't be able to resist, but the soft green would much better suit someone fairer. Like Elisabeth or you."

Gabrielle bit her lip as she set the green silk back in a lined basket with the same care she'd use for an infant. "I don't think Elisabeth or I have any call for a silk gown, but thank you for the compliment."

Neither the occasion nor the means, you thoughtless ninny.

"It's a shame, really." Claudine decided that apologizing might only make her blunder worse. "Your lovely red hair begs for a green dress. You looked so beautiful dressed up for the ball."

Gabrielle proceeded without acknowledging Claudine's words and draped the silk artfully over Claudine's frame. "To get a feel for the fabric, to see how the sheen catches the light. How it wants to drape and fold," Gabrielle had once explained, speaking as though the fabric were a living thing. Claudine had once thought the process of dressmaking dull and mindless work. A few hours paying attention to Gabrielle and her craft cured her of any delusion that her friend was anything less than an artist. After a quarter of an hour, Gabrielle seemed satisfied and placed the silk in the basket she designated for Claudine's projects and mending.

"Nicole will want the yellow, I'm certain of it," Claudine said as she looked over the selection, careful not to soil the delicate fabrics with the oils from her fingers. "She was to have been here more than a half hour ago. It's not like her to be late."

"No, it isn't," Gabrielle said, her brow furrowed. Almost as soon as Gabrielle spoke, Nicole emerged into the shop, Pascal hard on her heels.

"Gabrielle, I'm afraid I can't stay for a fitting." Nicole gasped her words, panting like she'd run from the Lefebvre house all the way to the shop in the hot July sun. "Papa is ill, Claudine. Stay here if you wish, but Maman asked Pascal to fetch me. She says she won't leave him."

Papa. Thomas Deschamps, the proud oak of a man, was never meant to topple. If Manon was called to help and wouldn't leave his side, it had to be grave.

"Of course I'm coming." Claudine folded the last length of silk with care, but not much precision. Gabrielle would see to it. "Please send word with someone to Laurent that I may be late."

"Consider it done." Gabrielle patted Claudine's elbow and opened the door for her company, accepting a distracted kiss on the cheek from her brother as he left. Under other circumstances, the brief display of affection between brother and sister might have given Claudine a pang of envy for her two big brothers left behind in France so long ago. Now she only wished to hurry the departure. She'd make up the inconvenience to Gabrielle later.

Claudine couldn't bring herself to chat over the pounding of the horse hooves over the dry earth. She clasped Nicole's hand in silence and willed the horse to fly over the hills to her parents' little stone house.

Once there, Claudine and her sister crowded into the bedroom with Manon and their mother, Bernadette. Thomas's face was ashen, but his breathing was even. He slept peacefully, so they spoke in whispers.

"I think it was something to do with his heart. His heartbeat seems strong now. . . ." *But you can't tell us if it will stay that way. Of course you can't, but thank God you were close by.* Manon applied a cool cloth to his wrinkled forehead, tanned from too many hours toiling in the sun. *Too much work and too few sons to help.*

"We should have hired some help for him," Nicole said, as if reading her sister's thoughts.

"He wouldn't have accepted it anyway. You know how stubborn your papa can be." Bernadette directed the words at her daughters but her eyes never left her husband's face.

"He'll have to after this," Manon said. "Once the heart gives a man trouble, it's likely to do worse in the future. Doubly so if he overtires himself."

"It will take some convincing, but he's nearly sixty. He can't work like a boy anymore." Nicole took on the stern voice she used with the children, even Alexandre at times when he was being contentious. She was likely adding up her monthly accounts to think where she could scrimp to allow for extra field hands.

Claudine nodded in agreement. *If you want to arrange all this, do so by all means. But what of Maman?* Bernadette's face had aged in the two months since Claudine had ventured to the farm. Her lines were deeper and her eyes fatigued. The slump in her shoulders never fully went away. Though Bernadette had always seemed "ancient" to Claudine, this was the first time she'd recognized that her mother had actually become an old woman.

It was a long trek to venture this far afield with any sort of regularity, but her parents had only seen little Zacharie four times that year. Winter was never far off and the visits would become less and less frequent.

I must do better. All I could think about for years was escaping the farm, and I never once thought of the hard work my parents endured to give me any sort of comfort. I must do better for them. I will do better.

By four in the afternoon the floor of the Deschamps farmhouse gleamed like the marble galleries of the Palace of the Louvre, or so Claudine imagined. The stew was warming on the fire and two big loaves of good Beaumont bread graced the table for the evening meal. Two weeks had passed since Thomas fell ill, and he was still unable to stir far from bed without fatigue. Bernadette used every last fraction of energy to tend to him, which left Georges and the house in need of attention. Claudine's younger brother, a sturdy lad of thirteen, helped without complaint, but by the end of the day, Claudine was so tired she was certain she would sleep a week, but knew she would force herself awake at dawn and be back before breakfast the next day.

"Stay for supper, sweetest," Bernadette cajoled. "You must be starving."

"I should get home to Laurent and Zacharie, Maman. They'll miss me if I don't join them for supper. I'll be back in the morning."

"Really, Claudine, you don't have to come so often. Georges and I can get by." Bernadette shifted an errant lock of hair from Claudine's forehead behind her ear.

"Papa needs you to tend to him, so someone needs to tend to you and Georges." The tone of her voice left no room for argument. *Nicole isn't the only one who can take charge. She's seen to your fields, I'll see to your house.*

"It's good to have Claudine back so much," Georges interjected from his seat at the table, where he sat figuring sums. Even with an ill father and a preoccupied mother, Claudine wasn't about to see Georges's studies fall behind. Rose would be furious with her former pupil for allowing the lapse, aside from the disservice she would be doing Georges himself. As the sun slipped low in the sky, she kissed her mother's papery cheek, and ruffled Georges's hair as she issued his standing orders:

"Help Maman, study, and don't get into trouble—or you'll have my wrath to contend with." Her admonition was met with a defiant raspberry from Georges's tongue and a roguish wink. For all his bravado, he was the most obedient of the Deschamps children, with the possible exception of Emmanuelle.

Laurent saw her equipped with a sturdy horse and wagon for her treks to and from the town. She wasn't much of a horsewoman, so driving the wagon was less daunting than riding on horseback. She clutched the reins, feeling the blood pulse in her hands at the exaggerated grip, and willed herself to stay awake the entire ride. *It would be my luck to fall asleep and fall out of the wagon and break my fool head. One more person to take care of. Exactly what the family needs now.*

By the time she arrived home it was a full hour past their usual dining time. She passed the horse and wagon off to the stableman without comment and walked into the house through the back door that the servants used for transporting groceries and firewood.

"There you are!" Laurent bounded over to her as she entered the foyer by way of the kitchen. "I'd been worried for the past two hours."

"Papa was worse today. I stayed late so Maman wouldn't have to make supper."

"Darling, you work far too hard. You look exhausted."

"I am exhausted, and I should be ashamed. A day of work never fazed me like this before. I've grown soft." She handed her basket off to the waiting maid and removed her cloak.

"I'm glad to hear it." Laurent wrapped his thick arms around her and kissed her forehead when she was free of her outer garments. "What else is a man good for if not ensuring that his wife's life is one of comfort?"

"Papa doesn't have that luxury. He never has." Claudine turned away to straighten the cloaks as they hung on their posts. Laurent took her hand and turned her back to him.

"That was insensitive of me. I didn't mean to insult how well your father has provided for his family."

"I know you didn't." Claudine kissed his cheek reassuringly. "You're the kindest man to ever draw breath, but they need my help. I can't ignore them. I haven't the duties that Nicole has, so I must do what I can for them. There's no one else." *Were Emmanuelle alive she'd be there day and night. And God forgive me, I'd have let her.*

"What do you need, my love?" Laurent whispered in her ear and kissed the soft patch of skin directly below her earlobe.

"Supper and bed." Claudine spoke into the breadth of his chest, but clear enough for him to call an order for the maid that Madame needed her meal at once.

"You will have already eaten," Claudine said. "You needn't keep me company."

"Of course I wouldn't dream of eating without you when you were expected home. Though I suspect Cook is angry with us."

"I'll make my apologies in the morning," Claudine said. "I can imagine it was an inconvenience to her."

"Never mind that." Laurent pulled back a chair for Claudine to the right of the head of the table and took his usual seat next to hers. The maid placed some roast ham and elegant little corners of toasted bread before her. It looked like it would have been far more appetizing an hour before, but Claudine made no objection. She picked idly at the food, and though she should have been ravenous, she could hardly bring herself to eat. Claudine made an attempt to converse with Laurent, but her responses were scattered and vague. The battle to keep from yawning at the table took the majority of her concentration. As soon as the meal was cleared away, Laurent stood and offered her his arm.

"To bed. And, my dearest love, you must promise me to stay home tomorrow. I won't have you falling ill yourself."

"You know I can't. Maman needs me." She clutched to his arm as they began their ascent up the stairs.

"Others need you as well, darling. And none more than me." He patted her hand that he cradled in his arm.

"You're so sweet—"

All she felt then was falling against him and his strong arms lowering her to the floor before she collapsed.

* * *

"She'll need her rest, but she'll be well in time." Manon's calm voice pierced the blackness. Claudine's eyes protested against the light. She tried to sit up, but the wave of nausea thrust her back against her pillow, hoping the contents of her stomach would remain where they belonged.

"Don't try to sit up," Manon urged, approaching the side of the bed.

"I won't, I assure you." The room still spun violently, and Claudine shut her eyes against the spinning.

"Laurent tells me you were overtired, but did anything else ail you?"

"I've not had much of an appetite," Claudine confessed. "I've been working harder than I'm used to and so tired, I suppose I just haven't felt much like eating."

"Why don't we delay the questions for now until she's had some rest?" Laurent's tone was sharper than she'd ever heard, his face white with fear. *I'm going to be fine, my dearest. Don't fret.*

"Just one more. How long ago did you last have your courses?" Manon's dark eyes looked ready for calculation. Claudine's widened with comprehension at the significance of the question.

"I . . . I haven't really kept track." She sat up, waving against Laurent's protests. This time, her supper made no threats to reappear. "Oh heavens. It was May. Mid-May."

"Well then, I expect you'll be welcoming Baby Robichaux sometime in February. Our little ones will be playmates." She patted her own small bump with a smile. *You and Pascal wasted no time. You'll be rocking your cradle by Christmas.*

Claudine lay back against the pillow. *It was only a matter of time. This is why women marry, after all.*

"Do you feel faint again, my dearest?" Laurent's eyes searched her face for any clue as to how he might help her.

"No, no. Just surprised, I suppose. It didn't occur to me. . . ."

"You've been far too busy with your family to think about yourself." Manon gripped Claudine's hand reassuringly. "I'm sure you'll feel just fine if you rest. I promise I will see to your father as often as I can. I'll be back to check on you later in the week."

"Th-thank you." Claudine wiped her hair from her forehead as

Manon left with a quick smile. *Papa and Maman. What terrible timing, little one. My energy is needed elsewhere. You'll have to learn to share.*

"Are you sure there's nothing I can get for you?" Laurent took her hand, sitting gingerly on the side of the bed, careful not to jostle her. "Anything you want. It's yours."

"Just you, my dearest. Come lie down with me." She took his hand, kissed the back of it two or three times, and rubbed it against her cheek.

"I don't want to hurt you or disturb your rest." Laurent returned the gesture to the back of her hand, concerned, but not ready to leave her alone.

"I'll rest better with you by my side, love. I swear it."

"Very well, you little vixen. You know exactly how to get what you want from me." He stood, removing his cravat and waistcoat, placing them on the bedside chair for the maid to attend to.

"It's easy when it's something you crave as well."

"You speak the truth. I *do* crave you." He crawled into the bed, wrapping his arms around her. "Truly you feel well?"

"Tired and overwhelmed, but yes, I do feel well enough. I'm surprised little Baby Robichaux has been so long in coming." Claudine curled herself against Laurent's warm body, kissing the bare skin where the neck of his chemise gapped.

"I confess I was wondering what was taking so long myself, but I admit I was a bit relieved with the delay. I hate to say it, but it's true."

"My love, just because it happened to Emmanuelle doesn't mean . . ." Claudine took Laurent's hand in hers and pressed her lips to his knuckles.

"I know. It just frightens me. . . ." Laurent tucked her hair behind her ear and pulled her close to his chest.

"Then don't think of it, beloved. Think of our child. He or she will be healthy and happy and well cared for. The most beloved baby in New France, along with our little Zacharie, of course."

"I'm going to insist you keep your word, Madame Robichaux." Laurent rolled so his torso was over hers and kissed her deeply. "And you must promise to rest. We'll find a way to tend to your parents without you going out there every day."

Claudine wanted to protest, but she was too weary to consider a trip into the country the next day. She would send a maid with some food and instructions to help with any chores that needed tending.

It wasn't long before Laurent's breaths grew deep and even in restful sleep.

I love you more than you know, dear man, though I've no idea what I've done to deserve you.

CHAPTER 28

Gabrielle

July 1679

I am his mistress.

It was the hour before dawn, and Gabrielle stretched against René's muscular frame as he languished next to her in the warm bed. The words tumbled over and over in her head, but she forced them away. The occasions for him to spend more than an hour or two alone in her company were rare, but Madame Savard had taken another brief trip to Trois-Rivières to visit friends, so the trysts grew longer and less guarded. Never before had she the luxury of waking in his arms after a night of lovemaking. She would not ruin their time together. There would be plenty of solitary hours later in which she could nurse her qualms and misgivings.

"I ought to get home before anyone notices my absence." His words sounded resolute, but he wrapped his arms tighter around her.

"You ought to, but I'd prefer you stay the day complete." Gabrielle buried her face in his chest, breathing deep. Clean, expensive soap . . . not the smell of horse and sweat that seemed to perfume other men.

"I'd love nothing better, little dove. A morning in your arms. A picnic by the river. A stroll through town with you on my arm. But I won't see you ruined." His lips found hers and drank their fill, though she still thirsted when he pulled away and pulled on his breeches.

"Will you be back tonight?" Gabrielle traced the sinews on his back that flexed as he pulled on his boots.

"If at all possible, sweet one. I'll be here after dark if she hasn't returned."

"She." He never uses her name. Out of respect? Contempt? Fear?

And as he'd done all week, he slipped from her bed out into the darkness, hoping no one would suspect where he'd been.

Gabrielle knew she was the only one with anything to lose, and aware that there was precious little left. Her reputation, and even that was tarnished. From the way people eyed her in town, they still wondered why she had sued for separation from her husband. Whether she was truly blameless in his death.

They cannot tarnish my happiness. They cannot take this from me.

He had been gracious enough to escort her home after the ball at the Robichaux house. Her head full of champagne bubbles, chocolate mousse, and dancing, she had invited him upstairs. Since that night, they found a spare hour whenever they could to indulge in each other. The guilt weighed in her stomach like a stone most of the time, but his smile and embrace were enough to keep her trepidation at bay long enough for her to make more foolish decisions.

It's all well until you find yourself with a bastard child to feed and no means to do so. Gabrielle chastised herself for the ungracious thought. She could never use such a term about a love child with René. René's child, surely a strapping boy, would be all golden curls and mischievous smiles. And René said he had been very careful not to risk a child. She wasn't sure what that meant, and was afraid to ask.

But he would still starve. No one would give you so much as a pair of trousers to mend if word broke out.

Gabrielle abandoned any pretense of sleep and ate her solitary breakfast in the weak light of morning that streamed into her minuscule kitchen. She was unimpressed with the radiant display of color that peered in through the small window. It seemed pale and gray in René's absence. Her bread and egg sated her appetite, but she wasn't sure she'd tasted a morsel of it.

Uncertain what else she could do to delay the start of the day, she set to cutting out the dark, inky blue wool for Claudine's winter suit. Manon had let her know of the impending arrival, so she fashioned the skirt and bodice to allow for her expanding stomach. The wool was some of the highest quality she'd come across in her life. It was a delight to sew on, being soft to the touch, but not nearly as temperamental as silk.

Just as she was about to take scissors to the fine wool, the shop door creaked open without preamble. She tossed the scissors down in frustration, but she was glad her start had not caused her to ruin the fabric.

"Are you Madame Patenaude?" A tiny woman, lilting and blond like a spring flower that would never weather a heavy rain, stood just inside the shop door. Her clothes spoke of generations of wealth and taste. Small wonder Gabrielle had not made her acquaintance. Gabrielle stood and crossed to where the woman stood and offered her hand.

"Indeed, I am. What may I do for you, Madame—?"

"Savard."

Gabrielle felt the color drain from her face and knew that René's wife would see the guilt there. *Be calm. Don't act as if you've done anything wrong. She'll never make him as happy as you do.*

"A pleasure to meet you, Madame Savard." Gabrielle forced a smile. "I do believe I have some mending for your house. Shall I fetch it for you?"

"Yes. And don't expect more work from us. The servants will get on as they did before—you." *She knows. She must know everything.* Gabrielle fetched the parcel with a few of René's chemises he'd brought for mending as a pretext for visiting.

"Was some of my work not up to your standard, madame?" *It was perfect. Every stitch.*

"Your services are superfluous. We already have the staff to do the work."

Of course you can't be bothered to do it yourself, you lazy cow.

"Very well, madame. But do feel free to call on me if ever you're in need of any mending or sewing."

"Good day, Madame Patenaude. We won't have occasion to see each other again."

Gabrielle watched Madame Savard leave the shop, carrying the parcel out from her body with two fingers as though it contained a decaying carcass rather than her husband's clean shirts. Gabrielle always kept the shop door unlocked during daylight hours as a point of pride, but she barred the door behind Madame Savard and rushed up the stairs to her room before anyone walking on the street below could see the tears streaming down her face.

She knows everything. She will ruin me if I step near him again, or him near me. Why would God dangle him before me just to take him away?

Two days later, as Gabrielle stood to bar the door for the night, a gentle rapping sounded before the door swung open.

"What are you doing here, René?" Gabrielle busied her hands sorting some scrap fabric she'd left on her worktable.

"Annette said she'd been here." He made no move to approach her, didn't embrace her as he had done every time they'd been alone for the past few months. She'd been expecting this visit since his wife left the shop, but it didn't lessen the pain she felt in the center of her chest.

"She had her friends spying on me for weeks. It seems her trip to Trois-Rivières was just a pretense for her to give you and me time alone . . . so her old crones would have a chance to catch us. . . ."

"Heavens above, what a charming woman." Gabrielle flung the last of the scraps in the appropriate basket and shoved it back on the shelf. "How many times are we women told to look the other way if our husbands stray. To accept responsibility for their infidelity. To end it, if possible, by making home a haven of comfort and affection. Has she transformed into an angel of domestic tranquility since her return?"

René snorted and rolled his eyes. "Hardly. She's been a proper shrew since she came back."

"Then why do you tolerate it? For pity's sake, you're a man and can do as you please, whether it's fair or not to your wife or any other woman."

"Dearest one, you must understand . . . I simply cannot afford to anger her father. She's threatened to write to him. If she does, he could ruin me. I should never have agreed to bring her here. She wasn't always quite so . . ."

"Surly? Unpleasant? Cruel?"

"I'm sorry Annette came to see you. I would never have allowed it if I had learned of her plan."

"So you're casting me out. Leaving me to my cold bed for the rest of my days, then?"

"Don't be like that. Don't be like her. I'd spend the rest of my life with you if I were free. But I'm not. I only thank God that I haven't gotten you with child and that I leave your reputation intact."

"My reputation. My reputation. What of yours? I wasn't here alone all those nights."

"Don't you think there wouldn't be consequences for me here in town if things were to come out in the public eye, Gabrielle? I'm a deputy of the governor. I cannot afford to have a scandal attached to my name. Even someone like you must understand that."

"Someone like me? What, pray tell, do you mean by that?" Gabrielle slammed a bolt of fabric down on her workbench with an unsatisfying *thunk*. She wished her pots and pans were in closer proximity to make a proper clatter.

René raked his fingers through his hair and stared at the ceiling, perhaps willing it to provide him with patience. "Someone who doesn't live in the public eye, someone who doesn't live in the first circles. A private person, so to speak."

"A nobody." *I will not make this easy on you.*

"That's not what I said, woman, and you know it. I loved you. This is killing me and you're mocking me."

Loved. The tears stung so painfully she grimaced against them. "Then go, René. Go and be well and we can pretend to be utter strangers when our paths cross. Go home and be with her if that's what you want."

"That's what I'm trying to tell you. Our paths won't cross, Gabrielle. Annette and I are going back to France. She insisted, and I agree with her. I wouldn't be able to be an honorable husband with you nearby and she will be happier back in Paris. I'm certain of it."

Gabrielle looked up and finally locked her gaze with his.

"You're leaving me."

"I don't see how things could have ended any other way. I wish things could be different." His eyes cast downward. *At least you feel some shame. I'd hate to bear it all alone.*

"Things could be exactly as you want them to be, but you're letting her lead you about like a wayward horse. You refuse to use your crop and rein her in." She turned her eyes, looking for something to tidy on her workbench, but found nothing out of place.

"You're being incredibly unfair." René's arms crossed over his broad chest, shielding himself against her accusations.

Gabrielle looked up from her well-ordered worktable. "Honestly, René? You think of the three of us that *you're* the one being treated unfairly? Do you hear yourself?"

"I know. I'm sorry. So desperately sorry."

"As am I. I thought you were a man."

René crossed the room to her, cupped her face in his hands. She allowed herself to fall into the softness of his kiss. *This will be the last time he kisses you, enjoy it.*

"Good-bye, my love," he whispered.

"Good-bye." She choked on the word, the pain stealing the air from her lungs.

For several minutes, perhaps longer, she stared at the door that René shut behind himself. She might see a glimpse of him from time to time in town. He might bow, almost imperceptibly, if they passed on the street. He would never speak to her again. She would never hear the rich baritone of his voice directed at her, but she might hear him address others more worthy of his notice if she happened by him in the settlement.

Those scraps of René would only last for a few weeks. Days, more likely. No more than a month if they were to find a ship returning home that year.

At least your last word wasn't spoken in anger. At least his words were tender ones.

The supper she'd planned forgotten, she ascended the stairs to her bedroom. She clung to the faint smell on her sheets of the perfumed soap that he must have brought over by the trunkful from France.

Not his. His wife's. It was her soap.

The revelation kicked her in the gut, but she refused to give in to her misery. She had the luxury of a spare set of sheets, so she leaped from her bed, stripping the bed clean with one fluid motion. She pulled the pillows from their cases to replace them with unoffending linens. She would remove every trace of his scent—every trace of him—with boiling water and plain soap the next morning.

She climbed back into her bed, which now smelled of innocent pine boughs Elisabeth sewed into sachets for her linen drawers. *I must remember to thank her.*

But the image of her loving mother gave way to Annette Savard's angelic face as she wrestled with sleep. *Annette is his wife . . . you ought to put yourself in her place. How would you react if you found out your husband had been untrue?*

Gabrielle thought of Patenaude and snorted to herself. *I could have only been so fortunate. She could have borne some of the misery with me.*

But René was not Patenaude. He was a kind man who owed his wife more consideration than he gave her. Try as she might, she could not despise Annette Savard for her outburst in the shop.

She felt bruised as she settled into her bed, but hopeful that sleep would come, blissful in the knowledge that she greatly preferred pine to exotic spices and flowers that could never flourish in their frozen forests.

As Gabrielle predicted, René and his household were gone a week and a half after he bade her farewell in the shop. She spent every hour of daylight with mending in her hand or crafting the odd new garment. Elisabeth had commissioned a new everyday dress that was a much welcome diversion. Evenings were harder. She would sit before her thin soup and hunk of bread. *Eat, you dolt. There are many without. Open your mouth and just eat it.*

She no longer took solace in embroidery after a day hunched over with her mending. She would have enjoyed a visit with Claudine or Manon, but married bliss had claimed them both. She had taken to long meandering walks since the August sun set so late and the warmth of the evening did not chase her back to her hearth. She took the little paths east of town, breathing in the air, free from the scent of sweat and excrement that never really dissipated in town, especially in the heat of summer.

Not anxious to return home, Gabrielle saw a patch of late-summer wildflowers in a secluded field. She gazed over the field, ablaze with orange and red blooms punctuated with embers of blue and purple. There was not a soul to be seen, so she ran out into the field and rolled in the middle of it, carefree as a horse let loose to run after a long stint cooped up in a stable.

She lay on her back, looking up at the sky, streaked with the first shards of pink sunset. She breathed in the delicate scent of the wildflowers . . . not as pretentious as the roses and lavender true ladies preferred. They smelled of grass and earth and goodness. She used to escape to fields like this when she was a girl. When Raymond Giroux had taken to drink or was in a foul mood. Either she'd come out to escape his wrath or recover from it when she was too late.

She'd not done so after Patenaude's outbursts. The lands near their homestead were not so lush and verdant as this. As if he'd chosen the rockiest, most inhospitable patch of land in all of New France out of spite. *It suited him.*

For a while she wondered what it might be like to stay the night, ensconced in a bed of wildflowers and willowy grasses, but her pragmatic nature reminded her that the chill of night would soon chase her home and it would be better to find her way before the light died completely.

I will take the meadow home with me. I deserve some beauty there at least. She took her mending shears from her apron pocket, rarely leaving home without them, and cut a massive armful of flowers to brighten the somber timbers of her shop. She was careful to cut a few flowers from a patch and move on so that the effect wouldn't be ruined for the next passerby, and so their seeds might produce another splendorous display the following year.

She arrived back home well before dark settled in earnest, and was glad for the prudence of her decision.

"Out awful late, aren't you?"

The flowers erupted from her arms in a cascade of color as she jolted from the shock. Bailiff Duval sat in her best chair by the window, legs crossed as though he'd been prepared to wait the night.

"Pardon me, Bailiff, you startled me." Gabrielle knelt and began gathering up the discarded blooms.

"I was surprised not to find you at home at such a late hour."
Don't offer to help. Don't apologize. Fat oaf of a bastard.

"It's not yet dark, monsieur. I like to take a brief walk after my supper."

"I see. Some might think you're up to trouble."

"Gathering wildflowers from an empty field, monsieur? Surely there's no crime in that. Nothing worrisome, even for you."

"Maybe. Maybe not. I've come to ask you a few questions."

"Has the judge sent you, monsieur?"

"No, but don't be surprised if he does."

"I will be happy to answer his questions when the time comes, monsieur. I don't believe I'm under any obligation to do so now."

"I'd watch my tongue if I were you, young madame. It's come to my attention that Monsieur Patenaude might not have died in an accident. That you might have wished him ill so that you might have been free to dally elsewhere. Say, with our recently departed deputy?"

The stems of the flowers she had picked up from the floor now cut into her hand. She forced herself to loosen her grip before she destroyed her harvest completely, the blood rushing painfully back through her whitened fingers.

"Monsieur, do you realize I never made the acquaintance of the deputy until several months after my husband passed away? I was living out on a homestead and never ventured back into town. He visited here once on the governor's bidding and commissioned some mending a handful of times after that. You're being remarkably presumptuous." Gabrielle wished she could have swallowed back her words as soon as she'd spoken them. *Duval isn't a man who likes to be argued with. And he's in no real position to make your life worse. That's for the judge. He's merely a complication.*

"Might be, but your making doe eyes at the deputy didn't help but to feed the fires, so to speak."

"And does idle gossip now constitute grounds for a formal inquiry?" *Fling the flowers at his fool head. The vase, too.* Gabrielle gripped her hands behind her back to keep her less noble thoughts from realizing themselves.

"People say you kept a musket with you, and none of Patenaude's hunting companions ever gave any sort of account of what happened."

"Monsieur, my husband was a hunter. A fur trapper. He was gone for weeks at a time. Do you honestly think it wise for a woman alone to stay out in the wilderness unarmed? Would you have Madame Duval do so?"

Gabrielle was careful not to let a smirk cross her face. Duval had risen from farming stock and abhorred any comparison to those who worked the land.

"Just know, questions are being asked. Were I you, I'd be prepared."

"Thank you ever so much for your warning, Bailiff. If that is all, I suggest you find your way home to supper. Madame Duval won't appreciate your tardiness on my account."

Gabrielle did not dignify his presence with words any longer and held open the door into the darkening night.

As she shut the door, with a resounding *crack* behind Duval, there was no wondering why, after all these months, her innocence had come into question.

What a kindly gift your wife has left me, René. She's done her best to send me to the gallows, and you'll never know if I swing.

CHAPTER 29

Manon

September 1679

Why did I not take Mother Onatah's advice and learn how to cook properly? Manon fumbled about the kitchen as she attempted to prepare breakfast for Pascal and Théodore. Every mealtime she missed Mother Onatah in a way she never anticipated. She spent the years when she'd have learned to keep house learning how to mix herbs and concoct fever remedies instead. She was a passable seamstress, thanks to Rose, but in all other respects, she was helpless as a housekeeper. She was raised by Mother Onatah to be a healer and by the Lefebvres to be a lady. In the end, she was not destined to live either of those lives.

She toasted some bread over the fire and fried up some eggs and a ham steak. The odor was pleasant and the smoke not too bad for once. The eggs looked fluffy and yellow as they should; the ham steak looked well browned, but not charred. *Success at last!* The smell of the sizzling pork stirred both man and boy from their beds, staggering bleary-eyed to the table.

"It smells good," Pascal said tentatively, eyeing the food cautiously. *Too many failed attempts. The poor boys will starve if I don't improve.*

"Better," Théodore pronounced, chewing slowly.

"Better," Pascal agreed.

"What's wrong with it?" Manon asked, her sigh of exasperation audible.

"It would help ever so much if you cooked the meat through. It's lovely and crisp on the outside and raw in the middle."

"I swear I'm cursed. It's either raw in the middle or completely burnt. I'll never get the handle of it." She crossed her arms over her chest in defeat. A small kick from her midsection protested her decision to stop eating.

"You're learning, my darling. It just takes practice."

"All well and good so long as you two don't waste away in the meantime."

"We'll manage. We always do." Pascal kissed her cheek and left as soon as his plate was cleared, Théodore chasing after him.

Poor man. I must find a solution.

There was mending to be done, but she'd saved enough pocket money to hire Gabrielle to do the work. Pascal wouldn't have need of the wagon and the horse, so she decided that it would be as good a day as any to deliver the basket of clothing.

When Manon entered the shop, Gabrielle had several customers, so Manon left the bundle of clothes on the workbench with an approving nod from the busy patroness. *She's managing well despite the threats hanging over her head.* Manon and Claudine had assured Gabrielle that the bailiff's warnings were all a bluff, but indeed the judge had begun investigating Patenaude's death in earnest. More questioning was certain, and it set Manon's teeth on edge to have Gabrielle still tortured by the evil man she'd married.

At the Lefebvre house, she found Nicole was out on social calls, and she was sure Alexandre would be too busy to be bothered with a visit. The children would be engrossed in their studies, and oughtn't be disturbed either. The sound of well-ordered clanging and banging of the experienced cook, Madame Yollande, came from the kitchen along with the enticing aroma of the meal that would be served at midday.

"The young madame come back to see us!" Madame Yollande cried. The two had rarely had occasion to chat, but she always welcomed Manon into the one corner of the Lefebvre house where the rest of the Lefebvres rarely ventured. "Might I fetch you something to nibble on, madame?"

"I don't think I could refuse," Manon admitted, thinking of her subpar breakfast and the insatiable appetite of the life within. "Thank you."

"And how are you getting on all the way out there, madame?" Madame Yollande placed an appetizing meat pie and a mug of cider before Manon. She felt the need to restrain herself as she ate, else risk appearing as savage as many in town thought she was. The cook's face was lined with sympathy as if Manon had been sent to the moon itself rather than a well-ordered farm that sat a relatively easy distance from town in fair weather.

"Things are going quite well," Manon said in between the small bites she forced herself to take. "You're an artist with food, Madame Yollande."

"Oh, you're too kind, madame."

"Not at all. I'm a miserable failure as a cook. I never seem to get it right." Manon set down her fork with a sigh. She'd had an enjoyable meal, but poor Pascal and Théodore would have to get along with her poor efforts.

"Now, madame, why don't you stay on this morning and watch me as I put together luncheon. You might pick up a trick or two."

"Are you certain I wouldn't be in your way?" Manon stammered at the woman's thoughtful gesture.

"Not in the least bit, madame. Have a seat right there and I'll talk you through it all as I go along. You can rest your poor feet while you learn."

Manon's eyes stung, and she wiped away the evidence before the squat woman with flyaway gray hair could notice. *It's the onion. Else perhaps the fatigue of carrying a child. She doesn't need me weeping in her kitchen.*

For over an hour, Manon watched as Madame Yollande chopped, measured, stirred, and simmered. She narrated the meal preparation as simply as she would explain the process to a child. There was no end to her patience with Manon's questions and her bumbling attempts to imitate Madame Yollande's techniques that had taken the talented cook years to master.

Manon realized her own men would soon be in need of their midday meal, so she was forced to take her leave of her culinary patroness.

"Thank you so much for all your help." Manon embraced the woman briefly. Madame Yollande patted Manon's hand, one brow arched in mild surprise. A Lefebvre would never have made such a gesture to a servant, no matter how kind the deed.

I needn't worry about rank and station anymore. I am a farmer's wife, though he aspires to be so much more. It's as freeing as a barefoot walk on spring grass.

Manon returned home, extra meat pies and bread thrust upon her by Madame Yollande after Manon promised to come back as often as she could for more lessons. *At least Pascal and Théodore will eat well this afternoon, little thanks to me. I will return for lessons from Madame Yollande. I owe them that much.*

Manon felt her shoulders drop slightly as the stone buildings gave way to lush pastures. *The settlement was good to me, but this is home.*

Manon took example from her first schoolmistress, Rose, and taught her class out of doors. Though the Lefebvres had done what they could to "civilize" Théodore, to turn him into a well-behaved French child who played indoors with toy soldiers and wooden horses, Manon was pleased to see that the Huron had not been completely bleached out of the boy. He loved the craggy hills and rugged trees. He loved the freedom to scamper unfettered like the babbling brook that wound through their land. He was a proper boy of eight with scabbed knees and energy that Manon envied as the baby within began to tax her stamina.

"*Yearonta,*" she called out as they passed a thicket of trees.

"*Yearonta,*" he echoed, his pronunciation better than it had been even a week before. The Wendat words came back to him quickly. They wandered farther afield that day, as far as the river, where he yelled out triumphantly: "*Yeandawa!*"

"Yes, the *Yeandawa* is mighty today. But we must return soon or Pascal will be hungry for his *datarah*."

"Bread. Can't we just live on the scenery? It will be sleeping for the winter soon." Théodore looked as though Manon were dragging him away from a friend from whom he would be separated for years. In a sense, it was true. Winter would be there within weeks and he'd spend more hours indoors than he cared to. She smiled at the thought of the snowshoes that Pascal had bought for him in town that they would present him with at the first sign of his winter melancholy.

"It fills the soul, but not the stomach, my boy. Let's head back."

Théodore reluctantly returned back to the path Pascal had cleared and maintained, which was just barely wide enough for the two of them to walk side by side.

"You're happy you came with us, aren't you?" The question had been dancing in Manon's mouth, waiting to escape. *You love me, dear brother, but do we make you happy?* Manon was content with the isolation, but Théodore might have a different take on the solitude.

"Of course, sister." Théodore slipped his hand in hers. "Where else would I be, but with you?"

"I worried you might be lonely without your friends in town."

"I miss them." His eyes darted downward for a fraction of a second. "Frédéric, Pierre, and the others are great fun. But if you were my mother, would you have left me behind, even if I would miss my friends?"

Manon released his hand so she could wrap her arm over his shoulders. "Never."

"I want to be with you. It's what Mother—*aneheh*—would have wanted. Pascal is great fun, too. Did you know he promised to buy me a pony?"

"I had heard something about that, yes." *And wondered where the money would come from, but goodness knows there's no arguing with Pascal once he gets an idea in mind.*

It was shortly after their wedding that Manon realized Pascal and Théodore had barely spent five minutes in each other's company and never alone. It wasn't unusual for the children in a family like the Lefebvres to dine separately from company, but the realization that she'd completely neglected to consider how the two would get along had sickened her. Pascal eased her nerves by taking the boy on a fishing trip for an afternoon. Théodore came back with a basket of fish ready for supper and a more ebullient smile than she'd ever seen. Pascal returned having much less luck with the fish, but a great deal of admiration for the sweet-natured boy.

Pascal took to the role of father figure with more enthusiasm than she would have expected. That he waited with impatience for his child who grew in her womb, she expected completely. She had not anticipated the level of patience he showed when teaching Théodore the basic tenets of husbandry and farming, how to hold a knife properly when whittling, how to lead horses without spooking them. He was a born father. Manon rubbed the skin that stretched over her bulging abdomen and smiled to herself. *You will have a loving mother, father, and brother. You're born with some lovely advantages, little one.*

"I do have a question for you, sister." Théodore scuffed the dirt with the tip of his boot as he walked alone.

"Of course, my sweet boy. What is it?"

"I was wondering . . . I know they gave me the name Théodore so that I might fit in better with the French. We don't really live with them anymore. Do you think you could call me Tawendeh again? I could always go by Théodore in town."

Manon stopped in her tracks and pulled him into her arms. "Tawendeh, my curious, funny little otter, we will call you whatever it is you want to be called."

"Do you miss being called Skenandoa?"

"It's been so long since anyone has used it, it almost sounds strange to me," Manon admitted.

"I know what you mean. I think it fits you better than Manon, though. And I think Giroux is a nicer family name than 'Big Turtle clan.' You're too fast to be a turtle."

"Ah, never underestimate the turtle. He can swim like a fish. He's not meant to be on land like you and I. His place is in the water."

"I suppose it's hard to understand something when we never see it in its proper home." He again scuffed the dirt with the toe of his boot as he walked.

"You're too smart for your years, young man." Manon ruffled his hair and tried to ignore the tears that stung at her eyes.

Manon thought of the rude woman from the cheese shop, the old man who used to scoff at her in church when she was a girl, even Alexandre and Nicole. If they saw her with her own people, how would they think her different? Would they see the grace of the turtle's glide through water, or would they forever see his plodding movements on the hard, unforgiving earth?

Manon and Tawendeh arrived home as the light began to fade and the air grew crisp. Pascal, she expected to be home and waiting for them, but did not expect the whole of the Alexandre Lefebvre family to be waiting as well.

"Don't you fret," Nicole greeted, kissing Manon's cheeks, then moving on to Tawendeh's. "We've brought supper with us. It's warming now. You needn't feed the whole Lefebvre army without notice. Madame Yollande sends it along with her compliments. I never knew you'd been so friendly."

"It's a recent friendship." *Very recent.* "And bless her. I'm thrilled to have you, but managing dinner for so many would have stretched my skills, to be sure," Manon chuckled, kissing the top of Hélène's mop of golden brown curls. Tawendeh and Frédéric quickly fell into a conversation that looked to Manon's intruding eye as serious as the peace talks between the great clans of the Iroquois Nation. Little Sabine and the twins played on the floor with Pascal's new pup he was training up for a hunting companion.

Nicole served the hearty chicken stew and crusty bread as she used to do alongside Sister Éléonore at the convent before Alexandre whisked her off to become a society wife. Manon smiled at her foster mother and passed the bowls brimming with the rich mixture of meat, vegetables, and broth around the table. *This life suits you better than you remember, Nicole. It's wonderful to see that you haven't forgotten that entirely.*

Alexandre and Pascal dominated the conversation with discussion of the tenants and farming, the children interjecting as they so rarely had occasion to do. Manon studied Alexandre's face, surprised not to find a trace of annoyance there. He looked completely at ease, dining without ceremony or splendor. *Your kind tend to be malleable, I will say that. The obdurate would never rise as far as you.*

"And how are *you* feeling, darling?" Nicole eyed Manon significantly. Alexandre's momentary lapse in formality would not extend to an open discussion of Manon's condition.

"I tire easily, but nothing one wouldn't expect." Manon patted the top of Nicole's hand.

"You must promise to let me know if you need help. I can come as often as you need, or else you could let us hire a maid for you."

"Do you really think you could find a maid wanting to live so far out of the way? Never mind that we'd be awfully crowded with another adult here."

"The house will need expanding before long, it's true." Alexandre wiped the corner of his mouth with his cloth. "We'll be sure to allocate some of the rent from the other farms for the expenditure."

"That's generous of you," Manon said, eyes wide. The home was no longer Alexandre's responsibility to maintain, but part of Pascal's duty as a landowner in his own right.

"Not at all." Alexandre dismissed her praise with the wave of a hand. The expense was nothing to him, but would mean a good deal more comfort for Manon and her family.

The meal continued long into the dark until at last Alexandre announced that he'd better set to yoking the matched horses to the small carriage.

"Let me come hold the lantern for you," Manon offered, grabbing her shawl and the lamp before Pascal could offer.

They walked the first few steps to the barn in silence, but Manon found her tongue at last.

"I've never thanked you." Manon's voice was unsteady, her eyes focused on the path ahead rather than on Alexandre's reaction. "For this land. For giving Pascal a job he might never have aspired to. For taking me in when you married Nicole, for that matter." *You have been ungrateful. Despite his flaws he has been good to you.*

"My dear, it's the sort of thing one does for family."

"You'll forgive me, but I got the impression you didn't think of me that way." Manon held the lantern high now that they'd reached the stable, so Alexandre could see to the task of yoking the horse to the cart. *You're better at this than I expected from a man with an army of servants at his disposal.*

"Whatever gave you that impression, my dear girl?" His eyes were on the wagon's rigging, but his tone conveyed that Manon had his full attention.

"I heard you telling Nicole that you didn't think of me as a daughter like you did Hélène. Years ago before I went back to the Huron village."

"I never dreamed you heard that. I'm heartily ashamed." He patted the horse and looked up at Manon, regret in his dark gray eyes.

"Don't be. I am *not* your daughter and I had no right to expect you to think of me as Nicole did. She's more given to sentimentality than you are."

"That she is, but all the same, I didn't ever intend for you to feel unwelcome in my home."

"I was oversensitive. It doesn't matter now. I've been ungrateful and ought to have thanked you before now."

"No thanks are needed, my dear Manon. I may not have thought of you like a daughter. Hélène happened to be the very image of a favorite young cousin of mine. Perhaps it's what made it easier to feel as a father to her. She was also a baby and you were not. All that withstanding, I always thought of you as something like a much cherished niece. I know it ought to have been more, but you mustn't feel like I have no affection for you at all."

"I don't think I ever felt that way. Not really." Manon gave him a quick embrace. She'd never dared before. She'd always offered him the same prim kiss on the left cheek, never quite touching lips to skin.

"I'm glad we've come to a better understanding. I hated to see the rift between you and me cause any unhappiness for Nicole." Alexandre took the lantern with his left hand to guide them back to the house as he led the horse with the right.

"I feel the same. And please, let me thank you. What you've done for Pascal, for Tawendeh, for me. Thank you."

"I can't say the generosity is all selfless." Alexandre chuckled softly. "Pascal is one of the best estate managers in all of New France, I'd lay wages on it. Despite his young age, he knows the land and the tenants and has the skill to manage both. Not to mention his work ethic. Giving you land and keeping your home in adequate condition will keep you both happy, and hopefully dissuade you from giving up on this enterprise of ours for a good long while."

"I think you're safe in that. Pascal has never seemed more content than in the months he's been here. The out-of-doors is good for him."

"A good wife and a strong, strapping son—adoptive or no— and another child on the way have done more than this parcel of land. Though far be it from me to contradict a lady."

"I'm sorry for the way I've acted toward you, Alexandre. You've been kinder to me than I deserve."

"Say no more of it. And while we're in the moment for making heartfelt confessions; daughter or not, there is no young lady who could have made me prouder."

Manon looked down at the earth beneath her feet, ignoring the dark splotches that now formed on it from her tears. That those words should be so important for her to hear after all this time was perhaps ridiculous, but she could not alter how she felt.

"Come now, you mustn't carry on so. It's not good for the little one. And now that the subject is at hand, my dearest wife had asked me to persuade you to come to us for your travails. It would make her easier knowing you were nearer to help should the need arise."

Manon nodded. "Thank you, Alexandre . . . for everything."

CHAPTER 30

Claudine

October 1679

Claudine stood over the kitchen worktable, taking her mother's instructions on how to preserve cranberries in sugar for their enjoyment throughout the spring. The morning had been spent salting fish and a freshly butchered hog. There were winter squash and potatoes to store in the root cellar and beans to dry. The orchestra of smells transported her back to their ramshackle farmhouse outside of Rouen where she'd spent her girlhood. September and October were always months defined by labor. She'd helped her mother in the harvest season before, but never had the bounty been so large.

Papa's farm in France really was *depleted. Just twice the amount of land here, but five times or more the harvest. In two or three years we might have starved.*

Claudine shuddered at the thought. She'd cursed her parents for taking her out of France when she was twelve and she realized how remote her life would be still. Farther away from the fine dresses and courtly manners she had imagined were the norm in Paris. Even the more rustic version of sophistication she'd seen in Rouen would be lost to her. It had broken her heart and she'd howled like a beaten dog every time they had to come home from Nicole's house in town. Emmanuelle always tried to comfort her, but in those years, there was nothing that could have soothed her.

As she wiped up the filled jars with a clean rag and set them in crates for the hired boy to take to the cellar, she conjured up her childhood image of Paris. Every woman wore silk from the Orient and yards of hand-spun lace and carried a ridiculously small dog. Every man was dashing, wore an intricately embroidered *justaucorps,* and had family money to spare. After close to a decade in New France, that old image of luxury and refinement seemed a distant dream. Not to mention, ridiculously inaccurate. Rose and Elisabeth had shattered her childhood fantasies with their descriptions of the poverty and hardships in the capital. The grandeur wasn't wholly imagined, from what she'd learned of Rose's early life, but it existed amidst squalor. She knew now she wouldn't enjoy it.

I will never visit Paris to see for myself. She'd known it in her heart for years, but to own the knowledge so openly was new. She found it didn't sting like she expected it to. While she wouldn't refuse the chance to see the fine buildings and glimpse the Palace of the Louvre and its elegant courtiers, the lure of Zacharie's chubby toddler smiles, Laurent's midnight embraces, and the insistent kicks from her midsection called to her more than the busy streets of the capital.

"How is your back, darling?" Bernadette clucked over her youngest living daughter with more anxiety now than she ever had when Claudine was a girl.

"Aching. Still." *Perhaps it's because of what happened to Emmanuelle. Perhaps she's worried for the little one. Remember, you'll be the* maman *someday and your little ones will be just as annoyed by your worrying.*

"I'm sure we can manage for a bit. Why don't you lie down in your old room and rest awhile?" Claudine wanted to melt into a puddle as her mother rubbed her aching back, but the mountains of work in front of her kept her from seeking out the comfort of her old bed. She was certain she wouldn't wake before morning once her head found the goose down pillow.

"I'm fine, Maman. Really. There's a lot to be done and we can work faster together than you can alone. I don't want Papa to see any work unfinished. It will just upset him more."

"I doubt your father will notice the goings-on in my kitchen to that extent, my dear." Bernadette made light of her daughter's concern but the downturned corners of her mouth showed the astuteness of her daughter's observation. Thomas had been reduced to overseeing the harvest and giving orders for the first time since he was old enough to lift a hoe. The effort to plow alongside the hired hands would be the undoing of his weakened heart, but the feeling of uselessness was killing him just as surely. Claudine could see the frustration lined in his face. He was not meant to sit idle.

As if cued by her thoughts, Thomas chose then to enter the house and sit at the end of the table now covered in freshly harvested produce and a good helping of the earth from which they'd been plucked.

"You're back early, Papa. Would you like some cider? Some bread and jam?" Claudine kissed the top of his sunburned head as he stretched back in his chair.

"Save the food for the working men," Thomas spoke absently. For a moment, Claudine wondered if the statement were aimed at her or not.

"Papa, you've been in the fields since dawn and only taken a short break for luncheon. Surely you're hungry."

"Giving out orders. Overseeing things. It's not hard labor."

"But necessary work. Who knows this land better than you?"

"No one, and that's why it ought to be me who cultivates it. Not just hiring it out."

"Papa, you know you're not a young man. You've never been the sort to conceal your age or act younger than you truly are. Other men retire from their labors. It's time you do, too."

"What will I do with myself?" Thomas folded his hands in his lap, the schoolboy waiting for an answer from the master. "I can't spend the rest of my days on my duff. I have to have work."

"Papa, we can find you something to occupy your time. I swear it. But think of Maman and Georges before you take up the fool idea that you might be formulating about running a plow with the others. Think of Nicole and me, for that matter. You won't earn anyone's respect by making yourself a martyr."

"Very well. Though I'm not sure how I can stand this much longer." He placed his hands on the table, his fingers still laced as if in prayer, his face just as solemn as when he addressed his confessor.

"You weren't built for leisure, Papa. I understand. But *you* must understand that if you continue to work as you have been you will die. You will leave Maman and Georges all alone. We would do what we can for them, you know this, but we cannot replace you. No more than I or Nicole have been able to replace Emmanuelle."

Thomas took Claudine's hand and kissed the back of it. "Darling girl, no. You haven't replaced your sister, but I wager you inherited some of her sweetness. From the time you were knee-high I worried about your ambition. I'm just a farmer and I wasn't able to give you the life you wanted. I was convinced that you would never settle for less and you'd spend the rest of your life resentful. I'm glad I've lived to see you happy and well married, even if it wasn't of my own doing."

Claudine kissed his cheek, rough like tree bark. *I hope what Papa says is true, Emmanuelle. Yet, you had sweetness enough to spare when you were alive. I should have been wise enough to accept it then.*

Claudine glanced up the stairs with a longing to make the long climb and find the warmth between the covers, preferably with Laurent at her side to rub her aching back and whisper sweet things in her ear. Instead, she tossed a worn skirt atop the mending basket and walked to Gabrielle's shop. There was a shorter route on the side streets, but Claudine always took the front roads where more people could see her and know where she was doing business. The subtle compliment of a lady's custom was the best endorsement for a business like Gabrielle's. Claudine had seen her sister be the making of a business, and on occasion, the end of one. Claudine didn't see herself exercising her influence at every whim, but had no reservation about using it when it was warranted.

Gabrielle sat in her usual chair by the window, a pair of tattered gray breeches over her lap. She affixed patches to the knees, worn so thin Claudine could see Gabrielle's fingers through the fabric that wasn't covered by the scrap. Lines of fatigue encircled Gabrielle's green eyes, though her hands moved unwaveringly as she wove the needle through the layers of fabric.

"Are you sleeping any better?" Claudine said, refusing Gabrielle's offer for a beverage. She didn't want the weary woman to go to the effort on her account, and her own ankles weren't fond of any extra exertion.

"Some nights aren't too bad."

"Last night wasn't one of those."

"No," Gabrielle agreed, cutting the thread on the breeches with a vicious clip. "The judge sent that damned Duval around with more questions." She scanned her surroundings as an afterthought; probably scanning to make sure Duval or one of his cronies wasn't lurking in hopes of hearing just such an insult.

"If there isn't any proof, I don't see how they can do anything." Claudine sat back in her chair. *She needs a footstool or two for her little work nook. I'll have to find her one.*

"Don't be naïve, Claudine. The courts will do exactly as they please. If they uphold justice, it's merely a happy coincidence."

Claudine remembered the sham of a hearing where Gabrielle was sent back to live with Patenaude. The judge knew without question that Patenaude was a brutal man, his temper volatile, yet he sent Gabrielle back to live with him without the slightest concern for her welfare. Claudine doubted there was a person with less confidence in the servants of the law in their settlement than Gabrielle, and she'd been given good cause.

I want to offer you some assurance, but we were certain we could protect you last time. Thinking of nothing intelligent to say, Claudine traced the pattern on the arm of her chair with her index finger. Gabrielle didn't prod her into conversation or hint at her to leave. Claudine imagined it was a lonely life for her in the shop at times, and chitchat or not, another warm body in the house was welcome.

"Deputy Savard can't have known what she did," Claudine mused aloud after a few minutes. "He wouldn't have allowed it. If in fact it was she."

"You underestimate her hold over him. He may not have loved her, but he wouldn't dare to cross her. Nor can I think of anyone else who would bother to sully my name. No one mourns Patenaude enough to see me hang for his death, responsible or not. But I do agree with you on one matter. I don't think he knew. He would have tried to do something about it, somehow." Claudine saw Gabrielle take the briefest of pauses from her mending to look out the murky glass window.

"I wish I knew what else to do. Of course Laurent and Alexandre will do what they can. . . ." *But it didn't do much good last time.* The words were unspoken, but hung heavy in the air.

"You're doing exactly what I would ask right now." Business and company—and being seen doing both.

"I'm just sorry it's all happening. You deserve better than this." Claudine knew that Gabrielle's dealings with the deputy weren't blameless. Another time, she might have cast down Gabrielle as a harlot with the rest of the town, but she knew better. She knew how Gabrielle had suffered, first at her father's hands, then at Patenaude's. She'd known love from the Beaumonts and Pascal, but never the warmth of a lover. Claudine could imagine that René's sweet temper and affectionate disposition would have been irresistible to Gabrielle. A brilliant stroke of color in Gabrielle's gray world.

"There's no sense in talking about what anyone deserves. What's happened has happened whether I am deserving of it or not. People far more innocent than I have borne guilt before me, and I am certain I won't be the last."

"The judge will find you innocent. Must." Claudine would have stamped her foot to punctuate her fervor, were they not too swollen for the gesture.

"Even if he does, do you think the people of this town will acquit me so easily?" Claudine scoffed, ripping out a careless stitch. "They still haven't forgiven my attempt to separate from Patenaude while he was alive. If there is the least glimmer of doubt in their minds, no one will have anything to do with me no matter what the judge says."

Claudine opened her mouth to protest, but clasped it shut again. It was true. The judge enforced the law of man, but the town had different standards. The damage was done and Gabrielle would never be welcomed, embraced in town like she should.

"Whatever happens, you might think to go to Ville-Marie. Start over there. Alexandre will release you from any obligation to him. I'll see to it Laurent helps you get a start there. He travels there a few times every year. I'll come with him and visit you when I'm able."

"You're kind, Claudine." Gabrielle leaned forward and embraced her from the side. "But I'm not sure I have it in me to leave my home and everyone behind. I was born here."

"How many of your acquaintance have traveled across an ocean to start anew? Myself included. People are capable of far more than they give themselves credit for." Claudine rubbed her abdomen reflexively. "Once you start on the impossible journey, you'll be amazed at how far you travel."

"Madame, supper is waiting for you."

Claudine didn't recognize which of the two maids had called her from the doorway, so deep was her slumber. She'd hoped for a short nap after her visit with Gabrielle, but based on the moonlight pouring in her window, she'd lost the rest of her afternoon. *Do I stay and have her fetch a tray, or act like a lady and join Laurent for dinner?* The first option beckoned like a temptress, but she didn't want to give Laurent any cause for worry.

She threw back her covers, examining her ankles before swinging them over the side of the bed. Still twice their normal size, though she'd been resting for two hours. Dr. Guérin had said it was perfectly normal. Manon was less convinced that her level of swelling was usual, but admitted most every woman suffered swelling to some extent. Shaking her head, she stretched and stood at the side of the bed, motioning for the maid to come straighten her hair and make her presentable for supper. She thought of the ease with which Manon seemed to bear her own pregnancy and felt a stab of envy. *She's stronger, fitter than I am. I should never have let myself grow so weak.*

Claudine clucked her tongue at the bags under her eyes and her ashen pallor. Her hair lacked its brilliancy and she looked like a shadow of her former self. *You're draining me, little one. I'll be glad when you make your appearance.*

Claudine clutched the railing as she descended the steps, her growing belly making her awkward as she walked.

"So sorry to keep you waiting, my love," Claudine said by way of greeting.

"If I'd known you were sleeping, I wouldn't have sent for you. I've told the staff not to bother you when you're napping under any circumstances from now on." Laurent circled his arms around her and kissed her forehead and cheeks with his soft lips.

"I have to eat, my love. It's just as well. I wanted your company."

"Then sit and eat and we can retire early." Laurent held her chair out for her and she grabbed his hand and kissed it before he took his place.

"That sounds lovely."

"I'm afraid you've tired yourself out at Madame Patenaude's today. You ought to have invited her here if you wanted company."

"She has work to do, and I needed to drop off the mending. It was just as well that I went to her." *And her shop is more visible than our home. It did her more good.*

Laurent's fork clattered against his plate. "Do you mean to tell me that you carried a hamper of clothing all that way? Surely you asked one of the servants to do it. Tell me you weren't so foolish."

"Laurent, it was a small basket with a few chemises and a pair of breeches. I wasn't about to trouble the staff for such an errand. Besides, Manon says I need to get plenty of exercise and fresh air. The weather was remarkably fine today."

"Please don't change the subject, dearest. I don't want you carrying anything heavier than your evening bag until the child is born and you're well recovered."

"You're being silly, Laurent. I promise I'm being careful."

"Claudine, I know I'm being silly. Worse, I'm being illogical and unreasonable. But you won't sway me in this. I beg you, for the sake of my sanity, you must promise to rest. You must promise to ask for help. I can't bear to see you so exhausted."

"I'm sure it's all perfectly fine, darling. Manon thinks I might be further along than I thought I was, based on my size. Perhaps we'll have a baby before Christmas after all. I admit it would be a relief."

"For both of us," Laurent said, picking at his food.

"Would you be . . . disappointed if we were to take a long pause before we do this again?" It was the first time she'd dared broach the subject. They were Robichauxes. They were supposed to set the example for the settlement. First and foremost, that meant large, healthy families. Any deliberate attempt to thwart childbirth risked questioning eyes in town—and possibly troublesome questions with the Church.

"Not at all. While I'd love to have a noisy clan of children, I'm not sure how many more times I can bear this."

Claudine bit her tongue until she felt the twinge of blood trickle in her mouth. *Fool. Don't make him any more terrified of this than he already is.*

"There's no need to be so anxious, my love. I know given the events of last time you're entitled to be nervous, but with each child I'm sure you'll grow less and less so. Forget I said anything. I'm sure the first child is the most exhausting. Not knowing what to expect and all."

"I hope you're right, my angel." Laurent brushed his thumb along her cheekbone. "I know I'll rest easier when this little one is here and tucked in safe and sound with his brother in the nursery."

"That will make two of us," Claudine said, caressing the hand that lingered on her face. "I do promise to ask for help. Truly. But do promise to relax as best you can. Everything will be well."

"You can help me relax by curling up against me for a good night's sleep and whispering all those loving thoughts you store up for me all day long." Laurent stood and helped Claudine stand on her swollen feet. She was embarrassed to realize that while his gesture was borne of his gallant nature, her condition made his assistance necessary.

"That sounds decadent, my love." Claudine stood on her tiptoes and kissed him softly before they ascended to their bedchamber.

She leaned heavily on Laurent on the way up the stairs, the effort more taxing than she cared to admit. There would be no trip to see Gabrielle the next day, nor any ventures as far as her parents' farm for some time. *A fantastic lot of good you are to everyone. Spending all day in bed.* There were crops to preserve and a winter to prepare for. This was not the time to give in to her fatigue.

Laurent served as her lady's maid that night, helping her from her bodice and skirt into her nightgown, then brushing her long brown hair into soft waves that cascaded down to her buttocks. He gently rubbed her back, causing little groans of pleasure to emit involuntarily from her lips. He led her to the warm bed, where she watched him undress before he climbed in next to her.

She pressed the length of her body against his, letting his warmth soothe her aching muscles. Her hands traced the familiar slopes and curves of his back and she felt her desire swell. He would never agree, given her condition, but she missed the intimacy of his midnight caresses.

Children or no, I'll never be able to resist you, Laurent.

CHAPTER 31

Gabrielle

November 1679

Gabrielle sat upright in her bed, drenched in frigid sweat despite the bite of the November night air. Since Patenaude's death—even before—she'd been plagued by nightmares. As the date for her questioning drew near, they increased in frequency and vividness. Sometimes it was Patenaude attacking her for a burnt meal or a snide remark. Sometimes it was reliving the horror of when her baby died.

Other nights, like tonight, it was imagining her life if the baby had lived. Little baby Gilbertine. She never told anyone that she knew it was a girl. Never told the Beaumonts that she wanted to call her after Gilbert, the first man to show her kindness. In her dream, Gilbertine was born healthy and beautiful. Gabrielle doted on her, cared for her every need with the love and gentleness that she'd never known as a child.

And every moment she lived in fear that Patenaude would hurt the baby . . . the scenarios played over in her mind after she awoke. Sometimes it was an act of carelessness, such as leaving a trap about on the floor. Other times, he would hit Gabrielle and cause her to fall on the baby. Occasionally he would hurt Gabrielle so badly she was unable to attend to the child and he was unwilling to help. The worst were the images that appeared when she thought of him grow-ing impatient with her squalling. Slapping, shaking, punching... One time she imagined him leaving the shrieking baby in the snow and tying Gabrielle to a chair so she couldn't save her. When he untied her, a frozen blue baby just outside their doorstep was all that re-mained of her precious daughter.

The last scenario was grisly, even for Patenaude's temper, but the rest were more than plausible. They were the reality she'd been fortunate enough to escape. Every single day, she ached for Gilber-tine. Felt cheated that she never had the chance to hold her in her arms properly. Felt betrayed that she wasn't able to give her baby a proper funeral. With René returned to France, she had nothing to keep these harrowing thoughts from coursing through her mind. Right or wrong, their brief affair had given her an escape from her grief.

She took her pillow to her chest and bit down furiously. She imagined it was Patenaude's bicep and dug her fingers in, thinking with satisfaction of the sensation of driving her nails into his flesh and ripping his muscle with her teeth. She stopped only when she heard the rent of fabric. She'd enough mending to do and did not want to be picking feathers from her bed for weeks to come.

It was an hour before dawn, but as winter was upon them and the sunrise quite late, Gabrielle decided she would allow herself to wake in earnest. She pulled herself out of bed and forced herself to eat some breakfast before bothering to dress. Food didn't really help all that much, but it did serve to bind the frayed edges of her nerves for a short while.

As she dressed, her hands shook. The judge had summoned her for questioning. This could be her last day of freedom before she swung from the gallows. She chose her clothing carefully. Her skirt and jacket were unassuming brown wool. They were clean and tidy, well cut and well made, but had no frills or embroidery. She looked modest and respectable, but avoided anything that would lead the judge to believe that she'd ascended too far in the world since Pate-naude's death. She couldn't have him thinking the truth—that she was better off since he died.

She examined her reflection in her small looking glass and gave herself a grim smile. Gabrielle could at least be confident in the knowledge that she was innocent. She had not pulled the trigger that killed Patenaude, even if she'd wished she had. *Even though I'd been prepared to. Even though his careless accident was the greatest kindness he ever offered me.*

A rap at the door sounded to let her know the Beaumonts had arrived to take her to the courthouse. It wasn't a trial, just a questioning, but the result could be the same. If the judge was persuaded she'd killed her husband, he could ensure she never breathed fresh air or saw blue sky again.

And a pox on you, Annette Savard. You've thoroughly complicated my life with one cruel flick of your insolent tongue, but you won't have the satisfaction of ending it.

Manon and Claudine, both comically large in their pregnancies, arrived with the Beaumonts. They approved her choice of clothing, restyled her hair, and held her hands until it was time for her to depart for the small building where the judge heard his cases.

This time, they offered no false assurances. She loved them for it.

"Whatever happens, thank you," Gabrielle said, taking them both in her arms. "I'm so glad you're my sister, Manon. And you might as well be yourself, Didine."

Claudine made quite the show of fussing with the cuff of her sleeve in an attempt to cover her tears, but Manon shed none.

"None of this," Manon said. "You are innocent and you must not demonstrate any doubt before the judge."

"Am I truly innocent, Manon?" Gabrielle asked. "In truth, I plotted to kill my husband. I coveted another woman's legally wed spouse. How can I claim to be innocent?"

"Gabrielle, you are accused of killing Olivier Patenaude. Did you kill him?" Manon's tone was closer to the growl of a grizzly than her own usually melodic tones.

"No," Gabrielle answered.

"That's all that matters," Claudine said, taking Gabrielle in her arms. "Just remember that."

"How often does the truth really matter in these sorts of proceedings? There is more than enough reason to cast me out of the colony forever. To hang me, even."

Neither Manon nor Claudine supplied a response.

"Promise me you'll take care of my brother, Manon," Gabrielle said, taking Manon's hand in hers. "I could not have asked for a better wife for him. Just be good to him and I will be happy."

Manon nodded, the tears spilling over her cheeks.

"And, Claudine, if things go . . . badly, please write to René. I am sure Laurent or Alexandre can get his address from the governor's office. He's sure to have left his information. Let him know what his wife has done."

"I swear it." Claudine nodded.

"Then let us go to court. I could ask for nothing more than you have promised me."

Gabrielle sat before Judge Arnaud, the same wizened old man with a martyred expression who presided over her trial against Patenaude. Manon and Claudine, both round with child, sat on either side of her, the picture of maternity and matrimonial duty. This was not happenstance. Elisabeth and Gilbert looked pale with fear, her hand clutching his until her knuckles gleamed white in the seats behind Gabrielle. Pascal sat behind his wife, next to the Beaumonts, his arms crossed and expression surly. The entire court looked up and began whispering as Sister Anne entered the room and sat in the row behind Gabrielle, going so far as to offer her a reassuring pat on the shoulder. *Your presence means more than you know, dear woman. Please God that none of the Savard woman's friends come to negate all the benefit of your support.*

"Madame Patenaude, if you would please stand for questioning." The judge rubbed the bridge of his nose, with a look of annoyance as if he'd already heard a dozen cases that day, though she was the first and only matter of his day.

"I wasn't aware that this was a trial." Alexandre stood, his hand preventing Gabrielle from standing. "Else we would have prepared differently. You have no need to treat her as though she's been accused of anything." For two weeks, Gabrielle heard him curse the King's edict that forbade attorneys in the colony. She couldn't deny she'd feel better with experienced counsel.

"Seigneur Lefebvre—"

"No, *Monsieur le Président*. I insist Madame Patenaude remain seated," Sister Anne demanded, standing tall next to Alexandre, her arms straight at her sides in defiance. The nun's eyes flashed in anger and, out of the corner of her eye, Gabrielle could see the muscle flexing in Alexandre's jaw.

"Very well, Sister. She may remain seated, but I warn you I will not tolerate outbursts in my courtroom. Even from the pair of you." Sister Anne and Alexandre offered the judge a curt nod of the head and took their places on the rigid bench behind Gabrielle. "Now, madame, tell me the events that transpired the day your husband died."

Gabrielle, in painstaking detail, recounted every event of that day from the moment she awoke until she departed the house, musket in hand, prepared to kill her husband. She'd fabricated a story about hauling in water from the river to boil for laundry. It would explain the snow on the floors of the cabin, the used snowshoes, and her breathless demeanor.

No one could have known that the fire wasn't stoked enough to boil water, nor that she'd done the laundry the previous day. Or so she hoped. Her voice was steady as she spoke; her hands trembled, but not excessively so. The judge's placid face gave no hint as to whether or not he believed her story.

"The bailiff tells me that you acknowledge keeping a musket of your own in the cabin. Is that correct?" The judge shifted positions in his unyielding chair with a grimace. *At least you're no more comfortable than the rest of us, you pompous ass.*

"That's not precisely accurate, *Monsieur le Président*. Olivier, that is, Monsieur Patenaude, had a spare musket that he left at home. I don't believe it was in working order. I wouldn't have known how to use it well enough to find out, I'm afraid. Had there been trouble when my husband was out hunting, I would have been left to brandish the musket and hope the robbers were foolish enough to think I could use it."

The judge silenced the titter of laughter in the courtroom with an acrid glare.

"And where is the musket now, madame?" the judge all but grunted in annoyance. Gabrielle kept her face from falling. It was likely a rusted mess hidden in brambles after a year of snow and rain if it could be found at all.

"I could not tell you, monsieur. My family sold most of Monsieur Patenaude's belongings to help me reestablish myself, and I expect it was among the items sold. The settlement doesn't need another penniless widow to support." Alexandre rapped his knuckles on the wooden bench in support. *Exactly what the judge wants to hear. Hard-working. Self-supporting. A woman with the desire to help the settlement.*

"Can you not remember who purchased the firearm, madame? For one with the reputation of being a fastidious businesswoman, that seems unlikely."

"Monsieur Beaumont and my brother saw to the sale of my late husband's effects. I was in no condition to see to those matters myself. They kept no record of the items or who bought them, monsieur."

"That would be a likely story for one trying to conceal the offending weapon."

Dear God. The judge has found the scrap of information he needs to keep me here. A functioning musket was all he needed. The blood rushed in her ears, making her glad Alexandre had insisted she remain seated for questioning.

"*Monsieur le Président,* even if we traced the musket back to the man who purchased it, how could you be certain it was the weapon that killed Patenaude?" Alexandre now stood, arms crossed.

"It seems to me, that both the absence of the weapon and any confirmation of the story from Patenaude's hunting companions makes Madame Patenaude's story rather suspicious given her attempts to separate from her lawful lord and master in the past."

"You see here, young man." Sister Anne stood next to Alexandre; her height wasn't considerable, but she made the most of every inch. "Just because a woman, rightly, wanted to be freed from a cruel husband does not make her a murderess. You ought to be ashamed of yourself."

"Sister, I really must insist—" The judge opened his mouth to speak, but a clerk entered the courtroom and crossed to the judge's bench to whisper in his ear.

"Very well, show him in."

Jacques Verger, as scruffy and fragrant as he'd been on Gabrielle's wedding day and the day he delivered Patenaude's body to her home, entered the courtroom and removed his hat.

"My clerk informs me you have something to add to the proceedings, monsieur . . . ?"

"Verger," he said with a nod. "I was with Patenaude the day he died. My boy and I were out hunting with him when the fool took aim at a rock instead of a deer and he ended up with a ball in his chest. He was never much of a shot when he'd been in the bottle, nor could a man reason with him not to drink on a hunt."

"Why have you not come forth before, monsieur?"

"I didn't know there was reason to harass this nice lady over everything. I didn't figure anyone other than her'd miss old Patenaude enough to take the trouble. I'm just sorry you folks decided to give her more grief before I could come and set things straight. My boy can tell you the same thing, but he's in La Chine for another week or more."

"I'll be sure to speak with him when he returns. See to it that you send him to me." The judge wore an expression of grim determination. "Very well. I suppose there can be no grounds for further investigation for the time being. You're free to go, madame."

Gabrielle held her smile until she left the courtroom. As soon as they were free of the building she fell into Elisabeth's arms, the tears refusing to remain at bay.

Sister Anne whisked away almost immediately with a very brief embrace and a "Go with God, my daughter. Start a new life in His name" for Gabrielle and polite nods for the rest.

"It's all going to be well, sweetheart." Elisabeth kissed Gabrielle's temple as she rocked her back and forth. "It's all as it should be."

Gilbert wrapped his arms around his wife and Gabrielle, wordless with relief.

"I meant what I said in there, madame." Verger took several paces back, but spoke in a clear voice so the rest of the assembly could hear. "I'm awful sorry they pestered you about all this. Patenaude weren't worth the trouble. If I'd known that you were a real lady, I wouldn't have let you walk down the aisle without warning you off."

"We thank you greatly for your coming to Madame Patenaude's aid," Alexandre said on their behalf. "Your testimony has saved Gabrielle from a dire fate. Will you please do us the honor of joining us for luncheon?"

"I couldn't be a trouble, Seigneur. I do have a rusty old musket in my wagon the young lady might do well to keep track of."

Gabrielle looked at the old man. How much had he guessed? "Keep it," she said. "Give it to your boy. Destroy it. Do whatever it is you like."

"As you wish, madame. I was asked to deliver this letter to your hands as well." Verger extended a crisp white envelope with his dirt-crusted hands. He'd clearly taken pains to make sure the missive arrived to her in pristine condition. Gabrielle broke free of her embrace with the Beaumonts and wrapped her arms briefly around the grubby man and kissed his brown cheek.

"Thank you, Monsieur Verger. I owe you my life."

"Well then, you can repay me by living it right and enjoying it as best you can," he said. He leaned in closer to whisper, "I'm plenty glad the fool did the shooting for you."

The kitchen staff bustled about the dining room, serving the impromptu luncheon with a bit less flare and style than the usual company meal at the Lefebvre house, but none of the assembly much cared about the lack of ceremony.

"To justice." Alexandre raised a glass of Burgundy so rich that the lush brown-red liquid looked as warm and soft as velvet in the candlelight.

"Justice," the rest chorused in unison.

For the first time in weeks, Gabrielle found herself equal to eating a meal out of hunger rather than habit. The delicate quail and sautéed vegetables were far more refined than her usual fare. She might have preferred a beef stew or chicken pie, but she ate the elegant meal with pleasure.

"You'll finally be able to go about your life as before," Rose said with a pat to Gabrielle's shoulder. *Can I really? Would I want to?*

"I imagine your shop will benefit from all this," Laurent said, his hand on Claudine's. "That will be a bit of a relief I should think. Verger's testimony will silence a lot of tongues. Sister Anne's support, as well."

Gabrielle nodded. She'd not had trouble keeping food on the table, but she hadn't much means for any sort of luxuries or comforts.

"And perhaps you'll have time to meet a more—deserving—young man." Nicole winked over her plate in Gabrielle's direction, and she felt the meal churn in her stomach.

Patenaude had been gone for almost a year. No one in the colony would question her for remarrying. They would likely think all the better of her for it. No one, apart from Manon and Claudine, officially knew about René. Gabrielle imagined others suspected some partiality, perhaps an innocent romance of sorts. Annette's friends had mercifully kept their mouths closed. It seemed that once Annette was no longer there to offer favor, they were far less concerned with Gabrielle's comings and goings. There were still glances, however, and Gabrielle wondered if the time would come when they might decide to cause her trouble out of sheer spite.

Forget him. Forget the very idea. You've a business to run and a life to rebuild.

She picked up her fork once again and resumed the pretense of eating. Seated about the table, there were ten other adults, all happily partnered. *Is there something wrong with me for not wanting a family? For enjoying my solitude?*

As she chewed and pretended to acknowledge the conversation she wondered how much she truly enjoyed being alone. Was it the privacy she appreciated, or the freedom from her wretched marriage?

As the dessert course appeared Gabrielle found herself willing the minutes away so she could slink back home and, with luck, find some dreamless sleep before facing the world again. More pressing, the letter Verger had passed to her itched to be read, and she would only sate her curiosity in the privacy of her room. In the end it was Claudine who mercifully broke up the party by claiming fatigue. Laurent whisked her away the same moment she voiced her need for rest, his brow furrowed.

"I believe I'll follow her example, if you don't mind too terribly much. It's been a taxing day."

"I imagine so," Nicole clucked. "We'll send over a hamper with some good things for your supper late in the afternoon if you like."

"That would be lovely." Gabrielle nodded with a forced smile.

"Why don't you come spend the night in your old bedroom?" Elisabeth offered.

"Perhaps another time? I'd not be much company tonight." Gabrielle grasped Elisabeth's hand, hoping she understood the need for solitude that night.

"We'll depend upon it," Gilbert said, silencing Elisabeth's unvoiced protest with a hand on her shoulder.

"Soon," she promised, kissing his cheek.

Back at home, she climbed up to her bedroom, shucked her clothes in favor of her nightgown, and prepared to climb into bed, though the sun was still high in the afternoon sky. The pristine white letter that Verger delivered to her fell to the floor with a soft *whoosh* as she draped her skirt over her dressing chair.

She claimed the letter off the floor and curled under the covers with the missive. She loosened the wax seal with her finger and saw René's bold scrawl across the page. They'd had only a handful of occasions to exchange notes of any kind, but the script seemed as familiar as her own.

> *My dearest love,*
> *I pray this letter reaches you in safety and happiness. If you read this, then you must be aware that Annette has, despite my direct orders, spoken horrible rumors against you to cause an inquiry. Perhaps worse. I know these rumors to be unfounded. You are too good, too kind, too gentle to commit such an atrocious act, even against a monster of a man who would have deserved no better.*
> *It is only hours before my departure to France, and I have only just learned of her disgusting plot. I haven't the time to settle matters on my own before the ship sails back home, so I have enlisted one of my assistants to uncover the truth in secrecy. I have also charged him with delivering this note to someone unconnected with me so that you might know the truth. There is a large part of my heart that wishes to see Annette board the ship and never see the like of her again. Alas, I cannot abandon her. I wish to say it is from the nobler part of me that strives to honor my vows. It comes, sadly, much more from the part of me that recognizes I am neither resourceful nor clever enough*

to carve a place for myself in the world without the wealth
and influence of bigger men.

I will think of you every day for the rest of my life, my
darling Gabrielle. Would that I were free to claim you as
my wife and be the husband you deserve. Alas, I must con-
tent myself with the lot I have chosen, and you must find
yours. Be happy, my love. If I cannot be, you must be
happy for both of us. There will be a time when your heart
is so full of others, that you'll have no room to remember
me. I long for that day, for then I will know my memory
no longer causes you pain.

Good-bye, Beloved. And God Bless You,
Your,
René

Gabrielle held the letter up from her lap so there was no risk of her tears smudging his words. He loved her. He had tried to protect her. Despite his flaws, he was the good and true man she'd longed for. Others would only see his infidelity, despite to an honorable, if unloving, wife. They would be blind to the brief moment of happiness he'd brought to Gabrielle's dreary life.

And she would never be able to tell him how grateful she was for those stolen moments whose memory faded more each day.

His scent was gone from her pillow. The precise shade of his eyes was vanishing from her memory. In time he would be but a specter to her. She did not long for that day, as René wished for her. She knew, deep inside, that she would not be free of him when he became a ghost of himself. She would be haunted by him.

Chapter 32

Manon

December 1679

Manon grew restless in the confines of the Lefebvre house, but pushed the anxiety from her thoughts. Every time she felt her nerves fray, the child inside began to kick her furiously as a reminder to calm herself. It wouldn't be long now. She had given her word to Alexandre and Nicole that she would come to town for her lying-in, though she began to question the wisdom of it as the time drew near. Pascal reasoned with her that the roads would be too treacherous to cross quickly if things went badly; that the trek was too long even when the weather was fine. After a week into their stay, she felt the walls grow closer and closer together. *Fool, you'd be trapped inside at home just as you are here. At least this way Tawendeh is with his friends and you have company and care as well. Be grateful.*

Manon spent much of her time in her old bedroom near the nursery, behind Alexandre's massive old desk in the company of her books. When she spent her time among the others, they watched her constantly, waiting for the child as if Manon were in imminent danger of collapsing in spasms. She looked over her old volumes that remained in the room as a sort of shrine to her girlhood. Each precious book as familiar as an old friend. She would have to remind Alexandre to have them moved back to his library where the others could access them more readily.

Knowing the midday meal would soon begin, she heaved a sigh and left the quiet of the peaceful haven behind. She took one step down the stairs and gripped the railing as she felt a sharp cramping in her midsection and a flow of warm fluid down her legs. From what she could see it was clear and not tinged with blood. *A very good sign.* Rather than descend the staircase unaided, she returned to her old bedroom and rang the servant bell for help. It was the first time she'd ever bothered with the bell pull, but she knew she shouldn't risk another surge as she walked down the stairs.

Rather than a maid or a footman, Nicole came to investigate the cause for the summons.

"It's not going to be long," Manon said, taking deep breaths between her words to slow her heart and relax her tensing muscles.

"I'll send for Gabrielle and the midwife. Let's get you changed and in bed." Nicole looked pale and frazzled as she absorbed Manon's words. Nicole had brought five children into the world, but had never served as a midwife before.

"Changed, yes. Bed, no. I want to walk." Manon held on to Nicole's arm as they traversed the corridor to the guest room that had been designated as Manon's birthing chamber. It suited Nicole's understated style—pale pinks and grays contrasted with deep-red mahogany. It was light and pleasant, which was as much as Manon could ask for. It had seen four healthy babies born in it—a good omen to anyone.

"Darling, don't you think you ought to lie down and save your strength? This could be a long business." Nicole busied her fingers with the laces of Manon's loose bodice and pulled the gown over her head. She stopped Nicole from pulling the clean chemise over her as a wave of pain slammed into her like a wall.

"I need to walk," Manon said as the surge eased. Nicole fussed over her remaining on her feet, but Manon insisted on pacing the room and walking the corridor. Every time she attempted to lie down she felt like she was just slowing the baby's progress. After a half hour of pacing, the surges came so close she was panting just to keep the air in her lungs.

"Now" was all Manon could utter, discarding her chemise. Though made of the softest fabric, it still felt oppressive in her current state. She pulled back the bed linens under her own strength and climbed onto the bed. Rather than lie prostrate, she gripped onto one of the posters that held the canopy and let her body work with her. "The baby isn't going to wait for the midwife."

Manon vaguely heard Nicole's requests to lie down and let her cover her, but she could not find her voice to contradict her. The surges were on top of one another, and all she could do was grip the solid mahogany post and let her body move as it willed. She was completely at the mercy of her own flesh. It was an uncomfortable reality, but she let her body complete its task without letting her mind hamper her progress.

"Now," she said again. With a surge stronger than all the others, she emitted a cry as fierce as any warrior's and felt Nicole catch the child as it entered the world.

She crumpled onto her side and breathed evenly, relieved that the surges had finally subsided. She heard the lusty sounds of her child's cry. That the baby was well and that her own pain was over was all she needed to know.

"A boy," Nicole said, her voice quivering. "A strong Giroux lad if ever I've seen one. And the quickest birth of a new mother I've ever heard of."

Because I wouldn't lie down and do things your way. "Let me see him." Manon situated herself on the bed, not bothering with her chemise, but covering with the sheets. Nicole handed off a well-swaddled, clean lad just a few moments later. Manon unwrapped the blankets and held the naked baby to her bare chest so he could find her nipple and suckle. The little one flickered his eyes open for a few seconds and cooed, happy to be free from his confines.

"Welcome, *cheahhah*." *Welcome, child.* She murmured words of love in her native Wendat. *His first words will be those of my people. May they ring true in your perfect ears.*

A soft rap at the door announced that Pascal anxiously awaited his first glimpse of his son. Nicole had wanted to clean the sheets and see Manon dressed and ready to receive her husband properly, but Manon called her permission for him to enter.

"You can help me clean up before Tawendeh sees me," Manon assured Nicole. "Pascal will be fine to see me as I am."

"Very well." Nicole leaned in and kissed Manon's forehead and stroked the baby's brow before leaving the parents alone to admire their child.

"He's beautiful, my love." Pascal kissed her deeply and wrapped his arms around mother and son. "And so fast. You must have been having pains all day and told none of us."

"Nothing more than a persistent backache." Manon kissed his scruffy cheek softly. "He is a lovely baby, isn't he?"

"Indeed, darling. Though I think we're incredibly biased."

"As well we should be."

"You're right as always, my darling. Shall we give him a proper Huron name, do you think?"

"No," Manon spoke decidedly. She had not discussed the naming of the child aloud, not counting on blessings before they were hers to hold; however, she'd given it a good deal of thought. "His papa is French and so should his name be. But we can give him a second name in Huron so he will remember where his *maman* comes from."

"I'm partial to the name Julien, if you don't mind. It was my uncle's name, and though I only met him a handful of times, I remember him as being a man of great kindness. Or at least generosity. He always had a pocket of molasses taffy for us."

Manon smiled at the sweet memory and nodded her agreement. "Julien *Scanonie* Giroux. Do you think it suits him?"

"It's a mouthful for such a wee man, but he'll grow into it." Pascal took the baby into his own arms and placed a kiss on the downy skin of his son's cheek. "Peace?"

Manon blinked, surprised her husband recognized the Huron word she'd given as her son's name.

"It's the greatest thing I can hope for him," Manon said. "The greatest wish any mother can have for her child."

"A better name I couldn't think of, my darling."

Manon could hear the whispers of the rest of the family gathered outside the door, all clamoring for their chance to welcome baby Julien to the family and congratulate the new parents. With a smile she allowed Pascal to place the baby in his cradle so Nicole could help her dress for company.

My sweet little boy, welcome to the world. I hope it will be as kind and gentle to you as you deserve.

Manon cursed her thickened waist and discarded her favorite dress with delicate embroidery in favor of a plainer, looser gown she'd worn in pregnancy. Little Julien was three days old, and he was due for his christening. Manon had hoped to be dressed in her best, as all eyes would be on her as she and Pascal, along with Julien's godparents, Laurent and Claudine, presented the child to the Church.

Ridiculous ceremony. My child is free of sin and has no need to be forgiven . . . but this is the price of raising the child to be French. Or at least mostly French.

She looked in the mirror, not pleased, but not too disheartened by the reflection. She heard stirring in the halls that meant most everyone was ready or nearly so. *I'll have to do.* She went over to the cradle where Julien slumbered and lifted him into her arms. He was none too pleased as she replaced his plain swaddling clothes with the elaborate baptism gown Gabrielle had made. Lace and ribbon over every inch of fabric so that Manon could hardly find her sweet boy's full cheeks and chubby fingers in the ocean of white frills.

"Come, my pumpkin, let's go to church. Your papa and Nicole are anxious to show you off to the town. Just don't listen to the townsfolk too closely. Some are lovely. Many are not."

Manon wrapped a warm blanket of soft wool over the baby to protect him from the December cold better than the thin white linen of the gown.

Alexandre readied a veritable caravan to the church to escort Julien to his baptism. Manon rolled her eyes at the excess of three large sleighs pulled by fine horses, but she held her tongue. It was his way of displaying affection, and she had to give him his due. He'd cooed over Julien like a proud grandfather, holding him for a solid hour once he'd been given his chance with the little one.

Claudine, looking almost too pregnant to be seen in public, held Julien before the priest. The choice of an expectant woman to serve as godmother caused some whispers in the congregation, but so did Manon herself. Laurent supported Claudine with his arm, his face somber and distracted, looking as though he paid little attention to the priest's words. Manon could feel the assembly take a collective breath as the priest approached the child to anoint his forehead with holy water. Would he remain asleep on his godmother's bosom or explode with shrill cries to echo off the church walls?

Manon could not conceal her smile as he slumbered through the ordeal, unaware that he was being welcomed into their community. Gabrielle, seated next to Nicole and Alexandre in the first pew, smiled back up to her. Manon was old enough to remember her own baptism, shortly after she'd come to stay at the convent with Nicole. The Sisters could hardly allow an unredeemed native child to stay among them, and Manon would have done anything to please Nicole and the Sisters in those days.

There had been cake and a fine stew that night in honor of her baptism. And hearty congratulations from the Sisters as well as a rosary and a prayer book from the much lamented Sister Mathilde. It almost made up for the wary glances of the churchgoers who viewed her baptism as somehow insincere. She was too old, too brown, to take the sacrament seriously.

Your papa is French. Your skin is only a degree darker than his. You could pass for one of the Frenchmen near the Mediterranean with their olive skin and dark eyes. The Provençal with their lilting accents. No one will doubt your sincerity, your piety, to the point where you question it yourself.

Manon felt her shoulders lower as the priest offered a final benediction to the congregation and dismissed them to the frosty December day.

Nicole would not hear of a quiet celebration *en famille* to commemorate the event. All the elite of the town had been invited to a fine dinner that had taken every member of the staff, along with half of the members of the Robichauxes' as well, two full days to prepare. *At least this will take the place of the Christmas ball and we will be spared a second spectacle.*

"Congratulations, Madame Giroux," said a deputy—or assistant deputy—or some far-flung secretary of the governor's, who then kissed her hand with pomposity. "May this be the first son in a large family devoted to the glory and honor of His Majesty."

"Th-thank you," Manon stammered, not knowing how to address the absurd compliment.

"What a lovely christening gown," the deputy's wife breathed as she looked into the baby's curious black eyes.

"Thank you. Madame Gabrielle Patenaude made it." Manon glanced over in Gabrielle's direction with a pointed smile. Her decision to commission the baptism gown from Gabrielle rather than use a Lefebvre family heirloom was a strategic one.

"Oh, I see." The woman gave a sideways glance toward Gabrielle. "You being out of town much of the time, you might not have heard about the terrible to-do with the late Monsieur Patenaude."

"Oh, but I have, madame. How fortunate that Monsieur Verger was able to answer everything about the terrible accident to Judge Arnaud's satisfaction. It must give poor Madame Patenaude such solace to hear the full truth spoken without any equivocation. And how fortunate for all of us that our justice system is so rigorous."

"Quite." The woman's expression grew cold as she registered Manon's meaning.

"It's such a shame the man was careless enough to drink while hunting. Don't you think? Then again, alcohol really is the devil's own handicraft, isn't it?"

It had not escaped Manon's notice that the wrinkled woman had a glass of port in her hand, though it was barely past the noon hour. The woman looked down at her glass with an indignant blush, claimed to see an acquaintance with whom she needed to speak, and made her leave. *Yes, go. And sleep sound in your bed knowing that dangerous criminals like Gabrielle Patenaude are not on the loose.*

Nicole, having overheard the conversation, offered her a mischievous wink. *Well, if I've learned the art of turning a phrase on its end, I learned it from you.*

By the time the last well-wisher had passed on his praise of the child to mother, father, and the rest of the extended family, Manon was close to tears from her fatigue. The nanny ushered the baby to Manon's room and, for once, Manon did not feel the prick of annoyance at the woman's interference.

"You were magnificent this afternoon," Pascal whispered into her ear as the family gathered in the parlor with warm cider and spiced biscuits from Elisabeth's kitchen.

Manon kissed his cheek and followed him to the small settee. *It was torture, but my son will have a place here. If I have to endure a throng of Nicole's guests for his sake, so be it.*

"Have you recovered from the festivities?" Nicole asked, popping her head in Manon's room the following morning. Despite the repeated offers to hire a wet nurse, Manon insisted on nursing Julien for as long as she could. She sensed Nicole wished to argue the point, but Manon knew Nicole had nursed Hélène before she married Alexandre. She wondered if she would have done the same for the rest of her children had Alexandre not paid so much credence to fashion and style.

"Fairly well," Manon said, offering her a small smile from the comfortable chair.

"I hope it wasn't too much for you."

"It was lovely," Manon allowed. "Thank you for all your trouble."

"I know it wasn't the quiet affair you wanted. Thank you for indulging me." Nicole leaned over, kissed Manon's forehead, and took her place in the spare chair.

"I don't mind. Really. If it gave you pleasure and helped to introduce my Julien to society, I'm not one to stop you."

"I'm surprised you feel that way. I know you aren't enamored of some of our traditions."

"Nor am I of all the traditions of my own people. I want to raise Julien to have a place in the world. I don't think that there will be much of one with the Huron. It makes sense to see him welcome with yours."

"Sensible. Sad, but sensible."

"He won't be ignorant of where his mother came from. I will do my best to teach him of my people. Our language. Our customs. It won't be the same as growing up among them, but at least he will have an idea that there is more to the world than just what the French would have him believe."

"Quite so." *The response of a Frenchwoman who knows not what to say.* "Tell me, my darling. Do you regret having come to us?"

"No," Manon said without hesitation. "I owe much to the education I received here. I have no idea what life would have held for me if I'd never left the Huron, but I can't imagine it would be as rich as the life I have now."

"I'm glad. There were days after you left that I wondered if I'd been cruel to ask you to stay with me at all."

"No, but I confess I am glad that I went back, too. It erased any doubt in my mind that I had no place there. But if I had never stayed with you, my childhood would have been a much less cheerful one than what I had. I am grateful to you."

"That warms my heart. But please don't feel grateful. Caring for you was one of the great joys of my life."

"I am sorry my leaving hurt you." Manon looked down at her son and knew that he could devastate her in the same way she'd wounded Nicole when she returned to the Huron.

"It's all over now. Just promise that you'll not leave for so long again. Having the four of you back here this winter has been wonderful."

"I'm glad to brighten the short days for you." Manon gripped Nicole's hand briefly and released it. "Did Alexandre tell you of the talk we had?"

"Only that the two of you had mended some fences, so to speak."

"We did. I've been unfair to him for a long while. He's a good man." Manon took Nicole's hands in her own.

"That he is," Nicole agreed. "Though he could have been warmer to you."

"He was honest with me. While I may not have understood that as a child, as a woman I know the value of it."

"I'm glad the two of you were able to talk things through," Nicole said, discreetly dabbing the corners of her eyes with a handkerchief.

"As am I." Manon now as a wife and mother imagined how pained Nicole must have been at the tension between her husband and the girl she loved. "I just wish my being here hadn't caused you difficulty. It doesn't seem right that your kindness to me should have been rewarded with contempt from others."

"Perhaps not, but don't think it mattered to me in the least. No one would have been openly rude to our faces, not with Alexandre's position. I can't pretend I didn't see the cold looks and callous stares, but they meant nothing to me compared to you. It only hurt to see how it made you feel unwelcome."

"I underestimated you, Maman," Manon said, wiping her cheek with her sleeve, not caring that the gesture was unladylike.

"It's been too long since you called me that." Nicole abandoned any pretense of decorum and wrapped her arms around Manon and the sleeping infant.

"Yes, it has."

CHAPTER 33

Claudine

December 1679

"May I please help with the decorations at least?" Claudine pouted from the settee where she rested, her aching feet elevated and a cold compress against her throbbing forehead. She felt miserable, but hated to be left out of things, no matter how her back and everything else troubled her. Laurent and Nanny Simon, along with the Deschamps, Nicole, Gabrielle, and Manon, took to ensuring that every corner of the house was prepared for Christmas and the New Year, not to mention the arrival of Baby Robichaux at the end of the following month. Though the child wasn't expected for another six weeks, Laurent insisted that every safeguard be in place. Dr. Guérin could not be persuaded to attend the birth for any sum of money, however, claiming he was no common midwife. Manon and Nicole promised to attend until babe and mother were fully recovered, with Gabrielle supporting their efforts, as her work would allow.

"Rest, my love," Laurent said, following Nanny Simon's orders on how to arrange the evergreens on the mantelpiece.

"Here, string the cranberries onto the thread to drape over the greens." Manon handed her the bowl of red berries, a spool of thick beige thread, and a needle large enough for tapestry work.

"She really ought to rest," Laurent objected.

"I think it best she have some sort of occupation, my dear Monsieur Robichaux. If I know her well, and I believe I do, she'll run mad without one," Manon reasoned.

"Very well, but you must stop immediately if you feel overtired." Laurent eyed the bowl of berries with disdain.

"Of course, darling." Claudine tossed aside the compress from her head and began the task. It was a little better than sitting idle, but not much.

Thomas offered his daughter a sympathetic grunt from his chair. His heart was stronger, but he'd never be able to work as he had before. Despite the protestations from the family, he considered himself a useless husk of a man now. He didn't have to say it; it was etched in the deep lines on his face.

"How pleasant it is to have all my chicks under one roof," Bernadette said, knitting needles flying as she spoke. Claudine saw a flash of pain in her mother's eyes. Two of her chicks were still in France, both well and with growing families of their own as of the last letter they'd had six months before. And there was the little chick that would never join them for a Christmas meal again.

How I miss you, Emmanuelle. Wish you could be here to help me welcome my baby to the world. How impossible this all is. If you were here, my baby wouldn't exist. Laurent wouldn't be mine. How can I wish to have you both when I never could? She looked at her husband and a sharp pang hit her chest. She could imagine a life without his quiet gentleness and sweetness. She could, but it pained her so much she couldn't bear it for long.

"It is pleasant, isn't it?" Nicole said as she readjusted all the greenery that Laurent had set out. "Just imagine how much more we could see of one another if you were in town?"

"Enough of that. Not today," Thomas barked from his chair.

"But, Papa—" Nicole began.

"Papa is right, Nicole," Claudine interrupted. "It's the season of good cheer after all."

The subject of moving the Deschamps into town to live with Nicole or Claudine had been broached several times, and each time

Thomas refused to leave the land and make way for new tenants. Claudine would have welcomed them to her home with an open heart, but knew within herself that it would be the beginning of the end for her father.

"At least one of my children knows how to listen to her father. Though heaven knows I never thought I'd be saying it of Claudine." Thomas spoke in nearly a growl, but his lips softened to a smile as his remark was met with a gale of laughter from the room.

"Thank you ever so much, Papa." Claudine shot him a wry look as she balanced the bowl of cranberries on her crowded lap.

"Well, so far as I've stuck my foot in it, I'll keep going. I thought Robichaux was in for a time of it when he married you, my girl. But you grew into a lady rather than a shrew. And I had more than a few doubts on that score."

Laurent bent and kissed his wife on her forehead. "Thank heaven indeed, but I don't think she cast aside all traces of her shrewishness. She kept just enough to make her beguiling."

"And allowing for my newfound sweet and obedient nature, I'm going to ask Manon to reclaim the cranberries so I can lie down for a while."

As soon as the words had escaped her lips, Laurent took the bowl, passed them into the nearest hands that reached out for them, and helped Claudine to her feet.

She looked up at her husband but could not focus on his features. She gripped his arms as she felt the darkness crush down upon her.

Light shone through the polished glass of the windowpane as Claudine struggled to open her eyes. The lids felt glued to one another and left a sticky film over her eyes. She blinked a dozen times or more before the room came into focus.

"Thank God!" Laurent cried, bounding to her side from his chair by the fire. His usually swarthy complexion was white as bleached linens, excepting the black circles under his eyes. *Things haven't gone well.*

"Th-the baby?" Claudine tried to sit, but Laurent eased her back on her pillow.

"Our daughter is well, my love. She's cooing happily in Nanny's arms and has bewitched the house with her charms already. She is most assuredly your daughter, my darling."

"I want to see her—please."

"Of course." Laurent called out a flurry of orders to the staff that must have been camping in shifts waiting for orders from the master.

She looked down, distressed to find that her bulging stomach had not disappeared. Lessened, but still considerable.

"Dr. Guérin says that many women look as though they're expecting still for a few weeks. He says it's nothing to worry about."

"He came? What in Christendom did you do to persuade him?"

"I went to his home myself and threatened to beat him with my own horsewhip if he refused to get his lazy arse out of bed. Worse, I promised to ensure he'd never see another paying patient again under penalty of the gallows if he didn't attend you."

"Good for you." Claudine kissed his hand. "I would have liked to have seen that. You show your anger so rarely."

"You'd prefer I rage at you, my beloved? I don't think I have that in me."

"Perhaps not. But I wouldn't mind seeing you rage at others when they're deserving. It might be amusing." Claudine offered her husband a fatigued chuckle, but no mirth shone in his eyes.

"I'll make sure you have a good view the next time, my love. In truth, I *ought* to rage at you for the fright you gave me."

"I'm sorry for that, dearest one. How did I manage to bring forth a baby when I was blacked out?"

"You weren't blacked out for the entire time. You had moments of lucidity. You wouldn't let me leave you." Laurent's face blanched as he recalled his daughter's entry to the world.

"I'm sorry I don't remember her birth at all." Claudine gripped his hand, though she hadn't the strength to hold it for long.

"And I'm sorry to remember it so clearly. You seemed to be in agony and there was nothing I could do for you."

"You did precisely the right thing by staying at my side. Many men wouldn't have the stomach for it. I'm proud of you." She smiled up at her husband. *You really are remarkable. How could I have ever thought you a stolid old man?*

"Anything for you, my angel." Laurent bent down and kissed her mouth. She felt a tingle of desire—a mild one—despite her exhaustion and discomfort. *Perhaps I will be myself again. Thank heaven for that.*

"I believe you would like to meet your daughter." Manon stood at the doorway, a bundle swaddled carefully in her arms.

"More than anything." Claudine opened her arms and took the sleeping infant against her bosom.

"She's a sweet thing," Gabrielle said from behind Manon, a small pang of regret—perhaps even good-natured jealousy—sounding in her voice. "I ought to go tell Nicole and your mother you're up and well. They retired for some sleep not two hours ago, but I promised faithfully that I would fetch them when you stirred." *When or if?* As Gabrielle exited the room, Claudine had to wonder how close her brush with mortality was. Laurent still seemed to shake, but he was, understandably, sensitive to the dangers of childbirth.

"Thank you for taking care of her for me, my dear girls. Truly. I wouldn't entrust her to anyone else."

"Our pleasure," Manon said. "I hope you don't mind, but I had to nurse her myself. The wet nurse couldn't make it for the snow. It seems your little one brought a squall with her."

"She had to make an entrance, didn't she?" Claudine said with a wink. She peered down at the face, Laurent's proud nose, her grandmother's wise brow, and her own stubborn chin. She felt a cascade of warmth pour over her. *You are the reason I was born, my precious girl.* She kissed the downy skin of her forehead and traced her soft cheek with her finger.

"She's perfect," Claudine declared to her husband. "Absolutely perfect."

"Indeed she is, my darling. What should we call her?"

"I was thinking Marie-Emmanuelle . . . for my sister. Unless you think it would be too hard for you. Marielle for short."

"No, my beloved. She would have wanted to be remembered. I think it's a lovely tribute."

"As do I," Manon agreed.

"I don't want to cut your first embraces short, but it might be best if you give our little Marielle back to Manon so you can get more rest." Laurent kissed her brow softly.

"I think you might be right." Claudine placed a few more kisses on her daughter's cheeks and passed her back to Manon's capable arms.

"Are you unwell, my dear?" Laurent's brow crinkled again as he pushed a tendril of hair from her forehead.

"Something doesn't feel right at all," Claudine admitted. Just then, she felt her midsection contract, shooting pain through her already exhausted body.

Manon shouted for a maid and passed the baby off with orders to return her to Nanny Simon. She crossed over to Claudine and felt her hardening abdomen.

"Another child." Manon didn't look up. "That fool Guérin thought *this* much swelling was normal? I should have ignored his orders and stayed in the room."

"I'll have his head," Laurent growled. He returned to the door and barked for someone to fetch the doctor back, by the scruff of his neck like an unruly dog if needed.

"He won't be here in time," Manon predicted. "This little one will be here much quicker than his sister."

"Thank God," Claudine gasped. She followed Manon's orders, gripping a bedsheet and pushing with what little strength she had left. *At least I may remember bringing this little one into the world.*

"Another girl," Manon declared after a few more pushes. Claudine heard soft cries a moment later and felt her body sag in relief.

"She's so tiny," Claudine spoke, but her words slurred.

"Her sister took her fair share of the nourishment and gave this little one the scraps. But don't fret. She'll be just fine."

"Is there something wrong with her foot?" Laurent asked.

"Nothing that will have any lasting impact on her health," Manon snapped, her eyes glaring at the new father. She passed the baby off to Nanny Simon, who had appeared when the news reached her of a second impending birth.

"What's wrong?" Claudine asked. No one answered. "What's wrong?"

"She's mumbling something. I can't understand her." Laurent was looking in Manon's direction, not her own.

"She's bleeding. Badly."

"God, not again." *Not what again?*

"What's wrong?" Claudine asked more insistently.

Why can't they hear me?

CHAPTER 34

Gabrielle

January 1680

Gabrielle looked over the cradles where Claudine's twin daughters, little Marielle and the even smaller Benjamine, lie swaddled. Marielle slept peacefully, while Benjamine examined the room with her inquisitive blue eyes that already showed signs of darkening to her mother's rich shade of brown. *It will be something of her to live on, even if she could not.* She relished her visits to the girls, sparing extra affection for little Benjamine. She was curious and lively already. Her small stature and bent foot would be a challenge for her in life, but Gabrielle hoped extra caresses in her infancy might help prepare her for the hardships ahead.

Gabrielle wiped an errant tear from her cheek and bid Nanny Simon farewell. The old woman, the most devout caretaker in all of New France, still looked gaunt and sober-faced since her mistress's passing. The hours that Claudine had spent mothering Zacharie when he was motherless had endeared Claudine to the kindly woman, who felt there was no calling greater than the care of children after her own were grown and established in the world.

She walked slowly back to her shop, despite the January frost. The solitude, once welcome, had become oppressive. For the first time in her memory, she felt a pang of longing in her breast at the sight of babies and small children. She had loved Gilbertine because she was hers, but never before had she wanted a family for its own sake. She'd eaten more frequently at the Beaumonts' of late, and while Elisabeth delighted in her presence, Gabrielle had no wish to cast her sadness over the family that night. It was one of the days where the loss of Claudine—the injustice of it—stung too much for her to endure company.

Back in her shop, she cast aside her cloak and gloves to dry on the rack next to the fire. She stood before the hearth, adding a log and stirring it with the metal poker before lingering to warm her chilled fingers. She heard the muffled sound of crunching snow beneath winter boots in front of her window. She turned back and saw two women, seemingly well dressed from the look of their cloaks. Gabrielle offered them a smile and a friendly wave, though neither came from her heart.

They appeared to whisper to each other, and neither returned Gabrielle's overtures of kindness. They walked past the store, one glancing back and casting a look of disdain in Gabrielle's direction. *So you were friends with Annette Savard, then. Have a nice day.*

The piles of mending were small, but she took a chemise from atop Rose Lefebvre's basket and began rebinding the frayed hem. She'd have the order done two days ahead of schedule, but it was better to gain a reputation for completing her work two days early than two days late. She'd become so adroit with her needle that the hem was the task of a half hour. The rest of the contents of Rose's basket was already mended, folded, and ready to return.

While it was customary for Gabrielle's patrons to fetch their own mending, there was so little left to do that she decided that providing the extra service to Rose would be a better use of her time than patching the two pairs of breeches left in her pile. *Let's hope the Lefebvre children of both houses continue to damage their clothing at regular intervals or I will be without a roof over my head.*

Basket in arms, Gabrielle crossed back to the fashionable part of town where the Lefebvres and Robichauxes lived. Gabrielle didn't yearn for the luxuries they had, despite perhaps the absence of worry about where money would come from for the next meal or bolt of cloth, but she did enjoy the sight of their fine things and gracious homes. Manon and Pascal were already preparing their return to their homestead, but Gabrielle hoped the snows would keep them in town for several more weeks at least.

Known from her time as one of Rose's pupils, the maid escorted her to the parlor without ceremony.

"Oh, how lovely to see you, my dear!" Rose exclaimed at the sight of Gabrielle in the doorway. The maid whisked away the basket of mending and took Gabrielle's cloak with the same courtesy she would offer a duchess.

Gabrielle saw Rose hastily stow a handkerchief in her apron pocket.

"Claudine?"

"Yes. I'm afraid it's one of my bad days."

"Mine as well. I'm sure it's why I contrived a reason to visit."

"Well, I'm glad for it, though you know you need never *contrive* anything, my dearest girl. I was just thinking of my own little Henriette almost a year old, healthy as an ox with two loving parents. It doesn't seem fair that poor Laurent should have three motherless babies."

"It *isn't* fair. I miss her."

"We all do. She grew into such a lovely young woman." Rose gave up her pretense and pulled out her handkerchief again. "For all her wild notions growing up, she became so kind and caring. I always hoped that spark in her would take hold."

"It did," Gabrielle said, staring down at the rug beneath her feet. "And once Manon goes back to their homestead—"

"You'll be alone."

"No one will befriend me now. The questioning did nearly as much damage as the Savard woman might have hoped for."

"Almost." Rose rubbed the skin of her neck. It could have so easily gone much worse than it had.

"I keep thinking of a suggestion that Claudine made before she died."

"What was that, my darling?"

"She thought I might have a chance, at least a hope, of some happiness if I were to settle in Ville-Marie."

Rose stared into the fire for a long moment. "That's so far, my dear. It would all but kill poor Elisabeth."

"I know. It's the only thing that keeps me here. Aside from

Pascal—and of course Manon and Julien . . . not to mention little Zacharie and Claudine's girls."

"They would miss you terribly. Could you bear to be parted from all your dear nieces and nephews—both by blood and otherwise?"

"They're dear children, but if I stay here, I'll never have babies of my own." *If such a thing is even possible.* She could not voice her worst fear aloud.

Rose wanted to contradict her; Gabrielle could see it in her teacher's face. But there was too much truth in the words for Rose to speak against her.

"Perhaps it might be worth a visit at least. Henri could take you when he next has commissions in town. Would you like that?"

Gabrielle crossed over to Rose's settee and took her in her arms. "The thought terrifies me, but I feel like I must try."

"Put the chair over by the window, just as before." Gabrielle surveyed the shop with a careful eye to detail. It was important to get everything in the right places now before she lost her access to the muscled help. Rearranging a chair or an end table was a simple enough matter. If her workbench ended up out of place, there it would remain for months to come.

Gabrielle's shop in Ville-Marie was perhaps not as large as the premises Alexandre had rented to her in Quebec, but it had one distinct advantage: It belonged to her alone. With the funds she'd squirreled away from her mending, the savings she had from selling Patenaude's belongings, along with the incredibly low price Henri negotiated for her from the building's proprietor, she purchased the shop and the upstairs apartment with a little money left over to ensure she'd be well fed while she reestablished business. Alexandre and Henri had secured space on a trading vessel between Quebec and Ville-Marie for the Beaumonts and Gabrielle, also securing a large compartment of the cargo hold for her household goods and the contents of her mending shop. Manon, Pascal, and the children came as well to see her well settled.

"Don't you like the table there?" Gabrielle asked Elisabeth, who stared off blankly.

"Not particularly, I must confess. I much preferred it back in

Quebec and you with it. But I won't question you, my sweet girl."
It had been four months since Elisabeth raged at Gabrielle's proposal to move to a new town and start afresh. She'd come to an uneasy understanding that Gabrielle had to be free from the associations to her name and character. To make the decision even more painful, Elisabeth had discovered she was with child again for the first time in over three years.

"Don't you want to be here? To be a part of the baby's life?"

"Don't you want me to have the chance to make a family of my own? Don't you think I deserve happiness of my own?"

Elisabeth hadn't come up with a solid argument against that.

Pascal, Manon, and Tawendeh all did their part to ensure Gabrielle's shop was prepared to open. They followed her instructions without question and Gabrielle could not hide her smile. This was her domain and they let her reign there. From the wink Gilbert offered her, he was just as proud about it as she was.

"You'll come home as often as you can, won't you?" Elisabeth began wringing her hands as the wagons, once heaped with her tailoring notions, now stood empty.

"Yes, and a full month before this little one is expected and I won't come back until she's happy and drooling in her cradle and you're back on your feet and baking. I promised."

Elisabeth wrapped her arms around Gabrielle. "You say 'she' as if you're certain."

"You've got two boys. Pierre and Fabien need a sister to civilize them in a way you're too gentle to do."

"You make this poor babe sound to be a relentless shrew and she's yet to be born." Pascal shot his sister a wry look.

"And she will be a shrew. No girl born to a house of brothers could be raised up otherwise."

"She makes a fair point," Gilbert conceded. "My own sister was the sixth child born into a family with five sons and there wasn't a boy in our village who hadn't sported a black eye of her design at some point in his life. Myself included."

"No doubt you had it coming," Elisabeth said, laughing through her tears.

"I did at that. I seem to recall loosing a jar of spiders in her bureau drawer." Gilbert's eyes shone at the memory.

"A black eye seems like a merciful judgment on her part," Gabrielle snorted. "Now go off with you and get home before the boat leaves without you."

"The shrew speaks sense," Pascal declared. "Let's get underway."

The good-byes that Gabrielle had been dreading were just as tearful as she expected. Elisabeth gave her a bolt of the most beautiful green wool Gabrielle had ever seen. No doubt something Laurent had procured. *Was it to be for Claudine?* Gabrielle preferred not to think of it. Her dear friend would have no use for it now. She knew Claudine would have wanted her to have a beautiful garment of her own, and Laurent wouldn't want the reminder in his house besides.

"Make something for yourself with it, or I'll be furious," Elisabeth warned with tears streaming down her face.

"I swear it, Maman." Gabrielle hugged Elisabeth close. "And I'll wear it home in less than six weeks so you can admire me." *Bless Henri and his generosity. Receipt of payment for three passages home before next winter—more than I'd ever hoped for.*

"We're holding you to it." Gilbert spoke manfully, but Gabrielle could hear the crack of emotion in his voice.

"It's going to be a boy, you know," Elisabeth whispered in her ear.

"How could you possibly know?" Gabrielle asked, her brow arched.

"Because you are my daughter. The little scamp that came to mend my broken heart after my little Adèle died. I can't imagine having another."

To this Gabrielle could say nothing, but embraced the woman who had been kinder to her than her own mother, until the others insisted on their farewells.

"Good-bye, Manon," Gabrielle said, kissing her cheeks, trying not to jostle little Julien.

"Good-bye, my sister. I will miss you so terribly much, but I am proud of you. Starting a new life takes courage."

"And no one of my acquaintance would know that better than you." Gabrielle kissed Julien's cheek as well, causing his eyes to flutter open for only a brief moment.

"I'm not sure how true it is. Most everyone you know has started his or her life anew. Elisabeth, Gilbert, Rose . . . all of the others began their lives in France and started over again here. But it's an exciting journey for you. Be safe and well."

"And the same to you. Take care of my nephew for me."

Manon nodded solemnly and took her place in the wagon by Pascal's side.

Alone in her shop, Gabrielle had thought she would collapse in her bed for a long night's sleep before opening her doors the following morning. Instead she ran her fingers over the length of green wool. Her mind spinning, she grabbed her scissors, pins, needle, and thread and let her creative impulses run unchecked through the night.

Two days later, a crowd of a half dozen women stood in front of the shop as Gabrielle sat prominently in her window for all to see as she worked at her mending, wearing her newly fashioned green gown. There was nothing outlandish about the gown, but every line was crisp. Every tuck was artful. The cut of the sleeves that reached just past the elbow, the curve of the fabric over the hips . . . it was all meant to showcase a woman at her most beautiful. Contrasted with the overdress of evergreen was an ivory stomacher from a short length of soft muslin left over from a commission. The customer had given her the fabric in lieu of extra payment for rushed mending, and Gabrielle was now grateful for it.

Three times in the course of a morning, she had to tell customers that the gown she wore was not for sale at any price, but that she would be pleased to fashion one for them from the fabric of their choosing. She had a dozen women enquire about mending, nearly half of whom returned with baskets overflowing with tattered chemises, skirts, bodices, trousers, and jackets all in need of repair. It would keep her in food for a month.

But even if the work didn't come, she had a roof over her head and a place to call home. It was no small comfort. Though Alexandre was the kindest of landlords and the Beaumonts would never have let her suffer, the security of her home and shop made her feel more at ease than she'd felt in years.

Later in her first afternoon, a man appeared with a rumpled-looking sack.

"May I help you, Monsieur . . . ?"

"Tolbert. Gaspard Tolbert. I-I believe so," he stammered. "I understand you're a seamstress?"

Gabrielle nodded and he placed the pouch on her worktable, blushing as if it contained an intimate secret rather than a pair of work trousers in need of hemming.

"I haven't any skill with a needle, you see. Nor any wife to tend to these things."

"I've salvaged worse, monsieur. Have a seat by the fire and I'll see them mended in less than a quarter of an hour. Or come back in the morning if you prefer?"

"I'll wait if it's all the same to you, madame."

"Suit yourself, monsieur."

She coaxed the shy man into conversation as her fingers nimbly rebound the fraying threads of fabric into a neat cuff. His answers were monosyllabic until she asked him of his trade. He was a carpenter and passionate about his work. He cast his eye around the room until it landed on her workbench.

"It's too tall for you," he observed. "You're a petite woman and need something better suited to your height. It must be dreadfully uncomfortable for you."

"It was a worktable at my—parents'—bakery. My father is a tall man. It was built to suit him."

"I could adjust it for you. It might take an afternoon, but it wouldn't be complicated work."

"I'm afraid I haven't the means to pay you for your services, monsieur. Not quite yet." Gabrielle forced herself to not look down. Her lack of funds was no cause for shame. They would come in time.

"I could do it in exchange for the mending."

"A full afternoon of labor for fifteen minutes of stitching?" Gabrielle's eyes widened at the overgenerous offer.

"I might have other garments in need of repair. I trust you to be fair."

"You have a bargain, monsieur." *Because I imagine you won't accept a refusal.*

"Would tomorrow be too soon to start, madame?"

328 • *Aimie K. Runyan*

"No, monsieur. I think it would be ideal."

"I look forward to seeing you again, madame."

"As do I."

Gabrielle watched him as he exited the shop and walked back down the narrow lane, mended trousers in hand. She smiled softly at the realization that she meant what she had told him. She returned to her mending, and for the first time in many months, she looked forward to tomorrow.

EPILOGUE

Manon

September 1680

Manon stood on the steps of their farmhouse, taking a few moments to admire the fiery orange sunset streaked with purple as little Julien snored softly against her back, oblivious to the natural beauty before him. He had spent a good part of the day in his pack while Manon worked aside Pascal and Tawendeh to bring in the harvest. The French had yet to invent a device that kept a baby as contented as the cradleboards that the Huron women used to keep their infants safe as they labored. When he was first born, Manon had tried keeping him at her feet in the baskets like French mothers used, but he was not a child to be tucked away to sleep and dream while the world passed him by. Manon crafted the cradleboard out of desperation before he was two months old.

"God bless the Huron women and their ingenuity," Pascal had said when the baby had gone a full day without hours of plaintive wails or demanding every moment of his mother's or father's attention during the long winter days trapped indoors. "That contraption is the single greatest work of genius to come from the human mind; I'm convinced of it."

When the cradleboard continued to keep him pacified after a few weeks, Manon was convinced of it, too.

At nine months of age, Julien was getting too active for long stints in the device, but he tolerated it well enough while his family culled the spring wheat and harvested their potatoes, carrots, and a very few apples from the small orchard Henri had started during his tenure, which had been neglected in the years since. Apples— be it applesauce, apple butter, apples preserved in jars for use in pies or cakes—would be a welcome touch of sweetness in the midst of the long winter that lay ahead. The next week they would sow the winter wheat that would be harvested in July. It would break up the work of harvest a great deal, and for this, Manon was grateful.

"Have you fallen asleep on me, Wife?" Pascal asked, wrapping his arm around her and the sleeping babe.

"No, just admiring the view, my love." Manon stretched up on her toes to place a kiss on his stubbly cheek. The harvest was no time to worry about trifles like shaving, but the bulk of the heaviest work was done, and the preparations for winter wouldn't begin in earnest for another few days.

But first, there would be rest. Tonight they would bathe and prepare their best clothes. Manon would forsake her beloved braids and wear her hair up as the French women did. Pascal would leave behind the moccasins Manon had fashioned for him, which he wore every moment his labors didn't require sturdy boots to protect his feet. Tawendeh would be called Théodore, and he would trade his buckskin trousers for woolen breeches while in town.

In the morning they would hitch the faithful horse to Pascal's wagon and make the trek back into town so they could see Gabrielle Patenaude wed to her carpenter, Gaspard Tolbert. While not numerous, Gabrielle's letters over the past months in Ville-Marie had been long and encouraging—and increasingly sentimental about this Tolbert. When Gabrielle sent word about the impending marriage including her fervent request that her brother and Manon stand as witnesses in the small ceremony, none in the Giroux house was surprised at the news. Gabrielle knew the timing would be difficult with the harvest, and as a seamstress's and carpenter's duties were less affected by the season, they agreed to celebrate their marriage in Quebec, where it would be possible for Manon and her family to attend without losing a week or more for the festivities. Not to mention, it spared them the trouble of spending days traveling by trade ship with little Julien and Elisabeth's newborn daughter, little Elisabeth, or Lisette for short.

After a simple supper of ham, bread, cheese, and cider, Manon saw the freshly scrubbed children tucked into their clean beds and padded up behind Pascal's chair, where he sat putting the finishing touches on a dainty wooden box intricately carved with roses that he would present to his sister on the occasion of her marriage. She used her strong hands to knead the knots from his work-weary shoulders and stooped down a few inches to embrace him from the back, enjoying the sensation of his muscled back against her chest.

"It's beautiful, my love." Manon kissed his temple and moved lower, kissing every inch until she reached his whiskered mouth. "You're in need of a shave before tomorrow."

"Then light an extra candle or two and turn me back into a civilized city man." Pascal blew the stray wood shavings from the box, placed it in the middle of the table, and leaned back to let her lather the soap on his stubble.

Gently she moved the razor with the grain of his beard, removing two weeks' of growth and restoring a decade of youth back to his appearance.

"There is my handsome husband. I knew he had to be under there somewhere." She sat in his lap and kissed his freshly smoothed skin.

Pascal wrapped his arms around her and kissed her deeply before tucking her head to his chest.

"Do you miss town? The bustle, the gossip, the people?" Pascal asked, kissing the top of her freshly scrubbed hair and breathing in the scent of soap.

"Oh, in odd moments, I miss having news. But when I am there, I miss our peace and quiet," Manon said, sitting up straighter in his lap. "I love our little cabin and our little family. And very soon I shall have the very last thing I could ever want."

"And what, my sweet, would that be?"

"A daughter."

Pascal blinked a few times with comprehension, then held her closer to his chest. "I was hoping you might be.... But how can you be sure it's a girl?"

"Because a mother knows these things. She just feels like a girl. She should be here in April, so no spreading the news for another two or three months yet."

"I hope you're right. And I hope she's just like her mother in every way."

"Oh, I hope there is some of you in her, my darling man. I want her to know the best of both our worlds."

Gabrielle stood before the small mirror in Elisabeth and Gilbert's bedroom, smiling softly at her reflection. Her riot of red curls was tamed in a knot at the nape of her neck.

"Beautiful," Manon proclaimed, wrapping her arms around Gabrielle and kissing her freckled cheek. "It gives me more joy than you can imagine to see you happy, sister."

"Thank you, Manon. I didn't think it was possible for the longest time, but Gaspard is a good man as ever breathed and our businesses are thriving. I don't believe the Queen in her palace could ask for more happiness than I have today."

"And I can think of no one who deserves it more. I only wish Claudine could be with us to share today. She loved you and would have been so pleased to see you well settled."

"She is, Manon," Gabrielle spoke with certainty. "This dress was made from the wool Laurent gave me for her sake. It was the dress I wore when I opened my shop and met my Gaspard. She was with me then, and she'll be with me today."

Though Manon did not completely trust the French notions of the afterlife and the idea of heaven and hell, she hoped this once that Gabrielle was right.

"Let's get along to church, sweetheart. Your young man is waiting," Elisabeth announced at the doorway.

Gabrielle nodded and they descended into the shop below. Gilbert had borrowed one of Alexandre's smaller carriages and had it hitched to their two good-natured workhorses. It was nothing so grand as Manon's own parade into town on her wedding day, nor even the subdued elegance of Claudine's wedding that was shrouded in mourning for Emmanuelle. But as Gilbert helped Gabrielle into the carriage, more than a few neighbors peered out to see the beautifully dressed bride on her way to church.

Pascal and Manon rode behind Gabrielle along with the children and the Lefebvre family. Nicole glowed to have Manon back at home for a few nights at least. As much as Manon grieved for Claudine, no one missed her as much as Nicole, with the sole exception of Laurent. The Robichaux pew would be empty that day, and Manon could not blame him for not being able to participate in the joyous celebration.

At the front of the church, Gabrielle and Gaspard pledged themselves to each other. As they spoke their vows, Manon felt the warm grip of Pascal's fingers lacing in hers. The couple smiled broadly to the small crowd assembled as they walked back down the aisle to the world beyond. Manon could not help but echo that smile, for her dear friend would have her measure of happiness. It might be fleeting, but Manon held out hope that Gabrielle would have many happy years before her.

She took Pascal's arm to follow the newlyweds down into the street below and rubbed her abdomen where her precious secret grew into a child. A child who would someday grow to be a young woman. Manon looked at her friend, bathed in the autumn sunlight, as she kissed her husband's blushing cheek for the entire colony to see.

I hope you know a love like this one, my little dove. It will be second only to the love I have for you.

DUTY TO THE CROWN

Aimie K. Runyan

ABOUT THIS GUIDE

The suggested questions are included
to enhance your group's reading
of Aimie K. Runyan's
Duty to the Crown.

DISCUSSION QUESTIONS

1. We open with Manon's forced reentry into French society when the tenant farmer discovers her gathering herbs. Why do you feel she was so reluctant to tell the man about her connection to the landlord?

2. Why does Claudine find herself so frequently frustrated with Emmanuelle? How do you think Emmanuelle feels about Claudine's treatment of herself and others?

3. Gabrielle has lived as a sort of adopted daughter of the Beaumont family for many years, but doesn't feel like she is fully part of the family. How does this manifest itself and why is this the case?

4. Sometimes the treatment of Manon by the townspeople is clearly hostile, but do you feel some of the mistreatment is imagined or exaggerated—even preemptively—by Manon? Is her hypersensitivity warranted?

5. We see Claudine evolve from her self-centered ways throughout the course of the book. What do you think is the turning point (or points), and what motivates her to change?

6. Why does Gabrielle accept marriage to Patenaude? Do you think her past made her more likely to accept his offer? Why do you feel she had resisted courting in general?

7. What inspires Claudine to tell the truth to Laurent about her reasons for not devoting herself to her marriage entirely?

8. Do you think Manon's hesitance to form a real relationship with Pascal is justified? How does Pascal's pursuit of Manon differ from Heno's?

9. Gabrielle's tryst with René was exceedingly risky to her already precarious social status. Why do you think she chose to take the risk, considering the potentially disastrous consequences?

10. Why does Claudine insist on helping at her parents' farm herself rather than sending (possibly more capable) help?

11. What does Gabrielle's mending business represent, as well as her move to Ville-Marie? What do you think was the catalyst that allowed her to accept the possibility of a new life?

12. Does Manon succeed completely in finding a life among the French that allows her to embrace her native heritage? Do you think her ultimate decisions will permit her to be happy?

Connect with  U s

Visit us online at
KensingtonBooks.com
to read more from your favorite authors, see books
by series, view reading group guides, and more.

Join us on social media

for sneak peeks, chances to win books and prize packs,
and to share your thoughts with other readers.

facebook.com/kensingtonpublishing
twitter.com/kensingtonbooks

Tell us what you think!

To share your thoughts, submit a review,
or sign up for our eNewsletters, please visit:
KensingtonBooks.com/TellUs.